BETTER DEEDS THAN WORDS

GEORGINA GUTHRIE

OMNIFIC PUBLISHING
LOS ANGELES

Omnific Publishing
1901 Avenue of the Stars, 2nd floor
Los Angeles, CA 90067
www.omnificpublishing.com

First Omnific eBook edition, May 2014
First Omnific trade paperback edition, May 2014

The characters and events in this book are fictitious.
Any similarity to real persons, living or dead,
is coincidental and not intended by the author.

Library of Congress Cataloguing-in-Publication Data

Guthrie, Georgina.
  Better Deeds Than Words / Georgina Guthrie – 1st ed.
  ISBN: 978-1-623421-17-5
  1. Contemporary Romance — Fiction. 2. University — Fiction.
  3. Shakespeare — Fiction. 4. Forbidden Romance — Fiction. I. Title

10 9 8 7 6 5 4 3 2 1

Cover Design by Micha Stone and Amy Brokaw
Interior Book Design by Coreen Montagna

Printed in the United States of America

For my husband, with love.

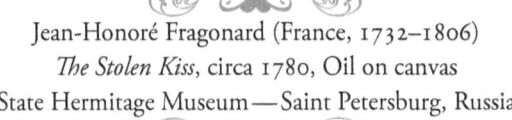

Jean-Honoré Fragonard (France, 1732–1806)
The Stolen Kiss, circa 1780, Oil on canvas
State Hermitage Museum—Saint Petersburg, Russia

CHAPTER 1

Faithful Friends

Words are easy, like the wind;
Faithful friends are hard to find.
(*The Passionate Pilgrim*)

Saturday morning. Hallelujah. No need to leap out of bed, no reason to move. I dragged the blankets over my head and stretched.

This is what it's like in heaven—Saturday every day.

Then I realized that this couldn't be heaven because Daniel, along with his whiskers, his hands, his lips, and his tongue, would have to be here too.

I closed my eyes, thinking about the night before. Daniel had dropped me off at Bay Street at eleven. My feet should have been killing me as I walked back to Jackman, but I was almost certain they hadn't been touching the ground.

What a crazy night. I'd arrived at the frat house expecting nothing more than a distraction from the horrible week I'd had. Then Daniel had shown up, and between his apology and his shocking story about what that Nicola girl had done to him at Oxford, my head had started to spin. The next thing I knew, I was meeting his grandmother, being invited for Sunday dinner, and sharing a first kiss with Daniel in an abandoned parking lot. Talk about plans going in an unexpected direction.

But how the hell was I supposed to enjoy the memories of Daniel's warm tongue and roaming hands with the unholy racket coming from down the hall? It sounded like Chef Ramsay was out there having a conniption.

I pulled on some PJ bottoms and made my way to the kitchen where Matt was creating a tower with our frying pans. Stranger still, he was wearing his hockey helmet and had his athletic supporter on over his track pants. His hockey stick was lying across the stove.

"Dude, what in the living fuck are you doing?"

He whirled around, grabbing his hockey stick and backing up, blocking my access to the frying pans. "Stay back." He held the stick out to protect himself.

"Have you lost your mind? What—?"

"Don't hurt me, Aubrey." He cowered in the corner, one hand over his crotch.

Oh, *now* I saw what this was all about. What a lunatic! I decided to play along.

"Lose the cup. I'm about to claim your first born." I edged closer to him, my eyes narrowed and hand outstretched.

"I mean it, stay back."

I tried to continue with the charade, but he looked ridiculous. I laughed so hard I gave myself a stitch.

"I guess that means you're not gonna castrate me for telling Daniel everything yesterday?" he said.

"Holy shit, dude," I gasped. "What's with the getup?"

"In case you came after me with a pan. Protecting the noggin'." He tapped the helmet.

"I think your noggin's safe, spaz." I wiped the tears from my eyes.

"And my gonads?"

"Safe too. For now." I grinned and filled the coffee maker with water.

"That's a relief." He sighed, tossing his helmet on the counter. He was about to follow suit with his jockstrap when I held up a hand.

"Ew, get that nasty thing out of here."

He took his hockey equipment back to his room while I put the frying pans away. He returned and leaned against the doorframe. "So?"

"So what?"

"*So*...Did you guys work everything out?"

"Yes."

"And everything's cool?"

"Everything's very cool. Thanks, Matt. I don't know what to say."

"You don't have to say anything." He gave me a giant bear hug. "I'm glad you guys got your shit together. And that you didn't punch me in the junk."

"Me too."

"But if he screws you over again, I swear to God—"

"I know. Don't worry. He's suitably remorseful. And he appreciated what you did. We both do."

"No worries. By the way, I told Shawn and Jo you left the party because you weren't feeling well."

"Thanks for covering for me."

"Hey, I'm gonna shower, and then I have a shitload of reading to do. Will you let me know when the coffee's ready?"

"I'll bring you a cup. It's the least I can do," I said, punching him lightly on the arm.

"Oh, this ain't over. Payback's a bitch, Aubs," he said, his toothy grin lighting up his whole face.

"How altruistic of you, *friend*."

"Don't mention it," he called over his shoulder.

I slouched against the counter, watching the coffee drip into the pot. Was I seriously going to try to get work done today? All I could think about were Daniel's lips and whiskers; his hands sliding around my hips, pulling me hard against him...

How would I control myself for the next six weeks? Keeping my hands off him now that I knew what I'd been missing was going to make graduating with distinction look like child's play.

I poured coffee and left a cup on Matt's dresser before returning to my room. Saturday morning. Time to email my mom and dad. I wrote a long message, telling them about Julie and Matt and talking up my social life. Mom always worried I was spending too much time on school work.

Next I turned my attention to my French homework. Emails from my group members with their contributions to our upcoming presentation waited in my inbox. I hadn't even started writing my own part yet, so I played catch-up for the next hour. I was snapping my laptop shut when my phone rang.

My heart leapt.

Daniel.

"Good morning, beautiful," he said.

"Hey! You sound out of breath. Been thinking of me?" I asked, my voice low and sultry.

"You know I have. Unfortunately, I've also been lugging furniture around Brad and Penny's house for the last hour. I'm helping them move."

"Sounds like fun."

"Not so much. What are you up to?" he asked.

"Trying to get caught up on school work. A certain asswipe threw me into a tailspin this week."

"Guilty as charged." He sighed dramatically. "Is there anything Mr. Asswipe can do to help?"

"I'll be fine. I work well under pressure."

"Good. I thought we should finalize dinner plans for tomorrow. Are we still on?"

"Of course."

We hashed out the details before Daniel had to go.

"Can't wait to see you," he said.

"Me too," I said. My face warmed at the thought of being with him again. I hung up, smiling goofily.

I wandered back out to the kitchen. Matt was sitting in the armchair, highlighting a textbook, but he caught the dreamy expression on my face.

"Ah, young love," he said. I flicked his ear as I passed him with my snacks. "Ouch. What happened to gratitude?"

"I left it on your dresser earlier. Help yourself to a second cup," I said breezily, kicking my door closed behind me.

A Merry Feast

Small cheer and great welcome makes a merry feast.
(*Comedy of Errors*, Act III, Scene 1)

What do you wear to dinner at your TA-slash-boyfriend's grandmother's house? This question plagued me as I stood in front of my closet the next day, staring at my woefully underwhelming wardrobe. What had Daniel said? "*Nice pants and a sweater.*" Not jeans. Black pants and my chenille wine-colored sweater? It was snug and soft and screamed *touch me!* Definitely what I was aiming for. Decision made.

Ready to go, I went to the living room. Matt was flopped in front of the TV. I updated him on my plans for the evening.

"Wow. Extended family? That's serious."

"Please don't, Matt. I'm nervous enough."

"Don't worry. She'll love you. Hey, what if Jo comes back tonight to do laundry or something? What should I tell her?"

I groaned as I slipped on my coat and boots. "I haven't told her about Daniel yet. Can you say I'm out with Julie or something?"

"Sure, I'll cover for you."

"Thanks."

I walked to the subway, and at twenty to five, I was picking my way through a snowdrift in front of Dundas West Station to get to Daniel's car like we'd planned. He leaned over to push the door open for me.

"Hi," I said as I hopped in.

"Hi yourself, gorgeous. Get over here." He leaned across the armrest. "I haven't kissed you in over forty hours. I can't wait another minute."

He pressed his lips to mine, forgoing sweet and tender in favor of hot and passionate. He was delicious and smelled divine—whiskery and freshly-cologned. I moved my hands up to his face, and he frowned at my gloves.

"Take these off," he grumbled, plucking them from my hands and throwing them over my shoulder. I tickled his scruff and curled my fingers in his soft hair. I could feel him smiling against my lips.

"Better?"

"Much," he said. Then we were on our way, Daniel quizzing me about my day as we drove to the heart of a High Park neighborhood. A few minutes later, we turned into the narrow driveway of a two-story brick house with a wide porch and traditional white-fenced front yard.

"This is it," he said. "You ready?"

"I think so."

He retrieved a bag from the back seat before coming around to help me out of the car. He turned the handle on Patty's front door and poked his head inside.

"Hello?" he called. "Patty?"

"Yes, Daniel, coming!"

Patty bustled out to the front hall, quickly hugging Daniel before turning to take my hand.

"I'm so glad you were able to come," she said. Without missing a beat she added, "Where's the wine?"

Daniel handed her the bag. "I grabbed two one-liter bottles. There's no way we'll make our way through both tonight. Put one bottle aside for another time."

"I suppose that's an acceptable compromise," she said with a tart smile. "I'm slicing the roast. Dinner will be ready shortly."

"Let me get some of the snow off the sidewalk," Daniel said. "You don't want the city issuing you a fine. You'll be okay for a minute?" he asked me, taking my coat and hanging it up.

"I'll be fine."

"Be right back."

I took off my wet boots and made my way through to the kitchen. The house was not at all what I'd been expecting. After seeing Daniel's parents' house, I'd imagined something similar. This house was nothing like the Grants' Forest Hill mansion. Patty's house had character and charm. The rooms were smaller, slightly cluttered, and homey.

In the kitchen, she moved between the stove and a giant cutting board where a carved prime rib waited to be served.

"Is there anything I can do to help?" I asked.

"No, no, dear. Everything's under control. Make yourself at home. There's quite a rogues' gallery in the hallway there if you're interested in family photos," she said.

I stepped through the doorway at the back of the kitchen and saw the wall she meant. It was full of pictures in a mishmash of decorative frames. I scanned the rows, taking particular interest in the photographs of Daniel, Brad, and Jeremy.

"You have a beautiful family, Patty," I said when she joined me. "Is it okay if I call you Patty?"

"Of course it is, as long as you don't expect me to start clapping my hands and chanting nursery rhymes." She smiled. "You know the story behind that name?"

"I do." I laughed.

"How disappointing. One less anecdote I can embarrass Daniel with. But yes, please, call me Patty. And don't ever let me catch you referring to me as 'Nan' or 'Nanny.' I'm not a goat."

"Got it." I smiled and turned my attention back to the pictures.

"That's my Gail." Patty gently placed her fingers on one of the frames. "She died, you know."

I nodded. "I'm terribly sorry. I can't imagine…" I trailed off, unsure what else to say. Poor Jeremy.

"One of the most horrific things a parent can endure. But thankfully we still have our Jeremy. He's so much like Gail. Compassionate and kind."

I continued to examine the photos, tracing Daniel's transformation from a pudgy baby to a pink-faced toddler and eventually a good-looking, lanky schoolboy. My eyes landed on a picture of Daniel with his arm around a pretty brunette with sparkling blue eyes. My heart lurched. They were both dressed formally. He couldn't have been any older than sixteen or seventeen. Patty saw me gazing at the picture.

"That's Sabrina. She was Daniel's first real girlfriend, I think. She went to Havergal, the private girls' school. That was Havergal's prom. Daniel came home from Oxford three times during his first year of university to visit her, but then he built a new life for himself in England. It's not easy to maintain a long-distance relationship at that age. Not terribly advisable, either."

"No, I suppose not." I tore my eyes away from the photograph. There was no point being jealous of Daniel's past. He wanted *me* now. That was all that mattered.

We returned to the kitchen, and Patty went back to stirring the gravy. Daniel ducked inside, noisily stomping the snow off his feet. As he hung up his coat and slipped off his boots, I noticed he was wearing the same outfit he'd worn the day he'd made me dissolve into a hot mess in the Hart House Library. Those black jeans paired with the sex boots could potentially cause my early death. He ran his hands through his hair, shaking out the snow.

Breathtaking.

"Thank you for doing that, Daniel," Patty said. "Now, I'm not going to stand on ceremony. Why don't we dish everything up in the kitchen?"

"Good idea." Daniel smiled and rubbed his hands together. "Ladies first," he said, handing us both a plate.

"Everything looks wonderful," I said as Daniel spooned food onto my plate.

"Patty's an awesome cook," he assured me. "Best gravy in Toronto."

I pointed to a muffin tin with little puffy, doughy things in it. "What are those?"

"Those are Yorkshire puddings," Patty said. "You have to have Yorkshires with a roast."

"You've never had one?" Daniel asked.

"Not to my knowledge."

Daniel dropped two of them on my plate. *I'll never eat all this.*

"I'll top up the gravy and bring it in. Can you take the salad?" Patty said, handing me a bowl.

I made my way to the table, which was set for three. Patty sat across from me, leaving the other chair for Daniel. He set his over-flowing plate down before opening one of the bottles of wine and pouring us each a glass. He sat, and I paused before reaching for my cutlery. Would Patty want to say grace?

"Enjoy," she said, picking up her knife and fork. "Try the York-shires, my dear. I'm interested to hear what you think."

Okay, no grace in the Wright household. Fair enough. I cut off a piece of the fluffy pudding and popped it in my mouth.

"Mmm, that's wonderful," I said.

"Told you," Daniel said.

I dipped some potato in the gravy — Daniel was right. It was amazing. Everything was delicious. Not glamorous in the slightest, but absolutely wonderful all the same. We ate quietly for a moment before Daniel broke the silence.

"So, tell me about Gerald, Patty. How long has this been going on, young lady?"

"Don't patronize me, Daniel," Patty said. "He's a lovely man, wid-owed for three years. I met him at Florence's house over Christmas. We have a lot in common. He enjoys dancing and playing bridge. He's a gentleman, and I like his company. *And* he has all his own teeth."

Daniel laughed and shook his head.

"Good teeth are imperative," Patty said, gesturing with her fork. "Do you floss, Aubrey? It's very important."

"I try to remember," I said.

"Try harder. You'll be glad you did when you reach my age. Noth-ing worse than kissing a man with dentures. Always worry they're going to pop out and bite you. More roast, Daniel?" She dropped another slice of prime rib on his plate.

Daniel regarded her with amusement, then glanced over at me, perhaps trying to imagine what I must be thinking.

I loved her. She was a hoot!

Patty held out the salad tongs. "Daniel, take more tomatoes."

"I already have a few. I'm fine."

She tossed three more tomato wedges on his salad plate. "Lyco-pene. It's good for the prostate," she said.

Daniel rolled his eyes and sighed.

"Prostate cancer," Patty said to me in a hushed voice. "That's what got Bradford — my husband. Never ate a tomato in his life. I'm convinced that's what did him in. Although I read an article recently about the importance of regular ejaculations as well. Not that Bradford had a problem with that."

I bit my lip to stifle a laugh. Daniel stared at her in stunned silence.

"You are having your oil changed regularly, I hope?" she asked him.

What the hell? Penny had said Patty was a corker, but nothing had prepared me for *this!* She was awesome! I blinked back tears as I tried not to burst into laughter. Daniel, on the other hand, was choking on a mouthful of roast beef. I clapped him on the back and handed him his water glass.

He gulped some and cleared his throat. "Jesus, Patty. That's a rather personal question."

"It's uptight people who impede the distribution of important information. Don't you think, Aubrey?"

"Oh, I couldn't agree more," I said, casting a meaningful glance at Daniel, who narrowed his eyes at me.

He turned back to his grandmother. "Are you implying I'm uptight?"

"Implying? No, no, I was stating it as a fact. I happen to believe you need to extricate that rather long pole from — well, there's no need to discuss the sordid details at the table," she said.

Daniel put down his fork and looked back and forth between the two of us. "Huh," he said, miffed. "Okay then. Allow me to put your mind at rest. My oil is being changed fairly regularly. There. Satisfied?"

He picked up his fork and forcefully stabbed a carrot. I hoped his comment wasn't intended as an admission that we were involved in an intimate relationship. Patty quirked an eyebrow at me, and I held up my hands as if to say, "Don't look at me." She surveyed Daniel expectantly, and he cleared his throat.

"Unfortunately, I'm decidedly, um, self-employed, at the moment," he said.

Oh. My. God. Was he really sitting here at the dining room table with his grandmother and admitting to masturbating? Regularly? Patty remained unfazed. We could have been discussing the current price of pork tenderloin.

I couldn't hold my tongue any longer. "Well, Daniel, this is very interesting. How is business these days, if you don't mind me asking?"

"Business is booming," he said, his sardonic grin betraying his amusement.

I bit my lip.

"Well, that's a very sad state of affairs for a young, handsome man," Patty said, eyeing us. "But I understand. These things take time. Just promise me that until someone *hires you on permanently*, you'll keep business ticking over for the sake of your prostate health."

"Patty, I don't have a lot of choice in the matter at the moment. Now can we *please* change the subject?" he asked.

"Well, all right." Patty dabbed her lips with her napkin. "So tell me, where did you two meet?"

Daniel pursed his lips. "At school," he said. Suitably vague.

"You're studying at U of T?" she asked me.

I nodded, chasing down my mouthful of food with some wine. "I'm graduating this year. I'll have a specialist in English and a minor in French."

Her eyebrows shot up. "Well, I can see how you two would have a lot to talk about. It can be tricky keeping up with Daniel sometimes."

"Oh, don't worry about that. Aubrey keeps me on my toes," Daniel assured her.

"I'm happy to hear that. Your grandfather would approve," she said.

Daniel smiled at me warmly. "Yes, he would."

"I see no reason to keep the young lady under wraps. Surely your parents would be pleased with your choice," Patty said.

Daniel shot me another quick glance and rested his knife and fork on his plate.

"Thing is, Patty, it's a little *complicated*." He looked at her with a strange expression. She gave him an equally inscrutable gaze in return, like they were communicating telepathically.

"I see," she said at last, taking a sip of her wine and sitting back in her chair.

She did? What did she see? What had just happened?

"Would you like to hear about how I met my husband, Aubrey?" Patty asked. Daniel relaxed, his shoulders settling noticeably.

"I'd love to hear about him."

She pushed her plate to the side and pulled her wine glass forward before clasping her hands on the table in front of her and embarking on her story.

"I went to Queen's University," she said. "Queen's was a very forward-thinking school in my day. Did you know that it was the first non-maritime university to accept female students?"

"No, I didn't know that," I said.

"Well, my parents insisted I attend university. Not that I resisted. I've always loved learning. Anyway, Bradford was my history professor at Queen's."

Suddenly I understood exactly where this story was going. This wasn't simply a nostalgic courtship tale. I glanced at Daniel. He raised an eyebrow and nodded slightly.

Patty had married one of her professors.

CHAPTER 3

Precious Time

I have no precious time at all to spend,
Nor services to do, till you require.
Nor dare I chide the world-without-end hour
Whilst I, my sovereign, watch the clock for you…
(*Sonnet 57*)

"Bradford was a wonderful teacher," Patty said. "He was quite a bit older than I was. I think I was twenty-two when I was in his class, so that would have made him thirty-one. But, goodness, he was devilishly handsome. He scared the liver out of me, but I never let *him* see that. Everyone knew he was engaged to be married. That didn't stop me from mooning over him, mind you."

When she stopped to take a drink of wine, I was afraid to move. I could hardly believe my ears.

"I thought I was being discreet in my admiration. We'd meet to discuss assignments and essays, and we'd end up chatting for hours. I flattered myself enough to think he found me interesting, but never once allowed myself to believe he saw me as anything more than a star student. You can imagine my surprise when he sent a bouquet of roses to my house on my graduation day."

Patty's eyes had glazed over. She was somewhere else, seeing her husband in her mind's eye.

"He'd broken off his engagement. Told me he'd been counting the days until my graduation, hoping and praying I wouldn't take a beau before he'd have a chance to tell me how he felt. He'd wanted to tell me his feelings many times, but he knew any admission would complicate our relationship. Once I'd graduated and he wasn't my professor any longer, he couldn't wait another moment. The whole thing caused quite a kerfuffle, especially in those days. We courted that whole summer. Had a wonderful time together. We were married on September first."

Patty's eyes came back into focus.

"So, you see, Aubrey," she said, "I'm quite familiar with *complicated* relationships."

"Were there any repercussions? Did he get in trouble?" I asked, looking first at Patty and then at Daniel.

"He hadn't truly done anything wrong, my dear. Unfortunately, he did break his fiancée's heart. And there was a lot of talk. But after we were married, we moved to England. He got a position at Oxford. We stayed there until nineteen sixty-seven. Gwen and Gail were born in England. He was so pleased when Daniel decided to go to Oxford to get his degree."

Daniel leaned over to refill our empty glasses.

"At any rate, that's the skeleton that rattles in my closet from time to time. You're not the first to find yourself in a complicated relationship, and you most certainly won't be the last."

"Thank you for telling me," I said. Daniel smiled, his eyes kind.

He continued to gaze at me from time to time as Patty shared more tales about her life in England with her husband and their years of traveling before they had children. She regaled me with stories of Daniel's childhood, embarrassing him numerous times with her anecdotes. She also talked a great deal about Bradley and Jeremy, the very picture of a doting grandmother.

We sat at the table for close to an hour and a half. At last she finished her third glass of wine and said, "Goodness, my lips are a little numb."

"I'm not surprised. Maybe you should come and sit over here," Daniel said, helping her up and leading her to an armchair. "Besides, *60 Minutes* is on soon." Daniel flipped on the TV. "You relax. Aubrey and I will clean up, okay?"

"All right." Patty squeezed his hand.

While we cleared the table and filled the dishwasher, I was lost in my thoughts, but I could see Daniel watching me with interest. As I brought the last few dishes from the dining room and piled them on the counter, he stopped me and took my hands in his.

"Are you okay?" he asked.

"Yes, I'm just surprised. I didn't see that coming at all," I whispered.

"I respect my grandmother's privacy. That wasn't my story to tell. But now you know why I felt comfortable bringing you here. Of all people, Patty would be the last one to judge our relationship. That's why I wasn't alarmed when we bumped into her on Friday." He smiled sheepishly. "Sorry for holding out on you."

"I guess I'm starting to get used to the Grant family fence posts." I reached up to give him a quick kiss. "Let's finish this."

I piled up the saucepans and filled the sink with hot, sudsy water, watching Daniel push his sleeves up.

"Now, what's that smile about?" Daniel asked, standing behind me and wrapping his arms around me.

"I was just thinking about how much I love your forearms."

"You do?"

"Uh-huh. They're very furry."

He chuckled. "No one's ever told me that before. Why am I picturing cavemen?"

I smiled and turned around. He leaned against me, pushing my lower back into the counter.

"I happen to find it very masculine," I assured him, swirling my fingers in the hairs peeping out of the top of his T-shirt. "I like this too, though," I murmured, dropping soft kisses along the expanse of smooth skin between the stubble on his throat and his chest hairs.

"So do I," he said, claiming my lips and kissing me deeply, his tongue working its magic as it moved against mine, turning me into a puddle of goo.

I tried to talk between kisses. "We probably shouldn't do this right now—"

"Aubrey, Patty's snoring. It's nice not to be outside or in my car, don't you think? Throw me a bone." He kissed me again, moaning quietly against my lips.

"I'll give you a bone, all right," I teased.

"Too late. I think you already did," he said, smirking as he took in my superior smile.

"Not exactly a newsflash."

"What, and you're completely unaffected?"

"Did I say that?"

He cocked an eyebrow. "Typical country weather down south?"

I moved in close to his ear. "Typical *English* country weather."

He groaned, trying to adjust himself. "These jeans are killing me. Do you think having blue balls really is fatal?"

"Don't tell me you're not taking care of business when you get home." I laughed. "That was quite the confession at the table earlier. Very enlightening."

He smacked my ass playfully. "You're getting a little too cocky for your own good, you know that?"

"I know nothing of the sort. Now, would you get out of the way so I can finish the dishes?"

"Yes, ma'am," he said, picking up Patty's plate and scraping it into the garbage can.

While he was bent over, I took the opportunity to thoroughly check out his ass. His jeans were killing me, too. I watched the snowflakes landing on the hedge outside the window and smiled dreamily, overwhelmed with how easy this felt.

"I should wake Patty or she won't sleep tonight," Daniel said.

I wiped the counter down while he roused his grandmother. "I wasn't asleep. Just resting my eyes for a minute," I heard her say.

"Of course. Aubrey and I have cleaned up the kitchen. It's still snowing. I think we should head out before the roads get too bad."

I dried my hands and joined them in the living room. Patty started pushing herself out of the chair.

"No, don't get up. We'll see ourselves out," Daniel insisted. He leaned down to kiss her forehead.

"Do you mind if I pop into the washroom before we go?" I said.

"No, go ahead." Daniel motioned to the hall. "You know where it is?"

"Yes, I'll just be a sec."

I used the washroom quickly. As I rinsed my hands, I peered at my flushed face in the mirror. What was it about Daniel's passionate kisses that set me on fire?

I headed back to the living room and saw Daniel crouched before his grandmother, listening as she spoke to him earnestly. She was running her fingers through his hair, kind of tucking it over his ear as she spoke. They obviously adored each other. Feeling like I was trespassing on an intimate family moment, I stepped unnoticed into the hall again and closed the bathroom door with a loud click.

Daniel stood up and Patty smiled, beckoning me over. "Daniel, go put your coat on," she said.

In other words: *What I have to say is not for your ears.*

"How about I go out and start the car?" He tugged his coat on and dashed outside.

"Now listen to me," Patty said, squeezing my fingers. "Daniel is a good boy. He'll treat you well, but you mustn't be afraid to assert yourself. He's had his fair share of heartache, but he's not made of porcelain. Sometimes he can get quite uppity, but you're an intelligent young woman. If he gets up on his high horse, don't be afraid to push him off, all right?"

"Why do I get the sense you aren't just talking about your grandson?" I asked.

"You *are* quick." She winked at me. "Don't worry about David and Gwen. What they don't know won't hurt them. I gather your friendship with Daniel is special. Remember to be careful and, most importantly, always be discreet. And remind Daniel that Gerald isn't to be discussed with *anyone*."

"I will. And thank you for dinner. I've had a wonderful evening."

"It's been lovely having you," she said.

Daniel came back inside, stomping his feet on the mat. "It's still coming down out there. We should go, Aubrey."

I gave Patty's hand a final squeeze and joined Daniel in the hall. He helped me with my coat, pulling my hair free of my collar.

"Bye, Patty. I'll call you this week," Daniel said. "Thanks for everything."

"You're most welcome. Drive carefully."

Daniel followed me outside, locking her door behind him. Soon we were on our way, the car fishtailing a little as we pulled out of the driveway. Daniel gripped the steering wheel with both hands and turned to me with an inquisitive smile.

"So?" he asked as we made our way down Patty's street.

"She's amazing."

"She really is. She's had some incredible experiences. I wish my grandfather were still alive. You'd have liked him."

"I bet you're a lot like him."

"So I'm told." He squinted out at the falling snow.

"I'm so over this winter, you have no idea," I said.

"You're not a fan of snow?" he asked.

"Nope. Aside from Christmas, I can't find anything redeeming about winter at all."

"Huh. We're going to have to do something about that."

"Like what?"

"Hmm. I'll think of something."

He smiled mysteriously. Fine. Let him have his little secrets or plans. Nothing was going to change the fact that winter aggravated me to no end. Daniel made a sudden right turn.

"Where are we going?" I asked.

"I had an idea. Something I want to show you. You're not in a hurry to get home, are you?"

"Not really."

"Good." We continued along a meandering road and then a parking lot appeared around the bend. He pulled in and stopped.

"This is High Park, right?" I asked.

"That's right. Will your boots keep your feet warm if we were to walk along the paths?"

"My boots are fine. Yours? Not so much," I pointed out.

Authoritative-sounding and hellishly sexy? Yes. Practical? Not at all.

"Don't worry about me." He climbed out and came around to open my door. "Careful. It's slippery."

"I'm fine. It's just a bit of snow."

"Okay. Well, give me a minute."

The snow was coming down in thick, wet chunks. It was dark, peaceful, and, dare I say it, beautiful. While Daniel poked around in the trunk, I tried to find my gloves. Where had Daniel thrown them earlier? I rooted around on the passenger side floor of the car and found one, but couldn't locate the other one.

"Crap!"

"What's wrong?" Daniel asked as I continued to dig around under my seat. "Well, this is an unexpected treat," he said, stepping up behind me and putting his hands on my hips.

"Be serious for a second, would you? I can't find my other glove."

He laughed. "Wow, that's incredible. You've truly got a gift."

"Hey, this wasn't my fault. You're the one who threw them around earlier."

"You're right. I'm a cad. We'll look for it later, though, okay? Let's head out before it gets too late."

I sighed. "All right."

I slipped my single glove on and pulled my hood over my hair, tightening the toggles.

"You look adorable," he said, dropping a soft kiss on my lips. "And completely unrecognizable," he added with a wink. He tugged my bare hand into his pocket.

I motioned to the blanket hanging over his arm. "Do you always keep that in your car?"

"Winter survival kit."

"Of course. Very practical. Tell me, Mr. Grant, are you actually doing something spontaneous or did you plan this?"

"Me? Do something impulsive? Surely you jest."

"True. What was I thinking? You're so much like your father. Not an impulsive bone in your body."

"Well, maybe one," he said, laughing.

We walked on in silence for a couple of minutes. "It is a lovely night," I admitted at last.

"These are the best snowfalls, when it's not too cold and the snow sticks to the trees. It's so peaceful. Perfect. I missed this when I was in the UK."

I turned to smile at him, and he frowned. "What?"

"You're quite the sensitive soul, aren't you?" I asked.

"I'm not sure how to answer that. I wouldn't want you to think I'm a pussy."

"Why do guys make it seem like caring about things is a sign of weakness? So you appreciate nature. You love poetry. You care about your grandmother. You're sensitive and you do thoughtful things — why does any of that have to be construed as you being a pussy? I don't understand."

"That's because you're not a guy with two merciless brothers."

"What's that got to do with how *I* feel about you, though?"

"Nothing, I guess. Just so long as you don't rat me out," he said sheepishly.

Men. Regardless of how sensitive Daniel seemed, at the end of the day, he was a man. A gorgeous and incredibly sexy man. And miracle of miracles, he was *mine*.

"Okay, here we are," he said, approaching a park bench at the edge of the path. He brushed the snow off and then stretched the blanket out on the slats and sat down.

"You wanted to show me a bench?" I sat beside him.

"This isn't any old bench. Look." He took out his phone, leaned away from me, and shone the display at an engraved plaque fixed to the top slat.

"In loving memory of Bradford Daniel Wright. '*Kites rise highest against the wind — not with it,*'" I read.

Daniel smiled sadly as he pocketed his phone and slipped his arm around me.

"Your grandfather," I said.

"He and Patty used to come to High Park every day to walk, and they'd always stop and sit here. After he passed away, Patty made a donation to the municipality, and they put this plaque on the bench. The words are John Neal's. Gramps loved kite analogies. If Patty ever wants to feel close to my grandfather, this is where she comes."

"Thank you."

"For what?"

"For bringing me here. It means a lot that you would share this with me. This place is obviously close to your heart."

He pushed my hood back gently.

"You know you're making quite a home for yourself in my heart too, right?"

I swallowed thickly. Speechless again. I lowered my eyes, but he tilted my face up, kissing me tenderly, his tongue slipping warmly between my lips.

"Your nose is cold," I said as he pulled away.

"Your tongue is hot," he whispered.

I leaned into him, eager for more. He pressed his lips against mine, his hands caressing my face.

"I meant what I said a minute ago," he said. "You're all I think about. Sometimes I feel like I've known you forever, and other times you do or say something that reminds me how much I still have to learn. I wish we had more time together."

"I know what you mean." I snuggled into his neck as he held me close.

"*I have no precious time at all to spend, nor services to do, till you require,*" he whispered. "*Nor dare I chide the world-without-end hour whilst I, my sovereign, watch the clock for you.*"

"You wrote that sonnet out for me a few days before Mary's memorial service," I reminded him.

"It's a favorite."

"The sonnets aren't my specialty, unfortunately."

"You'd better brush up, Miss Price. I happen to know of an assignment that'll require some attention to Master Shakespeare's sonnets."

"Jeez, here we go. On with the TA hat." I sighed.

He laughed. "Oh, come on, I've avoided shop-talk all evening. I've been good, haven't I?"

"I'd say you've been *very* good." I raised an eyebrow.

"And you, my lovely, are incorrigible," he said, kissing me with an intensity that made my heart gallop. "Stay with me tonight."

I gaped at him, dumbfounded. "What did you say?"

"Stay with me. I want you to come home with me."

My heart pounded harder. "Daniel, that's not a good idea. You don't know what you're saying."

"I know exactly what I'm saying," he insisted, kissing my cheek. "I haven't forgotten your conditions and our compromise. I'm just as determined to take things slowly as you are. Like you said on Friday, I want us to spend time getting to know each other. I don't have some master plan to try to seduce you. Well, that's not entirely true, but I promise not to put it into effect tonight."

I rolled my eyes, and he grinned.

"I have a pull-out couch in my office. I'll sleep there, and you can sleep in my bed. All this sneaking around is getting old. Wouldn't it be nice to be together without looking over our shoulders?"

"You can't be serious."

"I've never been more serious."

He kissed me again. I couldn't focus, couldn't possibly be expected to formulate rational thoughts. I closed my eyes as he slid his nose gently along my jaw and nuzzled my ear. "Please say yes."

Oh God. Yes—yes to whatever you want! Anything!

"I can't," I said. "I have to work in the morning. And I have a huge PowerPoint presentation that I need to finish before Tuesday."

"I'll help you with your presentation," he said. "You can use my laptop. You can be home in plenty of time to get to work. I have to meet my dad in the morning, anyway." He kissed me again. "Say yes."

I could feel my resolve wavering. I was going to argue that I didn't even have access to the work I'd already done on my presentation, but I'd emailed the rough draft to my group members and could easily retrieve it from my outbox.

"But I don't have any clothes, a toothbrush…" I didn't sound quite as convincing as I meant to.

He looked at me earnestly.

"Now you're being silly. We'll swing by a store on the way home so you can grab a toothbrush, and you can wear some of my clothes—sweats or something." He paused for a moment. "Are you making excuses?"

"Maybe."

"Why?"

"I'm afraid it would be too easy to give in," I confessed. "You don't understand the effect you have on me."

My mind raced as I thought through the possible scenarios if I were to spend the night at his condo. All of the ways that everything could go horribly wrong—or magnificently right, depending on how you looked at it.

"I promise this isn't about me trying to push you to do anything. I want to spend time with you somewhere safe. And somewhere warm, damn it!"

He shivered and held me closer, as if doing so would eliminate the chill in the air. Somewhere safe. Somewhere warm. That *did* sound awfully appealing. And he was promising not to push me. He had no expectations.

"Okay," I said quietly.

He tilted my face up. "Okay?"

"Yes."

"Really?"

"You'd better stop asking, or I might change my mind," I said with a chuckle.

"All right, shutting up," he said, standing and holding out his hand to help me up. He tugged my hood back over my head and tucked my hair into the sides. "Okay then. Let's go home."

CHAPTER 4

Temptation

Most dangerous
Is that temptation that doth goad us on
To sin in loving virtue…
(*Measure for Measure*, Act II, Scene 2)

I rode the elevator alone. Daniel had decided this was the discreet thing to do, heading up to the condo before me to await my arrival. The depraved part of my brain despised this prudent decision. There was something incredibly hot about a quick clutch and grope in an elevator. Thwarted again by good sense.

We'd swung by a pharmacy where Daniel had insisted I buy everything I would normally use at home, including whatever products made me smell "so fucking delicious." He'd handed me some money, insisting that it was his treat. He smiled and winked at me when I climbed in the car with the bag full of toiletries, satisfied that I'd done as he'd asked.

Now I was at his condo, trepidation and excitement blending in the pit of my stomach. When the elevator announced its arrival on Daniel's floor, I stepped out and stopped for a minute, resting my forehead against the wall and taking a deep breath. What the hell was I doing? Was I actually entertaining the idea of staying over? It wasn't too late to bail. I could stay for an hour or two and then insist he take me home.

My waffling was cut short by the sound of a clicking latch down the hall. Daniel's head popped out of a door about twenty feet away. He moved to stand in the doorway, one arm against the frame, his other hand seeking his pocket.

"What are you doing?" he asked, his voice echoing in the empty hallway.

I leaned against the wall. "Chickening out?"

He approached me cautiously and sighed, frowning as he twirled a lock of my hair around his finger. It wasn't a frustrated or impatient sigh, but rather one that said, "Please don't go."

He relieved me of the plastic bag and took my hand in his. His eyes were locked on mine as if I was a shy deer he didn't want to startle. My feet ignored the warning messages from my brain as he led me slowly through the door of his condo and into the entryway.

"Daniel, this is crazy."

My heart hammered a crazy staccato agreement.

He closed the door without pulling his eyes from mine. "Yep. Completely insane." His chest rose and fell rapidly. "Don't leave?"

I shook my head, and he carefully unzipped my coat, slipping it down my arms and tossing it on a bench against the wall. I placed my hands on the nape of his neck, angling my face up to kiss him softly.

"I'm not going anywhere," I whispered.

"Thank God."

He gathered me close, and I yielded to the heat of his insistent kisses, quivering and desperate for more. He really was the most incredible kisser. I pressed my body against his, and he pulled me closer still. Finally he took a step backward, his eyes heavy with unconcealed longing.

"Holy fuck," he breathed.

"No kidding."

"I seriously need to get the hell out of these jeans. I'd like to be able to procreate one day."

My eyes traveled down to his zipper. "There certainly doesn't seem to be a lot of room for—*movement*—down there."

"As I've said on a couple of occasions—"

"Yeah, yeah, I know. I'm sure John Holmes has *nothing* on you."

He raised his eyebrows. "Wow, I didn't know you were a big fan of seventies porn."

"Are you sure? I thought I mentioned that when I introduced myself at the first tutorial," I said.

He laughed and mimicked me. "'*Hi, I'm Aubrey Price, I live in rez at Vic and I'm a huge fan of John Holmes' giant dong'*? I think I'd remember that." He gave my ass a pinch.

I swatted at his hand. "I see we have a lot of ground to cover. Clearly you don't know me at all. I guess it's a good thing I agreed to come over."

"Apparently." He grabbed my coat and hung it in the closet. "How about I show you around?" he said. "Then I *have* to get out of these fucking jeans."

He retrieved the bag of toiletries and led me into an open-concept living room, dining room, and kitchen area. The stainless steel appliances and marble counter tops in the kitchen, the soft brown leather couch, the cherry wood dining set and the stereo with top of the line speakers—everything said, "I am Daniel Grant. Only the best will do." What really drew my eye were the floor-to-ceiling bookshelves running the expanse of the far wall. He had quite the library for someone his age.

Daniel waved his free arm around. "Kitchen, obviously. Help yourself to whatever you want. Dining area—"

"Incredibly beautiful bookshelves," I interjected. "You've read all those books, no doubt?"

"Yeah, they do sort of take over the room," he said with a sheepish smile. "Books are my guilty pleasure." He took my hand and showed me down a hallway, then knocked on a closed door. "Powder room." He pushed open the door across from the bathroom and I poked my head inside. "This is my office. It's more of a den, I suppose."

He shrugged self-consciously, and I stepped into the room, casting my eyes over the built-in entertainment unit with more bookshelves, a big screen TV in the center, another oversized couch with a coffee table in front of it, and on the far side of the room, a large, uncluttered desk with a laptop and a few books neatly stacked on one side. An acoustic guitar was propped on a stand beside the couch.

"So, this is where the really important stuff happens," I said, gesturing toward the desk.

"No, that would be in here." He led me to the next door — his bedroom.

I laughed. "No, this is where the *magic* happens."

"*Will* happen," he said. "You'll be happy to know nothing even remotely magical has happened in this room in the six weeks I've lived here."

"I am happy to hear that." I surveyed the room. The bed was neatly made and covered in a lovely chocolate brown and white duvet. "King size?"

"Yeah, I guess that seems self-indulgent too," he said, ducking his head.

"And another TV?"

"Sometimes I fall asleep with it on at night. Makes the place seem less empty."

My heart ached for him. I'd never lived by myself for any extended period of time. What would it be like, rattling around in a condo this size all alone? It was beautiful, though. I couldn't help wondering if the interior decorating was Gwen's handiwork. There was a touch of elegance, a softness to the design that, while not overtly feminine, still betrayed a woman's involvement.

"Okay, I have to ditch this bag. I can't wait to see what you've got in here. Feels like you bought a bowling ball. Washroom's in here," he said, leading me to the ensuite bathroom.

"Wow, this is beautiful."

The clean lines and dark tiles of the oversized tub and glassed-in shower stall were masculine and tasteful. And everything was so clean. There's no way Matt could keep a bathroom this spotless.

Daniel started pulling items out of the bag, examining them before lining everything up on the counter. He unscrewed the lid of the shampoo, smiling as he waved the bottle under his nose. "This is what you usually use, right?"

"Yep. Sweet pea and jasmine."

"God, no wonder you smell so delicious. Do you seriously use all this stuff every day?"

I crossed my arms. "You know, you're kind of blowing my feminine mystique out of the water by analyzing the shit out of everything."

He chuckled. "You're right, I'm sorry. This is a bit of an invasion of your privacy, isn't it?"

"I'm only kidding," I assured him. I was actually hoping he'd keep unpacking the bag because there was one particular item I'd bought as a joke. Unfortunately, I'd made him self-conscious and he'd stopped.

He opened a deep drawer under the vanity. "You can put everything in here," he offered.

"Okay, I'll hand stuff to you, and you can put it away," I suggested, starting to hand him things. Then I reached into the bag and gave him the tube of K-Y Jelly.

He pulled his head back sharply, his brows furrowed. "What the fuck is this?"

"What does it look like?" I asked, trying to keep a straight face. He squinted, reading the product description on the back label.

"'*Apply to areas of body where sensational personal lubrication is needed.*' Is this for real?"

"Well, I didn't buy it for tonight, but, you know, one day — "

Daniel backed me up to the counter and lifted me so I was sitting on the vanity. He stood between my legs.

"Excuse me, but what happened to typical English country weather? If you ever need to use this, I'll eat my fucking hat."

He tossed the tube on the counter and drew my hips forward, rubbing against me purposefully. I closed my eyes and breathed deeply as Daniel's tongue parted my lips and darted playfully against mine. His teeth tugged on my lower lip, and then he gently sucked on my earlobe, his warm breath sending a delicious shiver down my spine.

I wrapped my legs around him, and his fingers sank into my hips. A series of images flickered through my mind: Daniel's tongue running down across my breasts, pausing to flick over my nipples before traveling lower and finally coming to rest between my thighs where he would surely drive me to the brink of ecstasy —

He stepped away from me, resting his hands on my thighs, mighty pleased with himself. He'd made his point. Soundly.

"Well?" he asked, raising an inquisitive eyebrow.

I sighed and regained my composure, then admitted defeat. "Torrential rains. I guess you're right." I reached for the tube of K-Y, prepared to drop it in the garbage pail, but then another idea occurred to me. "Maybe you'd like to keep this for your own personal use? A little lube to go with the oil change? Self-employed people are often looking for business write-offs for income tax purposes. I *did* keep the receipt." I smiled innocently.

"All right, move your cheeky ass, young lady."

I hopped off the vanity. He opened the mirrored cabinet beside the sink and tossed the lube inside, shaking his head and smiling. Then he held out his hand. "Toothbrush."

I handed it over, and he stowed it in the cabinet. There was a row of prescription pill bottles on the top shelf—he sure was keeping some pharmaceutical company in business. I considered asking him if he suffered from migraines or something, but he closed the cabinet with such a decisive click that my question evaporated. When the rest of my toiletries were in the drawer, he took my hand, and we went back into the bedroom.

"Before you start your school work, do you want to change into something cooler? You must be boiling."

I pulled at the neck of my sweater. "It is a little warm in here. And humid." I winked.

He laughed. "Ah, crazy legs, what am I going to do with you?"

"I'm sure you'll think of something."

"You know me well."

"Do I?" I put my hands on his chest, thinking about the reason Daniel had wanted me to spend the night with him.

"You feel like you *don't* know me?"

"I think there's a lot going on in here that I haven't even begun to understand," I said, patting his heart. "Not to mention in here." I gently circled his temple.

"You may be right. How about this for a plan? You work on your presentation for a bit, and then we'll make Julie proud. We'll curl up in bed—"

I raised an eyebrow.

"Okay, we'll curl up *on* the bed, fully dressed," he amended. "You can tell me your whole life story."

He retrieved a pair of striped, cotton men's pajamas from his dresser drawer.

"Here," he said. "Give these a try. I'll go change in the office." He grabbed a pair of blue jeans from the closet and crossed to the door. "Did you want something to drink? A beer, a glass of wine?"

"If you have some red wine, I'll have a glass of that."

"Done. Take your time." He closed the door.

I undressed and piled my folded clothes neatly on top of the dresser. At home, I would've tossed my clothes on a chair, but there wasn't a single stray item to be seen on the two club chairs beside the bed. Damn, he was neat.

I put the pajamas on over my bra and panties, rolling the waist band over a few times. Imagining Daniel wearing stripy PJs made me smile. Actually, imagining Daniel doing *anything* made me smile.

I sighed and looked at myself in the mirror above the dresser. "How in the hell did you manage this, Aubrey?" I whispered to my reflection. It had no ready answer.

I headed into the hallway, adjusting the cuffs as I walked. A side table lamp cast a dim light in the office. Daniel was leaning against the windows looking out at the view, a glass of beer in his hand. He'd taken off his sweater, revealing the white T-shirt he'd worn underneath. He'd swapped the fertility-threatening black jeans for my favorite holey ones. His feet, like mine, were bare.

"Hey." He turned as I walked through the door.

"I thought you said you weren't going to try to seduce me tonight."

He laughed. "What do you mean?"

"You know what those jeans do to me."

He snapped his fingers. "That *had* slipped my mind, but now that you mention it…" He smiled. "Comfortable?"

I looked down at myself, shrugging awkwardly. "I guess."

"You look very cute."

"What I *feel* is ridiculous," I admitted with a sheepish grin, looking around the tidy room. "Hey, Daniel, your place is spotless. How do you keep this up?"

He chuckled. "Are you a slob, sweetheart?"

"A slob? Well, that's a rather strong word. I'm not OCD about tidying, though, that's for sure."

"OCD? Now *that's* a strong word! Are you suggesting I have some sort of neurosis?"

He smiled, still leaning comfortably against the window, but his eyes were narrowed. I sensed an unspoken challenge. I took in the even piles of papers and books, the neatly aligned pens and pencils on his desk, the strategically placed photographs on the bookshelf, the obvious lack of clutter. I couldn't help thinking of his BMW — always immaculate, inside and out.

I sauntered over to the coffee table to examine the carefully stacked magazines.

Daniel watched as I bent over and pushed one of the magazines off the pile. I raised an eyebrow. He shrugged, but didn't move. I took two magazines off the pile and threw them on the couch. He sighed deeply, but remained standing where he was. I waited a moment more, biting my lip, and then pushed the whole stack over on the coffee table. Daniel stiffened and dropped his arm from the window sill.

"What are you doing, Aubrey?"

"Making the place look lived in," I said, jutting out my chin.

"That's supposed to bother me? Is that it?" he asked, a strange glint in his eye.

"I don't know. Does it?"

He took a quick swig of his beer and put his glass down on the desk as he walked over to join me. "What if I said no?"

"I'm not sure I'd believe you."

He looked from me to the scattered magazines. I leaned over and slowly pushed the most recent issue of *Maclean's* onto the floor. He stood in silence for a few seconds, then swept every magazine onto the floor with a flourish. He turned to me, triumphant.

I squealed and flung my arms around his neck to stop myself from falling backward when he whisked me into his arms without warning, but I needn't have worried. He held me securely, pulling my shoulder forward as he kissed me with wild abandon. He dropped onto the couch, lips still locked onto mine, magazines crunching under our weight as we fell back onto the cushions. His tongue was warm and tasted of Guinness. Absolutely delicious.

He propped himself up on an elbow, brushing my hair off my face. "I can't tell you how many times I've imagined this. I can't believe this is actually happening."

"You know what I think?" I said.

"What?"

I grabbed the neck of his T-shirt and pulled him toward me. "I think we should talk later."

He grinned, drawing his legs up onto the couch and pulling me toward him so we were lying side by side.

At last.

He shifted my body slightly, his lips moving against mine. A magazine beneath me crackled and ripped as I rolled onto my back. He pulled away and sighed.

"Move your ass for a sec," he said.

I lifted my butt, which brought our hips firmly together.

He moaned. "See what you do to me?" He pressed against me and tossed the mangled magazine unceremoniously onto the floor.

"I don't know what I was thinking," I said breathlessly. "You're not the slightest bit neurotic."

"I knew you'd see it my way."

He covered my body with his own, deliberately pressing against me and looking into my eyes. I laced my hands in his hair, closed my eyes, and kissed him, teasing his tongue and enjoying the hoarse sound of his moans as he moved against me in a slow, measured pace.

Bliss. Pure, hot bliss. This was so wrong and so incredibly right. Strangely, I found myself repeating a line from The Lord's Prayer over and over again in my mind:

Lead us not into temptation, lead us not into temptation...

But it was too late. Temptation was leading *us*, and we were skipping along behind it like a couple of kids chasing an ice cream truck. Who knew a fully-clothed make-out session could be so hot?

His hand traveled from my hip, down my thigh and under my knee. He pulled my leg up, and the button-fly on his jeans rubbed me at just the right angle, at just the right speed, and God help me, in just the right spot. I was losing my grip, forgetting myself as I strained toward him, matching the pace of his movements.

His lips and tongue were everywhere—on my mouth, on my neck, sliding down to the hollow of my throat, grazing my collarbones. My husky breaths joined his desperate moans. I ran my hand down his side and found my way under his T-shirt, sliding my fingertips slowly up the smooth, taut muscles of his back.

Remember this moment. Remember how incredible his skin feels under your fingers as you touch him for the first time.

"That's amazing," he sighed.

He'd dropped his head forward, eyes closed, drinking in the sensation of my hands on his skin. I gently traced a path down his spine with my nails. His eyebrows came together, and he shivered.

"Fuck, yes, harder," he breathed. "Scratch me so hard that tomorrow I'll know I didn't just dream this."

His eyes clouded over with desire, and his open mouth hovered over mine, our breath mingling. I darted my tongue out to lick the cleft of his chin, dug my fingers into the hollow between his shoulder blades, and then dragged my nails firmly down to the small of his back.

He arched his back and let out a low guttural moan. "So fucking sexy, Aubrey."

He rubbed against me, his pace quickening and his breath following suit as his hand held my hip firmly in place, when suddenly the most ridiculous series of thoughts flew through my mind.

I don't know his middle name, his birthday, how he takes his coffee, his favorite flavor of ice cream. I don't even know the topic of his PhD!

I remembered Julie's words of caution, recalled the reason why I'd agreed to come over tonight. My brain echoed Daniel's words from earlier that evening: "*I haven't forgotten your conditions and our compromise. I'm just as determined to take things slowly as you are. Like you said on Friday, I want us to spend time together, getting to know each other.*"

I froze.

"Daniel," I gasped. "I think you should get off."

"What do you think I'm trying to do?" he said huskily, eyes closed, fingers anchored around my hipbone.

"No, I think you should get off *of me*."

He collapsed against my shoulder, chest heaving. "I was hoping that wasn't what you meant," he groaned.

He rolled onto his side, eyes shut tightly. I placed my hand over his heart and felt the thumping rhythm under my palm.

"Please don't hate me," I whispered.

He shook his head but didn't look at me, his hand now over his eyes. "Why would I hate you?" he asked, sitting up and dragging himself to the other end of the couch.

I quickly refastened the top button of the PJ top. I didn't even know he'd undone it.

"I don't want you to think I'm purposely being a tease." I sat up and slid down to the end of the couch to rest my chin on his shoulder.

He ruffled my hair affectionately. "I don't think you're a tease. I got carried away. It's my fault, not yours. However, if we're going to have a hope in hell of making it through the night, I think I'd better go grab a shower." He rubbed his face with both hands and sighed in defeat. "Will you be okay for a few minutes?"

"I'll be fine. You just go ahead and, um, do whatever it is you need to do. Maybe I'll get started on my stupid PowerPoint." I tried not to laugh. He looked so pained.

"How do women do that?" he asked, an expression of genuine curiosity on his face.

"Do what?"

"You know, walk away and do the damn dishes or something. I'm in agony here."

I ran my fingers through his hair. "I think we're wired differently, sailor."

"I don't know." He sighed, giving me a chaste kiss. "Fortitude of a saint, if you ask me. Feel free to use my laptop." He winked at me and made his way out the door.

How *was* I managing to keep a grip on myself? Wired differently, my ass. I slid Daniel's chair up to the desk and logged onto my email, rolling my shoulders as I waited for the program to load. I'd need to get at least an hour of work in before we could chill. I found the message with the attached Word document containing everyone's research information. While it opened, I sipped my wine and thought about Daniel in the glass shower stall, the doors coated with condensation as he soaped himself up…

Okay, not a good idea at all.

I cleared my throat and forced myself to sit up straight, focusing on the document in front of me. I was frowning and reading one of my group member's analyses when movement in the doorway caught my eye. Daniel was watching me as he rubbed the back of his neck with a towel. His face was flushed. He'd changed into a pair of PJ bottoms but still wore his white T-shirt.

"How's it going?" he asked. "Getting a lot done?"

"Just proofreading and editing. How was your shower? Did *you* get a lot done?"

"I accomplished what I set out to do, yes. Thank you for your concern," he said, smiling self-deprecatingly.

He joined me, resting against the desk. "Hey," he said. I looked up at him. "You probably think I was lying my face off earlier now that I've proven myself to be a complete horn dog."

I couldn't help laughing. "You think I'm just realizing *now* that you're a horn dog?"

"This is true. Seriously, though, I got caught up in the moment. Thank you for stopping me when you did." He laughed. "I never thought I'd hear myself say that. Anyway, I think I've got my act together now, so I promise to conduct myself appropriately for the rest of the evening."

"That doesn't sound like much fun."

He leaned over to kiss me softly. "Now who's the horn dog?" he whispered.

"Guilty as charged."

I stole another quick kiss before peering back down at the laptop.

"How can I help?" he asked, looking over my shoulder.

"I'm okay with the content. It's all the transitions and animations in PowerPoint that I get frustrated with."

"I'd be happy to help you with that. Let me grab another beer first." He turned back to me when he got to the door. "Oh, and make sure you're saving that. My laptop can be temperamental sometimes. Use the flash drive."

Having lost my fair share of important assignments over the years, I clicked on his USB drive and attempted to save the document as "Aubrey."

A dialogue box opened up.

The file "Aubrey" already exists. Do you want to replace existing file?

Daniel had a Word document saved with my name? Okay, that was kind of weird. I clicked "no" and tried again, this time using my full name.

The file "Aubrey Price" already exists. Do you want to replace existing file?

What the hell? I frowned and opened the flash drive menu. Six main folders popped up.

One of the folders was called *Aubrey*. I nibbled on my nail for a second and then clicked to open the folder. Inside there were three documents: *Documentation, Aubrey Price,* and *Aubrey.* The temptation to open the files was overwhelming. I tapped my foot and heard Daniel whistling as he came back down the hall. I closed the file folder hurriedly, yanked the flash drive out of the USB port, and tossed it across the desk. It landed beside a paper weight — a glass figure of Sisyphus pushing a shiny metallic boulder up a crystalline mountain.

Daniel strolled back into the room, and I looked up with a start.

"Everything okay?" he asked.

"Yeah, yeah, everything's great." I forced myself to smile.

I looked again at the flash drive, and my eyes were drawn back to the paper weight and the words etched in silver script along its mahogany base:

The truth shall make you free.

Love is All Truth

Love surfeits not, Lust like a glutton dies;
Love is all truth, Lust full of forged lies.
(*Venus and Adonis*)

"**R**ight, let's take a look," Daniel said, squeezing my shoulder as he pulled a chair over to sit beside me.

I avoided looking at him, quickly copying and pasting the entire text I'd edited into an email and re-sending it to myself before closing all the programs.

"You know what? I think I'll work on this tomorrow. I don't want to waste time when we could be relaxing and talking," I said.

I needed to get away from this desk. Away from Sisyphus and his eerily pointed message.

"Besides, I don't have the novel, and what I need to do next is look for quoted support, you know, to back up my own points, so I should probably wait until I'm home…" I trailed off, wishing Daniel would say something because I was quickly approaching Aubrey-who-can't-lie-without-turning-red-as-a-beet territory.

"Really? What's the book?" he asked.

"*Madame Bovary.*"

"I think you're in luck." He pointed to the top of his book shelf. "That's all French lit. I'm sure I've got it if you want to check."

I had no desire to start looking for quotations in *Madame Bovary*, but I decided to humor him and distance myself from Sisyphus at the same time. I got up and scanned the book shelf, mumbling titles as I read the spines.

"Here it is." He reached over my shoulder. "Right here, beside *L'Invitée.*"

He handed me the book, and I glanced at the next few volumes on the shelf.

"Daniel, are these arranged in alphabetical order?" I asked.

He crossed his arms and rested against the bookshelf with a smirk. "Maybe."

"Wow, you are *so* much like your father," I said.

"I'm going to choose not to be offended by that observation."

He reached up and gave the bookshelf a little shake. "One day we'll test out how solid this is," he said with a saucy wink. "So, did you enjoy it?" He pointed at the novel in my hand.

"It's okay. Not my favorite, but it's all right." I slid the book back into its spot on the shelf. "There's no way I can do anything else tonight, Daniel. Can we just curl up and talk now?"

Not so appealing was the first topic I planned to broach, but we'd made a pact on Friday. *No more secrets.* If I wanted to know what was in those files, I'd have to ask. If he wanted to be open with me, he'd answer.

"Are you sure you got enough done?"

"I'll be fine, honestly."

"Okay. It's your call." He freed himself from my arms and moved over to the desk. He located his USB drive on the other side of the desk and held it up. "So, you don't need this?"

I waved my hand. "I didn't save anything on there. I cut and pasted the text into an email and sent it to myself."

"That works."

He opened the top drawer and was about to drop his flash drive inside, but instead he pulled out another USB stick almost identical to the first. His face registered first confusion, then panic.

"Shit. Did you open any folders on this flash drive?" He held out the one he'd suggested I use.

Oh, hell. Here we go.

"Sort of," I said.

He dropped into the chair, looking like the wind had been knocked out of him.

"I meant to give you this empty one." He held up the other stick. "What did you see?" He looked truly panicked.

Holy shit, what was in those documents that would make him react this way?

"Nothing. I didn't open anything. I saw the *names* of the files."

"Fuck, this is exactly why we shouldn't be doing this." He dropped his head in his hands. "You honestly didn't open anything?" he asked, glancing up at me again.

"I told you I didn't open the files. I ripped the damn thing out of the drive before I could see anything. Which wasn't easy, by the way. There I was, innocently trying to save my work under my name, and I kept coming across these damned files already named after me."

He frowned and mouthed a few words without sound. Finally he found his voice. "What? No, I'm not talking about *those* files. I'm talking about the tests, the sample exam questions, all of the stuff from my meetings with Martin."

I stared back at him, equally confused. "I didn't see anything like that. I was a tad distracted by all the *Aubrey* files."

He expelled a gusty breath and put his hand over his heart. He bent forward and breathed deeply several times before sitting back up. "You're sure you didn't see anything?"

"Don't ask me that again, Daniel. I mean it."

He tossed the flash drives in the drawer and slammed it. Then he joined me on the other side of the desk.

"I'm sorry," he said, unlocking my crossed my arms and coaxing me into his embrace.

"Don't let me anywhere near your computer or your flash drives again until the course is over," I mumbled into his neck. "That was the dumbest idea ever. What if I *had* come across something by accident?"

He relaxed back against the desk, and I stood between his legs, eyes level with his.

"I don't know what I was thinking. I guess I *wasn't*. I have too many USB sticks, and I got them mixed up. I'm sorry I accused you. That was uncalled for."

"I understand why you had to ask. Although *once* would have sufficed," I added. "But now I have to ask—are those files with my name on them for school too? Do you have files on everyone?"

"I have records of the students in the class, but they're generic attendance and participation records. The files aren't labeled for each individual student."

"So, what are the ones with my name on them?" I asked.

"Would it be enough for me to tell you there's nothing reprehensible in those files? Would that satisfy you?"

"Not really. Relieve me? A little."

"Relieve you? In what way?"

"Well, it did cross my mind that maybe there was something creepy or stalkerish in there. Like maybe you've got access to my personal records or something."

As soon as the words were out of my mouth I realized how awful they sounded.

"Stalkerish? Wow." His hands loosened around my waist.

"Okay, that didn't come out right. But wouldn't you be weirded out if you were me and you came across a bunch of files on my computer with your name on them?"

"Since I know what those files are, it's hard for me to think about that question objectively." He shook his head. "I can't believe you thought I would invade your privacy by accessing your personal files."

"I can't believe *you* thought I would open documents that were obviously tests or exam questions," I retorted.

He sighed, re-clasping his hands behind my back. "We did it again, didn't we?"

"Did what?"

"Jumped to conclusions, over-reacted, failed to give each other the benefit of the doubt."

I took a step back, freeing myself from his linked hands. "It's a little disconcerting, isn't it?"

He wrinkled his nose at me like he was trying to solve a difficult puzzle. I wandered back to the bookshelf, needing a momentary escape. I scanned the titles of three large hardcover books at the end of one of the shelves: *A Clinical Guide to Anxiety in Adults, Managing your Mind, Mood Disorders.* Before I could even begin to reflect on the significance of this odd set of books, Daniel was beside me.

"I'm sorry I doubted you. You must think I don't trust you at all."

"Do you?"

"Of course I do. I guess I keep hearing my father's voice — like screwing up is inevitable. Maybe part of me worries he might be right."

"I would never do anything to hurt you," I assured him. "If me being here is messing with your head, I'll get dressed and go home right now."

"Stay. Please?" Daniel leaned over his desk to grab our drinks. "Come on," he said. "Let's go in the other room." I followed him into the bedroom, that familiar mixture of anxiety and excitement churning in my stomach again. He put our wine on the dresser and turned to hug me, drawing my face into the crook of his neck. After a few moments he murmured into my hair, "You know what I noticed the other night?"

"What?"

"You fit perfectly right here."

"I kind of do, don't I?"

He let go, and we crossed to the chairs beside the bed. I sat, tucking my feet under me as Daniel flopped into the chair beside me, lost in thought.

"Well?" I prompted him.

"Do you want to see those files?"

I groaned and palmed my forehead. "I feel horrible about what I said. I was out of line."

"It's not a big deal." He held his hand over the arm of the chair. I reached my hand out, and he laced his fingers tightly with mine.

"What if I said I didn't want to see them?" I asked.

"Then I'd say you are the most exasperating woman I've ever known." He tugged at my hand. "Come here."

I sat on his lap, throwing my legs over the side of the chair.

"Those documents are personal, but I wouldn't think twice about showing them to you if I knew it would put your mind at rest," he said. "No secrets, right?"

I wasn't entirely sure I did want to see them now. His willingness to share them blew any remaining discomforting feelings out of the water.

"How about we compromise," I said. "Why don't you give me a vague idea of what they are, and we'll leave it at that?"

"All right." He shifted in the seat. "I started one file on the day you signed up for tutorial. It's called 'Documentation.' It describes our conversations and exchanges."

"That sounds official."

"That's exactly how it started. I was recording the things I'd said to you and the way I'd behaved when I was with you, especially when we were alone. To be honest, I was covering my ass. I sensed some—interest—from you, shall we say, that Tuesday morning. When you signed up for tutorial?"

"Was I that obvious?"

"Well, the blushing and stuttering, not to mention the drool—"

"Fuck off." I laughed. "That was the most epically mortifying first impression I've ever made."

"Not at all. You were charming."

I wasn't sure if should feel insulted by the fact that he'd thought I could potentially threaten his position in the way Nicola had, but I suppose I'd have been equally paranoid if I were in his place. And he hadn't known me at all.

"So, when you were doing this so-called documenting—did you write about your feelings for me?"

"No, of course not. I was in denial. I wrote about how professional I was being. Keeping you at arm's length, not allowing myself to be alone with you in a room with the door closed, never calling you by your first name—that sort of thing."

"So, tell me, Mr. Grant," I said, dropping my voice. "Are you still documenting?"

"No, I'm not, Miss Price. At least not in an official capacity."

"When did you stop?"

"February thirteenth. I wrote one last entry justifying why I'd driven you home after you were sick at the play. Later on, I lay in bed for ages, but I couldn't sleep so I got up and wrote more, but this was very different."

"In what way?"

We were both whispering now.

"Well," he said, trailing his fingers gently along my cheekbone. "I started a new file. It's called 'Aubrey Price' and is hardly something I'd share with a university tribunal." He laughed softly. "I wrote about how much I wanted to kiss you when we were in the theater that night and how helpless I'd felt when you were sick. How insanely jealous I was of the fact that Matt got to spend time with you and I didn't. That's when I understood the hold you had on me."

"Really?" I whispered.

He nodded. "From that point on there was no more documenting. I was trying to come to terms with my feelings, which I knew were completely inappropriate and imprudent," he said, gazing at me from under his lashes.

God, he was so sweet. He cradled my face and rubbed his thumb along my cheekbone.

"I suppose I was joking on Friday when I told you I thought of March thirteenth as our one month anniversary, but that night in February was pivotal in terms of my feelings for you. The usher at Hart House asked me if I wanted her to check on you in the bathroom. She called you my *girlfriend*. I couldn't help wishing it was true."

"Well, all signs do point to that as our first date," I confirmed. "There's no denying it. You've got it in writing."

"I guess I do." He smiled. "Do you want to know more?" he asked. "I'll tell you about the third file if you want, but I'd like to preserve some of my pride."

"No," I said. "I don't need to hear another thing. I do need to get out of this chair, though. My ass is starting to get pins and needles."

He chuckled. "Okay, but we need ground rules before we head over there to curl up," he said, gesturing toward the bed with a bob of his head.

"Ground rules?"

"So things don't get carried away again."

"Wow, this sounds serious."

"It's extremely serious," he said, assuming an expression of mock sternness. "Rule number one. No come-hither lip-biting and raising your eyebrow in that sexy way you have."

"In that case, rule number two. No panty-melting dimply smiles and winking in that sexy way *you* have," I countered.

"Panty-melting? I like the sound of that," he murmured, pushing my hair over my shoulder and kissing my neck, nudging the collar of my PJs aside to caress my shoulder. "Tell me, do these panties match your black bra?"

I squirmed away from his lips. "Rule number three. No doing *any* of that shit you just did."

He laughed again and helped me up as I tried to wiggle out of the crevice between his leg and the arm of the chair.

"I guess I'll have to imagine they match," he said.

"Oh, they match, don't you worry." I rubbed my tingly butt as I crossed to the bed. Daniel followed me, possibly hoping to help me rub away the tingles, when his phone rang.

He grinned as he looked at the display. "Hello, Penny. How are things at the homestead?"

Moving to stand behind me, he wrapped one arm around me and rested his hand on my stomach as he continued his conversation. He swayed me gently as he talked, his side laced with giggles, sounds of surprise, and affectionate expressions, his lovely English lilt getting stronger the longer he spoke.

"How's Penny?" I asked when he'd hung up.

"Good. Worried that Brad's going to give himself a hernia, moving gigantic pieces of furniture around. And she told me to say hi to you when I spoke to you next. So, hi from Penny," he said.

"What was that about going over there to help with something next Sunday?"

"The former owners painted the kitchen walls sea-foam-green. Penny's dying. Jer and I are going over to help repaint. Maybe you could come along?"

"That sounds fun. And speaking of," I said, dragging him over to the bed, "can we? I mean, are we allowed to cuddle now? Or are there more ground rules?"

"How about we use our common sense? After you." He gestured to the bed.

I threw myself onto the comforter and flapped my arms around as if I was making a snow angel.

"What are you doing, woman?" he asked, perching his knee on the edge of the mattress.

"This bed is huge! I love it!" I scooted up toward the throw pillows and flopped against them. "Ah, this is the life." I beckoned, and he stretched out beside me, taking my hand and resting our entwined fingers on my stomach. He looked down at me, his eyebrows drawn together.

"What is it, sweet knees?" I asked, rubbing his bare foot with mine.

"Penny asked if I'd seen you since Friday, and I said I hadn't. I don't think I've ever lied to her before."

"Why didn't you tell her I was here?"

"I'm not sure. Maybe I wanted to keep this between us. Keep it *for* us."

I scanned his face. "That's one of the most wonderful justifications for a lie I've ever heard," I said. "Although, the truth *shall* make you free, Daniel."

"Oh, don't start with that. You saw that paperweight?"

"I did. What's that line from?"

"'*The truth shall make you free*'? That's from the Bible. John 8:32. Any guesses who gave me that as a gift?"

"Your dad?"

"You're a quick study, Miss Price. He gave it to me last year for my birthday. After everything that had happened, he said I needed to remain true to myself and, in the end, everything would work out. I think he was trying to be helpful or inspiring. Most of the time, looking at it makes me think too much."

"In what way?" I sat up a little.

"Usually it makes me wonder if he really does think I'm lying about what happened at Oxford. Sometimes I get philosophical, thinking about the definition of truth. There's a big difference between, 'what is *the* truth' and 'what is truth.' You know what I mean?"

I didn't have a clue. Maybe if it wasn't well after ten o'clock on a Sunday night and I wasn't lying in bed with Daniel, I'd be able to focus on the question.

"You're hurting my brain."

"You want a sore brain, try writing my PhD paper."

"What's it about?"

He sighed and folded his hands under his head. "In a nutshell, it's about Jungian individuation in Shakespeare."

"That's a heavy topic."

"It's fascinating when I'm in a good head space, but crippling when I'm not. I had to walk away from it after the fiasco with Nicola. Then I spent a month re-reading what I'd written before. It was like someone else had written it. It was almost like starting from scratch."

"I can't imagine."

"Then I had to prepare it for acceptance here at U of T. Nothing I'd done at Oxford guaranteed I'd get the go-ahead over here."

"I hate that girl. When I think of the way her false accusations have affected you, it's…" I shook my head.

"You don't know the half of it."

"What do you mean?"

"Nothing. Old wounds."

He held me for a few moments, and we lay there in silence. Then I remembered something.

"Hey, Daniel?"

"Hmm?"

"What's your middle name?"

"Garrison. Same as my dad's."

"That's a cool name."

He smiled up at the ceiling. "What's yours?"

"Lynn."

"Aubrey Lynn. I like that."

"Thanks. Okay, what's your favorite flavor of ice cream?"

He shifted slightly to look down at me. "Seriously?"

"Yes, seriously. Remember I told you I was thinking about crazy stuff earlier before I cock-blocked you? This is what I was thinking about. I need to know."

"Hang on. I was on the verge of jizzing in my jeans, and you were thinking about middle names and ice cream?"

I laughed. "I was caught up in the moment, but it was hard to lose myself in the throes of passion when there are so many things I don't know about you."

"Of course. How ridiculous of me. Vanilla. That's my favorite flavor of ice cream. No scratch that, *French* vanilla. What's yours?"

"Chocolate. I love anything chocolate. When's your birthday?"

"June twenty-sixth. You?"

"December thirteenth. And get this—I was born on a Friday."

"Seriously? Then it's official. I fucking love Friday the thirteenth," he declared.

"Yeah, I think maybe I'm won over, too," I said. "Okay, one last question. I take my coffee with milk and sugar. How do you take it?"

"Black."

"Ew, really?"

"Yeah, I don't like it all creamy."

I snickered, unable to contain my naughty smile.

He rolled me onto my back and propped himself up on his elbow again. "Do you have to turn everything into a dirty joke? No wonder Penny likes you so much. You're cut from the same cloth."

"And you adore her, so I'm not about to change now."

"Good. I love you exactly the way you are."

"Do you mean that?" I asked.

"Of course. You're perfect just the—"

"No, the *other* part. The *love* part," I said, squirming a little.

"Well, I don't know," he said. "It's sort of a figure of speech, isn't it? What do you think? Can you see yourself falling in love with me one day?"

The room was extremely quiet all of a sudden, making my breathing and my pounding heart seem very loud. I looked into his beautiful blue eyes and shrugged self-consciously. "I don't know. Maybe it's already happening." I held my breath, waiting for his reaction.

"Maybe?" he asked.

"I'd say a definite maybe, yeah."

"I'll take it," he said, kissing me softly. "And God knows I shouldn't say this, but since I already suggested as much when we were out for our walk earlier—I definitely maybe feel the same way."

"Really?"

Daniel Grant is definitely maybe falling in love with me! I kissed him enthusiastically, but he pushed me away gently.

"I can't breathe." He laughed.

"Sorry," I said, unable to contain my smile.

"Don't be. You're wonderful." He brushed my hair over my shoulder. "So, do you have your phone with you tonight?"

"Yes. It's in my coat pocket."

"Mind if I grab it?"

"No, go ahead."

He left and returned a moment later with my phone. He dropped back onto the bed.

"Will you do something for me?"

"Sure."

"Call or text Matt to let him know you won't be going back to the apartment tonight?"

I questioned him with my eyes, and the corner of his mouth crept up. "He worries," he said, winking at me.

CHAPTER 6

Patience

…thou must be patient.
(*Measure for Measure*, Act IV, Scene 3)

I brushed my teeth, smiling like a loon.

Was I falling head over heels in love? Absolutely. Definitely *maybe?* Pfft! More like definitely *definitely*.

I carefully cleaned up and put my toothbrush in the medicine cabinet. That's when I noticed the prescription pill bottles were gone. Daniel had moved them. Did he have some sort of embarrassing condition that he was afraid to tell me about? I frowned at my reflection. Regardless of how much we'd cleared up, I had so much more to learn about him.

I slipped my bra out of my sleeve. No way was I sleeping in it. Plus, something about having Daniel's pajama top against my bare breasts was rather titillating. When I returned to the bedroom, Daniel was sitting on the edge of the bed, frowning as he watched the nightly news.

He watched me place my bra on top of my pile of clothes, then eyed my chest. He wasn't even remotely subtle as he checked me out, no doubt noticing the way my nipples were pressing against the soft cotton fabric.

"Are you warm enough, my lovely?" he said.

"Whatever do you mean?" I asked, walking over and standing in front of him. He reached out for me, resting his forehead against my stomach. I ran my hands though his hair, making it stick out in different directions.

"Mmm. Why does that feel so good?"

I gently rubbed his scalp with my nails, and he moved his head like a spoiled cat.

"It feels good because *apparently* you like being scratched," I said.

"You've got that right." He reached up to stop my hands. "Be still for a second," he whispered, turning his head and pressing his cheek into my cleavage but leaving his hands at my waist. Oddly, even though his face was nestled between my breasts, there was nothing remotely sexual about it. In fact, it was one of the most exquisitely tender moments I'd ever experienced. I dared not move. After a few moments, he looked up at me.

"What was that all about?" I asked.

"I was listening to your heart."

My heart. The very same heart which was now flipping over and diving into my stomach to do somersaults.

"Daniel—"

"Yes, poppet?"

Instead of trying to find appropriate words, I held his steady gaze and took his left hand with my right, slowly guiding it to where I thought my heartbeat might be. Daniel closed his eyes and took a long steady breath. I did the same. He was now holding my breast, but his hand was gentle, unmoving.

"Your heart is racing," he whispered.

"I'm not surprised."

His lips gently parted as he slid his hand back down to my waist, grazing my nipple with his thumb as he moved. I swallowed hard, and my legs went rubbery.

He flicked the TV off and turned to me with a smoldering expression. "You're so beautiful," he said, gathering me into his arms and lowering me onto the bed where he proceeded to kiss me with a tender passion that swept me away.

As we kissed, I gave my hands license to roam, running my fingertips up his arms, taking in the sculpted lines of his biceps and shoulders. Time slowed as we moved against each other.

I'm actually melting in slow motion.

Having reduced me to a quivering mess, he rolled away, his eyes clouded with desire.

"I thought you said you were going to behave appropriately for the rest of the evening?" I said. "And what about all the ground rules?"

"In addition to any other horrible character flaws I already had, it seems I've now become a pathological liar," he said. "You're an amazing kisser."

"Hey, it takes two to tango, baby," I whispered, dropping feathery kisses along his upturned jaw. "Though it might actually be possible to tango alone, at least if you're in the shower."

He shook his head gently. "You enjoy torturing me, don't you?"

"Immensely," I said.

A gentle growl rumbled in his chest. "I don't think my Achilles' heel has ever ached so badly before. There's not a physiotherapist in the world who could treat it now. It's beyond repair." He moaned and shifted his weight. "Seriously, I want to lie here and kiss you senseless all night," he said. "Why do you have to be so irresistible?"

The most amazingly hot guy found me irresistible, and I wasn't supposed to be pursuing a romantic relationship with him. The scenario was beyond frustrating.

"Do you think I should go home?"

Daniel's hold on me tightened. "No, and please don't suggest it again. This isn't easy, but I'm not going to cross a line. The timing isn't right. I want our first time to be what you deserve."

We lay quietly for a few moments, and Daniel gently rubbed my back. I was so comfortable, and his touch was soothing. I tried unsuccessfully to stifle a yawn, and he chuckled quietly.

"We should get to sleep," he said, kissing the top of my head.

"No, not yet. I want to enjoy this for a while longer." Sleep meant tomorrow would be upon us in no time, and reality would intrude once again.

He shifted his position so that we were lying side by side. "In that case, can I ask you a question?"

"Sure."

"I'm not sure how to ask this delicately, so I'm just going to ask."

"Okay…" I frowned. He looked so serious.

"Are you on the pill?" He grimaced almost immediately. "I'm sorry, I shouldn't have asked."

"No, it's okay. That's an important question. I've been on the pill since I was seventeen."

"Is that when you, you know, lost your virginity?"

"Yes," I said, smiling at his uncomfortable expression. "I was seventeen, and the guy was eighteen."

"Interesting."

"Why?"

"Well, that's the exact same scenario for me. I was seventeen. She was eighteen."

She.

"Sabrina, right?"

Daniel flinched. "How the hell do you know about Sabrina?"

"Whoa, easy there. It was Patty. I was looking at her photographs in the hallway, and I saw a prom picture of the two of you. She said Sabrina was your first girlfriend, that's all. Don't worry—your deep, dark past remains a mystery."

He fell back against the pillows. "There's nothing deep and dark about it, believe me. You just took me by surprise."

"So, she was your first?" I asked.

He nodded.

"Patty said you tried to keep things going with her even after you moved to England. You must have liked her a lot."

He frowned. "She was a nice girl. Spoiled rotten by her dad, though. We stayed in touch, but the distance made it next to impossible to maintain a relationship."

I didn't want to hear about how nice she was. I wanted to hear more about how she was spoiled and rotten. Yes, I'd taken artistic license with Daniel's words, but I was okay with that.

"There's absolutely nothing between us now, you realize that, right?" he said.

"You sure sounded nostalgic there for a second."

"Aubrey, *you* are the one in my bed and lying in my arms right now."

"I know. Am I allowed to ask a couple of questions, though?"

"You won't upset yourself?"

This was a good point. Did I really want to hear about this nice girl to whom Daniel had lost his virginity? Yes, screw it, I did. Clearly I had a masochistic side that had long lain dormant but was now rearing its head with a vengeance.

"Patty said she went to Havergal. Is she rich?"

"Yes, her family is very well off. Sabrina was indulged. Spring break trips with her friends, a car for her sixteenth birthday, the jewelry, the clothes. She was accustomed to getting her own way. Bred a sense of entitlement in her that wasn't terribly attractive, but other than that she was a good person. Still is, I suppose."

"So, you still see her?" I asked. Wow, I was really asking for it.

Daniel exhaled. "I don't think we should talk about this. You're going to make something out of nothing."

"That's not true," I said defensively. "I promise not to make a mountain out of a molehill."

He looked at me indecisively.

"Does she still live in Toronto?" I pressed.

He hung his head in resignation. "No. She moved away a little over a year ago."

"Away? Where?"

Daniel's jaw twitched. I tried to stay calm.

"She lives in Ottawa," he said at last.

Ottawa. A five-hour drive. How inconvenient. I smiled inwardly, but then a latent memory flashed in my mind. Hadn't Daniel's Reading Week plans included a trip to Ottawa? A trip that had been canceled at the last minute—a cancellation that had resulted in his unannounced arrival at his parents' house and a night of excessive drinking, complete with a sexually charged snooker lesson?

"Is that where you were supposed to be that weekend? When we had dinner at your folks' place?"

He anxiously rubbed his eyes. "Figures you'd remember minutiae like that."

Was he pissed off at me for having a good memory?

"I remember a lot of things, Daniel," I said quietly.

"So do I, sweetheart. That's what happens when you write everything down." His smile was sad. I tried not to let him throw me off course.

"You haven't answered my question."

"Answer something for me first?"

The vague beginnings of irritation worried at the edges of my mind. "Okay."

"Are we arguing? Because if we are, we should move. My mother always says never argue in bed."

I had to laugh. He was so earnest. My irritation dissipated as quickly as it had begun.

"We're not arguing. We're having a conversation. You're being evasive, and I'm being insistent."

He relaxed against the pillows.

"Besides," I added, "it's convenient arguing in bed—you know, for when you move on to the make-up sex."

He laughed. "Make-up sex is a great deal more satisfying when it's *not* in a bed."

"Oh? Preferences?"

He rubbed at his whiskers. "Well, against a wall, for instance."

"Or a bookshelf?" I suggested.

"Absolutely." He was looking at me with the most salacious expression. Then I realized he'd completely distracted me.

"Nicely done," I said, crossing my arms. "You managed to avoid answering my question. Well played."

"Oh, come on, don't be like that." He sat up, resting his arm on his bent knee. "Go on, ask away. I can't even remember what the question was."

"Liar," I said, trying not to sound sulky. I stared at him until he cracked.

"Yes, I had planned to visit her in Ottawa." He looked at me grimly, perhaps expecting me to flip out. I tossed his confirmation around in my mind, unsure of how I felt about it. I remained calm.

"But your plans fell through?"

"Yes. She came down with the flu. The swine flu, actually. She was quite sick."

Thank God for pandemics, I thought, then reprimanded myself. The swine flu was no laughing matter.

"Is she okay now?" I asked.

"As far as I know, she's made a full recovery," he said. "I haven't spoken to her in a few weeks."

"And do you talk to her a lot?"

He reached out to stroke my cheek. "Not nearly as much as I used to," he said. "I called her the evening after we met at the Gardiner to let her know I hoped she was feeling better, but that I wouldn't be rescheduling my visit."

"Oh," I said, my voice small and far away.

Daniel reclined against the pillows, and I followed him down. He gently pushed my hair away from my face.

"Listen," he said firmly. "I was going to Ottawa to escape. I had to get away from a certain young lady. Everything I looked at, everything I did here reminded me of this girl. I wasn't supposed to be thinking of her in the way that I was. Then my trip to Ottawa fell through, and I paid my parents a visit. Imagine my shock when the young lady was at my parents' house. My resolve crumbled, and I knew there was no escaping her, no avoiding my feelings because I'd discovered she might feel the same way about me. I was happier that night than I'd been in months."

My heart leapt into my throat. "I'm sorry, I didn't mean to —"

"It doesn't matter. Sabrina doesn't matter. Only you. You're all that matters now."

Sabrina was forgotten, and Daniel's beautiful eyes, ablaze with longing, were all I could see.

"I should go in the other room right now and get the pull-out couch ready," he said, tearing himself away.

No, no, no!

"Daniel, please don't sleep on the couch. I want to fall asleep in your arms."

"There's no way I can stay in here."

"Please don't leave me in here by myself."

He growled, torn. "If I'm staying in this bed with you, then we need to take *serious* emergency measures."

"Such as?" I asked.

"Such as you covering up. I can't be allowed anywhere near your incredible skin." He dragged my top down over my hips.

Rolling onto my back, I took the two sides of the shirt and tied a knot at the bottom so he wouldn't be able to sneak his hands underneath, then I tightly cinched the drawstring of the bottoms and triple knotted it.

"There. Fort Knox." I smiled smugly.

"Don't you mean Fort Knots?" he asked with a sly smile. "Either way, wholly ineffectual. I was a kick-ass Boy Scout. Knots were my specialty."

"My goodness, sailor," I said. "You're so accomplished. Is there anything you can't do?"

"Resist *you*." He smirked and rolled off the bed. "I've got a brilliant idea, though." He headed into his walk-in closet and rustled around inside. He came out holding a gaudy, hot pink sleeping bag.

"Very pretty. Tell me that didn't get you in some hot water on Boy Scout camping trips."

He narrowed his eyes. "Watch it, smartass. This is Penny's. She bought it in December when Brad told her he wanted to take her up to our cottage. It's never been used."

"They didn't go?"

"Oh, they went, but you don't need sleeping bags up there. I don't think Penny fully understood the concept of a *winterized cottage*."

"Ah, I see." I could only imagine what the Grant family cottage looked like. "So, how come you have it?" I asked.

"A few of her boxes got mixed in with mine at my mom and dad's. So," he said, unrolling the sleeping bag onto the bed with a flourish, "you sleep in here on top of the blankets. I'll be underneath the blankets where I can't get at you."

"Daniel, you realize that's absurd, right?"

"Hey, I'm serious. You want me to stay in here or not? I can't be held responsible for what my hands do when I'm asleep. And God knows what mischief *you'll* get up to. Humor me."

He crawled back over to join me on the bed, kissing me playfully. I took his hands in mine.

"You could restrain me. Tie my hands to the bedpost so I can't get at you." I bit my lip and looked at him demurely.

"You little vixen," he said, pushing me back against the pillows and lying beside me, trapping my hips with his leg. "I thought we were trying to figure out how to *avoid* getting carried away. But that sounds incredibly hot."

His eyes hungrily searched my face.

"No one's ever called me a vixen before," I said. "There's another V-word to add to the list—Venus, velvet…" Feeling playful and extremely sexy trapped under his thigh like that, I decided to live up to this new name, taking my fingers and placing them in a V against his lips. "And now vixen."

He gently grasped my wrist, holding my fingers still and slowly licking down one finger and up the other.

Torrential rains officially upgraded to tsunami alert.

"Daniel," I breathed, shifting my hips under his leg.

He grasped my hands and clasped them above my head. Then he kissed me again, hot and wet and breathy.

I melted against him as he purged whatever demon was spurring him on. I struggled to free one of my hands, eager to touch his face, his hair, his thighs, his back. I wanted to scratch him again. But he held me still and worked his magic with his incredible lips before letting go of my hands and rolling onto his back, throwing his folded arms across his face.

"You're killing me," he groaned. "Get in that sleeping bag right now."

"What?" I asked, rolling over to peek innocently under his forearms.

"Don't play coy with me, Miss V." He looked at me from under his arm. "Let me know when it's safe to come out."

I pouted and slid into the sleeping bag, pulling the thick fleece up under my arms.

"Okay. I'm in."

He dragged himself to the edge of the bed. "I'm going to look at some pictures of geological rock formations, or something equally unstimulating, and then I'll set the timer on the coffee maker. What time should we be up?"

"I'll shower back at my place, if that's okay? I should be back there by quarter to eight at the latest. Can you drop me off at Union Station at seven thirty?"

He nodded and then headed off to the kitchen while I folded my hands under my head, staring at the ceiling with a stupid grin on my face, basking in the glow of—well, not what I wished I was basking in, but I basked anyway. When Daniel came back into the bedroom, he sat on the edge of the bed beside me, fiddling with the alarm clock.

"You look adorable," he said.

"I feel like a burrito."

"Well, you certainly do look good enough to eat." He kissed me chastely and crawled under the covers. He moved over to lie close to me and draped his arm across my stomach. "Can you reach the light to turn it off?" he asked.

I flicked the switch, and a deep darkness enveloped the room. I snuggled up against him, content.

He groaned suddenly. "Shit, I forgot something."

He reached over me to turn the lamp back on and opened the top drawer of the nightstand. He pulled out a calendar—the exact same calendar he'd bought me. He looked at me and winked, removing the cap off a red pen with his teeth. Using my stomach to lean on he drew a decisive X through Sunday, March 15th. One more day down.

He tossed everything back in the drawer, turned the light off, and settled in again.

"Forty-six," he whispered, kissing the top of my head.

I groaned. "I can't wait."

"Patience," he said softly.

"Patience, shmatience," I grumbled, resting my hand on his chest. I felt, rather than heard, his gentle laugh. As tired as I was, I couldn't stop my brain from replaying the evening, and I thought uneasily of the prescription pill bottles as I listened to Daniel breathing in the darkness. Was he already asleep?

"Daniel?" I whispered.

"Hmm?"

"Would you consider yourself healthy?"

"What?" He chuckled quietly again. "I'm as healthy as a horse."

"Okay. Good. Good night, sailor."

"Good night, poppet. Sleep well."

And I did.

Until exactly 3:20 a.m.

CHAPTER 7

Conscience

Love is too young to know what conscience is;
Yet who knows not conscience is born of love?
(*Sonnet 151*)

woke with a start, completely disoriented. Something was crushing my shoulder. Then I remembered—I was at Daniel's. He was still curled up against me, and it was his hand that was squeezing near my neck like a vice. He was moaning, repeating, "No, I didn't do it," over and over again.

He was having a bad dream.

I unclasped his fingers from my shoulder and drew his head to my chest, stroking his hair. His hand settled on my abdomen.

"I didn't do it," he mumbled.

"Shh, I know you didn't," I said.

"Why are you doing this to me?"

There was pain and disbelief in his whispered words. Was he awake? Asleep? Could he hear me?

"It's okay. I'm here. It's Aubrey. Everything's all right."

"I didn't do it." He snuggled up to me.

"I know, go back to sleep," I whispered, gently running my hand through his hair and over the nape of his neck, but he couldn't hear me. He was already out. He'd probably been asleep all along, talking while he dreamed. He snuffled and sighed, then relaxed against me.

My heart clenched. What had he been dreaming about? More fallout from his troubles with Nicola, even over a year later? I wanted to smack that girl so hard! I continued to rub his back, listening to him snore.

I blinked into the darkness. Holy crap, I was roasting! Why was it so frigging hot?

Without jostling Daniel too much, I worked at the knot on my PJ bottoms with one hand and wriggled out of them, pushing them down with my feet until they were balled up in the bottom of the sleeping bag. I rolled the sleeping bag down to my waist. I could feel a rivulet of sweat between my breasts. Charming.

Having Daniel's warm body pressed against me wasn't helping, but I wasn't about to move him. I may have been hotter than hell, but I was happier than a pig in muck. I settled back into the pillow and tried to regulate my breathing, and I soon drifted back into a deep, dark sleep.

When I awoke a few hours later, I was instantly aware of my surroundings. Although I'd fallen back to sleep with Daniel snuggled up against me, I was now lying on his warm, bare chest. I'd kicked the sleeping bag off completely, and Daniel had relieved himself of his shirt. The soft hairs on Daniel's chest tickled my cheek. My right hand rested on his stomach, and my right leg was slung haphazardly across his hips. His hand firmly grasped my thigh, very close to my ass.

Wowza.

Without moving my hand too much, I felt the sprinkling of hairs above his waistband. Glorious. As for what I could feel trapped under my thigh? Well, *that* was beyond glorious.

I shifted and squinted at the alarm clock. Six fifteen. My movements roused Daniel, who sighed sleepily and opened his eyes, blinking at me groggily.

"Good morning, beautiful." He kissed my forehead and glanced at the clock with a groan.

"Morning yourself, handsome."

He peered down at our entwined bodies, taking in the position of my leg and gently rubbing my thigh.

"Not that those aren't some fantastic black knickers, but where the hell are your pajama bottoms? And what happened to the sleeping bag?"

"Excuse me, I could ask the same of you. Where's your T-shirt?"

"Bloody hell, I woke up a couple of hours ago sweating like mad. You were like a furnace."

"I know! I was roasting. The sleeping bag had to go."

He laughed and shifted his hips under my leg. "Christ, that's a little too close for comfort." He gave my upper thigh a squeeze. "It's nothing short of a miracle that we made it through the night. I think you'd best move your luscious leg right this minute."

"Like this?" I asked, moving my leg up and down, feeling him harden even more beneath my inner thigh.

He moaned and grabbed my leg, pushing me away decisively. "No, like *that*," he said as I rolled onto my back, laughing. He flicked on the bedside lamp and stood, looking down at me, his hands on his hips. I stared at him stupidly, distracted by his bare chest, arms, and toned abdomen, not to mention the tent pole down below. He seemed oblivious to my ogling, casting his own eyes up and down my bare legs. "Are you, um, sure you don't want to shower here? If you do, you can go ahead."

"No, I'll wait till I get home," I said, snapping out of my trance. The thought of showering and then having to put yesterday's clothes back on was particularly distasteful.

"Okay. Well, I *have* to shower. The coffee should be ready if you want to grab a cup. And help yourself to food if you want something."

"Have a good shower," I said, raising my eyebrow knowingly.

"I intend to." He rubbed at his chest hair absently. "Did you drool on me?"

"Probably. I'm a total mouth breather when I sleep."

He smiled and shook his head. "That explains the dragon breath."

"Fuck off!" I threw several pillows at him. He dodged them, running for the bathroom door and slamming it behind him. "You'll get yours, Grant!" I hollered.

"Promises, promises, Miss Price!" he yelled back. I heard him chuckling to himself and then turning the shower on. I made my way to the kitchen, feeling surprisingly happy for a Monday morning.

I breathed in the tantalizing aroma of freshly brewed coffee. There were two mugs on the counter in front of the coffee maker, along with a spoon and a bowl of sugar. Daniel had done this last night. Apart from these items, the counters were bare. He was such a neat freak. This whole extreme organization thing was daunting.

I poured us both a cup, leaving Daniel's coffee black while helping myself to sugar and milk, noting the spotlessness of the fridge as I put the milk carton back on the shelf.

Did I feel like eating? I opened the cupboards to see what might appeal to me. In one I found numerous soup cans, neatly lined up with the labels all facing forward. In the next one, boxes of cereal were arranged smallest to largest. I decided to wait until I was home to eat, but I couldn't resist twirling the cans so that the labels were no longer uniform and rearranging the order of the cereal boxes — a little something for Daniel to remember me by.

On the way back to Daniel's bedroom, I lingered beside the couch, checking out a shelf full of DVDs. He had quite an impressive collection of movies. I strolled back into the bedroom with the two mugs of coffee. The shower was still running. Tempting. Oh, so very tempting.

Don't do it, Aubrey, a little voice chirped in my ear. Oddly enough, it sounded an awful lot like Julie. What the hell? I stayed away from the bathroom, flicking on the TV instead and turning to the Weather Network. The forecast for the coming week was horrid.

The shower turned off as I sat on the edge of the bed, sipping my coffee and rubbing my shoulder absently, my thoughts turning to Daniel's bad dream. He hadn't mentioned it and had seemed quite cheerful when he'd woken up. If he didn't remember it, I wasn't about to bring it up. Grabbing his cup, I made my way over to the bathroom door and tapped gently.

"You decent, sweet knees?"

He opened the door.

"I'm not sure. Am I?" he asked. He was wearing nothing but a pair of navy blue boxers, and his hair was sticking up, still wet from the shower. There was a blob of shaving cream on his cheek.

Decent? Good lord.

"I, uh, brought you a cup," I said, trying not to lose my cool entirely as I took in the sexy line of hair under his navel.

"What a treat." He put the mug on the counter and continued to lather his face.

"Do you mind if I stay?" I rested against the doorframe.

"I'm okay with it if you are." He gestured to his state of undress. "If you can control yourself, that is." He smirked through his shaving cream.

Well, that was a challenge, wasn't it?

"I think I can manage." I sounded far more confident than I felt. I slipped past him and perched on the vanity. "I'm a little disappointed that you're shaving."

He ran his razor under the hot water.

"I can't let it grow indefinitely. If I shave now, I can let it go all week, and by Friday it'll be the way you like it again."

I sipped my coffee, eyeing him over the edge of the mug. "You want to do this again next weekend?"

"I'd love it if you could stay tonight—every night this week, for that matter. But I know that's not realistic."

"Probably not."

I looked at him appraisingly. *Daniel Grant is standing in front of me in his boxers. This is surreal.*

"Is it odd that I want to lick your face?" I asked.

He chuckled. "This is shaving cream, not whipped cream."

"True. Put whipped cream on your grocery list—for Friday." I winked at him.

"Deal." He stretched his neck taut, scraping the razor gingerly down his throat.

"Daniel, are you religious?" I asked.

His eyes flickered to mine curiously. "Why do you ask?"

"I guess I'm thinking about your dad. He used to make you go to church when you were a kid, right?"

"I wasn't prepared to take everything at face value, but, yes, we attended church regularly."

"So, is there a higher power that guides your actions?"

"I don't know." He moved the razor across his right cheek. "My conscience guides my actions. I'd like to think I behave the way I do because it's right, not because some entity is judging me or waiting to catch me screwing up. How you live when no one is watching is the true test of your morality," he clarified.

"No one's watching you right now."

"I see what you're getting at." He sighed and stepped back. "You're absolutely right, and it's making me crazy because you being here doesn't feel wrong. That's not good. I mean, shouldn't I feel guilty as hell?"

"I don't like the idea of you wrestling with your conscience because of me."

"I'm not. That's my point. I was, but I'm not anymore."

"How do you just turn your conscience off?"

"It's not like that," he said, the razor temporarily forgotten. "It's—well, take the whole objectivity thing. Martin decided he wants me to mark this Friday's test. I was freaked out about it at first, but the more I think about it, the more sure I am that I can be impartial. It's like a switch flips in my brain when I think about marking your work. I don't know how to explain it."

"I get that. You have this strange aura in tutorials. It's cool. I look at you, and you're under there somewhere, but you have this different vibe. So, is that all there is to it?" I asked.

"No, there's the power dynamic aspect. But I'm not trying to manipulate you with my authority, so that doesn't feel like it applies either."

"You've thought about this a lot."

"You have no idea how much time I've devoted to batting this around in my head. I needed to come to terms with everything."

"And you have?"

"I think so. I've tried to see what we're doing as morally repugnant, Aubrey, but I can't do it. Having you here like this—just the way we are now—feels so comfortable. It feels *right*."

"I think so too. Last night was perfect."

"Ups and downs and all?" he asked.

"Absolutely. I think we did great. And I'm so proud of us for not crossing the line."

"Me too."

He smiled as he splashed his face clean and patted it dry with a hand towel. He stood in front of me, squeezing my waist. I hung onto his shoulders as he kissed me and gently rubbed his cheek against mine.

"You need some cologne, Mr. Grant."

"You're right. Mind your legs?" he said, gesturing to the drawer beneath me. Instead of swinging my legs to one side or the other, I opted to move them apart. He shook his head and reached into the drawer for his cologne, spritzing himself and then replacing the bottle, no doubt getting an eyeful in the process.

"Clothes — *now*," he said, decisively pulling my legs together. "You can get dressed in here."

He walked out to the bedroom to collect my clothes, and that's when I noticed the scratch marks.

"Gosh, what happened to your back?" I asked, feigning surprise.

"Whatever it was felt great, and I sure hope it happens again," he said with a salacious grin. He handed me my clothes, and I took one last look at him in his boxers, capturing the picture in my mind for later reference before the door closed between us.

I dressed and freshened up, peeking at his cologne before leaving. *Burberry*. Where the hell had I gotten sandalwood from?

I pushed the drawer closed and went in search of Daniel. He was in his office, already dressed and looking out the window with his cup of coffee. He seemed so relaxed as he surveyed the skyline. I was reluctant to bring him out of his reverie.

"Hey, there you are." He turned as I crossed to his desk. "I topped up your coffee. We still have a few minutes."

"Thanks." I grabbed the mug and took a sip, wrinkling my nose as the coffee mixed with the toothpaste taste in my mouth. I wandered over to sit on the couch.

The couch.

"That's a nice guitar," I said. "I can't believe I was here all night and I didn't get you to play it for me."

He smiled and walked around his desk to grab it, perching his foot on the table and balancing the instrument on his knee. Who was that smoking hot at seven o'clock in the morning? Honestly?

"How about I play you a little something I learned for someone when I was a teenager? You ready?"

"Absolutely." I leaned forward eagerly.

He played a few bars of a song, strumming the strings expertly. I had no clue what the song was, but he looked delicious. As soon as he began to whistle, I clued in — it was Guns N' Roses' "Patience." Daniel continued to strum, whistling like his life depended on it. I tried to join in, but the serious look on his face made me laugh.

"You're a fantastic whistler," I said between giggles.

"Helps when you have something amazing to whistle at," he said, wiggling his eyebrows.

"So, I'm your whistling muse?"

"Yes, among other things." He played a few more bars, singing the opening lines of the song, but then he abruptly stopped playing. "Huh. Who would've thought the lyrical stylings of Guns N' Roses would be so pertinent to my life?"

"I know. Clearly we need more patience," I said.

"This is true. I think I should switch my PhD topic. I don't think anyone has come close to unearthing Axl Rose's lyrical brilliance."

Daniel placed his guitar on its stand.

"So, who was this someone you learned the song for?" I asked, almost afraid to hear the answer.

"Bradley, of course." Daniel rolled his eyes. "And I think I know Rush's entire repertoire. He forced me to learn all their songs so he could pretend he was Neil Peart."

"That's right. He plays the drums."

"Brad's only aspiration in high school was to bang things."

"I bet," I said with a knowing smile. "Too bad no one ever told him guitarists are way hotter than drummers." I ran my nose along his freshly shaved jaw.

He kissed me slowly, all hot and wet and coffee-tasting. When he drew back, he was grimacing uncomfortably.

"I'd better get you back to Vic before I end up throwing you down on the couch and ravishing you." He picked up his laptop bag and motioned for me to follow him. "Come on, crazy legs, let's go." He ushered me down the hall to the front door where he helped me with my coat, slipping my hair to the side to place a gentle kiss on my neck. "I miss you already," he whispered.

"Daniel, I'll see you downstairs in two minutes."

"I know. And we have class in a few hours, but it won't be the same." He sighed and cradled my cheek in his hand. "Promise me we'll do this again on Friday?"

"*Definitely*," I promised.

He pulled me into a tight hug. "Okay. Head on down and wait for me in the lot. I'll be there in a few."

"No problem."

Despite my level-headed façade, I knew exactly how he felt. Friday seemed like a lifetime away. I took one last look at Daniel's orderly living room.

"One second," I said, stepping back through the door.

"Did you forget something?"

"Uh-huh."

I couldn't help it. The temptation was killing me. I walked over to the coffee table and pushed the pile of magazines over, watching as they slid haphazardly across the shiny surface.

"There." I smiled brightly and rejoined him at the door. He grinned and shook his head as I slipped out into the hallway. "See you in a couple of minutes."

I was passing the steps of Old Vic just before eight thirty when I saw Dean Grant making his way toward me along the path. He waved, then motioned to my single glove.

"Good morning, Aubrey. Is this your homage to Michael Jackson?"

Oh, David, you're such a square, I thought. But then I felt guilty. Would I have thought this of Dean Grant before meeting Daniel's grandmother and hearing her prattle about his shortcomings? I wasn't sure.

"Merely another glove that's lost its partner," I confessed. "I'm afraid losing gloves is my tragic flaw."

"Well, you're the Shakespearean expert, but I don't think any of the tragic heroes spiraled to their downfall as a result of a lost mitten."

"No, I suppose you're right."

"That's too bad, though. They were a gift, right?"

"Yes, I feel bad about that."

"Well, if a lost glove is your biggest concern, then I suppose you're doing okay. I'll see you in about half an hour. I'm meeting Daniel for coffee to make sure everything is fine with him."

Oh, he's fine, I thought. *Tired, but damn fine, indeed.*

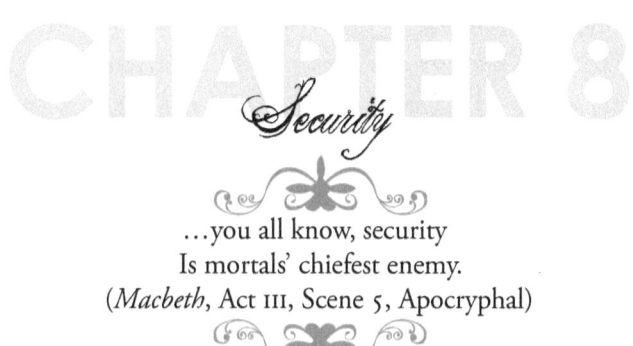

Security

…you all know, security
Is mortals' chiefest enemy.
(*Macbeth*, Act III, Scene 5, Apocryphal)

I floated through my three-hour shift in a haze, visions of Daniel in his boxers distracting me from every task. At eleven thirty, I leafed through the few remaining items in the inbox. Anticipation tickled my stomach when I locked up for the lunch hour, and I was practically skipping by the time I reached the stairs.

I was almost out the door when my phone alerted me to an incoming text message.

Before you leave, head down to the basement. -D

Wait, was Daniel down there waiting for me? I doubled back and dashed down the stairs to the Northrop Frye basement. As I reached the landing, the double doors to the underground passageway to Old Vic swung closed. Daniel was striding down the corridor. Was I supposed to follow him? My phone buzzed again.

Look under the stairs. See you soon. -D

So, he *didn't* expect me to follow him. I continued to the basement and peeked under the stairs where I found a bag tucked underneath. I pulled it free and turned to sit on the bottom step. Inside the bag there was a large tissue-wrapped box with a Louis Vuitton logo on the top. Crap, now what was he up to? This was way more expensive than a calendar or a silly pair of mitts. There was a note from Daniel inside the box.

Hi, sweetheart,

I realize this is the second Monday in a row I've done this, but I wouldn't want those delicious fingers getting cold as you walk across campus. I mean it, though — no more. God forbid I become predictable. ~D

I separated the tissue and found a pair of gloves in a muted charcoal color, the back of one adorned with the signature LV logo. They were soft and woolen and lovely. I dug around in the tissue and found a Vuitton umbrella, another note tucked into the strap. All it said was:

The weather's been terrible round your parts.
Thought you might need this.

Round my parts! The note may have been cheeky, but the gift — not cheap by any stretch of the imagination — was proof that he wanted to spoil me. This was something I needed to get used to.

Unfortunately, I didn't have time to sit and gawk at the gifts. I had to get to class — where I could sit and discreetly gawk at Daniel. I disposed of the packaging and stowed the umbrella in my knapsack. I hurried toward Queen's Park where I could see Daniel ahead of me, about to cross University Avenue. I struggled to text while following the uneven path.

> **Daniel! Louis Vuitton? Are you crazy?**
> **You know my track record! -A**

He replied almost instantly.

> **I don't care, sweetheart. You're worth it.**
> **Do you like them? -D**

> **I think maybe I love them. -A**

And the umbrella? -D

**I love it, too. No doubt it'll come in handy…
maybe on Friday. -A**

Maybe, Aubrey? -D

Definitely, Daniel…see you in 5 min. -A

I pocketed my phone and put on the gloves, grinning like an idiot. By the time I got to class, my face was burning, not from being out in the cold, but from anticipation. It had only been a little over four hours since I'd said goodbye to him at Union Station, but I couldn't wait to see his face again.

Julie was already settled in her spot in our row when I arrived. Daniel sat at the front, leaning back in his chair. I couldn't look at him now without images of his toned body in those blue boxers flashing before my eyes.

"Hey," Julie said as I shrugged out of my coat. "Wait, hold the phone!" She reached for my hand. "Are those Louis fucking Vuitton gloves? Since when can you afford *those?*"

"Shh!" I shook my head, avoiding Daniel's eyes.

"*Oh,* I get it. Peace offering?" she asked quietly, glancing at Daniel, who was smiling at his notebook.

"Something like that," I whispered, stowing the gloves safely inside my knapsack.

Professor Brown arrived and launched into a quick review lecture. My mind wandered, along with my eyes. I caught Daniel's gaze several times, but as usual, he was masterful in his nonchalance, writing in his notebook and looking around the room.

After about twenty minutes, Professor Brown assigned a couple of practice questions to work through with a partner in preparation for Friday's test. Daniel circulated, reading people's answers and offering suggestions for improvement. Julie and I pushed our desks closer together and veered off topic almost immediately.

"Guess where I'm going after class," she whispered.

"I don't know. Apartment hunting with Jeremy?"

"Ha, not quite. I'm going to the clinic. To get *a prescription.*" She lifted one of her eyebrows.

"I see. Things heating up in paradise?"

"Just a smidge."

"I love smidges."

"Me too." She covered her face with her hands to hide her telltale blush. Adorable, Julie. Simply adorable. "And tomorrow, he's finally taking the plunge and going car shopping."

"That's awesome! Tell him I said 'safety first,' okay?"

Our conversation was cut short by Daniel walking up behind us. I felt his presence before he actually spoke—a strange warm buzzing in my stomach. He bent down between the two of us, peering at our notebooks.

"Ladies, I don't see much written here," he said dryly.

Julie tapped the side of her head. "It's all up here, Daniel."

"Ah, I see. And you, Miss Price?"

"Don't worry about me, Daniel. I've got this bad boy locked up."

"Oh, you think so?" he said. "Don't allow yourself to be lulled into a false sense of security." Then he bent down to whisper, "I hear the guy who's marking these is an uptight prick," before moving off to the other side of the room.

Oh, not anymore, he isn't. I watched him lean over to take a look at Trina's work, giving me a stellar view of his ass.

Julie nudged me. "Subtle as a flying brick, baby doll."

"Right," I said, quickly turning back to my notepad.

"I gather things have improved since last week?" she whispered.

"Just a smidge," I said with a wink.

When class came to a close, Julie packed up quickly. "I'd suggest coffee or something because I feel totally out of the loop with you, but I have to get to the clinic pronto."

"We'll catch up later. Drop me an email or let's chat online or something. I'll be on my computer all night in PowerPoint hell. I'll welcome the distraction, believe me."

I hugged her, and she dashed off, remarkably excited considering she was about to be violated by a cold, rubber-gloved hand. Daniel was at the front of the room, avoiding my eyes and doing the infamous three-paper shuffle. I was on the verge of going up to engage him in conversation about the test—anything so I could talk to him before he had to go downstairs—but I was stalled by a hand on my shoulder.

"Hey, Aubrey, you're feeling better, huh?"

I turned around reluctantly. "Shawn, hey. Yeah, sorry I bailed on the frat party Friday. I wasn't feeling up to it."

"Yeah, you weren't there long. Too bad, 'cause you looked, well… really great."

Oh, please don't do this.

Out of the corner of my eye, I saw Daniel leave. I struggled to tear my eyes away from the sex swagger.

Damn you, Shawn Ward.

"Um, that's nice, Shawn. I, um—" I mumbled, hoping to begin the painful process of letting him down easily.

"Look, I'm glad you're feeling better," he said, interrupting my awkwardness. "See you on Wednesday?"

"Sure." I tried not to sound too relieved. "See ya then."

As I watched him leave the room, my phone vibrated in my pocket. I smiled gratefully as I answered.

"Hello, there," Daniel said smoothly. "Is there a damsel who needs rescuing?"

"You're about thirty seconds too late, but thanks for the intervention."

"Oh, don't thank me. It was completely self-serving. Tell me I don't have to worry about him."

"You don't have to worry about him. You don't have to worry about *anyone.*"

"What an outstanding answer. I wish I could talk to you all day, but I'm about twenty meters away from a group of people who are desperate to wheedle hints out of me about Friday's test. I'll call you tonight?"

"You'd better," I said. "I have a PowerPoint marathon ahead of me. I need something to look forward to. Have a good tutorial."

I went back to Jackman, dreading my work, but once I got started, things quickly fell into place. When Daniel called at ten thirty, I was in the home-stretch, previewing the slideshow to check transitions. We chatted for an hour, talking about everything and nothing. We spent most of the time laughing. He was so frigging funny when he allowed himself to relax. I was tempted to call Patty to tell her the pole she was so worried about seemed to have completely vanished.

No more than ten minutes after our phone call, I received a good night text from Daniel. All it said was:

Forty-five. -D

But only four till Friday…sweet dreams, sunshine. -A

And no nightmares. I placed a large X through Monday, March 16th, on my calendar.

I'd been in almost constant communication with Daniel throughout the week, but I couldn't wait to be alone with him at his condo. Texting and talking to him on the phone every day had been wonderful. He'd been so playful all week, full of innuendo and flirtation — so much fun. But nothing was a match for spending time with him alone.

And now that it was Thursday, all I could think about was that I'd be in Daniel's arms the next day. Yeah, I was beyond excited. First, however, I had to get through my damn French presentation. I was well prepared for my part of the seminar, but my stomach was cramping with nerves, a sensation which worsened as I walked to Vic for my French class.

As if he'd sensed my anxiety and knew I'd need a pep talk, Daniel was there waiting for me, resting against the Gatehouse wall. I wanted to run to him so he could scoop me up. Instead, I sauntered over, and he greeted me with a smile.

"Good afternoon, Miss Price."

"Good afternoon, Daniel."

"T-minus seven minutes and counting. Are you ready?"

"I'm ready but a bit nervous."

"You'll do great. Can we chat after class? You're done at three, right?"

"Actually, my French lecture on Thursdays is an hour, and then I have a class at University College from three to five."

"God, you must be exhausted. Your schedule's brutal."

"It's okay. I'm used to it."

"Well, can we talk for a few minutes before you head over to UC? There's something I'd like to run by you. I'll be in the reading room at the library."

"Pratt?"

"Who are you calling a prat?"

I rolled my eyes. "See you in an hour, Daniel."

"Good luck, Miss Price. I'm sure you'll do well."

Daniel was right. I did do well. My entire group did. The professor spent most of the twenty-five minutes while we were presenting nodding his head and didn't spend any time clarifying our points once we'd wrapped up, two sure signs we'd covered the material effectively.

After class, we patted each other on the back and someone suggested a celebratory coffee at Starbucks, but I begged off, using my next class as an excuse. Instead I walked to the library where Daniel was waiting for me, sitting by the window. When he saw me approaching, he stood and moved toward the end of the stacks in the corner of the reading room. I followed.

"How did it go?" he said once I'd caught up with him.

"It was great. Everything ran like clockwork," I whispered.

"I knew it would. I'm glad the time you lost working on it on Sunday didn't have any negative repercussions." He paused for a moment. "I know you're going to have trouble with this, but I got you something, and I'd really like you to accept it graciously."

He handed me a small envelope. I opened it and found a gift card for Holt Renfrew. I'd window shopped at Holt's but never actually bought anything. It was out of my league entirely.

"Why are you doing this, Daniel? I don't need anything. You don't have to spend your money on me to prove you care."

"That's not why I'm doing it. It makes me happy. Anyway, I think you *do* need to buy a few things. I'm taking you away tomorrow night, if you're okay with that."

"Taking me away? What do you mean? Where?"

"I should have checked with you first, but I wanted to surprise you. You've worked so hard this week. I've booked us a chalet at a resort up north. It's called Taboo. It used to be Muskoka Sands?"

"I'm familiar with it. I mean, I've seen pictures…" I trailed off, embarrassed. Taboo was not the kind of vacation spot my mom and I would ever have been able to afford.

"You don't sound particularly interested." His face fell.

"It's not that. I would have been fine with staying at your place, that's all."

"I know, but I thought it would be nice to be far away from here so we can go out and have fun together. We can rent some cross-country skis and curl up by the fire. Find something redeeming about winter." He smiled and rested his hand on the shelf beside us, close to my cheek but not quite close enough.

"So, what's this for?" I held up the gift card.

"I don't know. Maybe you could buy a dress, some new shoes. I'd like to take you out for dinner. And there's an indoor pool and hot tub. Do you need a new bathing suit?" Now he looked embarrassed. "I'm sorry, poppet. I want to spoil you. Please let me?"

I sighed and turned the card over in my hand. There was no dollar amount on it.

"Buy whatever you want, and they'll bill me. That's how I set it up. Will you do that for me? Please?"

He looked at me beseechingly. God, how could I resist?

"All right. You win. But I'm totally doing this under duress."

He smiled beatifically.

"So, tomorrow—when would we leave?" I asked, feeling a glimmer of excitement despite my initial reluctance.

"As soon as you're able to get your things together after tutorial. You can take the subway up to Yorkdale, and I'll pick you up there. If we leave by three, we can be up north in time to go out for dinner. Maybe we can ski on Saturday and be home after dinner. Penny's expecting us on Sunday to help with painting, if you're still interested."

"I see you've got this all planned."

"I've been thinking about what you said last Sunday—about hating winter. It'll be beautiful up there with all the snow we've had this week. There's supposed to be quite a snowfall tonight too."

I put the gift card in my pocket and zipped it up. "Okay, well, thank you. You're very…generous," I said, still not entirely comfortable.

"One other thing—please don't be frugal."

He knew me so well already.

"That's going to be hard. Frugal is hard-wired into my DNA."

"Do your best. For me?"

I sighed. "Okay."

"So, um, what do you think about swimming up at Taboo, or at least checking out the hot tub?"

"I'd say that sounds pretty damn appealing, sweet knees."

"I was hoping you'd say that. Do you have a bikini?" he asked.

"I'll add it to the shopping list."

He cast his eyes downward, moaning quietly.

"You okay?" I whispered.

"Yeah, just desperately trying *not* to get a visual."

I couldn't help laughing. "So, how's business been this week, anyway? Lots of *jobs* on the go?"

"Oh, you have no idea the number of jobs I've had to do all by myself. I'm seriously considering hiring some help. You know, a right-hand gal. Can you think of anyone who might be interested?"

"What if she's left-handed?" I asked.

"Nope. She has to be right-handed. Part of the terms of *service*."

"Well, I happen to meet that particular condition. Do you suppose I should apply?"

"I don't know. When can you start?"

"How does tomorrow sound?"

Now it was his turn to laugh. "Aubrey, you're a corker, you know that?"

"I'm going to choose to be flattered by that comment."

"As you should be."

"Good. I'm sorry, Daniel, but I really have to get going."

"Yeah, me too. I need to get the oil changed—in the car," he added, shaking his head self-consciously. "Patty. Jesus."

I smiled. Neither one of us moved.

He licked his lips meditatively. "I *really* wish I could kiss you right now."

I stared longingly at his mouth. "I wish you could too."

The air between us crackled.

Daniel sighed, breaking the tension. "You have a class to get to."

I nodded reluctantly.

"I'll call you tonight," he said. "You can tell me all about your shopping trip."

I stepped backward reluctantly. He leaned against the shelf, his hand in his pocket as I left. When I turned to look back at him, he flashed his lovely dimpled smile, and I grinned before hefting my knapsack higher on my back and finally escaping into the crisp afternoon air.

I'd never have thought I'd be able to shelve my frugal tendencies and treat myself to a frivolous spending spree, but women obviously have an innate talent for shopping, because several hours later, I was back at Jackman, packing a sexy dress, fantastic new shoes, and a killer bikini in my small suitcase with everything else I thought I might need for an overnight stay up north with Daniel.

Taboo. The irony of the resort's name didn't escape me.

After packing, I studied for the following day's test and waited for Daniel's good-night phone call. I was glad I took the time to read through my notes because I stumbled across a word I couldn't even remember writing down.

Apocryphal.

What the hell did that mean? Apparently I'd been daydreaming about Daniel during that lecture. I flipped back and forth a few pages, and then I found the definition and an example:

> Apocryphal - Authorship of doubtful origin. For example, Hecate's speech in Macbeth, possibly not attributable to Shakespeare. Excerpt from speech:
>
> "...you all know, security is mortals' chiefest enemy."

Wow, I really didn't remember writing that. I threw myself into studying with renewed vigor. Obviously I wasn't as comfortable with the course content as I'd initially believed. I continued to read through my lecture notes and didn't give the meaning behind the excerpt from Hecate's speech another thought.

In retrospect, I suppose I should have. Whoever had written those words was very wise indeed.

CHAPTER 9

Accidental Things

But all these poor forbiddings could not stay him;
He in the worst sense construes their denial:
The doors, the wind, the glove, that did delay him,
He takes for accidental things of trial...
(*The Rape of Lucrece*)

Friday morning, I woke up with that strange feeling I got when I wasn't sure what day it was. I pulled the sheets over my head and groaned when I remembered I had to go to work. But it was Friday, and Daniel was taking me away for a romantic retreat! I squealed and threw the covers back, doing a little happy dance in the bed. A three-hour shift, a test which I had studied my ass off for, a tutorial—with Daniel, and therefore not a chore at all—and then off to paradise. *TGIF.*

I stretched and yawned as I scrolled through my phone messages. Julie had sent me a text.

> **You'll NEVER believe what Jer and I are doing this weekend. Can't wait to talk to you! -J**

I smiled. Those Grant boys sure knew how to make their women spin. I typed out a quick reply.

**Can't wait to hear all about it, bun-head.
See you in a few....-A**

Next, I opened my Yahoo account. There was an email from someone I'd never heard of named Jung Willman. I considered deleting it, but I opened it to scan the contents, just in case. And thank goodness I did because it was one of the most amazing emails I'd ever received.

From: Jung Willman
To: Aubrey Price
Sent: Fri, Mar 20, 6:37:06 AM
Subject: Almost definitely...

Good morning, my lovely. I'm sure you're surprised to hear from me like this. I've had your email address since the course began, but you must be wondering what my pseudonym is all about. Last year I got rid of all social media accounts that would allow Nicola to contact me using my real name. I created this one, and only my best friends know the address. I didn't think it was advisable to use my university email to send you this message. I'm sure you understand.

I've been wide awake since five a.m., and I don't know what to do with myself. (I know exactly what you're thinking, by the way—always straight to the gutter.) After lying in bed for an hour thinking about you, I had to get up and write. I hope you don't mind that I'm emailing you rather than writing to my flash drive.

I can't wait to take you away from Toronto, away from prying eyes, away from the obstacles keeping us apart. I know we'll enjoy sharing some quality time, and I want to treat you to some much-deserved fun.

I don't think you understand how much I admire your work ethic. I wish there was something I could do to ease the burden of responsibility in your life. I'm amazed at how prepared you are to meet challenges with so little support from your parents. I'm in awe of your strength.

I'm counting the minutes until we're alone again. I hope you're excited, too. You sounded a little more enthusiastic when we spoke on the phone after your shopping trip. I can't stop thinking about how sexy your dress sounds.

Tonight we'll go out for dinner and drinks. Then afterward we'll curl up in bed and watch a movie. I can't wait to kiss you and fall asleep with you in my arms. I'm even looking forward to you drooling on me!

Tomorrow we'll go skiing, and then when we get back to the chalet we'll sit in front of the fire and drink hot chocolate with Bailey's. Winter's great, right?

I wish you could see the smile on my face as I write this. Even Sisyphus can't ruin my mood. I suppose I shouldn't hold you up any longer—you have to get to work.

I'll see you in a few hours. Until then, please know that on a scale of "maybe" to "definitely," I'm getting awfully close to the latter.

Your sailor,-D
xo

P.S. Please pack some very conservative PJs and make sure they're warm. I'll be leaving a window open tonight. Pajamas must stay on! Having said that, I'm stoked to see you in that bikini.

I had to read the whole thing twice, afraid I'd missed something important the first time as I'd scrolled through it quickly. This email—it *epitomized* Daniel. His confession about trying to hide from Nicola after her betrayal was poignant and distressing, but then the tone of the email changed as he regained his playful flirtatiousness and took great pains to communicate his feelings. I didn't have a hell of a lot of time, but I had to answer him. I wanted him to know I shared his excitement about our escape up north and that I felt just as strongly about him as he seemed to feel about me. I didn't bother turning on my laptop, opting to type out my quick response on my phone.

From: Aubrey Price
To: Jung Willman
Sent: Fri, Mar 20, 7:31:36 AM
Subject: Most definitely...

Good morning, sunshine. What a wonderful greeting to wake up to. I could get used to that. I am so excited to go away with you, Daniel. Sounds like you have a fantastic getaway planned for us. I can't wait.

I studied hard for the test today. Good thing I did—I didn't remember half the notes I took. There must have been something awfully distracting in that classroom while I was trying to listen to lectures.

I wish I could write more, but I have to get ready for work. My boss is even more uptight than his son, if you can believe it. ;) Can't wait to see you.

Your poppet

P.S. Now, those are some mixed messages, Mr. Grant. I guess I'd better unpack my silk negligee and try to find some flannel PJs. Do they make flannel bathing suits?

P.P.S. As for "almost definitely"? I'll do you one better. Most definitely.

By eight twenty, I was smiling to myself as I quickly got my things together for the day, leaving my suitcase at the bottom of the bed so I could grab it and run when I came home after class. I crossed the quad quickly, still on cloud nine.

I stomped my feet on the mat inside the doors of Northrop Frye Hall and went up the stairs and into the darkened office. Dean Grant hadn't arrived yet. Hopefully he was okay. The roads were probably gross this morning. I flicked on the lights, logged in to my email, and got to work sifting through messages. About fifteen minutes later, I was in the middle of sorting the mail when Dean Grant finally came in. His face was drawn and pale.

"Good morning, sir," I said hesitantly.

He didn't return my greeting. "Gwen will be here shortly. Tell her to come right in, would you?"

He pulled his door office closed with a resounding click. That wasn't good. Some sort of marital turbulence, perhaps? Should I take him a coffee or leave him alone? I opted for the second course of action. I didn't want to be on the receiving end of that simmering temper.

I was printing off envelope labels for people staying in residence over the summer when Gwen rushed in. She smiled at me, but it was forced. All the warmth she'd exuded when we'd first met had dissipated.

"Good morning, Mrs. Grant. Your husband said you should go right in." I couldn't bring myself to call her by her first name.

"Thank you, Aubrey," she said, heading straight into the office and closing the door behind her.

I shifted uncomfortably in my chair. Something was certainly going on. A momentary flutter of panic swept through my stomach as I wondered if it had to do with Daniel and me. But then I remembered how I'd gotten myself all worked up when Dean Grant had called me in to speak to me the day he'd found out about Mary, and I'd wrongly assumed he'd wanted to confront me about Daniel. My conscience was making me paranoid.

I shook my head resolutely to chase away my gnawing anxiety. It was difficult to distract myself from the unnerving silence of the office. If Daniel's parents were arguing, they were sure making quiet work of it.

When Daniel crashed through the door, my anxiety roared back.

"Daniel!" I rushed over to the counter to meet him.

"Hey," he said quietly. "What the fuck is going on?"

"What do you mean?"

"My dad called half an hour ago *demanding* I come in to see him. He hung up on me before I had a chance to ask any questions. I dropped everything and bolted. Is he in there?" he asked, motioning to his father's office.

"Yes, he is. So is your mother," I whispered.

"What? Christ. I hope everything's okay. Why do I have a bad feeling something's happened to Patty?"

"I don't know, Daniel. Something terrible *has* happened, for sure. You don't think—"

Before I could finish, the office door opened, and Dean Grant stormed through it.

"Oh, good, Daniel—you're here. Come in, please. And Aubrey? Can you lock the front door? We'd like to speak to you too."

Daniel set his mouth in a grim line as he held his hand up to me. "I'll get the door."

Daniel met us in the inner office and stood in the doorway, facing his father.

"What's this all about, Dad? You could have elaborated a little more on the phone. This wasn't exactly a great day to be driving with the fear of the devil in me."

"I'm sorry about that. Your mother just called your cell phone to tell you to take your time. Obviously your phone isn't on."

"I don't even have my phone. I dropped what I was doing and ran out of the condo like a bat out of hell."

"I'm sorry. That was careless of me. But you're here now."

Panic and dread mingled in my stomach. Someone must have seen us somewhere together and reported us. Dean Grant sat behind his desk. Daniel anxiously looked at me as we moved to sit side by side in the chairs across from his father.

Gwen was perched against the low shelf behind her husband's chair, her arms crossed. She didn't walk over to greet her son but simply stood there, her expression weary. Daniel leaned forward in his chair, eager to get to the bottom of things.

"Is Patty okay?" Daniel asked.

"Patty's fine, to the best of my knowledge," his father said. "I was at her house this morning, in fact. The high school kid who normally clears the driveway is away for spring break. I didn't want to wake her, but I swung by to shovel after last night's snow." He looked at each of us in turn. "I came across the strangest thing on the driveway."

He opened his desk drawer and pulled out my striped glove.

"I believe this is yours, is it not?" he said, turning to me and holding up my lost glove. He placed it on the desk.

My heart dropped into my stomach. I looked over at Daniel, who had his head in his hands. There was no mistaking the fact that this was my glove. And his father knew it.

"I, um, I don't know..." My head was spinning. "Daniel?" I whispered.

He glanced at me quickly before turning to his father. "Yes, that's Aubrey's glove," he said flatly.

He offered no further information. The two of them just stared at each other.

Gwen stepped forward and placed her hand on her husband's shoulder. "What does this mean, Daniel?" she asked. "What's going on here? Why on earth would Aubrey's glove be at my mother's house? Help me understand."

Daniel raked his hands through his hair. "I gave Aubrey those gloves," he said simply.

Dean Grant gaped at me. "So, this gift? These gloves, Aubrey? They were from my son? You've been hiding this from me?"

"Yes, sir," I said, shame coursing through me.

"I see." He paused for a moment. "You didn't answer your mother's question, Daniel. How did this glove get lost at Patty's?" Dean Grant's tone was growing steely. "I'd appreciate it if you could shed a little more light on what's going on here. *Please*." This last word was spoken through clenched teeth.

Daniel sighed in frustration and, ultimately, in defeat. "Aubrey came to Patty's with me last Sunday for dinner. She must have dropped her glove on the ground at some point during the evening."

Gwen's mouth popped open, and she steadied herself on the desk with her free hand. I thought for a second she might faint. I stared down at my lap, Dean Grant's words from Monday replaying in my mind, a mocking refrain:

"Well, you're the Shakespeare expert, but I don't think any of the tragic heroes spiraled to their downfall as a result of a lost mitten."

Apparently there is a first time for everything.

"So, let me understand this," Dean Grant said. "Despite my warnings. Despite my *clear* request, Aubrey," he said, looking at me pointedly, "the two of you have embarked on what can only be described as a clandestine *friendship*—a friendship close enough to warrant gift giving and at least one family dinner—without our knowledge? Is there anything else we need to know? Are you going out socially? Completely flouting all regard for university guidelines about fraternizing? Or, worse still, are you spending time together in private?" His mouth hardened. "Well?"

Though he was angry, his voice was barely raised. It was this quiet rage that frightened me the most.

"Aubrey and I have become close," Daniel said. "It's not Aubrey's fault," he clarified. "I forced the issue. I enjoy her company. We're very…compatible. It's been next to impossible for me to ignore…my feelings for her."

His feelings for me. As of two hours ago, he was *almost definitely* falling in love with me. They would never understand—*never* condone this.

Gwen covered her mouth with her hand, shocked speechless. Her husband, however, was not.

"Good God, Daniel. What are you *thinking?* Perhaps you've lost all regard for your reputation, but you could at least give your mother and me some consideration. Your behavior is beyond childish and immature. It's utterly selfish in the extreme."

He shook his head in disbelief.

"I can't believe you'd be so naïve to think you could get away with something like this. I've thought for a long time that you two would be well-suited for one another, but really, Daniel, to jeopardize your name—your standing here at the university—simply because your hormones are raging and you can't wait a few months?"

"David, really," Gwen said, her tone reproving.

Daniel glowered at his father. I kept waiting for him to say something, but he was completely silent. A muscle in his jaw twitched.

"No, he needs to hear this," Dean Grant said. "He's living in a dream world, behaving like a spoiled, petulant child who wants his Christmas presents in October. But this is not a game. And I'll be having a word with your mother about this too, Gwen. I have no doubt she's encouraged him in his pursuit of Aubrey."

I was dying of mortification and wanted nothing more than to take Daniel's hand and run out of the office, but that was obviously not an option. I didn't know where to look so I trained my eyes on my tightly clasped hands.

Dean Grant spoke softly, "I don't know what's happened to your moral compass. I don't think I've ever been this disappointed in you, son."

"David." Gwen's voice was firmer this time, but he held up a hand to her.

"After everything we went through in England to clear your name. The money we spent, the heartache of it all. You asked us to believe you unequivocally, and we did because we're your parents and we love you unconditionally. But for you to do something like this? It makes me think twice about—"

"David, that's *enough*." Gwen dropped her hand from her husband's shoulder and looked at her son, concern etched in her face. "Daniel?"

Daniel was rubbing his shoulder. His face was ashen and contorted in pain. He seemed to be having trouble breathing. Oh my God—was he having a heart attack or something? He bowed forward in his chair as Gwen rounded the desk.

"I can't...I can't," he gasped.

I jumped out of my seat, but Gwen knelt in front of Daniel, effectively blocking my access to him.

"I know, breathe, darling, just breathe slowly, that's it." She took his hand and rubbed it vigorously. "David, has this happened recently that you know of?" she asked, turning to her husband.

Has *what* happened recently? What the hell was going on? What was wrong with him? I was rooted to the spot, helplessly wringing my hands.

David moved to stand behind his wife. "No, I don't think so, at least not that he's confided in me. Which I'm becoming aware means nothing…"

I felt invisible all of a sudden. No one seemed to remember that I was standing there. They were so nonchalant. What the hell?

"What's going on? Daniel? Are you all right?" I said, trying to control the panic in my voice. Daniel didn't respond. He was bent forward, wheezing. "Is he okay?" I asked Dean Grant, my eyes darting back and forth between them.

Daniel was oblivious to my presence, one hand in his mother's clasped fingers, the other on his chest as he panted helplessly.

"Shouldn't we call an ambulance or something?" I suggested, my voice verging on hysterical.

Why were we all just watching Daniel as he fought to fill his lungs? A serious asthma attack—that's what this looked like to me. Standing around while he struggled to breathe was absurd and cruel. I leaned over the desk and picked up the phone receiver. Dean Grant took it gently from my hand and hung up.

"Aubrey, no. It's all right. That won't be necessary. Gwen, I'm going to get Aubrey out of here. You deal with Daniel."

"No! I'm not leaving—I can't leave! Not now!" I wanted to be the one holding his hand. I had to stay to make sure he was okay. How could I possibly leave him when he needed me?

But then Daniel motioned with his hand for me to go. He was rocking back and forth and waving me off, not looking at me, but dismissing me with a gesture that said, *Get out.* I took a few stunned steps backward, terribly hurt.

Dean Grant placed his hand under my elbow. "I'll close the office for the morning and put a sign up. Perhaps I'll see if Gisele can come in early. You can go home. Don't worry. Gwen and I will take good care of Daniel."

I walked woodenly toward the door. I didn't want to go home, but how could I possibly stay? It wasn't just his parents that wanted me out. Daniel didn't want me there, either. I glanced over my shoulder at him. His mother was rubbing his back and whispering to him. How could he dismiss me like that, knowing how I felt about him?

"Is he okay? Is he going to be okay?" I asked as we walked out of the office. I could barely formulate words. Dean Grant had taken my jacket off the coat rack and was helping me put it on.

"He's going to be fine. His mother and I have dealt with this many times," he said dismissively.

This what? *What is this?*

He was speaking cautiously and ambiguously, purposefully drawing a line around his family, stacking up the fence posts. I stood on the other side. The message was clear: *This is our business, not yours. You're an outsider.* I was crushed, but I knew I didn't have a leg to stand on. He'd asked me to stay away from his son, and I'd flagrantly ignored his request.

I grabbed my knapsack, and he led me out of the office. Actually, *dragged* might have been a more appropriate term. After locking the outer doors behind him, he helped me down the steps and held the front door for me. I stood on the pavement, squinting as the sun glinted off the snow. Dean Grant's eyes bored into me, and I shrank under his gaze, averting my eyes and staring blankly at the southern face of Old Vic.

"To say I'm disappointed would hardly do justice to my feelings at this moment, Aubrey," he said. As I looked back at him, his expression softened slightly. "I've come to think very highly of you. I've always admired your level-headedness and maturity. It's hard for me to believe you'd allow this to happen."

It took everything in me to contain my emotions as I was suddenly transported back in time — I was sixteen years old, and my mother was lecturing me about how foolish it was to experiment with smoking.

"I'm sorry, Dean Grant. I don't know how this happened. Daniel and I — we gradually became closer and closer. Your son is a wonderful man. We enjoy each other's company. I suppose we allowed ourselves to believe we weren't hurting anyone."

"That's a very dangerous misconception. If anyone were to find out how close you are, Daniel could end up getting very hurt. It's crucial for him to maintain his distance. You must know what happened to him last year? I gather he's confided in you?"

"Yes, sir. I know all about Oxford."

"Then surely you understand? You realize I'm not being unreasonable?"

I nodded. I'd never felt so ashamed.

"I need your word. You have to promise me here and now that you won't do anything that could hurt him."

I looked into his eyes levelly. "I promise."

"Are you telling me the truth this time, Aubrey?"

This time.

"I'd rather die than hurt Daniel. I guess I got caught up in my feelings for him. I really do care about your son, sir."

He looked at me soberly. "If you mean that, you'll need to cease all personal contact. I have no idea what the extent of this relationship is. Frankly, I'm afraid to think what's going on between you two. But I need you to cut everything off now — preferably until graduation, but at the very least for the next six weeks. That means no phone calls, no emails, and absolutely no visiting outside of the confines of the course. You might even consider taking your office hours with Professor Brown and not with Daniel. No point in making things more difficult for yourself."

I gestured back to the office. "Wait, Daniel — is he — "

"He'll be fine. We'll take care of him, don't worry. I know it looks bad, but in about fifteen minutes he'll be fine." He rubbed his face in exasperation. "As much of a mess as this is, Aubrey, I'm glad I'm the one who found out and not someone else. If one of your classmates or Professor Brown had discovered…I can't even entertain the idea. Look, I should get back inside."

"Okay," I said, my voice small and hollow.

What else could I say? He was right. I'd screwed up. Well, *we'd* screwed up. I certainly wasn't accepting full responsibility for the situation.

"You go on home. I'll see you on Monday. We'll talk more about how to proceed after the weekend."

So, that was it? I was supposed to go home as if nothing untoward had happened? He opened the door and left me standing there. Yep. I was dismissed. I watched him climb the steps and disappear into the far reaches of the office.

I turned slowly. People passed me, going about their routines — rushing off to class, meeting friends for coffee, running errands. There was no way I could join them or carry on with my day without knowing Daniel was okay.

I cut across the wide path between Northrop Frye Hall and Old Vic and jogged lightly up the south steps. I would wait. I would stand inside the door's archway and wait for them to come out.

And so I stood. I watched. I waited. Fifteen minutes went by, and no one emerged. My feet were getting cold, and my ears started to ache. I ducked inside the large wooden doors of Old Vic, peering out the window beside the door. I nibbled my nails impatiently, checked my phone for texts, even read a few random emails and Facebook comments. Another fifteen minutes, and still nothing. What the hell?

By ten forty-five, I started to get exasperated. I couldn't stand there all day. I *would*, just to know that Daniel was all right, but I did have a class to go to and a test to write. How would I be able to concentrate on a stupid midterm while I was worrying about Daniel?

I tapped my foot and continued to watch people walking between the two buildings. Screw it. I had to know. Without stopping to consider the consequences, I dashed across to the opposite building, running up the main stairs. The office lights had been turned off. There was a sign on the glass door that read, "Closed until 12:00." Peering through the glass, I considered letting myself in to make sure they were gone, but I didn't need to. I could tell they were no longer inside. How could they have left without me seeing them? Regardless of which exit they'd used, I would have seen them make their way to Dean Grant's car.

Then I remembered the underground passageway. Of course! That's the way they must have left, literally walking beneath me and most likely exiting through the west doors of Old Vic which led to the administrative parking area.

I ran outside, jogging to Old Vic's west exit. There were tracks in the snow, three clear sets of footprints coming down the steps and veering around to the north side of the building. Daniel had made it out of the building in one piece and presumably under his own steam. The asthma attack, or whatever it had been, had passed. I followed the footprints to where they stopped. Sure enough, all three sets of prints led to Dean Grant's parking spot. His car was gone.

I stood there for a few moments, then turned and started to go back to residence. What else could I do? Daniel was with his parents. Perhaps they were going to stay with him for a while to make sure he recovered. Maybe they'd take him home so he could get the things he'd need for the afternoon and return him to campus in time for class, which was a little over an hour away.

Regardless of the fact that he didn't have his phone—and certainly contrary to his father's wishes—I had to at least let Daniel know how concerned I was. As I crossed the quad, I typed a long text message.

I'm so sorry about what happened this morning.
I hope you're okay. You freaked me out with the crazy
breathing thing. What the hell was that? It kind of hurt my
feelings knowing you didn't want me to stay.
Has your dad calmed down? He's not happy with me.
We need to talk about all of this.
Maybe a quick chat after tutorial? -A

I read the message over a couple of times and then sent it. Now I'd have to wait. I let myself into the apartment. Matt was home. Music blared from his room. I kicked off my boots and dropped my coat and bag on the floor beside them, escaping to my room and closing the door behind me. I needed to be alone.

I surveyed my room, and there, silently mocking me, was my packed suitcase. I stood for a moment, sadly looking at it before unzipping the top flap. My beautiful new dress lay carefully folded on top. I lifted it out and sat on the edge of the bed, touching the soft fabric to my face, finally allowing myself the luxury of tears.

CHAPTER 10

Alone

Let me confess that we two must be twain,
Although our undivided loves are one:
So shall those blots that do with me remain
Without thy help by me be borne alone.
(*Sonnet 36*)

An hour later, I dragged my ass through the doors of the classroom, spurred on by the hope that, even though he hadn't responded to my text, Daniel would be sitting at the front of the room, relaxed and casual as always.

He wasn't.

Thanks to my meltdown at the apartment and the subsequent half hour it had taken me to get my shit back together, I was one of the last to arrive in the room. Test papers were arranged face down on every other desk, and Professor Brown was writing instructions on the chalkboard. Julie waved me over and moved her bag off the seat two away from hers. I quickly sat down, and she looked at me, frowning.

"You scared the shit out of me. I thought you weren't gonna make it," she hissed.

"Yeah. Crazy morning," I whispered back.

She questioned me with her eyes, but there wasn't time to explain. Professor Brown was standing behind the podium, rubbing the chalk dust off his hands.

"Well, then, ladies and gentlemen. I suppose we'll get started. Friday's seminar group, you'll need to pick up an extra assignment sheet from me at the end of class. I received a phone call from Dean Grant over at Vic. Daniel's a little under the weather and won't be able to conduct tutorial today."

Julie raised her eyebrow at me while Professor Brown sat in Daniel's usual spot. "Keep in mind, Daniel will be assessing these tests," he told us. "I certainly hope none of you have gotten on his bad side," he said with a playful smile.

Daniel doesn't have *a bad side*, I thought wistfully.

Forty-odd test papers rustled as everyone picked up their question sheets and answer booklets, flipping the pages open. I read over the whole test before starting. I recognized all of the quotations and had a firm handle on the context, meaning, and significance of each one. The hardest part would be deciding which five of the seven quotations to analyze. I brought my thoughts into focus, trying to put Daniel out of my mind. It wasn't easy, but in a way, I was actually writing *to* Daniel. I wanted him to be proud of me. I wanted him to read my work and be blown away by my answers.

I got lost in the test. To be honest, it was a relief to escape from the burden of my mortification over having so thoroughly disappointed Dean Grant. I wrote steadily, comforted by the knowledge that I was kicking the test's ass.

At quarter to one, Professor Brown gave us the fifteen minute warning. I glanced over at Julie. She was re-reading her test, gnawing on the end of her pen.

I was almost at that point, finishing up my analysis of the *Antony and Cleopatra* quotation. A few moments later, I was reviewing my answers, inserting missed words where my brain had moved more quickly than my pen. People around me began gathering belongings.

I waited for Julie to finish, and soon we were both handing in our tests and picking up the seminar assignment sheet before exiting quietly.

"That was a piece of cake," Julie whispered as she pulled on her coat.

"I know, eh?" I followed her down the hall.

She grabbed my arm, hooking her hand into the crook of my elbow and speeding down the stairs.

"Whoa, where's the frickin' fire?" I asked.

"Sorry, I'm just super glad this seminar got canceled. Not that I'm happy Daniel's sick, but I have *so* much to do before Jer picks me up."

"What's going on, anyway?" I asked her. "Where are you guys going?"

"Windsor—we're going to Windsor. Jeremy wants to meet my parents! I'm so excited I could puke!"

"Holy crap! This is serious! You've only been going out for a few weeks."

"I told him it seemed too soon, and he told me not to be dramatic. He wants to see where I grew up and meet my parents because that'll help him understand me better."

"Holy swoon!"

"I know!" She hopped from one foot to the other.

It was adorable and aggravating all at the same time. I wanted my relationship with Daniel to be this exciting—this *normal.*

"Is he staying at your parents' place with you?"

"Yeah, in the guestroom."

"You be careful, missy. First it's a smidge here and a smidge there, and the next thing you know…"

She laughed. "I know. Things are getting intense, but he's so cool with it, Aubrey. Jesus, I'm so lucky."

Are you ever. I swallowed my bitterness and smiled, doing my best to feel happy for her.

"What's up with you, though?" she asked. "How come you were almost late for class?"

I hesitated. I didn't want to spew my misery all over her. She was so damned happy, and it's not like there was anything she could do. Plus, she didn't even have time to hang around listening to my tale of woe.

"You know what, sweets? It was just a chaotic morning. No worries. You go do your thing."

"Okay, if you're sure…"

"I'm sure. Get out of here."

She hugged me and looked at me warily before taking a couple of steps away.

"Hey, tell Daniel I said I hope he's okay?"

"I will."

If he ever speaks to me again.

Even though I'd resolutely refused to unpack my suitcase, by nine o'clock that night it was clear that my trip with Daniel was not meant to be. I'd heard nothing from him.

It had also become obvious that Matt had been entertaining company the night before. I wished he would come home so I could ask him about the blond hairs I'd found on the vanity in the bathroom and the lipstick-smudged tissues in the wastebasket.

Sarah had long blond hair. Was it possible they'd gotten back together? Wouldn't that be ironic? Things between Daniel and me were falling apart, and Matt was back on track with Sarah. I'd have laughed if I hadn't been so incredibly miserable.

Matt had left a note on top of my suitcase telling me to have a great time up north and to be careful. I wasn't sure if he was counseling me to avoid a broken leg or a broken heart. Of course, he had no idea I wasn't going up north now. I hadn't seen him after this morning's disaster. He'd been holed up in his room during the hour I'd been home, music blasting the entire time, presumably *entertaining* his lady friend. And now he was out, perhaps with her again.

In Matt's absence, I raided his movies. I settled on *Shop Girl*, which I watched while eating chips, drinking beer, and clutching my phone, hoping that at some point Daniel would buckle and text me or call. It took every ounce of self-control I could muster to leave the ball in his court.

As I drank my beer, I tortured myself with thoughts of Daniel's delicious Guinness kisses. And speaking of torture, *Shop Girl* had not been a wise choice. By the time the final scene rolled around and Ray Porter's voice-over described how he felt connected to Mirabelle even though they were separated by miles and time zones, my heart was throbbing painfully.

Daniel, wherever you are, please call...

Daniel did not call on Friday or even after I broke down on Saturday morning and left a message on his cell phone.

So much for my promise to his father. What had he said to Daniel? *I don't know what's happened to your moral compass?* Apparently mine had gone berserk too. But surely this was different? I wasn't harassing him to say "Let's go out" or "Can I come over?"

I just wanted to know that the man I was falling in love with was okay.

Matt finally came home late Saturday afternoon. After having slept elsewhere on Friday night, he walked through the door looking mighty pleased with himself, but his face fell as soon as he saw me flaked out on the couch watching infomercials. I'd been lying there for hours, still in my PJs, watching drivel and dozing occasionally.

"Aubrey, what the hell are you doing here? I thought you were going away? Jesus. You look like crap."

"Thanks, Matt, I appreciate your comforting words."

But he was right. I looked and felt like shit. He flopped on the couch beside me to listen as I explained what had happened, including my attempts to reach Daniel and my lack of success at getting hold of him. It was a relief to pour my heart out. After being the good friend and not telling Julie a word, I'd been on the verge of exploding from holding everything in.

"So, he had some sort of breathing attack, and they booted you out, and that's the last you heard from him?"

"Pretty much."

"That sucks. Now you're wallowing in Magic Bullet infomercials?"

"Yep."

"I don't know, Aub, that's Stage Two if I ever saw it. That's *way* worse than Maury Povich."

He smiled sadly at me. I shook my head, recalling how I'd tried to joke around with Matt after his break up with Sarah. Now that the shoe was on the other foot, I was kicking myself for being such a smartass.

"Do you want me to call him?" he offered. "If he's screening calls, he won't recognize my number. Maybe he'll pick up. I can try to reason with him."

I didn't want to put Matt in an awkward position, but…

"It's worth a try, I guess."

He didn't miss a beat, handing me his phone. "Dial."

I punched in Daniel's number and gave Matt the phone. He stood up and paced, waiting for an answer. Then he shook his head.

"Yeah, Daniel, it's Matt. I'm here with Aubrey, and she'd — well, *we* actually, would appreciate it if you'd call to let her know what's going on. I warned you not to screw her around again. Leaving her in the dark like this? Not cool. Call her as soon as possible. I mean it." He hung up and tossed his phone on the table. "Sorry, Aub."

"Thanks for trying."

"Look, isn't there someone else you could call? Julie's dating his brother, right? Maybe they know what's going on."

I sighed. "Julie and Jeremy are in Windsor. They're having this big meet-the-parents weekend. I don't want to wreck her fun."

Matt looked at me, perplexed. "Why do you always do that?"

"Do what?"

"Worry about everyone else. They're your friends. They'll understand. That's what friends do for each other."

I chewed on the inside of my cheek, imagining how things might unfold if I called Julie. Either Jeremy would get dragged into the middle of things, calling Daniel and trying to intervene on my behalf, or he'd find out that Daniel wasn't well and feel guilty for being away for the weekend. Worse still, maybe he wouldn't be able to reach his brother either and he'd drive home in a panic from Windsor — he was a nervous driver in the first place.

I shook my head. "Nope. I'm not calling Julie."

Matt sighed. "You're so fucking stubborn."

"Daniel thinks so too."

"For once we agree on something." He paused for a second. "What about the English bombshell and Mr. Muscle? Can't you call them?"

"I tried earlier. No answer."

"Try again," Matt said.

I got Penny's voice mail after the fifth ring. I rolled my eyes at Matt. We weren't having much luck.

"Hi, Penny, it's Aubrey again. I'm sorry to be a pest, but I was wondering if you could give me a call back when you get a second. It's kind of important. Thanks."

I hung up and fell back onto the couch, sighing.

"Looks like you've done the best you can. Why don't you have a hot shower? Try to unwind a bit."

I allowed him to cajole me with the promise that he would make dinner while I got myself sorted out. After my shower, I dried off, bundled myself up in my robe, and stared at the lipstick-smudged tissues in the waste basket. It was Matt's turn to talk. I called for him to come to the bathroom quickly.

"What is it?" he asked from the other side of the bathroom door.

I held up one of the long blond hairs and poked my hand through the door.

"My hair. I think it's going gray from stress," I said.

"That's blond, not gray."

I whipped the door open, looking at him suspiciously as I held the hair aloft. "Spill."

He took the hair and dropped it in the garbage. "I'll give you three guesses, and your first two don't count," he said.

"Sarah?"

"Ding, ding, ding! We have a winner, folks."

Ha! I knew it!

"You want to talk about it?" I offered.

"Would you be mad if I said no?"

"Nope. Your call, dude. I don't mean to pry. You know I want you to be happy, right?"

He took my hand. "I know. I just don't want to jinx anything. I want you to be happy, too. I can't believe this is happening with you and Daniel. Actually, I *can* believe it. I've had a bad feeling about this since the beginning, but it's not my place to say, you know?"

"I know. Can I have a hug?"

"What kind of question is that?" He pulled me into a tight embrace, rubbing my back. "I'm glad you showered. You smelled kind of funky earlier."

"Fuck you," I whispered into his neck.

He laughed and stepped back. "Atta girl. Now get dressed. I'm in the middle of making you the most amazing mac and cheese. Best cure for heartache I can think of. Then you can spend all night watching infomercials. You should see if you can find one for a Tae-Bo DVD or something. You're getting a little doughy."

He playfully poked me in the belly and shook his head.

"One day we'll both be happy at the same time, Aubs," he said, heading off to the kitchen.

I tried to do homework Sunday morning, but it was an exercise in futility. I checked my email every two minutes for an answer to a message I'd sent Daniel. I'd tried to be straightforward, pleading for him to tell me he was okay so I could stop worrying. When my phone rang at noon, I almost put my back out leaping to reach for it.

Sadly, it wasn't Daniel. But it *was* Penny, and I was almost as thrilled to hear from her.

"Aubrey, I'm so sorry, love. I've only just received your messages. Brad and I went out for the day yesterday, and I had my phone off. So, is Daniel with you? He was afraid to call me back after he heard my message this morning, wasn't he? You're still up at that bloody resort, aren't you? I'll never get this house painted. First Jeremy leaves with Julie, and now Daniel's gone and buggered off too."

"Wait. You lost me—"

"You and Daniel. Aren't you two still up in the Muskokees?"

"Muskokas. And, no, we're not up there. We didn't end up going. At least *I* didn't go. If Daniel went, it wasn't with me. So, you haven't spoken to him at all this weekend?"

"No, that wanker. He was supposed to call me to tell me what time he was coming over today to paint. Why aren't you with him? He was beyond excited about going up there with you. You didn't have a fight, did you?"

"No, we didn't have a fight. Not really. It's kind of complicated."

"I'm all ears, darling."

I told her the whole story while she occasionally interjected an "Oh no" or sighed. Penny gasped when I told her we'd had dinner at Patty's. Once the words started coming, I couldn't seem to stop.

"I can't believe he hasn't called you, of all people," I said, after explaining how Daniel had waved me out and David had sent me on my way. "He tells you everything. Now I'm more worried than ever. What if this breathing thing got worse after I left? What if he's in the hospital or something?"

Jesus, why hadn't I thought of that earlier? He was probably in the hospital! That's why no one could reach him. But wouldn't his parents call to let people know? The whole situation was beyond weird.

My questions were met with silence, and then Penny said, "Oh, sod it," very matter-of-factly.

"What?"

"Well, it's just—oh, bugger—"

"Wait, don't tell me. You *do* know what's going on, don't you, and you can't say? What—is this *fence post?* Not your place to tell? Goddamn this family and their frigging secrets. Fuck the fence post, Penny!"

"That's inadvisable, love. You'll get slivers in places you didn't even know you had."

"You know what I mean. I'm going out of my mind. If you know something, please tell me!"

She sighed and grumbled unintelligibly.

"Penny?"

"You know, he's going to absolutely throttle me when he finds out I've told you this."

"You're killing me."

"I'm sorry, really. Look, by the sounds of things, I'm sure he's fine. David meant it when he said it would pass in twenty minutes or so."

"*It.* What *it?* Tell me what *it* is!"

"Panic, darling. Anxiety. Daniel has a mild anxiety disorder. Well, he *did.* He's been so much better lately. I've noticed a real change since I've been over here. I've only heard him complain a couple of times about it recently."

"Anxiety disorder? How long has he had it?"

"It's nothing to worry about, lovey. Sometimes he has these extreme reactions to stressful situations. Often, they happen out of the blue. Panic attacks aren't life threatening, but they can be debilitating if you don't deal with them early on. He's been having them since that bitch at Oxford dragged his name through the mud."

"Oh, Penny, why didn't he tell me? I had no clue."

"You know how proud he is. Plus, he's probably terrified of scaring you away. He's notorious for over thinking. I'm sure you've sussed that out as well."

"So, he's probably fine? He's most likely *not* in the hospital?"

"I'd be very surprised to hear that he was in the hospital, yes, so there you are. One fence post knocked over. Done and dusted."

This was a nice thought, but it wasn't exactly true. If the fence post was truly knocked over, I'd know precisely where Daniel was and why he wasn't answering any of my messages.

CHAPTER 11

To Be So Moral

'tis all men's office to speak patience
To those that wring under the load of sorrow,
But no man's virtue nor sufficiency
To be so moral when he shall endure
The like himself.
(*Much Ado About Nothing*, Act v, Scene i)

I walked across the quad on Monday morning, oddly full of dread and hope. Normally I'd have been thrilled about the sun's efforts to melt the last stray patches of snow, but I couldn't have cared less. Seeing Dean Grant was going to be uncomfortable. Seeing Daniel later—hopefully safe and fully recovered from his anxiety attack—would be the balm to ease the discomfort. Even if he didn't want to talk to me, knowing he was okay was all I needed.

The office was dark when I arrived. There was a note from Gisele outlining what she'd accomplished on Friday; from what she'd written, I gathered Dean Grant hadn't returned in the afternoon.

Preoccupied, I went on auto-pilot and worked my way through my morning's tasks. I kept reflecting on my conversation with Penny. We'd actually talked for over half an hour as she'd tried to calm me down and put my mind at ease.

Shortly after nine thirty, my musings were interrupted by Dean Grant walking through the door, a bleary-eyed Daniel on his heels.

"Good morning, Aubrey," Dean Grant said as he hung up his coat, his voice a touch more brusque than usual. He was wearing Dockers and a golf shirt. I couldn't remember a time when he hadn't come to work in a suit.

Daniel hung back, one hand in his pocket and the other resting lightly on the counter. A thousand emotions passed across his face as he met my eyes.

"Hi."

That was all he said.

How could one small syllable be imbued with so much feeling?

"How are you?" I asked. What an absurd question. I didn't know what else to say. His father watched us from his office doorway.

"Better, I suppose." He frowned and shook his head slightly as if calling himself out on the lie.

"Okay, come on in, you two," his father said, holding the door to his office open.

Daniel stepped around the counter and stood with his father in the doorway. "Dad, I'm going to talk to Aubrey first. Alone. I think she deserves the courtesy of an explanation from me."

Dean Grant seemed prepared to dig in his heels. His eyes bounced back and forth between us.

Please.

I willed him to agree with my eyes.

"Well—"

"I'm not asking permission," Daniel clarified, his voice steely.

Wow. Was this the same Daniel who'd fallen apart here three days ago?

His father sighed. "All right, go in here." He motioned to a small reading room. "I'll be waiting in my office."

Daniel nodded grimly. "This might take a while. We have a lot to talk about."

I met Dean Grant's eyes, and he gazed back at me contemplatively. God only knew what he must have been thinking. Daniel gestured for me to enter the small room ahead of him, and he followed, pushing the door closed quietly and turning the lock. I stood beside the small round table in the center of the room, tracing the wood grain pattern on the surface with my thumbnail.

"Are you really okay?" I whispered.

"No, not really."

I stepped forward, my hands hanging uselessly at my sides. "I was so worried when I didn't hear from you, and I didn't know what was wrong or where you were—and now you come in here, looking like, God, I don't know, like you haven't slept in days…What's going on? You could have at least answered one of my messages. I just wanted to know you were all right."

He shook his head. "I'm so sorry. I had no control over what happened this weekend. I was beside myself worrying about you too, you have no idea…" He took a step forward, and I thought he was going to take me in his arms, but he didn't. He walked around the table and stood by the window looking out at the quad. "I've been with you for two minutes, and already I want to do all the things my father said I shouldn't do." He peered over his shoulder at me, his eyes pained.

"I'm sorry. I guess we're in the same boat. I promised your father I'd back off, and there I was, texting you, phoning you, emailing. Obviously that put you in an awkward position. Is that why you didn't answer me? You promised your father you wouldn't?"

He dropped into the chair on the other side of the table. "I promised my father no such thing. I didn't get any messages. I've been up at our cottage all weekend. I didn't have my phone, my laptop. Nothing. I had no way of contacting you, no way of leaving. We left there early this morning. I haven't even been home yet." He gestured to his scruffy clothes. "I insisted on coming here to see you first."

"That's why no one could get hold of you?"

He nodded. "After we left here on Friday, I was exhausted. I assumed they were taking me home. I closed my eyes in the car, and I guess I fell asleep. When I woke up, we were in fucking Bracebridge. Can you believe that?"

"Oh my God. I had no idea."

"Of course you didn't. My dad said I needed to make a clean break for a couple of days to clear my head—get some distance and regain my perspective. I had no say in it, and I was livid. I asked if I could use his phone to call you, and he assured me he'd told you I'd be fine and that you needed some time to think, too. I promise you, Aubrey, it was never my intent to leave you hanging like that. It was an awful weekend. *Tense* doesn't even begin to describe it."

I sat down across from him. "They didn't let anyone know where they were going?"

"Jeremy was away for the weekend. They didn't think they needed to call him. And with Brad and Penny on their own, they assumed they'd be none the wiser. No need to worry them unnecessarily."

I grimaced. "Well, I'm sorry, but they were worried by yesterday afternoon. I had to call Penny. She left you quite a few messages. I did as well. I think I started to sound a little hysterical by yesterday morning. There's a message on your phone from Matt, too. He was worried about me."

A gentle smile ghosted across his face, and he looked down at my hands. "Good old Matt."

"He's back together with his girlfriend, by the way. I thought you'd be happy to hear that."

"That is good news." He paused for a moment before taking a deep breath. "So, I guess you have a lot of questions. About my behavior on Friday, I mean."

"I did have lots of questions, but I think the most important ones have been cleared up for me."

"What do you mean?"

"I was desperate, Daniel. I was terrified when I couldn't reach you. Seeing you like that on Friday scared the shit out of me. I finally got hold of Penny. I thought she'd know where you were, but she said she and Brad were looking for you as well because you didn't show up to help paint. I ended up telling her what happened on Friday. I thought maybe you were in the hospital."

Daniel clenched his jaw, and a muscle in his cheek jumped. "What did she tell you?" he whispered.

"She told me about your panic attacks."

He rubbed his face. "I wish she hadn't."

"Well, I'm glad she did. I think it's important I know, don't you?"

"Yes, *of course* it is. What I mean is—I wish *I'd* been the one to tell you instead of her."

"Why *didn't* you tell me?"

He looked at me for a long moment, and then dragged his chair close to mine, perching his elbows on his knees.

"It wasn't my intention to hide it from you. I honestly didn't think there was anything to tell. I thought I was dealing better with all of the implications of our relationship than I actually was."

"Penny told me these panic attacks started after the situation with Nicola?"

"My tendency for anxiety goes way back. I've always been a bit obsessive—a perfectionist—and I've always felt extreme pressure to live up to my father's expectations. But the scandal with Nicola is what set off the actual panic attacks. Feeling like control is being taken away from you when you have a predisposition to anxiety…"

"So, did you have them a lot?" I wanted to know everything now. I knew Daniel's father was in the office next door, waiting for us to emerge, but he'd have to wait.

"I had my fair share. The first one scared the hell out of me. It happened out of the blue at a football match. A bunch of my friends were trying to cheer me up after my position at the university was suspended. Penny was there. It was crowded, and people were fighting and surging toward the field. I freaked out. I got these black spots in front of my eyes and a piercing pain in my shoulder, then my heart started pounding and I couldn't breathe. I thought I was having a heart attack. Penny and my friend Gavin took me to the hospital, but by the time we got there, I was feeling better. Tired, but better. It's the strangest sensation."

"So, that's what happened on Friday?"

"Exactly."

"Daniel, tell me about the prescriptions—the bottles you moved out of your vanity cupboard when I stayed over."

He smiled grimly. "You caught that, did you?"

"I didn't want to pry. I figured there was a good reason for you to move them. But now I'd like you to tell me about them."

He sat back in his chair and rubbed at his whiskers. "Okay. Well, brace yourself."

I nodded.

"Let's see, there's the anti-depression meds. I took them for a while last year, but they didn't agree with me. Terrible side effects.

Then there's the anti-anxiety meds. I wasn't a big fan of those either. Sleeping pills? Took those for months, too. I went through a spell where I couldn't fall asleep, and then when I did get to sleep, I'd suffer from nightmares."

"Are you still taking any of those prescriptions?" I asked, remembering the nightmare he'd had when I'd stayed over.

"No, I haven't taken anything for months. This was the first panic attack I've had in ages." He paused. "Actually, that's not true. I've had a couple of small ones over the last few weeks. Both times I managed to avert a full-blown attack."

"When?"

He closed his eyes and clamped his mouth shut. I thought he was going to refuse to tell me, but then he visibly braced himself and continued.

"After we met at the Gardiner that day? Once I'd dropped you off at residence, I was going to meet Jeremy, and I had to sit on a bench in the quad here at Vic and calm down. My heart was racing, and I had chest pain. After sitting for a few minutes, I was okay."

"What do you think brought it on?"

"I'm not sure. Perhaps deep down I knew the danger I'd put myself in, letting you know my feelings for you. I honestly can't account for it. I was ecstatic about the prospect of us having a relationship. The subconscious mind is a mysterious place."

He seemed completely bewildered. His explanation made total sense as far as I was concerned.

"And the other one?" I asked.

"The night I saw you and Matt at the Madison House. That one makes more sense. I wanted to beat him to a pulp. It was pure adrenaline. Thinking I'd lost you because of my stupid position had me gasping for breath by the time I got home. Luckily, that attack didn't progress either."

"How do you get them to stop?"

"There's not much you can do, really, except breathe and try to calm down. My parents know I need to be talked down. That's what my mom was trying to do on Friday."

"You didn't want my help," I said, my voice wavering slightly. Remembering how desolate I'd felt when he'd shut me out was bad enough, but now my heart was breaking for him.

"I didn't want you to see me like that. It's completely emasculating, falling apart like that. Not to mention being incapable of forming coherent thoughts. I wanted to give my dad a piece of my mind, but I was so focused on trying to calm down that I couldn't even speak."

"I thought you didn't want me there."

"I'm sorry. I figured I'd be home an hour later and we would talk and I'd explain everything before we had to go to class."

I thought back to how much I'd worried over the weekend. It was nothing compared to the way I felt now.

"What are you thinking?" he asked softly.

I sighed. "I'm thinking—I'm thinking you don't need instability in your life. You need things to be orderly and logical, not frigging chaotic and unpredictable. Correct me if I'm wrong, but our relationship is causing you a hell of a lot of anxiety."

He sat up stiffly, his eyes betraying his distress.

"I'm going to keep my promise to your father, Daniel. I'm going to back off. I'm not going to see you outside of the classroom until the semester is over."

"Aubrey, please—"

"Daniel, try to understand my position. I don't want to be responsible for causing you anxiety. I certainly don't want to be a source of conflict between you and your parents, not to mention the fact that I have a relationship with your father that's important to me. I'm supposed to be covering Gisele's three-week holiday in June. I can earn enough in one month to pay my parents back what I owe them."

His jaw clenched. I knew what he was thinking.

"It's not only the money," I said. "If you're going to be a part of my future, I need to stay on good terms with your parents. I made your father a promise. I don't want to go back on my word."

He shook his head, frowning. "Please don't speak about our future in hypothetical terms. I *am* going to be a part of your future. End of story."

"Okay. I'm sorry."

"You don't have to apologize, but I want to make myself clear. Assuming you want me to be a part of your life, I'm in, one hundred percent."

I smiled and nodded, my heart hammering its agreement.

"Now, tell me about this promise you made," he said.

"I told your dad I wouldn't do anything that could hurt you and your reputation, and if that meant backing off for a while and ceasing contact outside of class, then I was prepared to do it."

"I hate him for the position he's put you in. He's never experienced anything this frustrating. It's so easy to preach the moral high ground when you've got absolutely no concept of what someone is going through."

"He's trying to protect you and your family."

"He had no right to burden you with all this guilt. I'm not surprised, though. He's fucking masterful at it. He's been doing it to me for years."

"Penny alluded to that yesterday," I confessed. Penny had spoken of David as a good man, but one who was sometimes misdirected — especially in his dealings with Daniel, who'd always been so desperate to please his father.

"Poor Penny's had to listen to her fair share of me bitching about it over the years. He doesn't seem to realize I'm not the same kid who used to fall all over myself for his approval. It's like I was frozen in time while I was at Oxford or something. And you certainly don't need to answer to him."

I sighed. It wasn't that simple.

"I get it, though," he said. "You're in a difficult position."

"I'm torn right now."

"What can I do?"

"Help me meet your father's terms?"

"Which are?"

"I told him I wouldn't contact you. He expects us to limit our communication to classroom instructional time. He even said I should take office hours with Professor Brown instead of with you."

"That's just insulting. And there are going to be times in the next few weeks that we'll have to meet beyond the classroom simply by necessity, based on upcoming course assessments. I think you'd be drawing more attention to yourself by insisting on seeing Martin. He'd probably wonder what your problem was with me."

"I guess you're right."

"Good. I'm glad you agree." He looked at me thoughtfully. "Are you sure about this? I don't see the harm in you texting me or emailing.

No one would ever know we were in touch. I think it would make me more anxious not hearing from you."

"I don't know. That's what I told him."

"I can tell you right now that I can't promise to stop communicating with you. That's what got me through last week, you know? I don't think I could cope if I couldn't share my feelings with you. I can almost handle the idea of not spending time with you alone, but I don't like it. As far as I'm concerned, my position can't be put in jeopardy if you email me. No one would know unless you decided to report me."

"Daniel, don't be absurd." I scowled at him.

"I was joking," he said, smiling gently.

He grasped my hand on the table, rubbing his thumb across my knuckles. "What happened to our reservation at Taboo?" I asked.

"Money down the tubes. I wasn't able to cancel."

"I'm sorry."

He shrugged. "I don't care about that. I was looking forward to spending time with you. I couldn't wait to see you in that new dress."

"We'll have our chance soon. It's not the end of the world," I said softly. "In six weeks — thirty-eight days, to be exact — there won't be anything anyone can say or do to keep us apart."

"He wants us to wait to go public until after you've graduated, you know that, right?"

"Yes, but he also said at the very least until the course is over. There's no way I'm waiting until June to be alone with you, Daniel. As soon as that exam is over, I'll be all over you. Best prepare yourself."

"Hmm, in that case, what's to prepare? I can't wait." His eyes sparkled mischievously. I'd missed that.

"Six weeks might seem like a long time, but as long as I know you care about me, I can get through," I said.

He shook his head. "Aubrey, you have no idea."

He brought my hand to his lips and kissed it gently before pressing his cheek into my palm. I genuinely smiled for the first time in three days.

"Does that mean you forgive me for putting you through hell this weekend?"

"There's nothing to forgive. It wasn't your fault. And I suppose I understand why you didn't tell me about the anxiety attacks, but you can tell me anything. You won't scare me away."

He helped me to my feet. "Thank you. You may come to regret saying that. I can be a wordy bastard at times." He sighed. "I don't want to walk out that door. Things are going to be very different when we leave this room."

I nodded. "This was a wake-up call. What if it had been someone else who had found out?"

He closed his eyes. "Do you know how many times I heard that this weekend?"

"I'm sorry, but it's true."

"You don't need to apologize," he said, hugging me. "But someone does, and he will very shortly. If you don't mind, though, before we leave, I need something to think about for the next six weeks."

Before I could even think about protesting, he pressed his lips to mine with a passion that overtook us both.

Promise? What promise?

Daniel

This Sad Interim

Let this sad interim like the ocean be
Which parts the shore, where two contracted new
Come daily to the banks, that, when they see
Return of love, more blest may be the view…
(*Sonnet 56*)

God, it was good to be back in civilization. My dad's justification that it would be good for me to "get away from it all" for a couple of days after my attack had been laughable. I'm sure what he'd actually meant was, "I need to get you away from Aubrey for a few days." And it had been pure hell.

Now I was kissing her, having told her everything and fully expecting to be cast aside as not merely unavailable, but emotionally unstable. But had she balked? Not at all. She'd been compassionate and sensitive—stubborn as fuck, but wonderful as ever. Thank God. I don't know what I would have done if she'd pushed me away.

Being wrenched away from her on Friday morning had been particularly cruel, especially given the weekend plans we'd had. The thought of her turning me away after the progress we'd made was beyond contemplation.

I could have stayed in that office kissing her all day, feeling her velvet-soft tongue against mine, her hands in my hair, her breath coming in small gasps as she made those sweet whimpering sounds in her throat. From the beginning, I'd been so afraid to kiss her, knowing I'd be tortured by need as soon as my tongue touched hers. I'd been right to worry. Her kisses swept me away, and I imagined my lips roaming her skin, her body responding…

Jesus, this wasn't the time. I had to face reality.

I gave her one last kiss, trying to freeze it in my memory, then pulled away to look at her. She sighed and gently rested her hands on my chest, a sincerity in her expression that took my breath away.

"I guess it's time to see what's in store for us," she said.

"This should be interesting. We talked a hell of a lot this weekend. I'm not sure how successful I was at bringing him around to my way of thinking, though." I stroked her cheek. "*I would my father look'd but with my eyes.*"

"Daniel Grant, stop laying it on so thick."

"Sorry."

"No you're not. You know it makes me weak in the knees when you haul out the Shakespeare."

"Well, given the weak knees, I suppose I'm not the slightest bit sorry," I admitted. I unlocked the door. "Ready?"

She closed her eyes and exhaled shakily. "Okay."

I couldn't blame her for being nervous. I was dreading this conversation as well, but more than that, I was dreading being apart from her, especially now that I knew what I'd be missing.

"Whatever happens in the next six weeks, don't ever question my feelings for you, okay?" she said.

"I'll do my best. And that goes double for you," I said. "Let's get this over with."

We went to my father's office. He was gazing out the window over Queen's Park, his arms crossed in front of his chest. It was odd seeing him standing there wearing clothes he'd generally wear on the golf course. He seemed less imposing. I left the door open a crack, and he turned around, gesturing to the round table in the corner.

"Why don't we sit there?" he suggested.

Wonder of wonders, a flash of humanity. Sitting at the table instead of being lectured at from across his desk would be far less confrontational. I slid a chair out for Aubrey, and we all sat. I clasped my hands in front of me and noticed Aubrey had done the same. She looked at my hands, also taking in our simultaneous gesture. My father sighed.

"Look at the two of you."

"What?" I said, already on the defensive.

"How on earth do you manage to hide your feelings when you're in the classroom?"

Aubrey's cheeks turned pink.

"It's not easy," I said, "but I think we're coping admirably."

"Goodness, I hope so. I'm even more worried than ever about the two of you being seen together in public." He grimaced.

Were we really that transparent? Probably.

"Look, I have no desire to drag this on," he said. "We've talked ourselves out over the last two days, Daniel, but I know you're not happy with the way your mother and I handled things, and I don't want to let any bad feelings fester. You know we only have your best interests at heart."

"No, cutting me off from Aubrey and making it impossible for me to contact her to put her mind at rest was not in my best interest *at all*. Or hers."

His eyes shifted to Aubrey. "Were you really that concerned? I tried to reassure you that Daniel would be fine."

She met his eyes. "Your assurances were comforting to a point, but it's very difficult watching someone you care about suffering. I didn't know what was wrong with him. So, yes, I was concerned. In fact, I spent the better part of the weekend worrying, sir."

My father looked at her over his bridged hands. "I'm sorry. You know how much I prize discretion. I gathered he hadn't told you about his anxiety. It was Daniel's prerogative whether to share that with you. As for taking him up to the cottage, his mother and I wanted to keep an eye on him. We thought it would be wise to eliminate emotional stimuli that might set him off. It's been difficult for Gwen since Daniel moved out. She worries about how he's coping with stress. Daniel had a terrible episode of recurring anxiety in England last year, and we feared something similar might occur this time. Happily, that wasn't the case."

I grimaced at the memory of the few days of repeated panic attacks, one of the most frightening experiences of my life. Thank God my parents had been there to help me through that.

My father continued to plead his case, mostly to Aubrey. "What I've obviously drastically underestimated is the extent of the feelings you have for each other. Perhaps I was naïvely hoping what you felt was a casual attachment. I thought a few days apart would give you a chance to regain perspective. Clearly, I was wrong. I'm sorry to have worried you."

He said these last words looking down at our hands, which we'd both unclasped. I wanted nothing more than to hold one of hers at that moment.

"Do you accept my apology, Aubrey?" he said.

She gazed at him steadily. "I do. And I'm sorry for going against your wishes. You made it clear in February that you didn't want me to complicate Daniel's life, and I — "

"Don't," I intervened. "Don't apologize for your feelings."

"I appreciate that nonetheless, Aubrey," my father said. "Now I'm going to tell you something against my better judgment. I wasn't going to share this until I was more certain of the outcome, Daniel, but you obviously think I'm being harsh, worrying about the family name and your standing here at the school without due cause. The situation we dealt with last year is more than enough to warrant my uneasiness, but the truth is, I also have a selfish motivation for my concern. You see, the University of Toronto's vice president and provost is retiring in June. I've applied for the position."

My head snapped up as if I'd been slapped. "What? You're in contention for a U of T administrative position?"

He nodded. "There's a strong possibility I'll be named. I'd be realizing everything I've worked so hard for. I never dreamed the opportunity for advancement would present itself now. I thought maybe in a few years, but then I heard of this impending opening, and I thought I'd take a chance."

Holy shit! My father, vice provost of one of the most prestigious universities in Canada?

His eyes pleaded with me to understand why now, of all times, his name needed to remain unsullied, untainted.

"I don't understand," Aubrey said, looking at my father. "What does the provost do?"

I answered in his stead. "They oversee all of the portfolios of the university including the academic integrity and ethical standards of both students and faculty."

"Oh." Just one syllable, but the look on Aubrey's face revealed that she understood the implications of my explanation.

"Why didn't you tell me?" I asked, turning back to my father.

"If you were in my place, why might you have kept it a secret?"

"In case you weren't successful? You wouldn't want anyone to know you'd failed."

He smiled gently. "You see, son? We're far more alike than you'd care to admit. My pride was a primary reason behind my secrecy, but it's not the only one. Your mother tried to convince me to tell you this weekend, but I was reluctant to do that. I didn't want my aspirations to put more pressure on you. However, the more I thought about it, the more I feared you might believe I was being asinine just for the sake of it." He slid his hand self-consciously back and forth on the table. "I don't want to be seen as the enemy. You're my son, Daniel. I love you, and I want what's best for you. I want you to be successful beyond your wildest dreams. And I know that you and Aubrey will be wonderful together." He looked back and forth between us pointedly. "When the time is right."

And with those words, I grasped Aubrey's hand, squeezing it gently.

He noticed the gesture and sighed, recognizing the futility of arguing. "Okay, son, you should probably head home and get yourself sorted out. You don't have much time before you have to be in class. Aubrey and I have a few more things to discuss."

I didn't want to leave Aubrey alone to deal with him, but she was a strong woman who could fend for herself, and my father did seem to be in a more conciliatory frame of mind this morning. I stood and touched her shoulder.

"See you later? In class, of course," I added, more for my father's benefit than hers.

"Of course." She tried to remain composed. I knew how she felt.

Leaving this office would be like stepping off a ledge into a dark abyss.

I was distracted as I sat and marked at my desk that evening. I was still in shock about my father's potential promotion to vice president and provost. No wonder he was going off the deep end about my relationship with Aubrey. As if my Oxford debacle wasn't enough! Of course I was pleased for him; he was my father and I loved him, extreme reactions notwithstanding.

I tried to focus on the papers in front of me. I wasn't sure how much longer I could mark. Honestly — some people's fucking handwriting. Vince Costa's test looked like it had been scribed for him by a chimp hanging upside down from a tree. I tossed it aside. I'd look at it another time when my eyes were fresher.

I was purposely avoiding Aubrey's test, but I knew I'd have to grade it eventually. I was also avoiding checking my email and voice mail. I dreaded hearing her panicked voice and reading her desperate words. No, first I would take care of the test, and then I would deal with the messages.

I flipped through the pile, smirking as I remembered the smile on Martin's face as he'd dropped the tests in front of me at the end of today's lecture, wiping his hands as if to say "good riddance." The class had laughed at my expense, but it was all in good fun. Aubrey had smiled wistfully at me before leaving with Julie, who was nattering away excitedly. I gathered they'd been setting off to have coffee together. This was good; she needed the opportunity to vent to a friend. Someone *other* than Matt.

Finally, I reached Aubrey's test booklet. Her neat printing seemed relaxed, unhurried. Considering the frame of mind she must have been in while writing, her ideas were remarkably clear, her analyses precise and articulate.

That's my girl.

She had a firm handle on what had been discussed in lectures and seminars but always took her discussion to another level, offering further insights, more elaborate interpretations. Fuck, she was a good writer! Her prose was descriptive but not flowery, her arguments cogent but not redundant. She would make an amazing journalist or editor. I was hard-pressed to find a single grammatical error.

There were words inserted here and there with neat little arrows, and I could almost hear her frustrated, "*Gah!*" as she discovered she'd left out a word. I read her answers again, this time trying to assign marks. I looked at it numerous times but couldn't find a damn thing to penalize her for. But I couldn't give her a perfect score. How would that look?

I started splitting hairs over minor nuances, managing to find a couple of instances in which her logic could be found faulty if one considered an alternate perspective. Even so, I had to assign her twenty-eight out of thirty. Ninety-three percent. Would Martin object? We'd briefly discussed bell curving earlier in the semester, but I wasn't sure how he felt about students receiving such high marks.

Not sure what else I could do, I wrote her mark at the top of the page, along with the comment, *Clearly and concisely argued. A pleasure to read, Miss Price!* I smiled as I imagined her reading it, biting her lip and blushing as she thought about how proud I was of her.

I drained my coffee cup and retrieved my cell phone from my bag as I waited for my laptop to fire up. Time to check the weekend messages. I had texts from Brad, Jeremy, and Penny, in addition to Aubrey's, but hers were the only ones that interested me right now. I read her frantic text sent on Friday morning.

Heartbreaking. That's the only word to describe it. She'd sounded terrified and devastated, thinking I'd cast her off. Of course I hadn't answered, and then I hadn't been in class. She must have been a nervous wreck. I checked my voice mail, and there was Aubrey's voice.

"Hi, Daniel, it's me. I can't even — God, how can I explain how worried I am? It's Saturday morning, and no one else is home. You haven't answered my text. I don't know what's going on with you, but you're probably avoiding me because of everything your father said. I can't blame you, and I know I shouldn't ask this of you, but can you please let me know you're okay? I'm sorry, but please? I'm so worried. Okay. Bye."

The pain in her voice broke my heart. She was trying so hard to do the right thing, to give me the benefit of the doubt, while being beside herself with worry.

The next message was from Matt, pleading with me to call Aubrey. I had to give the guy credit. He was nothing if not loyal. Penny had also left a message on Saturday night, telling me she was going to a movie and that I should call her in the morning before *Coronation Street* to let her know what time Aubrey and I would be over to paint, presuming all of our limbs were intact. There was another from Penny — a rant this time:

"Where are you, you soddin' wanker? It's Sunday morning. You said you'd be back to help us paint. While you're shagging in a snow bank, I'm staring at these bloody hideous walls. Call me! But Corrie will be on in five minutes so wait till noon, all right? Bye, love."

Leave it to Penny to forego the sentimentality. I tossed my phone on the desk and opened my email. Among several, most of them school-related, was an email from Aubrey.

From: Aubrey Price
To: Jung Willman
Date: Sun, Mar 22, 8:13:24 AM
Subject: Very Worried

Either you've decided your father was right and you're not going to contact me, or you're so unwell that you're incapable of it. I don't know which of the two alternatives worries me more. All I need is two words. "I'm fine" would suffice.

Aubrey

How could she think I'd ignore her messages and let her worry all weekend on purpose? The thought made my heart drop. And she'd sounded so cold. I clicked on "reply" and composed a quick answer.

From: Jung Willman
To: Aubrey Price
Date: Mon, Mar 23, 10:07:29 PM
Subject: Re: Very Worried

Hi, sweetheart,

I've retrieved all of your messages, and I feel horrible that you'd think I'd purposely put you through something like this. Don't ever doubt my feelings for you again, okay?

I've been trying to avoid contacting you, but I've been thinking about you all day. I hope my father didn't give you a hard time this morning. You seemed relaxed in class. You and Julie went out for a coffee afterward, yes? I should call Jer to see how he enjoyed the weekend. Actually, I need to call everyone…but the only person I really want to talk to is you.

I'm having trouble focusing. I see you everywhere in my apartment. I can't even brush my teeth without picturing you sitting on the vanity watching me shave. Have you any idea the self-control I had to muster that morning, especially when you spread your legs, flashing those lacy black panties at me? You're so tantalizing.

I'll leave you for tonight. I feel strangely compelled to take a shower before turning in!

I hope to hear from you, but I'll understand if you can't write back. I miss you. Good night & sleep tight.

-D

I re-read the email before sending it. *I'll understand if you can't write back.* Understand? Of course I'd understand. But I sure as hell wouldn't be happy about it.

Many Days

I must hear from thee every day in the hour,
For in a minute there are many days.
(*Romeo and Juliet*, Act III, Scene 5)

By early afternoon on Tuesday, I hadn't heard anything from Aubrey, and I reconciled myself to the fact that she wouldn't be responding to my email. There was little I could do but take my cues from her and be respectful of her wishes. Of course, that didn't stop me from leaping for my phone every time it vibrated.

After several of these Pavlovian episodes, none of which resulted in a message from Aubrey, my response time began to lag. I returned to my marking, taking up residence at the dining room table. I was about to start in on Neil Hammond's test when my phone buzzed. I reached for it calmly, telling myself not to get my hopes up, when there it was—an email from someone called "Miss_V." I opened it hurriedly.

From: Miss_V
To: Jung Willman
Date: Tues, Mar 24, 3:32:44 PM
Subject: Two can play at that game…

Hey, sailor,

I'm not sure if you'll be surprised to hear from me. I was thinking about your email during my French lecture, and I decided to come home and open this new account. Using it feels safer for some reason. Is it naïve of me to think that? I can't bring myself to cut off all communication. I'm afraid that if we don't have some sort of contact, I won't be able to keep my promise. I guess I'm bending the rules on the smaller stuff so I won't screw up on the big stuff. I don't know if that means I'm a bad person, but, if so, I suppose I'll have to accept that judgment.

You don't need to worry—your father was fine after you left yesterday. He didn't say, "Go shout from the rooftops that you want to be together," but he wasn't nasty to me. We actually talked more about his new position (he's excited as hell, just so you know) and what would happen if he got the job, because it'll mean I'll end up working for someone else. I'm not too happy about that, but I need the money to repay my parents.

I suppose I should tell you why I owe them so much money. I know I told you a while ago that I was planning a trip overseas in the summer, but I don't expect you to remember that. My mom badgered my dad for some cash, and she went ahead and booked my flight to Europe for the end of July. She said she was afraid that if she left it to me, I'd decide not to do it at all. She knows me so well. So, now I owe them both money. I have some saved, but not nearly enough.

I know you're rolling your eyes, money bags.

Yes, I went for coffee with Jul. Got her up to speed and heard all about her weekend with J. I was insanely jealous and have been thinking non-stop about the time we spent together last week. If I close my eyes and really concentrate, I can taste your lips. You are the most fucktacular kisser (yes, I made that word up—zip it, Professor!). Nothing beats the feeling of your tongue teasing mine—at least nothing yet—and I look forward to all of the other things that'll feel even better.

Okay, I'm going to stop rambling and head to the library to work on my paper. Matt's girlfriend is coming over—the lovebirds need some privacy, and if I keep on fantasizing about you, I may need some privacy of my own! Self-employment truly does suck big time.

I miss you like crazy. Please write back if you get a chance. Reading over Romeo and Juliet again last night, I saw so many lines in a totally different light. For example, Juliet's words, "I must hear from thee every day in the hour, For in a minute there are many days," have a completely different meaning to me now. Was Shakespeare not the most brilliant man?

Can't wait to see you tomorrow, even if it is from fifteen feet away.

Definitely your poppet
xo

That was all it took to go from dejected to overjoyed just like that. I re-read it, smiling stupidly and so relieved. She'd sounded good — playful and upbeat. And this summer trip to Europe — what was that all about? It sounded like it might coincide very nicely with Brad and Penny's wedding. Did I dare hope?

I should have turned my attention back to Neil Hammond's test, but Neil was long forgotten. Instead, I clicked "reply."

After one of the longest weeks of my life, Friday finally arrived with the promise of an extra hour in Aubrey's company. Although she'd been true to her word, writing to me every day and insisting on a reply from me, I still sensed that she'd been trying to restrain herself. I'd done nothing of the sort, sending three emails for every one that I received from her. My behavior was bordering on pathetic, but I missed her so much and couldn't help myself.

Today's tutorial would be very different from the one we'd had two weeks ago. I was certain I'd never be able to read *Antony and Cleopatra* or *Othello* again without feeling physically ill.

I scanned the group assembled around the three tables, quickly checking off attendance in my notebook. Aubrey and Julie were sitting at the table opposite mine. Aubrey was tapping her feet. Was she anxious? Excited? I smiled and got the session underway.

"Sorry about last week, though I suppose you were happy to have some down time after your test. I gather you all picked up a copy of the sonnet assignment from Professor Brown?"

"Uh, yeah, can I grab another one? I lost mine."

Vince Costa. Not surprising. His test had been a meandering stream of consciousness. The ideas weren't bad, but organization was clearly not his strong suit.

I pulled an extra from my bag and handed it to Trina Collins to pass down to him. I looked up and down the tables. "Any questions about that assignment before we talk about *Romeo and Juliet?*"

Vince quickly scanned the paper. "Um, why is the mark split into two parts?" *Just read the damn sheet properly, you stooge.*

"I'll be assessing the first part. It'll be a conference," I clarified. "You'll read the sonnet out loud and go through your analysis, I'll ask you a few questions—help you to tighten up your examination of the poem—then you'll be on your own to write your analysis for Professor Brown. Make sense?"

"Okay, yeah. Cool, thanks."

"Don't forget the *Much Ado* live performance is next week, so if you didn't do the *Hamlet* piece, you'll have to select one of those days for viewing. I have a quick meeting with Professor Brown after tutorial to go over the tests from last week, but I imagine you'll get them back on Monday. So, let's take a look at *Romeo and Juliet.* Here's what I'd like you to do today: jot down the one thing about the play that frustrates you the most."

"Do we have to narrow it down to one thing?" Trina asked.

I laughed. "As difficult as that might be, yes."

I watched as everyone thought briefly and started writing. After a few minutes, everyone seemed to have something down.

"All right," I said. "Who'd like to start?"

Julie put up her hand. "For me, it's the behavior of the adults in the play. Everything they do is so ridiculous."

"Anything specific?" I prodded.

"A lot of things. Juliet's father threatening to kick her out if she doesn't marry the guy he's picked? That's insane. And the friar with the potion? What a nut. I can almost see the logic in her leaving temporarily to avoid marrying Paris, but pretending to be dead? That's loco."

"So, what's the reasoning behind those characterizations and decisions?" I asked, throwing the question out to the table.

"To isolate Romeo and Juliet and make their situation really desperate?" Trina said. "Right from the first page, the feud sets up the catastrophe. Their parents probably don't even know what they're fighting about anymore. I think Julie's right. The adults fail them miserably."

"Excellent points, both of you. I agree. Romeo and Juliet are certainly victims of the constraints of society and of their parents' expectations."

Why do all roads lead back there?

"What else drives you crazy?"

Aubrey leaned forward slightly. "The coincidences. It's like everything is conspiring against them. It's so frustrating to watch."

I sat back as a lively conversation broke out, everyone talking over each other.

"Oh, I know! Like he hears she's dead from someone who's seen the funeral procession…"

"Right! And he just *happens* to know of a guy who sells poison right when he's all suicidal…"

"And the friar guy, the other friar? How he can't send the letter because of the plague…"

"The worst is when Romeo takes the poison seconds before she wakes up. Did you see the Leonardo DiCaprio version, where she wakes up and looks at him and he's not dead yet, but he knows he's about to die any second? Man, that's brutal."

"Oh, I know, right? I love that movie." Cara sighed.

Why was I not surprised that Cara's understanding of *Romeo and Juliet* was tied to a film adaptation of the play? I held up my hands to regain control of the group. "Okay, okay! So, based on what I just heard, it's fair to say the coincidences ruffle a lot of feathers, yes? How do we justify Shakespeare's use of coincidence in the play?"

Aubrey looked around the table. "He's demonstrating the power of destiny. Nothing can go right for them because their stars aren't aligned. They're victims of a force more powerful than their love."

"Absolutely, Miss Price," I said. "The smallest events, the most seemingly insignificant things" — *a lost glove, for instance* — "can thwart our hopes. Destroy everything."

"It makes me wonder what they would have been like together if things had worked out," Trina said. "Once they got to know each other, they might not have even liked one another."

Lindsay frowned. "How long did they know each other before they got married?"

"Not even twenty-four hours," I told her.

"Really? That *is* kind of crazy," Lindsay said.

"Like anyone would fall in love that fast. It's the whole clichéd love-at-first-sight bit, right?" Vince said.

"So, you don't believe in love at first sight?" I asked him.

"What, you *do?*" Shawn piped up.

I tapped my pen for a second. On the spot again. I could tell him my opinion on the matter was irrelevant, but I decided to pursue the question.

"I suppose that depends on a number of factors, not the least of which is knowing yourself well enough to understand what type of person you're looking for," I said. "If you know which qualities you admire most in someone, you're more likely to recognize that person when you meet her…or him. I prefer to call it *recognition* at first sight."

I avoided looking at Aubrey, but I had to meet her eyes as she posed another question.

"In your opinion, what *are* the other factors contributing to this recognition at first sight, Daniel?" she asked casually.

All eyes were on me. "Frame of mind, I suppose. There are times when you simply couldn't fall in love if you tried because you're not in the right place in your life. The conditions surrounding the actual meeting might also hold some sway. Certain circumstances seem to set the scene for emotional vulnerability, and you get swept away in the moment."

"That's so true," Trina said. She looked almost wistful.

Again, I tried to bring the conversation back around to the play. "And that's the case for Romeo, wouldn't you say? He's fond of the notion of being in love, and once he sees Juliet at the ball and decides she's the one for him, he's doomed. That's the root of the tragedy. The only thing keeping them apart is the fact that they're from feuding families. The so-called 'rules' of their social situation, who they are—that's all that ultimately stands in the way of their potential for happiness."

Trina shook her head. "That sucks."

"It certainly does," I said.

Aubrey was aimlessly twirling a lock of hair while staring down at her notebook, lost in thought. *Thinking about us? Our predicament?* Fortunately, ours was neither fatal nor permanent. Somehow that didn't make the waiting any more enjoyable.

I steered the tutorial to safer territory, and then, all too soon, it was time to go. A feeling of desolation washed over me. Little black words on a screen—that's all we'd have for two days. I watched as everyone rushed for the door, thrilled to start their weekend, while I lingered, dreading mine. Aubrey and Julie gathered up their belongings.

"Have a good weekend, Daniel," Julie said as they walked toward the door.

"You too."

"Bye," Aubrey said, with a wave and a lovely smile.

I raised my hand and tried to smile back but thought, *Don't go. My car is right outside. Let's go somewhere, anywhere.* Of course, this couldn't happen. I had somewhere else I needed to be, and Aubrey was determined to keep her promise to my father.

I packed up my bag and left, checking my phone for messages as I walked. Not more than thirty seconds later, my phone vibrated—a text from Aubrey.

> **I'll miss you this weekend, but only 34 days left.**
> **That's all. We can do this.**
> **Have a good meeting and email me later, okay? -A**

I paused on the sidewalk to type out a quick reply.

> **Thanks, I needed that.**
> **I hated watching you walk away--except for the view.**
> **I'm going to miss you like crazy,**
> **and I'll be thinking of you constantly. -D**

I made my way to Martin's office. He was sitting at his desk, his door open wide.

"Daniel, come in and have a seat," he said. "Good tutorial?"

"Yes, it was. It's a nice class. There are some really fabulous students. Of course, there are a few needy ones thrown in the mix, too."

"That's usually the way. And you're good with the plan for the sonnet assignment?"

"I think so."

"Good. We'll talk more about that later. For now, I'd like to discuss these tests. I had a look through the pile while you were conducting your tutorial, and I must say, I'm a little perplexed."

"How so?"

Jesus, I'd frigging agonized over those tests. Where could he possibly find fault with them?

He tossed one of the booklets on the desk in front of me and jabbed his finger at the mark at the top, his forehead creased with concern. "How do you explain that?"

I leaned over to take a closer look. Fuck. It was Aubrey's test.

Aubrey

CHAPTER 14

Grace and Faults

Both grace and faults are loved of more and less;
Thou makest faults graces that to thee resort.
As on the finger of a throned queen
The basest jewel will be well esteem'd,
So are those errors that in thee are seen…
(*Sonnet 96*)

"Come on, Aubrey." Julie rested her chin on my shoulder as I typed. "It's time to take a break."

She'd been circling my room for fifteen minutes, waiting for me to finish a concluding paragraph for an essay. My thoughts weren't gelling, and her pacing wasn't helping.

"I told you I need to finish my term paper before all this other shit starts to pile up."

"What other shit? The sonnet analysis? You could write that in your sleep. Take a break."

I spun around in my chair, peering up at her. "Don't forget, we have to go see *Much Ado* this week and write a paper on that. Plus, I have four other lit courses to deal with. I'm starting to freak."

She tugged at my hand. "Just an hour of girl talk. Come *on*."

"You're killing me, bun-head." I groaned, letting her drag me to the bed where we both flopped onto our backs, staring up at the ceiling.

"You need to tell me about that LV umbrella hanging on your doorknob. Tell me it's not real."

"Um, actually, it is," I admitted.

"Let me guess—"

"Yes, Julie, it's from Daniel."

"Christ on a cracker! Gloves *and* an umbrella? He is *so* jonesing for a blow job."

"Are you suggesting that I'm allowing him to buy sexual favors from me? Because that's absurd."

"Oh really?" she said archly, rolling onto her side and narrowing her eyes at me.

"Yes, really." I paused for a moment for dramatic effect. "I would *totally* blow him for free."

Her laugh echoed around my room. She was still snickering as she reached over the side of the bed, grabbing her knapsack.

"While we're on the subject of gifts from Daniel—here." She handed me a Chapters bag. I peeked inside. It was Sarah Waters' latest book in hard cover. "Jeremy gave it to me last night," she said. "It's from Daniel. He knows you love her and that you wouldn't buy it for yourself."

I slid my hand across the smooth dust jacket. "I told him I couldn't afford it."

"Is money really that tight?"

"I owe my parents nearly a thousand dollars for my flight."

"Was your mom shopping around? My flight to Germany wasn't that expensive."

"Your dance studio booked over a year ago."

"This is true."

"You getting psyched about your trip?" I asked her, knowing she was probably stoked to go to Germany with the girls from the studio.

"Excited out of my gourd. The showcase will be stressful, but, once it's done, the rest of the time will be mine. I wonder if we can try to meet up somewhere."

"What, like somewhere in the middle, you mean?"

"Yeah, you know, in France or something."

"I'd love to go to France." I sighed, blinking up at the ceiling as I hugged the book to my chest.

"You miss him a lot, eh?"

"This sucks. His emails are wonderful, but I'd rather hear him say all that stuff to me in person."

"You should have taken my advice, Aubrey. Now that you've kissed him, you know exactly what you're missing."

"You're probably right. But honestly, if you'd been there that night at the Palais Royale, dancing and drinking champagne after he'd been so sweet and apologetic, you wouldn't have cock-blocked him either. It felt right, you know?"

"Don't get me wrong, I understand. I just think it's going to make the rest of the semester so much more difficult."

I cringed. I already missed him so much. How could things possibly get worse?

Later, I took a break from my pile of homework to email Daniel. I'd made a pact not to send him a constant flurry of messages, but I couldn't wait any longer.

From: Miss_V
To: Jung Willman
Date: Sun, Mar 29, 9:34:16 PM
Subject: Tipping the Velvet anyone?

Hiya handsome,

Thanks so much for the book. Julie came to visit today and dropped it off. When it first came out, I stood in the store with it in my hands, but I couldn't bring myself to drop 35 bucks. Did you know Waters has a book called Tipping the Velvet? That day in the library at Hart House when you told me your desire for me tasted like the sweetest velvet, were you plagiarizing by any chance?

Speaking of which, I'm almost ready to upload my term paper to the plagiarism-detection site. Will you be reading my paper at some point? I hope you don't think I'm a dolt. LOL.

Okay, I really have to get back to work, but I wanted to thank you for the book and tell you that I miss you. We're getting there, sailor. Very soon. You should probably start preparing yourself now. In 32 days, I'll be all over you like a bad rash!

Your poppet

I couldn't help laughing after I'd clicked "send." A bad rash? That didn't sound terribly appealing. What a doofus. I turned up the alert on my phone and then spent some time planning my wardrobe for the next day and putting away my laundry. True to form, Daniel's reply arrived with a *chirp* within twenty minutes.

From: Jung Willman
To: Miss_V
Date: Sun, Mar 29, 9:53:48 PM
Subject: Tipping the Velvet...

Hello, Miss V.

I'm so happy to hear from you! I hope you're not working too hard. I have heard of Tipping the Velvet. I love it. (The book's okay too...) But seriously, you should read it. If the idea of an erotic love story between two women doesn't turn you off, I think you'll quite enjoy it.

And you're right—when I said I wanted you so badly I could taste it, perhaps my use of the word "velvet" was borrowed from that book, and now that I've tasted your fingers, your neck, your lips, your tongue—let's just say I'm waiting with bated fucking breath to confirm that every inch of your beautiful body tastes of sweet velvet. And rest assured, I'll do much more than "play the tip." I suppose I'd best leave it at that before I get carried away. Goodnight, crazy legs, and sleep tight. Words don't come close to explaining the way I feel when I'm not able to see you.

-D

P.S. Will I need some topical cream to deal with this rash? Lubricant perhaps? See you soon.

I laughed, loving the way he would cheekily skirt around issues and then be so sweet and adorable. I could almost hear his voice murmuring in my ear as he'd done the night we kissed after leaving the Palais Royale.

I was right. You do taste like sweet velvet — the champagne chaser is definitely a bonus.

I snapped my laptop closed, quickly crossed off Sunday March 29th on my calendar, and crawled into bed. Closing my eyes, I imagined Daniel licking his way from my neck to my breasts, continuing down my body, his fingertips slipping purposefully between my thighs…

It's an unfortunate reality, but true. Sometimes the only way to deal with life-threatening sexual tension was to take matters into your own hands.

"Have you noticed that Daniel really likes to use his hands — when he talks, I mean?" Julie whispered to me in class the next day, a naughty expression on her face. We'd sat through our Monday lecture, and now Daniel was walking us through the sign-up procedure for the performance of *Much Ado About Nothing* and the sonnet conferences coming up the following week.

I kicked her foot, and she smothered a snort. She was echoing my own dirty thoughts, though. Daniel had one hand on his hip, but was gesturing animatedly with the other as he spoke. My face grew warm as I remembered how I'd fantasized about him the night before. I couldn't wait until *his* fingers brought me pleasure instead of my own. I continued watching him intently while he answered questions.

From somewhere behind me, I heard Lindsay's insipid voice. "Daniel, do you need to know what sonnet we're doing ahead of time, so you can, like, read it before our conference?"

"You can tell me if you'd like, but I'm fairly comfortable with the sonnets. I'm sure I'll be able to keep up. Feel free to surprise me if you'd prefer." He smiled indulgently.

I had to admit, he had his moments of cockiness. I may have been falling head over heels in love with Daniel, but I wasn't completely blind to his faults. This was a good thing.

"So, these are your tests. I don't have time to chat about them now, but you're welcome to make an appointment if you have any questions," Daniel said, fanning the booklets out on the front table.

Everyone took turns rooting through the pile. Some people dashed out the door without looking at their papers while others stood and leafed carefully through their test booklets. Julie glanced at hers, gave me a hug, and rushed off to a rehearsal.

I stared at my test, trying to decipher the writing scribbled across the top. There were two marks, one of them crossed out. Either my eyes were deceiving me, or it looked as though Daniel had given me a perfect grade. Holy shit! What the hell was he doing? Talk about losing his objectivity!

I waited for everyone else to filter out of the room, and then I stood in the empty aisle, watching Daniel collect his things. He looked up at me expectantly.

"Yes, Miss Price? Something you wanted to ask?"

I looked over my shoulder to make sure we were alone before approaching the desk.

"Daniel, what's this all about?" I held up my test. "What were you thinking?"

"Miss Price, I don't have time to talk about it right now," he said, all business. "I need to get to tutorial. Perhaps we could meet afterward to discuss it." He had a smug smile on his face.

"Very clever," I said softly.

"Why don't we meet at the Hart House library, say at ten past two?" he suggested, maintaining his business-like tone.

Did I dare venture back in there with him?

"Are you sure that's a good idea?" I whispered.

"It's a fantastic idea. See you at ten after two, Miss Price." He hauled his laptop bag up onto his shoulder and strode briskly past me, stopping at the door to turn and wink before continuing out into the hall.

I jammed the test into my bag and made my way over to Hart House. Daniel must have suspected I'd react this way. He'd been waiting for me to query my mark so he could suggest a meeting to discuss it, a meeting which wouldn't make me feel as if I were breaking my promise to his father.

While Daniel was in his tutorial, I grabbed a bite and read over some sonnets. At two o'clock, I bought us each a coffee and went to the library. With the exception of a girl working at a table by the window and a guy snoring on a couch by the fireplace, the room was empty.

I opted to sit in a small niche which allowed students to slightly sequester themselves from other patrons. It was a lovely little nook with four narrow stained glass windows lining the west wall.

When I was settled into a chair at a corner of the table, almost completely hidden from view, I unpacked my test and my anthology.

A few moments later, the door creaked. I peered around the wood panel wall, watching as Daniel scanned the library. He put one hand on his hip and ran his other hand through his hair.

"Pssst."

He spun around and rolled his eyes, his hand over his heart.

"I thought you'd changed your mind," he whispered, pulling a chair across the carpet to sit beside me.

"I considered it," I said quietly, handing him his coffee.

He took a gulp and sighed. "God, that's good. Thank you. So, did you really consider standing me up?" His eyes danced, and his hand rested near mine on the table.

"Briefly."

"I'm glad you didn't. I'd forgotten about this little area. It's surprisingly private, don't you think?" He traced a line along the outside of my wrist with his index finger.

I closed my eyes. "Daniel, please don't."

"Oh, come on, Aubrey. No one can see."

"Look, can you just put your TA hat on for a sec?"

"Well, I never thought I'd hear you say those words." He clasped his hands in front of him and sat upright. "Okay, Miss Price. Fire away."

I slid my test across the table. "I can't believe you gave me a perfect score. Isn't that dangerous?"

"I didn't."

I peered at the page. "That clearly says thirty out of thirty."

"You're right. It does. It's Professor Brown's writing."

"I thought *you* marked these tests."

"I did. Then he looked them over. He was displeased with my assessment of yours."

I squinted at the crossed out mark. "So, you gave me twenty-eight?"

He nodded. "I was afraid to give you full credit. I read it a few times. I guess I nitpicked a little."

"Wait, you *looked* for things to penalize me for? Jesus, Daniel! What the fuck?"

The muscle in his jaw jumped. "Let me get this straight," he said. "A minute ago you were upset because you thought I'd given you perfect, and now you're pissed because I took two marks off? That smacks of 'damned if I do and damned if I don't,' wouldn't you say?"

He sat back in his chair, resting his hands on his thighs and shaking his head.

"I'm sorry, it's just that I thought you'd have a hard time finding fault with my work, but now it sounds like you can't bring yourself to give me perfect, even if I deserve it. That's not fair."

"Give me a fucking break," he said in a heated whisper. "Don't forget, this was my first time marking one of your assignments. All I could hear was my father's voice chirping at me about *objectivity*. I'd appreciate it if you'd try to see it from my perspective."

I rubbed my temples in frustration. Of course this was hard for him.

"You're right. I'm being unreasonable." I looked at the pained expression on his face. "I overreacted. Forgive me?"

He turned in his chair so that he was facing me, his hand seeking mine under the table. "Of course I forgive you. This is all so fucked up." He laced our fingers together. I looked anxiously at the entrance to the room. "Aubrey, no one can see us. Let me hold your hand for a few minutes, please? We just had an argument. I need a make-up squeeze."

I couldn't help smiling. "A make-up squeeze?"

"Yes, right now, please."

I clasped his hand tightly, and he closed his eyes, breathing deeply.

"Better?" I whispered.

"Not as effective as make-up sex against a bookshelf," he said, tipping his chin at the wooden bookcases behind us. "But it'll have to do for now."

"Can we start again?" I asked.

"Do I have to put my TA hat back on? Because I'd really rather not."

"Fine. But tell me what happened," I said, gesturing to my test. "What did Professor Brown say?"

"He scared the living shit out of me. I thought I was going to have to defend giving you such a high mark, but then he told me it wasn't high enough. He said my expectations were inflated and you deserved a perfect score. You've made a good impression on him over the years."

"How did you explain yourself?"

"I grasped at straws. I told him I knew you and a few others in the class are in contention for dean's list standings, and I was afraid I might be letting your reputation for doing well cloud my judgment, and that's why I'd been particularly critical."

"Did he believe you?"

"I think so. He spent fifteen minutes lecturing me about criterion-based assessment and achieved learning expectations. I had to nod and play dumb. Something good did come out of all this, though—something that's put my mind at ease. My dad was happy to hear about it, too."

"What's that?" I took a sip of my coffee.

"Martin suggested students use ID numbers instead of names on the *Much Ado* paper, and he's decided that instead of splitting up the exams into two piles, I'm going to mark the first part of everyone's exam and he'll mark the second part so he'll be able to look them all over as he goes and make sure he agrees with my assessment. It's like a weight's been lifted off my shoulders."

He pulled his hand from mine and reached down to rifle through his bag.

"Speaking of a weight on my shoulders, I've been carrying this around since this morning." He placed a paperback copy of *Tipping the Velvet* on the table. "I picked it up before class. I should have given it to you earlier so you could have read it while you waited for me. It might've softened you up a bit. Maybe you wouldn't have given me so much grief about your test."

I rolled my eyes. "You think that was grief? You have no idea. Until you've watched my mom and dad argue, you have no concept of grief. And I'm warning you right now—I'm stubborn, sunshine. If that turns you off, you might want to cut your losses and make a speedy exit."

"I'm not going anywhere, Aubrey, so there's no point trying to frighten me away. And I happen to like it when you're sassy." He pushed the book forward. "Put this in your bag. I know you don't have time for personal reading right now, but as soon as you do, read it, okay?"

"Okay. Thanks. I'm excited to take a look at it, but you really need to stop spending money on me."

He frowned. "Are you kidding? This is nothing. If I have to put up with your sass, then you have to learn to live with me spending money on you. I'd say it's a fair trade."

"I don't mean to sound ungrateful, Daniel, but I can't afford to get you anything right now, so it makes me feel bad."

"All I want is a little of your time. Sitting here with you now, even a few minutes ago when you were pissed at me, it's the best I've felt all week. To paraphrase a tired old cliché, sometimes the best things in life are free."

"That's just something rich people say to people who don't have any money to try to make them feel better."

"That's the second time you've said something like that to me. Don't be cynical. Sassy, I love. Cynical, not so much."

His observations, while a little cutting, were probably accurate. I was allowing myself to feel contempt for "the other half" and disparaging him in the process.

"I guess you're right. But if you truly believe that, then stop buying me things for the next thirty-one days. No gifts."

"I can't buy you anything for the rest of the semester?"

"Nope. No Louis Vuitton, no Holt Renfrew, no books. Nothing."

He drew his eyebrows together. "I'm not a fan of that idea."

"You don't have to buy my affection, Daniel." *Or my sexual favors*, I thought, remembering Julie's comment from the day before.

"I'm *not* trying to buy your affection." He narrowed his eyes. "What? What's with the grin?"

"It's just something Julie said yesterday. It's nothing."

"Judging by the look on your face, that's not true. What did she say?"

I put my hand over my eyes and peeked at him through my fingers. "She said you were giving me gifts because you were jonesing for a blow job."

Daniel stifled what would most likely have been a Guinness laugh.

"I can't believe she said that." He leaned over to whisper in my ear. "It's a little worrisome, though. I certainly hope I won't have to bribe you to get a blow job. When the time is right, of course."

Ha! If he only knew how desperate I was to lick him from head to toe…

"You'll just have to wait and see, won't you?" I said with a naughty grin. "God, what is it about this room that always leads to us talking about oral sex?"

"I'm not sure. Do you suppose they rent the space out for dirty weekends? There are a hell of a lot of bookshelves we could work our way through." He scanned the walls around us.

"Oh, please don't," I begged him. "I'm dying over here."

"Well, at least I'm not the only one being tormented by pent up sexual tension." He smiled cheekily, tapping his fingers on the table.

"Who says my sexual tension is pent up?"

His tapping fingers stilled. "What do you mean?"

"You know *exactly* what I mean."

He cleared his throat. "Jesus. Really?"

"Yes, really. Especially after that email last night. All that talk about your fingers…"

He slowly licked his lips and then grasped my hand under the table again.

"These?" he whispered.

I nodded, and he closed his eyes, expelling a long, steady breath. "Fuck." He stood and walked over to the bookshelf, scanning the collection as though he'd just noticed the most fascinating volume of poetry. I wasn't fooled. I could tell that he was adjusting himself in his khakis. He dropped his head back and rolled his shoulders before turning back around to look at me pensively.

I smiled, and he smirked. The library door creaked open, and he sat back down, dragging his chair a little farther down the table. I watched a guy walk across the room and flop into a seat near the fireplace.

"We shouldn't tempt fate," I whispered.

"You're right. I have to meet Cara downstairs in the coffee shop soon anyway. We're going over her paper again."

"Sounds like fun."

"Indeed. She's an interesting young lady, that one."

"Interesting?"

Vacuous I'd give him. *Shallow, moronic, top-heavy*, yes, but *interesting?*

"I know she comes across as ditzy in class and during lectures," he said, "but she did fairly well on her test. I obviously can't discuss specifics, but I got the sense that she'd studied. And she's working hard on her paper. She's not what I'd call intuitive, but she's really trying."

I couldn't hide my surprise. "Good for her, I guess. I still can't help wondering what the hell she's doing taking this course, though."

"I happen to know the answer to that. She's been surprisingly forthcoming. Apparently, her mother didn't get a chance to go to university. She always wanted to study English, and she seems to be living vicariously through Cara's experiences."

"So, Cara is taking English courses to appease her mother?"

"Essentially. She loves her sociology courses, but she's taking the English minor for her mom's benefit. Her mother reads all the books so they can talk about everything. It's kind of sad."

I nodded. "It's hard to see past the boobs and the valley talk sometimes, you know? Maybe I've been too critical."

"I have to admit, it's hard not to talk down to her and Lindsay when they say such ridiculous things."

"I noticed that earlier. You need to rein in the condescending tone a wee bit, eh? There's a fine line between confidence and arrogance, sailor."

"Just as there's a fine line between skepticism and cynicism."

Touché.

"I probably shouldn't have told you that information about Cara," he said. "Keep that between us, okay?"

"Of course."

"I should go. Are you cool with what happened with the test?"

"Yes, Mr. Grant, I understand what happened."

"And you'll be sure to make another appointment if you need to discuss *Much Ado*, or your sonnet analysis, or your paper, or, I don't know, the difference between colons and semi-colons?"

I laughed. "Don't push your luck."

"Fair enough," he said, grinning wickedly all the same. "I'll be in touch. Excellent independent work, Miss Price. I'm impressed with how well you took care of that *problem* you were having without my *assistance*." He raised his eyebrow impishly and made his way out of the library.

Good lord, he was cheeky. And so damn sexy. I gathered my belongings and left, immediately feeling his absence and already looking forward to his evening email. As it turned out, I didn't have to wait that long. I was in the middle of Queen's Park when my phone chirped, and I stopped at the edge of the path to read the message.

From: Jung Willman
To: Miss_V
Date: Mon, Mar 30, 2:35:16 PM
Subject: Stress!

Hey, Miss Busy Fingers,

I really enjoyed chatting with you. Sorry again about the mark issue. I'll do better next time. You're not a "dolt" and deserved a perfect grade.

I hate arguing with you, but I love that we're getting better at talking things out. Most stressful of all is that I can't spend money on you for thirty-one days, yet I know that I'm not prepared to stop giving you gifts. I'm going to have to be creative.

Your favorite nitpicker,
-D

Brief Hours

Love alters not with his brief hours and weeks,
But bears it out even to the edge of doom.
(*Sonnet 116*)

"Okay, I think we'll leave it at that for today," Daniel said. "*Sonnet 116* is a favorite of mine, and I'd rather not beat it to death. Plus, some of you have to put up with me tonight too. Wouldn't want to risk getting tiresome."

As if. Daniel could read sonnets to me until the cows came home and I'd hang off his every syllable. He could probably read the phone book, and I'd still end up in a puddle at his feet.

Julie had spent almost the entire tutorial banging her knee against mine while Daniel read sonnet after sonnet. All the girls were similarly enthralled. Even Trina, who made no attempts to hide that she was a lesbian, was utterly rapt during his reading of *Sonnet 116*.

"*Love is not love which alters when it alteration finds, or bends with the remover to remove: O no! it is a fixed mark which looks on tempests and is never shaken…*"

So true.

"It's hard to believe we only have one more tutorial left. The semester is flying by," Daniel said, his eyes briefly meeting mine. "Does anyone have any questions before we go?"

Apparently no one did because everyone began pushing back their chairs.

Julie gave me an awkward hug. "Have fun at the play tonight. Wish I hadn't gone on Wednesday night without you, but rehearsals are kind of running my life right now. I'll be so glad when this show is over."

"A few more weeks and you'll have your life back." I snuck a peek across the room. *A few more weeks — a mere twenty-seven days — and he'll be completely mine.* I looked back at Julie. "You did grab me the tickets for your show, right? Two of them?"

"They're waiting at the box office. All *five* of them."

"Five? Why five?"

"Brad and Penny are coming too. No pressure!" she said, laughing ruefully as she left.

I slid my bag over my arm and glanced at Daniel. He was talking with Neil, eyebrows furrowed as he nodded. I turned, intending to make my way out of the room, and bumped straight into Shawn.

"Hey, Aubrey," he said. "I noticed when I signed up that you're going to the play tonight too. Maybe we can sit together?"

"Yeah, maybe," I said noncommittally.

"So, um, what sonnet are you doing for your analysis?"

"I'm still trying to decide. Sonnets aren't my specialty."

"Yeah, I hear ya. I prefer to have some plot along with the imagery. Still, Daniel made it seem straightforward today. I gotta hand it to him; he seems to be on top of things."

On top of things? There was only one thing I wanted Daniel to be on top of right now. He was still chatting with Neil but looking uncomfortably in our direction, displeased that, once again, Shawn Ward was hovering around me attentively.

Never had there been less justification for jealousy.

It seemed strange to leave without saying goodbye to Daniel, but at least I'd see him again in a few hours. He obviously felt as uncomfortable as I did because he'd already messaged me by the time I reached the entrance to Queen's Park.

**Sorry I didn't get a chance to talk to you before you left,
but I have to get home to work on a special project.
This not spending money nonsense is time consuming.
(Don't worry, there's neither a glue gun nor icing sugar
involved. Apparently creativity isn't always messy!)
And are your knee caps bruised from all the bumping
with Julie's? See you soon! -D**

I smiled as I responded.

**My knee caps are fine, thank you. They're remarkably
resilient. One day you'll see exactly what I mean.
(Are you messy now?) See you soon. -A**

Daniel was pacing in front of the theater doors when I arrived at Hart House that night.

"Sorry I'm late. I got a little sidetracked with an essay," I said, shrugging out of my jacket.

"You'd better get in there," Daniel said. "Here's your ticket. Give me your coat. You head on in."

I made my way into the theater, following the usher who led me to my seat. A few people I recognized from class were sitting together, all in one row. There were two empty seats at the aisle, and then Shawn. It appeared I had no choice. I forced myself to smile and sat down.

"Hey. I was wondering what happened to you," he said with excessive enthusiasm.

"Yep, here I am."

"I've heard this is a good production."

"Yeah, Julie enjoyed it." I flipped absently through my program.

"For sure. I heard her say that this afternoon. So, um, that's good."

When did talking to Shawn become so awkward?

Daniel arrived, rescuing me from my discomfort. I retrieved my notepad and pen from my purse and settled in, angling myself slightly in Daniel's direction. Shawn smiled at me, but before he could launch into any more banalities, the house lights went down. A moment later, the stage lights came up, and the action began.

I kept my eyes fixed on the stage, occasionally jotting notes. From time to time, Shawn's knee would bump against mine, or his elbow would brush against my arm. I tried to fold in on myself to avoid touching him.

On the other side of me, Daniel sat with his elbow resting on the armrest we shared. I perched my left elbow next to his so that our arms touched. Every now and then, he'd incline his head in my direction, and I was reminded of the night seven weeks before when I'd almost leaned over to give his neck a good sniff.

"The guy playing Benedick is good," I whispered to Daniel as the actor soliloquized about his love for the fair Beatrice.

"Unfortunately, I think he knows it," he said quietly. "As someone once told me, there's a fine line between confidence and arrogance, Miss Price." He made a point of gently blowing in my ear before reclining in his seat. I shivered and crossed my arms, poking his bicep with my index finger. He cleared his throat, and even though I couldn't see his expression, I was sure he was smiling.

When the plot came to its crisis and the false allegations against Hero were dealt with, I heard Daniel take a deep breath, and he shifted uncomfortably beside me. I thought about Nicola's wrongful accusations against Daniel, and I marveled once again at the way Shakespeare's themes spoke so eloquently to timeless issues. I rubbed his arm softly with my finger. He sighed quietly, and I smiled, pleased that I could comfort him with a simple touch.

When the house lights came up at the end of the performance, my throat ached with sadness. My time with Daniel was coming to an end, another lonely weekend looming. Daniel leaned forward to address our small group.

"Does anyone have any questions or comments now that the play is over?"

Everyone shook their heads, standing and stretching, probably eager to get on with their Friday night festivities.

"Well, you're free to go. Good luck with your papers."

Daniel moved to join the crowd leaving the theater. I followed closely and would have met him at the coat check, but Shawn was instantly at my side.

"So, Aubrey, we're all hitting the Kap party. You wanna come?"

"Um, I think I'll take a pass. I'm bagged. Up early for work this morning and all that."

"Are you sure?"

"Tempting as it is, Shawn, I think I'm gonna say no. But thanks. I appreciate the offer."

"Okay. Well. See ya."

"Bye, Shawn. Later, guys."

Shawn made his way to the door, followed by the others, while I hurried to the coat check.

"Where'd everyone go?" Daniel asked.

"Kap party."

"You're not going?"

"No. I think I'll head home."

He looked around uneasily. "Look, it's late. I don't like the idea of you walking back to Jackman alone."

"Daniel, I've been walking alone around campus for four years. I'll be fine."

He sighed. "At least let me walk you to the main road so I can see you on your way? I'm sure any decent TA would be concerned about the safety of his best student."

"Okay."

"It's a nice night," he said, pushing the theater doors open. "Do you suppose spring is finally on the way?"

"I sure as hell hope so."

We strolled along the sidewalk in front of Hart House, dragging out our time together.

"I've been looking forward to tonight all week," he said. "It was nice sitting beside you for a couple of hours, especially in the exact spot where we had our first date." He smiled, and I shook my head. He was so adorable. "But it's never long enough, you know?"

"The couple of hours we spend together in class are always the highlight of my week. The rest of the time just drags."

"For me too." He looked at me searchingly. "Did you enjoy the play? Do you have some ideas for your analysis?"

"I did like it. I got to thinking about the way Shakespeare dealt with the false accusation thing—you know, the faking of Hero's death? It's such a strange plot device."

"I think of it metaphorically. To me, it represents the social death that follows a scandal and the loss of reputation. You'd be amazed the stuff that goes through my mind when I read *Much Ado* now. Well, I suppose I see everything through a different lens these days." He sighed.

Would a part of his psyche be forever damaged by what Nicola had done to him?

"It would be so amazing if I could give you a good-night kiss right now, poppet," he said as we stopped under the streetlight at the top of the steps.

"You know that's not possible."

"I know. So, what's on the agenda for the weekend?"

"School work. I'm kind of panicking. I have so much to do before the end of term, so I made up a schedule for the next four weeks. The sonnet analysis has me freaked out."

"Anything I can do to help?"

"I don't think so. I guess I'm stressed about being alone in that room with you and not being able to focus. I don't want to screw up."

"I promise I'll have my TA hat on. You bring your A-game, and I'll do whatever I can to make the process work."

"Thanks. That helps a little." I stared out at the park, my hands tucked safely in my pockets. "How about you? Big weekend plans?"

"Not really. I need to finish that creative project I told you about," he said, flashing his dimpled smile.

"Any hints?"

"Nope. You're going to have to wait."

"More waiting." I sighed dramatically. "Always with the waiting."

"It's very character building," he assured me.

"My character is going to be enormous by the end of the semester," I said dryly.

"Then it'll be right up there with my cold water bill," he countered with a cheeky grin.

I yawned as I traipsed up the stairs to the Hart House meeting room Wednesday afternoon. The previous few days had been a whirlwind of writing, proofreading, and preparing for today's conference. I'd finally completed my term paper for Brown's class, and once I had this sonnet analysis written, I'd be finished with my work for the course. I wished I could write the damn exam now and get it over with, for more than just the obvious reason.

The glass-paned meeting room door was open. Daniel waved me in and told me to push the door closed. I sat beside him and assembled my notes on the table. It had been six days since we'd been in close proximity to one another. I'd missed him so much, but this was an assessment and I had to keep my cool. There was no way of maintaining anonymity in a conference.

He'd continued to assure me that he'd be completely professional today. I'd even noticed a lessening of the effusive affection in his emails over the last couple of days, like he was getting his head in the game. As soon as he looked up from his notebook, the TA wall was between us, and I breathed a sigh of relief. He started off with some small talk, perhaps sensing my nervousness.

"How are things?"

"I'm doing okay."

"I'm surprised you picked this time slot," he said, shuffling some papers off to the side.

"I considered doing it tomorrow, but Thursdays are crazy so I figured I'd do it now, then head to my night class after."

"So, how did this go for you?" he asked with a Daniel-the-TA expression.

"I think I took an unconventional approach," I said. "I hope that's okay?"

"Unconventional?" He flipped to a blank page in his notebook.

"Yes, I decided to take a look at the 'Palmer's Sonnet' from *Romeo and Juliet.*"

He raised his eyebrows and wrote the title in his notebook. "Mind if I ask why?"

"After your discussion of recognition at first sight during tutorial a couple of weeks ago, I went back to re-read Romeo and Juliet's first exchange, and then I remembered it was set up in the form of a sonnet. I thought I'd give it a whirl."

"Okay, fair enough. It's a dialogue, though. Awkward for reading. Want me to speak Romeo's lines?" He smiled. "Only if that would help, of course."

Well, that would certainly help me fall off my chair.

"Would I lose marks?"

"I don't see why. Do you have it committed to memory?"

"I think so," I said.

"Okay. Let's begin." He launched into Romeo's opening quatrain, completely off the top of his head. "'*If I profane with my unworthiest hand This holy shrine, the gentle sin is this: My lips, two blushing pilgrims, ready stand To smooth that rough touch with a tender kiss.*'"

I resisted the impulse to swoon, instead delivering Juliet's quatrain in a calm, steady voice. "'*Good pilgrim, you do wrong your hand too much, Which mannerly devotion shows in this. For saints have hands that pilgrims' hands do touch And palm to palm is holy palmers' kiss.*'"

"'*Have not saints lips, and holy palmers too?*'" he asked.

"'*Ay, pilgrim, lips that they must use in prayer,*'" I replied.

"'*O, then, dear saint, let lips do what hands do. They pray, grant thou, lest faith turn to despair.*'"

"'*Saints do not move, though grant for prayers' sake.*'"

"'*Then move not while my prayer's effect I take.*'" Daniel paused after delivering the last line of the sonnet. "Then what happens, Miss Price?" he asked.

"He kisses her."

"And her reaction?"

"Well, doesn't she begin what would have been another sonnet if she weren't interrupted by the nurse?"

"You're right. What does she tell him?"

"She says, '*You kiss by the book.*'"

"Meaning?"

"Either she's responding dreamily, telling him that he kisses well, according to the conventions of what makes a good kiss, or she's being critical, telling him that his kiss was too restrained, too concerned with rules, convention, and propriety."

"I agree. Okay, back to the sonnet. Let's hear what you've come up with. I'll take notes. Try not to let that distract you."

I took a deep breath and launched into my analysis of the passage and how Shakespeare's use of the sonnet form for their first exchange underscored the power of their chemistry, explaining the traditional themes pursued in classical Petrarchan sonnets.

I reviewed the diction and word-play, then discussed the interplay between religious devotion and Romeo's worship of Juliet's beauty along with the underscored erotic undertones. Daniel wrote in his notebook, glancing up from time to time as I spoke. At last, I was talked out, and Daniel put his pencil down.

"Let me ask you this," he said. "Everything you've said suggests a positive connotation to Shakespeare using a sonnet for their first meeting. Is there anything to suggest that it might *not* be a good thing that their first meeting is structured this way?"

Okay, that was a curve ball. How could a love sonnet be anything but good? It was inherently romantic and clearly showed their likeness of mind.

"I'm not sure what you mean."

"I'm playing devil's advocate, I suppose, but I think one could argue that their first dialogue being set up this way actually foreshadows ill for them."

I tried to follow his line of thinking but was stumped. "I'm sorry. I don't see where you're going with this."

"What are the critical underpinnings of the definition of tragedy? See if you can talk your way through it." He was guiding me, trying to nudge me toward understanding, as any good teacher would do, instead of presenting me with the answer.

"Tragedy? Well, you have a tragic hero with an inherent character flaw—usually hubris, there's nemesis, um, catharsis, tension, a sense of inevitability—"

"Now you're getting somewhere," he said. "Talk to me about inevitability."

"Usually the course the tragic hero is on can't be averted. In the case of Romeo and Juliet's relationship, fate is dictating their course, and they can't avoid—" Realization struck me. "Oh, I see. You think the sonnet form being rigid and prescribed shows the inevitability of the course of their love—in this case, a doomed one that unfolds within the confines of a predetermined fate?"

His eyes shone proudly. "Well done. There is a critical stance that looks at this fixed dialogue between them, not as utterly romantic, but as terribly tragic. The sonnet form doesn't allow for any movement or wavering from its ultimate course. If I were you, I'd do some reading about that and include it in your written analysis."

"Thanks," I said with a grateful smile.

"That's what I'm here for. So, is there anything you'd like to add? Anything you feel you've missed?"

"I think I'm happy with that."

"All right. Give me a second here." He took a few moments to write some more notes. "Okay, that should do it." He smiled, and I could see *my* Daniel there, just under the surface.

"Did I do okay?"

"You did great, poppet."

And there he was.

"You did great too, Daniel. You're going to be a kickass professor one day. Your grandfather would be proud."

"Thank you. That means a lot." His sad smile melted into a frown. "We're not going to see each other for a week, you realize that? Because of classes being canceled for Easter weekend? If you hold onto this promise you made my dad, next Wednesday in class is the next time I'll see you. I can't stand that."

"I know, but we're getting there. I'm keeping my promise to your dad, and no one knows anything. Personally, I think we're doing great. Just three more weeks. We'll both be so busy with end of semester stuff that the days will fly by."

"I hope you're right." He reached into his laptop bag and pulled out an envelope. "Now that your conference is over and done with," he said, "*this* is what's been keeping me busy this past week. I would've given it to you sooner, but I thought it was important for you to get through this assignment first. I think you'll see why."

"Should I open it?"

He looked over at the door. "Just take a peek inside."

He crossed his arms as I peeled the envelope flap open. There was a CD inside, along with several folded sheets of paper.

"For you to listen to tonight after class — or over the long weekend. I hope you like it. I already had the recordable CD and the paper," he said, his expression serious. "I didn't buy them especially for the occasion. I haven't broken any rules, you know."

"I'm impressed." I laughed. "And, I must admit, I'm curious. *You*, sunshine, are completely disarming."

"I aim to please, Miss Price."

"And you succeed every time."

He dropped his eyes to my lips.

"If there weren't glass panes on those doors, I'd be kissing you so hard right now."

"I'd be kissing you back and grabbing your ass," I added with a cheeky grin.

He chuckled. "All right, you should go so I can complete your evaluation rubric without being distracted by that beautiful smile, not to mention thoughts of your hands on my ass. Wait in the hall, and I'll bring your notes out in a few minutes. If Cara's out there waiting, tell her to hang tight."

"Okay. Thanks again for the recommendations for improving my analysis. And for the CD. I can't wait to listen to it."

"You're welcome."

I gathered up my belongings and made my way across the room. Cara and Shawn were hanging out on the other side of the glass door, chatting. I fixed my face in an expression that said "I'm so relieved that's over" and joined them, closing the door behind me.

"Hey, Aubrey. How'd it go?" Shawn asked. He looked nervous.

"Hi, Shawn. Hey, Cara. Daniel said to tell you he'll be out in a sec. It was fine. I'm sure you'll do great," I said, trying to alleviate his anxiety.

"I hope so. I don't think he likes me."

"Don't be ridiculous," I said. "It's not a popularity contest. It's a conference."

"I guess you're right. So, hey, I've been meaning to ask you — are you planning to go to the Kap formal at the end of April?"

Oh, Shawn, please let this go.

I tried to cobble together a decent excuse for why I wouldn't be attending, but my efforts weren't necessary. Cara sighed in exasperation and spoke on my behalf.

"God, why don't you give up, Shawn? She's already seeing someone. This is totally second-hand embarrassing to watch." She rolled her eyes, her arms crossed under her boobs.

Shawn scowled at her for butting in.

My heart seized for a second. Who could she possibly think I was seeing? Then I remembered. Of course! She'd seen Brad sitting with his arm around me on the night of the benefit. She thought *he* was my boyfriend.

Shawn turned to me in confusion. "You're seeing someone? But Matt said—"

I tried to speak calmly, in spite of my hammering heart. "Matt and I may be roommates, but that doesn't mean he knows all of my personal business."

"I'd like to get to know *his* personal business," Cara said, thrusting her chest out suggestively and looking at Shawn with a challenging expression. "I hope he's going to the pub tomorrow night. I think it's time to make my move before he goes back to B.C."

Oh, Jesus, no. Cara and Matt? I thought about the way Matt's headboard had crashed against my wall all weekend. At the time, I'd been fuming, cursing his erotic escapades with Sarah while simultaneously wallowing in a miserable pit of sexual tension. Suddenly I was extremely grateful for their amorous weekend.

Shawn held up his hands and backed away. "Okay, I really don't need to be hearing this. Sorry, Aubrey. I honestly didn't know you had a boyfriend. You can't blame a guy for trying. I'm going to grab a coffee before it's my turn to go in. See ya around."

"Sorry, Shawn. Hey, have a good Easter, okay?" I called after him.

He turned and smiled tightly before escaping down the hall.

"Aaaaawkwaaaard," Cara said dramatically as Shawn disappeared around the corner.

"Yeah, totally. He's the nicest guy, but he's so persistent. And like you said, I'm not even available."

I couldn't believe Cara Switzer had rescued me from Shawn Ward's determined advances. Well, one good turn deserved another.

"Cara, can I talk to you about something?"

"I guess."

"This probably isn't any of my business, but I wanted to give you a head's up. You'd probably be better off not going after Matt."

"What are you, his mother?" she scoffed. "I know you don't like me, but you can't tell him who he can and can't go out with."

"Look, I just thought you should know that he got back together with Sarah. I'd hate for you to make a move on him and—"

"Get rejected?" she said.

"Yeah, I suppose."

"Thanks for looking out for me. But FYI, I knew they were back together. I don't think she's good enough for him. And I totally doubt he'd reject me."

It took everything in me not to burst into hysterical laughter. Was this some sort of belated April Fool's Day joke?

"But you know what? Since you so were so sweet to offer me advice, I've got some for you, too." She leaned over to whisper in my ear. "You should be careful what and *who* you talk about in public washrooms. You never know who might be listening."

I shrunk back from her. "What's that supposed to—"

At that precise moment, Daniel opened the door of the meeting room, handing me my conference notes and cutting off my question.

"Here you are, Miss Price. I hope I didn't keep you waiting. I wouldn't want you to be late for your class. And good luck with your written analysis. See you next Wednesday."

I looked at him, my pulse thumping in my temples.

"Thanks. You didn't. I mean, I won't." My voice was barely audible, which was a blessing because what I'd said probably hadn't made any sense.

"Are you, ready, Miss Switzer?" Daniel asked looking cautiously from Cara's face to mine.

"Totally," she replied. "Talk to you later, Aubrey." She left me standing there, gaping after her.

CHAPTER 16

Shallow Fools

What your wisdoms could not discover,
these shallow fools have brought to light…
(*Much Ado About Nothing*, Act v, Scene 1)

"Jesus, Aubrey, why didn't you wait for her to come out after her conference so you could ask her what the fuck she was talking about?"

"I couldn't. I had to go to my night class."

"You know what? There are times when it's appropriate to be late for class. I'd say this was one of those times."

I walked another circuit around Julie's room. I was wearing a path in her area rug while she watched me from the middle of the bed.

"I wasn't thinking straight," I confessed. "I was in a daze. I might as well have skipped my lecture. I didn't process anything the prof said."

"So, what are you going to do now?" Julie asked, jamming clothes and toiletries into her suitcase.

"I don't know." I made another anxious lap of her room, sitting briefly on her roommate's bed before leaping up and pacing again. "But I need to know what she was talking about. Do you think I should try to track her down? She lives somewhere off campus with Lindsay, right?"

"I might be able to think straight if you'd stop moving. You're making me dizzy. I pirouetted my ass off for two hours tonight. I don't need to spin any more, thank you very much."

I sighed and slouched against her dresser. "I don't know what to do! When could she have possibly heard me talking about anything—in a *washroom*, of all places? I'm trying to remember if I've been at any events lately where I might have said something, but it's not like I've been wasted at a party somewhere spewing nasty rumors about someone. I have this horrible feeling it's about Daniel, but how could it be?"

"Unless you've been talking to yourself, I don't see how. You've only told Matt and me. Maybe you're making something out of nothing."

"I know! I don't get it. It's paranoia or my guilty conscience making me think it has to do with him, right? But you should have seen the look on her face. It was like she was mocking me and feeling sorry for me at the same time."

"Well, think back. Have you ever been anywhere with Daniel where you might have gone to the washroom and chatted to a stranger or a waitress—"

"A waitress?" I rubbed my eyes. I was driving myself crazy. "Seriously? It would have involved you or Penny, since you're the only females who know about us. It makes no sense. I don't hang out with Cara. I *never* see her outside of the classroom."

I was on the verge of dismissing Cara's cryptic comment, prepared to conclude that she was just trying to psych me out, when the expression on Julie's face changed. She brought her hands up to cover her mouth.

"Holy shit. Oh no, Aubrey. Fuck—"

"What? What is it?" I rushed over to the bed and dropped beside her, pulling her hands down. She looked at me, horror-stricken.

"Oh crap, Aubrey. Think for a second. When was the last time you remember seeing Cara outside of class—for a social event, I mean?"

"She was at the Kap semi-formal a few weeks back, but she didn't see me. I wasn't even there for ten minutes before I left with Daniel. And he didn't come in—"

"No, before that…go back farther," she interrupted, her face serious, her voice low and controlled.

"I can't think of anything. Wait, there was the memorial service for Mary. She sat behind us, remember?"

"And the next day?" Julie asked.

"Oh, right. The benefit at Brennan Hall. She was there, but we hardly—"

I stopped short, remembering that I *had* made two trips to the washroom that night. Julie had been with me each time, and Penny had been there for the second one. And we had *definitely* talked about Daniel. Both times. Not once had I paid any attention to the stalls. The blood rushed out of my face, and my own hands flew up to my face.

Julie nodded slowly. "Remember when I first arrived? After our fight, we went in the washroom to talk?"

"Oh, sweet Jesus," I breathed, horrified.

"I know. We were talking about how you hadn't told me about you and Daniel. I don't remember exactly how the conversation went down. Maybe we mentioned his name when we were talking. Do you remember looking around to see if anyone was in there?"

"No, I was too worried about our fight. I didn't even think twice about anything else. What if she was in there the whole time listening?"

"Oh my God. You know what? That would explain how weird she was when she came over to the table to say hi. Remember how she looked at us like we'd all grown two heads? And then on Monday, in class, she gave you that creepy look? You brushed it off, but I knew there was something up. Fuck, Aubrey, she *knows*."

I flopped on the bed, burying my face in my arm as terror gave way to acute anguish.

"Oh my God, what the hell am I going to do? Daniel is gonna have a shit fit!"

Julie nudged my arm away from my face. "Let's think this through. Why was she telling you?"

"To freak me out? To scare me? It's no mystery she doesn't like me."

"She's probably jealous. Maybe she wants the upper hand for once. Maybe she has no intention of doing anything with the information. If she was planning to use what she knows, wouldn't she have done something by now?"

That was a good point. If she meant to hurt me or Daniel, why would she wait weeks to do it?

Unless…

"Maybe she's biding her time to see if she needs leverage. Perhaps if Daniel assigns her a low mark she can use what she knows to blackmail him."

My thoughts flickered anxiously to Nicola. I couldn't discuss Daniel's history at Oxford with Julie, but there was a very real possibility that Cara had similar plans in mind.

"You need to tell him," Julie said resolutely.

"Don't you think I should get proof before I start throwing around accusations?"

"You don't have to word it that way. Tell him what she said and what you *suspect* she might mean."

"And then tell him that I was blabbing about him and our relationship indiscreetly in a public washroom? He'll kill me. Any hope of a relationship, out the window. Fuck, this is brutal!"

"I'm just as much to blame."

I tried to picture myself telling Daniel. I'd have to break my promise to his father and tell him in person. It's not like I could call him or tell him in an email. I imagined the look of panic on his face. All his worst fears and nightmares would be realized. What if he had an anxiety attack right there and then? What if I couldn't talk him down?

"Jul, I need to think this through and figure out what to do next. Please don't say anything to Jeremy, okay?"

"If that's what you want. I won't be seeing Jer until next week, anyway. I'll be on the train by ten o'clock tomorrow morning. Are you gonna be okay here alone this weekend?"

"I'll be fine. I'm planning to work my ass off to try to make a dent in these last three papers."

"Is Matt going to be around?"

"No. He's going to Sarah's until Sunday night."

"And Jo?"

I shook my head.

"That sucks. You should come home with me."

"I have three classes tomorrow. I can't miss them. I'll keep myself busy, don't worry."

She looked at me sadly. "Try to stay positive. I'm sure everything will be fine. Maybe Cara's just blowing smoke." She squeezed my hand. "You know there's a big Easter dinner at Casa Grant on Sunday, right?"

"Yeah, Daniel was telling me about it. They're going to church for the Easter service and then having an early dinner because Penny leaves for England Sunday night, right?"

"That's what Jer said. It'll be so fun when the semester is over and you and I can go to some of these Grant family events. I can't wait until they know about us and we can all hang out together," she said.

Julie, the eternal optimist, was looking ahead to the end of the semester as if nothing had changed. I wasn't as hopeful. The likelihood of the six of us having a great time together *anywhere* was now in question because I had foolishly committed the cardinal Grant sin: I hadn't been discreet.

An hour later I was sitting in the middle of my bed in fleece PJ pants and Daniel's black T-shirt. Cara's whispered warning made the hair on my neck stand on end every time I thought about it. Desperate for a distraction, I opened the CD Daniel had made me. He'd created a liner sleeve—a picture of a cherubic angel playing a lute. Across the top he'd included the words, "*If music be the food of love, play on.*"

I slipped the CD into my laptop and scanned the folded papers he'd included in the envelope. What I saw made my heart flip. It was a list of the songs on the CD, along with selected lyrics and a personal commentary explaining why he'd chosen each one. I took a deep breath and started the CD, alternately reading along with Daniel's notes and listening to the music as each new song began.

It was like a scrapbook of our relationship thus far, each song corresponding to an event from the past couple of months or tied to his feelings for me. He covered everything from the early days of our acquaintance to our mutual admission that we had feelings for one another and beyond.

He claimed to have included the second-to-last song, "Heart on My Sleeve" by Idina Menzel, because the words made him think of my willful independence. In the liner notes, he'd written, *Your combination of strength and vulnerability takes my breath away. You amaze me—every single day—without fail.*

Tears welled in my eyes, but they spilled over when the last song began. I'd never heard of it, but "You're the Best Thing" by The Style

Council was an old favorite of Daniel's, one which had suddenly come to mean more to him than ever before. His notation to accompany the song said, *You are the best thing that's happened to me, Aubrey. Mark my words—this is a song we'll make love to.*

I finally gave in to my tears, sobbing openly. If I'd listened to the CD before my conversation with Cara, I'm sure I would have reacted emotionally, but now the knowledge that she could do him serious harm if she went public with her allegations, or if she tried to blackmail him into giving her a better mark on her conference or her paper—well, that changed everything. She would ruin him and probably destroy any chances we would have for happiness by irreparably tainting our relationship.

Unable to string words together coherently enough to thank Daniel for his wonderful gift, I went to bed at midnight. My eyes were sore from crying.

On Thursday morning, I awoke just before ten o'clock. Prior to leaving for my class at St. Mike's, I managed to throw together a quick email to Daniel to thank him for the CD and to explain how deeply the songs and accompanying words had touched me. I also tried to impress upon him that this present meant more to me than any gift with high monetary value possibly could. I didn't mention anything about Cara or her ominous warning.

Daniel wrote back almost immediately to say he was so glad I'd written—he'd been worried when he hadn't heard from me the night before, but he'd assumed I'd been too tired after class to give the CD a listen. He said choosing those songs and writing about what they meant to him was one of the most enjoyable things he'd ever done for someone and that he wished he could make me a hundred more CDs just like it.

I thought I'd cried myself dry the night before. I was wrong.

By the time my French lecture came to a close that afternoon, I'd managed to forget and then subsequently remember Cara's cryptic advice too many times to keep track of. My mind would wander as I moved through my day, and then her words would come back to me with a sudden jolt and I'd cringe, my shoulders lifting as if to protect me from some tangible physical onslaught.

All day I vacillated between wanting to stick my head in the sand to avoid dealing with her threat and knowing I needed to face it head-on. As I made my way back to Vic after my final lecture of the day, I decided the best course of action would be to track Cara down at the campus pub that night. It was the only approach that would clear my mind and alleviate my anxiety.

With that decision made, I sat on a bench in front of Hart House to read the email Daniel had sent while I'd been in class.

From: Jung Willman
To: Miss_V
Date: Thurs, Apr 9, 3:15:43 PM
Subject: LONG weekends

Well, here we are, poppet, on the brink of a very long weekend. Normally these extra days off are such a boon, but I'm certainly not looking forward to it. The fact that I won't see you until next Wednesday has me feeling really lost.

I wish you were coming with me to my parents' for Easter dinner. My mom makes a mean turkey dinner—which you know—but Patty's bringing her famous pecan pie. It's to die for. I wish you could be right by my side, trying it for yourself.

April 13th was my grandfather's birthday. Easter was at the end of March last year, but this year, with the family dinner being the day before his birthday, I'm anticipating some melancholy moments at the table. I'll probably go to see him on Monday. Since you won't be sitting beside me on his bench this time, I'll feel even sadder.

God, I'm sorry, I don't know why I'm burdening you with all this. I wish we could talk face to face, but I know you're trying to do the right thing. You're so strong, my lovely.

Anyway, at the risk of putting undue pressure on you, I'm going to say this anyway...feel free to call me this weekend. But if you can't bring yourself to do that, then please email me as much as you like. Regardless of what I'm doing, know that I'll be thinking about you.

-D

xo

Daniel's words led to more pangs, and again tears clouded my eyes as I read. I typed out a reply on my phone, struggling to keep my tone light.

From: Miss_V
To: Jung Willman
Date: Thurs, Apr 9, 5:17:07 PM
Subject: Re: LONG weekends

Hey, sunshine, I know exactly how you feel. I'll miss you so much this weekend. I'm dreading all this time alone. On the bright side, I hope to get a ton of school work done, but that's not exactly something to look forward to.

I hope your dinner with your family isn't too gloomy. I'm sure Patty will feel sad — I bet she misses your grandfather so much. If you have a moment alone with her, tell her I said hi and I'm thinking of her. And when you talk to your grandfather on Monday, please tell him I think the world of his grandson, okay?

I'm heading back to Jackman now. I have a beautiful CD that I need to listen to eleventy-billion times. Talk to you later.

Your Poppet

CHAPTER 17

Truth

Out with it boldly: truth loves open dealing.
(*Henry VIII*, Act III, Scene 1)

"Are you sure you want to do this?"

"I have to, Matt. I can't sit and stew on it all weekend."

"Have you thought about what you're gonna say to her?"

"A bit. I'll probably end up winging it."

Matt and I were at the pub — Cara's Thursday night haunt. My goal was to find her and glean from her what she knew. I'd have to be careful. I couldn't risk telling her something she didn't actually know.

Over dinner, Matt had listened to my account of what had happened, his face revealing his growing concern as I explained what Julie and I assumed Cara was referring to. His response to my story had surprised me.

"There's no love lost between me and Daniel," he'd said. "But no one deserves to have their life torn apart because they've fallen for someone at the wrong place and the wrong time."

Again, I was struck by how lucky I was to have Matthew for a friend, and now here he was by my side as I tried to figure out how best to approach Cara. I could have saved myself the effort. As I did a circuit of the dance floor, liquid courage in hand, it quickly became evident that Cara wasn't there. I checked the bathroom, and Matt scanned the clusters of people smoking in front of the building, but she wasn't anywhere in sight.

"Do you think she'll come later?" I asked, leaning close to Matt's ear so that he could hear me over the pounding bass of the music.

He looked at his watch and led me to a quiet corner near the entrance.

"It's ten thirty. She's usually here by now. Actually, she's usually wasted by now. It's not like Cara to miss a pub night," he said. "She never passes up a chance to get sloshed and hit on someone."

"Hey, there's Vince. Maybe he's seen her."

I moved through the crowd and tapped Vince on the shoulder. He swung around, holding up two beer cups and smiling broadly when he saw me.

"Aubrey Price! Slumming it!" He had to shout to be heard over the music.

I smiled self-consciously. Was I beginning to get a reputation as a snob? God, I hoped not.

"Can I talk to you?" I said, standing on my toes to reach Vince's ear.

"Sure."

He followed me back to where Matt was standing.

"Hey, Matt, what's up?"

"Hey, man, not much."

I interrupted their pleasantries, wanting to get right to the point. "Vince, have you seen Cara tonight?"

"Yeah, she left about half an hour ago."

"Do you know where she was going?" Matt asked. "Another pub or a party or something? We need to talk to her."

"Oh, I know exactly where she was going. As for talking? Doubts, my friend," he said, elbowing Matt in the ribs.

"Meaning?" Matt asked.

"Meaning…she left with Shawn. They went back to her place." He wiggled his eyebrows.

"Shawn?" I said, not even trying to contain my shock. "Seriously?"

"Lauren told me Cara's been hot to trot for Shawn since second year. Can you believe that?"

"Are you sure? Just yesterday she was saying how hot she thinks Matt is. She said it right in front of Shawn."

Vince shrugged. "You know how chicks operate. She was probably trying to make Shawn jealous."

I thought about the way she'd looked at Shawn when she'd been talking about Matt. Holy shit! She'd been goading him! And this was another reason for her to dislike me. Shawn hadn't exactly been trying to conceal his interest in me. No wonder she'd been so eager to let him know I was "taken."

"Anyway, I'll see ya later," Vince said. "I've got someone to entertain." He held the two beer cups over his head as he wove through the crowd to join Lauren, who was sprawled out drunkenly on an ancient vinyl couch in the corner.

It looked to me like the last thing the girl needed was a drink. A blanket and a bucket would've been much more appropriate.

Like virtually everyone else on campus, Cara went home for Easter. I had to accept that her words would run on repeat in my head for four days.

Stuck at Jackman alone, my only respite from the excruciating boredom was the flurry of emails that Daniel and I bandied back and forth. I read his messages voraciously, drinking in his words and allowing them to gather in my mind, wishing they'd squeeze the less savory thoughts out of my brain. They didn't.

My sleep was disturbed on Saturday night by a strange dream in which Cara stood before Daniel and me, pointing an accusing finger and telling anyone who would listen that we were engaged in inappropriate actions. Then a mysterious girl was there, holding a voice recorder up to Cara's mouth, gathering damning evidence against us. Though I had no clue what Nicola looked like, somehow I knew that this girl in my dream was Daniel's accuser from Oxford.

Daniel's mother and father were there, too, shaking their heads in disappointment. Dean Grant was reading from an enormous book detailing the University's Code of Conduct. My mouth was moving, but no sound came out. Daniel gasped and clutched his chest, but my hands were bound to my sides—I couldn't even reach out to comfort him.

I woke with a start, stomach churning, the details of the dream haunting in their vividness. The dream lingered at the edges of my consciousness all day while Cara's whispered threat came back to me again and again.

At six o'clock on Sunday night, the silence of the apartment was interrupted by the buzzer—someone calling up from the lobby. My first thought was Daniel. He wouldn't risk coming here, would he? I pressed the intercom.

"Hello?"

"Aubrey, it's me, Penny. Can you pop down here for a minute?"

"Of course! I'll be right there!"

I quickly threw a sweatshirt over my T-shirt and slipped on some shoes. Why on earth would Penny be here? When I reached the lobby and pushed the door open for her, the look of affection and sympathy on her face just about made me buckle at the knees. She reached out to hug me with one arm.

"Happy Easter, lovey."

"Thanks. You too. This is a surprise. What are you doing here?"

She handed me a plastic bag.

"Special delivery."

"What is it?"

"Open it when you get upstairs. I guarantee you'll love it. Look, I can't stay. Brad's waiting in the truck. We're on our way to the airport in a couple of hours."

"That's right. I hope everything goes smoothly on your trip. Have fun, okay?"

"I will." She hugged me again and whispered in my ear, "Just a little over a fortnight and this will all be over. Keep your chin up. And if it makes you feel any better, Daniel's absolutely beside himself missing you."

I nodded. "This isn't easy on either of us." I held up the bag. "Thanks for this."

"Not to worry, love. Bye, then. Good luck studying," she said, pushing through the door.

"How long are you gone?" I called after her.

"Until the twenty-sixth. I want you to come over for lunch or something when I'm back, all right?"

"Sure thing." I waved as she left, wondering if that lunch date would ever come to pass.

I dashed upstairs, eager to see what was in the bag. I unknotted the plastic and found five foil-wrapped packages, two of them still warm to the touch. At the bottom of the bag, there was a folded sheet of paper—a note from Gwen:

> Aubrey,
>
> I imagine you may not think too kindly of me right now, and I'm sorry. My son's welfare has to be my top priority, but I realize you have neither malicious intent nor any desire to hurt him. He misses you, and your absence at our gathering this afternoon, although necessary, seemed wrong. I hate to think of you at your residence alone without your mother to cook you Easter dinner, so I prepared a little something. Consider it an olive branch. David doesn't know I've done this, so please don't mention it. I'm entrusting the delivery to Bradley and Penny. I look forward to the day when you can join our family for holidays and celebrations. -Gwen

I inhaled deeply, swallowing the lump in my throat and turning my attention to the warm packages—turkey and stuffing, mashed potatoes, carrots, green beans, and a small container of gravy. Next, I found a slice of gooey pecan pie. I smiled as I imagined Daniel's face when dessert was served.

I picked up the last two packages. One felt decidedly non-food-like. The other was a strange bumpy shape. I peeled open the foil of the bumpy one and found a chocolate bunny. I sat him on the counter while I opened the last package, which wasn't food at all, but rather a framed picture of Daniel with a small folded note stuck in the frame.

I pulled the paper away so I could look at the photograph—Daniel dressed handsomely in gray pants and a charcoal sweater with a white shirt and tie underneath. He was standing in front of an ivy-covered wall — this had to be at Oxford. I stood the photo on the counter and opened the note.

Hello, lovely,

See what this no spending money silliness is doing to me? Now I've had to resort to stealing things from my parents' home! Add to that the subterfuge of having Penny conceal this photo and the bunny (they were buy one get one free — I gave you the free one!) in the bag my mom was putting together for you, and I feel downright criminal!

I'll be visiting my grandfather at his bench tomorrow afternoon. It was dark when we went there last time, and I don't think he got a good look at you. I miss you so much. I hope you can come with me when I visit him again.

Enjoy your dinner, and I can't wait to see you in a few days.

Yours, Daniel

It's not easy swallowing turkey and stuffing with all the fixings when you're crying your eyes out, but somehow I managed. I sat at the kitchen table, Daniel's picture and the chocolate bunny propped up beside me, and ate every last bite of Gwen's peace offering. And Daniel was right. Gooey pecan pie *was* to die for.

"Thanks for brunch, Matt. It was nice to get away from my own thoughts for a couple of hours."

Matt draped his arm around my shoulders as we made our way up the subway steps, turning to look at me sincerely.

"It was nice to hang out, just us, you know? I've been kind of ignoring you."

"Don't worry. I get it. It's good that you got to spend the weekend at Sarah's. I wish I could do the same with Daniel. Now I don't even know if we'll ever get to that point."

Matt squeezed my shoulder as we walked on.

"You really think Cara's gonna blow the whistle on you guys? I still think you might be jumping to conclusions."

"I've gone around in circles about this all weekend. Part of me thinks she's messing with my head, and then part of me is sure she heard everything Julie and I said in that washroom and she's waiting for the right moment to pounce."

We reached the entrance of Northrop Frye hall, and I stopped, gesturing to the doors.

"This is where Daniel's dad made me promise not to see Daniel until the class is over."

I walked over to a low-walled planter and sat on the ledge looking up at Old Vic.

"Ah, yes, the dreaded promise," Matt said, sitting next to me. "Well, the way I see it, you need to break it. I think you need to tell Daniel what you suspect. And soon—definitely before class on Wednesday. Forewarned is forearmed, right?"

"I'm just terrified he'll have an anxiety attack and I won't know what to do. Or what if he decides I'm way too much trouble and walks away?"

"Aubrey, don't take this the wrong way, but I think you need to sideline your worries about the relationship. This is his *life*. His *reputation*. That's way more important right now. You'll have to take your chances that he'll handle it okay. Plus, look at the effect keeping this to yourself is having on you. Have you looked in the mirror? You're a mess."

It was true—I did look awful. My eyelids were puffy from crying so much over the weekend.

"I guess I'm selfishly trying to prolong the inevitable. It's weird—I can't stop thinking about his father's words. Daniel and I were so quick to attack his dad and call him unreasonable, but now that I know he was right to be concerned about someone finding out about us, I feel wretched."

I promise…I'd rather die than hurt Daniel.

How was I to know that when I'd said those words to Dean Grant, I'd already taken the misstep that would lead to disaster? Why did everything have to be so complicated? I wished there was some way of knowing I was making the right decision—some sort of sign.

I sighed and looked up at the southern wall of Old Vic, the ivy just beginning to show the promise of spring buds. As my eyes traced the curved arch and the path of the soon to blossom ivy, I frowned. Above the arched doorway of the building was something I hadn't noticed in the entire four years I'd been at U of T.

I don't know how I'd overlooked it, but as I sat wrestling with the difficult choice that lay before me, I knew without a doubt that this message nestled among the ivy buds was the sign I'd been looking for.

Daniel

CHAPTER 18

Words, vows, gifts, tears, and love's full sacrifice…
(*Troilus and Cressida*, Act 1, Scene 2)

What a beautiful day. Four weeks ago, Aubrey and I had sat on this very bench, watching the snow falling. It never ceased to amaze me the way the weather could change on a dime in this country; the season had turned in the space of a few days.

The clouds swept across the sky, urged on by occasional gusts of wind. Behind me, I heard the frustrated shouts of the boy who'd spent twenty minutes unsuccessfully trying to get his kite to take to the air. It was a good day for kite flying, but he hadn't mastered the technique. He'd run, dragging the kite along the ground, and give up before the wind had a chance to scoop it up.

I closed my eyes and breathed deeply. "It's a nice day, Gramps," I whispered. "You and Patty would've enjoyed your walk today. One day I'll bring Aubrey back here with me. I wish you could have met her. I think you would have liked her."

Sudden hoots of delight filled the air.

"Hey, Dad, I got it! Did you see that?"

I whirled around on the bench and watched the kid running as the wind took his kite higher. His father caught up with him, showing him how to play out the string.

Beyond the swerving kite, the clouds drifted by, changing shapes as they moved. But off to the west, darker clouds were forming. We were in for some rain. I'd have to leave soon anyway to make it to Brad's place for one o'clock. I passed my fingers across the plaque affixed to the back of the bench.

"I'll have to go in a few minutes, Gramps."

I looked around self-consciously. If anyone were to see me sitting here talking to myself, they'd think I was half-cracked. A woman I'd seen earlier was returning from her walk with her Golden Retriever. She smiled and waved as they made their way past me, the dog stopping occasionally to investigate various scents.

And that's when I saw her.

Aubrey.

She was standing in the middle of the path about fifty yards away. I rubbed my eyes. Was I seeing things? No. It was absolutely her. She was just standing there, looking at me. I didn't know what the hell she was doing here, but I swear I'd never been happier to see someone in my life.

I stood up, and she crossed the grassy expanse beside the path and headed off into the woods, glancing back at me before disappearing into the trees. Aubrey obviously wanted me to follow her, and I made my way through the trees. She didn't slow until she was well into the woods, and then she turned, dropped her bag on the ground, and rested against a tree, waiting for me to catch up.

Once I was about twenty feet away, I started jogging and scooped her up into my arms, lifting her off the ground. She flung her arms around my neck and knotted her hands in my hair roughly, holding on so tightly she might have taken a clump of it out.

"Oh my God, I missed you." I buried my face in her neck.

"Me too, like you wouldn't believe," she said.

I brushed her hair back from her face so I could get a good look at her. "What are you doing here? Not that I'm complaining, but are you okay? It's probably awful of me to say this, but you look totally wiped!"

There were dark circles under her eyes, and her eyelids were puffy.

"Rough weekend," she said, smiling weakly.

"You sounded so upbeat in your emails."

She chuckled humorlessly. "And the Academy Award goes to…"

I ran my thumbs under her eyes. "You were pretending? Why? What's going on?" She shook her head but didn't answer. "How did you get here, anyway?"

"Taxi. Matt loaned me twenty bucks."

"If you'd told me you wanted to come, I could've picked you up."

"I didn't know I was coming to see you until about forty-five minutes ago. This was kind of an impulse."

"I can't believe you're here. I never dreamed you'd break your promise to my father."

"I didn't either. Not that I didn't think about doing it every hour all weekend, but I was trying so hard to do the right thing. I had to come, though. I need talk to you about something."

"What is it?"

She looked around, biting her lip hesitantly. "I feel like we should sit," she said.

I gestured to a fallen tree trunk, taking her hand as we went over to the log. "Is your family okay?"

"Yes, everyone's fine. Well, as of Saturday, anyway. No, this is about you—about us."

I nodded, encouraging her to continue while a million possibilities raced through my mind.

"I don't know how to say this. Try to stay calm, okay?"

"Christ, Aubrey, the preamble is killing me. Just say it, please," I begged.

"Okay. Crap. This is even harder than I thought it was gonna be. It's just that—well, I think Cara knows about us."

She looked at me worriedly while I tried to process what she was saying. *Cara knows?* How was that possible?

"Why the hell would you say that?"

She took a deep breath. "I think she heard Julie and me talking in the washroom the night of the benefit at Brennan Hall. Remember we'd had that fight? When I was explaining everything that was going on to Julie, I think we might have mentioned your name. And it turns out Cara might have been in there, listening."

I leapt up as a surge of anger shot through me. "What? You've been keeping this from me for weeks, and you're just deciding to tell me now? Are you serious?"

She rolled her eyes. "No, of course not. She said something to me on Wednesday. I had no idea about any of this until she spoke to me."

"Okay, explain. I don't understand."

"Wednesday, after my conference, she told me that I should be careful what and who I talk about in public washrooms because you never know who might be listening. She said it like it was a threat or something. I didn't get a chance to question her. Julie and I talked later that night, and we figured the only time we've been anywhere in a washroom talking about our relationship was at the benefit at Brennan Hall. Cara was there that night. She must have been in one of the stalls, but I swear I didn't hear or see anyone."

"Aubrey, do you realize how irresponsible it was not share this with me right away? What were you thinking?"

As I spoke, I realized I sounded an awful lot like my father, not something I was particularly proud of. Aubrey stood up and stepped away, her hands clenching at her sides, eyes flashing.

"I'm sorry, that didn't come out right," I said, backpedaling.

"I was trying to protect you," she whispered, turning away and shaking her head.

"You should never keep something from me if it affects my welfare. I don't see how the hell that could protect me."

"I was afraid of your reaction. What if I broke my promise to your father and came to tell you, and you had a panic attack and I couldn't help you? I was scared."

I joined her, taking her hand, which she reluctantly unfolded. If only I hadn't come unhinged in front of her that day. My anxiety—it frightened her.

"It was bad judgment on my part, not telling you," she said. She paused for a second, and then she took my other hand. "If you want to know the truth, I thought this would be the last straw—that you'd be mad at me for being careless in that washroom and tell me to get lost. I couldn't face the thought of losing you."

"What? Jesus Christ, Aubrey! Where do you get these outrageous ideas? Come here." I pulled her into my arms, bringing her face into the crook of my neck as I tried to comfort her. "If I ever have an anxiety attack when we're alone together, all you have to do is stay calm. If you're calm, I'll be fine." The tension dissolved from her body as she nestled against me. "I'm sorry I snapped at you," I added, rubbing her back.

"I'm sorry, too. For everything," she whispered against my neck. "I was planning to tell you, but I thought maybe I should try to talk to Cara first."

I led her to the fallen tree and sat down again. "So, you haven't spoken to Cara?"

She shook her head. "I looked for her on Thursday night. I couldn't find her. And she went home the next morning."

"So, what made you suddenly decide to come here and tell me?"

"Matt. We went out for brunch and were sitting in front of Old Vic afterward, and he gave me shit. He told me you needed to know and I was wrong to keep it from you."

A smile spread across my face. "He's definitely growing on me."

"Between his nagging and the inscription over the south door of Old Vic, I knew I had to come and talk to you."

"There's an inscription over the door?"

"Yep. Get this. It says '*The Truth Shall Make You Free*' in the stone above the south archway."

"No shit? I've never noticed that."

"Me either. It totally freaked me out, especially after seeing the same inscription on the paperweight on your desk. I took it as a sign."

I couldn't help smiling. "A sign?"

"I know it sounds flaky, but it was like that inscription was confirming what I needed to do. Like it was telling me your dad would forgive this because it was something you needed to know. Now that I've told you the truth, I do feel a hell of a lot better. All weekend, I thought I was being stoic. Turns out I was just being stupid."

"You've been on quite an emotional rollercoaster."

"That's an understatement." She sighed. "What are we going to do? What if she tells someone? Of all people to find out, *Cara?* She really doesn't like me, Daniel."

I thought about my dealings with her—the insights I'd gained over the past several weeks.

"I don't think she'll be a problem. I doubt she'll say anything if she actually does know about us. It's possible you've misunderstood her meaning."

Aubrey drew her head back, examining my face.

"Why do you look so calm?" she asked. "This is *so* not how I imagined you'd react. I thought you'd go crazy. I mean, I really thought you'd go mental."

"Can I make a small request?" I asked, smiling wryly. "Can you avoid describing me with words like neurotic, OCD, crazy, and mental? I'm a little sensitive about that."

"Sorry." She grimaced.

"It's okay. I'm half joking."

"Fair enough." She nodded and then asked, "Should *I* talk to her, or do *you* want to? Or should we let it alone? I've considered this from so many angles."

"I don't want you talking to her. And the way I see the situation, it would be a case of your word against hers if it ever came up. She has no tangible proof."

"But your reputation precedes you. This is the type of thing the university is looking for. You told me that even the slightest *hint* of impropriety—"

"I'm convinced Cara won't say anything. I'm not sure what she's playing at, but I'm certain she won't tell anyone anything."

Aubrey looked completely amazed and more than a little worried.

"You trust me, right?" I asked her.

"Of course I do."

"Then let me handle this, and if she says anything else, plead ignorance. Don't let her bait you. I know she can be difficult to deal with, but she's got her weaknesses. Trust me. I'm sure we're fine."

I put my arm around her and tucked her close to my side.

"Maybe now that she's finally snagged Shawn, she'll be too busy to torment me," she said hopefully.

"Cara and Shawn?"

"Apparently she's been carrying a torch for him for years, at least according to Lauren."

"Huh. Well, that is good news." I stroked her cheek gently. "I don't want to waste any more time talking about Cara. Just promise me you'll never keep anything from me ever again? If you stub your toe, I want to know about it. Spare no details."

She smiled. "I promise."

"You promise? One hundred percent?"

"Definitely." She looked at her hands. "Most definitely."

Ah, yes. Definitely. Most definitely.

Was now the right time? The leaves on the trees were rustling in the breeze, and the only other sounds were the distant shouts of the little boy who was still having a great time flying his kite. It *was* a beautiful day.

I tipped her chin up so she'd look at me.

"You know what? I think I'm done with word games. So, in the spirit of being *completely* up front with you, there's something I need to say." I took her hand, tracing the veins on the back of it with my thumbs. "I've suggested as much with every word, every gesture, every gift, whether expensive or handmade. What I haven't done is spoken the words themselves, but they need to be said." I held her gaze. "I love you, Aubrey Price. I'm completely and totally in love with you."

She bit her lip, and her chin trembled. I held her hand tightly and forged on before she could get a word in edgewise.

"If, after everything I've said and done over the last few weeks, you still doubt my feelings, then I'm at a loss for what else to do. I'm not about to throw everything away because our relationship is complicated. Maybe we have to go to ridiculous lengths to steal a few moments together, but where my feelings are concerned, I'm not playing games. This isn't a passing infatuation for me."

She moved around to kneel in front of me so that our eyes were level, and then she took my face in her hands. "I don't know what I've done to deserve you, but I'm so damn thankful I did it, whatever it was," she whispered. "I love you too, Daniel. You are the most thoughtful, understanding, and amazing person I've ever known."

I pulled her toward me, beaming like an idiot. "You have no idea how happy it makes me to hear you say that, poppet."

She smiled sweetly, and before she had a chance to move away, I embraced her tightly and kissed her. It had been three whole weeks since we'd kissed in my father's office. How could I have forgotten how incredible her lips felt, how quickly I lost myself when her tongue touched mine? God knew what was in store for me once we were free to be together—*completely* together.

Reality intruded a few minutes later as several drops of moisture landed on my face. "Aw, shit." I peered up through the canopy of trees at the cloudy sky. So much for our beautiful day. "Quick, take my hand."

Aubrey grabbed her backpack before clasping my fingers tightly, and we ran for the cover of a leafy maple. I sat between two gnarled roots, and she settled close beside me.

"I should've seen that coming," I said. "The clouds were rolling in before you arrived."

"It's April. What can you expect?"

"That's true. What does the calendar say this month? *'The April's in her eyes: it is love's spring—'*"

"*'And these the showers to bring it on. Be cheerful,'*" she said, finishing the line.

"Do you spend as much time staring at that calendar as I do?"

"You have no idea."

We were both quiet for a moment. Aubrey broke the silence. "So, it's your grandfather's birthday today. Did you talk to him?"

"I did. I told him I'd be bringing you back to see him soon."

She smiled wistfully. "Soon."

"Very soon, sweets."

Seventeen days, but who's counting?

I rested my head against the tree trunk. "God, I love the smell of rain in the spring."

"I think it smells like worms." She wrinkled her nose.

"You are not a fan of nature, are you?" I laughed. "I've got my work cut out for me."

"I'm not a huge fan of rain, but I don't care what season it is, or whether it's raining or hailing, as long as I'm with you, sailor."

She sat astride me. I gave myself over entirely to her kisses as her soft, warm tongue explored mine. I pulled her hips forward and she moaned into my mouth and tangled her fingers roughly in my hair. The feel of her body pressed against me roused an uncomfortable pressure against the zipper of my jeans.

"I just want to go to sleep and wake up on May first." I tried to avoid noticing the way her jeans hugged her thighs. My imagination was going into overdrive.

"Me too." She ran her thumb along my lower lip. "I swear, sometimes it's all I think about—being with you. Unfortunately, I also have two papers and five exams to write between now and then, so I guess I don't have the luxury of fantasizing all day long. But I did procrastinate a little this weekend."

She grabbed her backpack and pulled out a CD, which she handed to me.

"What's this?"

"Reciprocity."

"Wait, you made this for me?"

"I wanted to return the favor. The CD you made me is one of the most wonderful gifts I've ever received."

I touched my forehead to hers. "It wasn't too over the top?"

"It was perfect, especially all the notes you wrote. I haven't had a chance to write anything for yours, but I'll email you something. I was going to wait until I had it completely finished, but I figured I should give it to you today." She bit her lip shyly. "Call it a two month anniversary gift — assuming you were serious when you said you considered February thirteenth as our first date."

"Of course I was serious. Damn it, I was so focused on my grandfather's birthday, I forgot about our anniversary. I don't have anything for you."

"I think all the gifts you've given me more than make up for it. Besides, you did give me something today." She placed her hand on my chest, over my heart. "What else could I possibly need?"

I felt her sweet smile against my lips and knew unequivocally that the next seventeen days would be the longest of my life.

"Thank you for the CD. It means a lot that you'd go to the trouble of making it, especially considering how busy you are."

"It was actually a good diversion this weekend."

I clasped her hand. "Can I say something, sweets, and risk sounding like a bombastic ass?"

"I suppose you've earned the right to be bombastic." She grimaced. "Go ahead."

"You said you thought you were being stoic this weekend. Sometimes it seems like your stoicism borders on finely honed martyrdom."

She looked at me steadily but didn't object.

"It's okay to let people help you. You don't have to shoulder everything yourself. There are people in your life who love you and want to help you. It doesn't mean you're weak if you let them."

She sighed and set her hands on my chest again.

"You're right. I've always thought that if you love people, you shouldn't be a burden — you should be prepared to make sacrifices, even if it means you have to do without something you want. Or if it eats you alive with worry. But Matt is always telling me the same thing you just said. I'm getting better at asking for help. I did talk to Julie after class on Wednesday, and when I told Matt everything, he came with me to the pub to help look for Cara."

"I'm glad you agree because all that shit about being a burden is absurd. I want to help you. I want to talk about your plans for the summer and how I can help with your job search after you graduate." She wrinkled her nose. I could almost feel her stifling her desire to object. "But we can talk about that another time, okay? Right now, I want to celebrate my anniversary with the girl I love."

We spent God knows how long kissing and snuggling under that tree, waiting for the rain shower to stop. I felt happier than I had in ages, despite Cara's potential threat. At last, I reluctantly pulled my phone from my pocket to check the time. I had two unread messages.

"It's two thirty, love. I told Brad I'd be at his place by one to help him put up some ceiling fans. He's probably wondering where I am."

Aubrey stood up with a sigh and wiped off her knees and the back of her jeans.

"I guess I should head back to campus anyway. I have to get some more work done." Before I could speak, she said, "I'll take a taxi back. The rain's stopped. I'll be fine."

I squinted up at her. A taxi was probably the safest course of action. I stood and took out two twenty dollar bills.

"I'll let you take a taxi on one condition. Take these. One is to pay back Matt, and the other one is to get you home. Please don't argue," I said sternly.

"I wasn't going to. Thank you," she said, smiling ruefully as she slipped the money into the pocket of her sweater.

I called her a cab and then I gathered her close again. The taxi dispatch had said a car would be there in fifteen minutes, and it would take about five to walk to the road from here. Ten more minutes alone with Aubrey. I wasn't about to waste it.

Later that evening, I sat at my desk, drinking a Guinness and staring at the CD Aubrey had given me. I wanted to listen to it, but she'd said she was going to write something to accompany the songs. I'd wait until I had those words in front of me before listening. I wouldn't bother her. She had enough on her plate without worrying about writing me love notes.

I looked out the window, replaying our conversation from earlier today. Cara Switzer. Did she really know about us, or was Aubrey jumping to conclusions?

I contemplated my previous meetings with Cara, trying to recall if there had ever been an indication that she suspected anything. I came up empty. I'd flattered myself enough to think she was grateful for my help, and we did seem to get along well. We'd been meeting weekly, sometimes twice a week, since the course began, and we had another meeting coming up on Wednesday to try to sort out her most recent difficulty in time for her to hand her independent paper in on Friday.

Strangely enough, despite her ridiculous behavior in front of everyone during tutorials, she'd never overstepped boundaries during our meetings, never said or done anything inappropriate. She was puzzling, no doubt about it. Just when I thought I'd figured her out, I would discover something else about her which would set me back.

Her strange warning to Aubrey was another twist in the plot. And now she was dating Shawn Ward? What a fortuitous turn of events — one which would hopefully put an end to Shawn's persistent effort to win Aubrey's affection.

I spun around in my chair, sliding Cara's independent study essay out of the folder on my desk. No, if she knew anything, she wouldn't tell anyone, even if she did harbor some secret resentment toward Aubrey. As long as I played my cards properly, I could be assured of her silence.

CHAPTER 19

Secrets

It becomes thy oath full well,
Thou to me thy secrets tell…
(*The Winter's Tale*, Act IV, Scene 4)

My confidence crumbled at precisely five minutes to twelve on Wednesday. After sending Aubrey several reassuring emails throughout the day on Tuesday and another one before she'd left for work Wednesday morning, I had us both convinced that Cara was not the slightest threat. But when Cara bounced into class on Wednesday, Shawn in tow, she made a beeline for Trina Collins and proceeded to whisper in her ear. Trina looked directly at me, eliciting a hissed response from Cara. Unless I was mistaken, it sounded an awful lot like, "Well, *don't* look at him!" or something along those lines. Jesus.

When Aubrey walked in with Julie a minute later, I tried not to betray my mounting anxiety, but I felt certain my guilty expression would tip off everyone in the room, revealing my misdeeds in all their sordid glory. Every day, it became clearer to me that I was not cut out for subterfuge. My conscience couldn't hold up under the pressure.

As usual, Julie waved before sliding into her seat. Aubrey stole a quick glance at me, offering up a small, reassuring smile. I didn't want to worry her, so I composed myself, settling back in my chair and breathing deeply a couple of times before jotting the date and the title of the final play for study at the top of the page.

All's Well that Ends Well.

Please, God, make that true.

I thought of the folder in my bag—the file that contained information which would hopefully guard me against any damning accusations Cara might be planning to make. *Might,* I reminded myself. *This is all speculation. Nothing is certain. For that matter, she might not even know anything.*

My paranoid musings were interrupted by Martin, who hurried into the room, apologizing for keeping us waiting and quickly getting the class underway. As usual, my mind wandered. It was virtually impossible not to think about Aubrey when she was sitting right in front of me. At one point during the lecture, my eyes met Trina's, and I realized I was smiling, probably inspired by some wayward love-induced thought. My spine stiffened, but then she smiled back at me. It was a genuine and friendly smile. There was nothing veiled in her expression—nothing that said "I just heard the most disgusting secret about you."

Was I was losing my mind? Just because Cara had spoken to Trina, that didn't mean they'd been discussing my misdemeanors. A guilty conscience was a frigging scary thing. What had Macbeth said when he'd started coming unhinged in the weeks after his terrible crimes? "*O full of scorpions is my mind…*"

I pretended to read my notes, snapping back to attention as Martin ended his lecture and people started approaching the front of the room to toss their *Much Ado* analyses and sonnet papers haphazardly across the desk.

"That should keep you out of trouble for a few days," Martin said, gesturing to the papers piling up in front of me.

"Yes, no doubt."

I leafed through a few. There were no names—just student numbers. Perfect. Glancing up, I saw Aubrey and Julie coming forward. I purposely looked away from the pile and continued to chat with Martin so that I wouldn't even see the title of Aubrey's paper, or Julie's for that matter. I didn't want anything undermining my objectivity.

"Once you've finished those, bring them in to the office," Martin said. "If I'm not there, leave them with the secretary. Give me a call if you have any issues."

I shuffled the papers and slid them in the side pocket of my bag, watching as Aubrey and Julie walked out of the room without a backward glance. I knew Aubrey was pouring on the pretense of disinterest in light of Cara's recent threat, but watching the person you love leave without a hint of a goodbye was fucking heart-rending. But then Cara was there, distracting me from my disappointment, rushing toward the front of the room with Shawn.

"Are we still on for two fifteen in the Arbor Room?" she asked.

"Absolutely. See you then," I replied, watching as they left, holding hands and whispering conspiratorially.

What are you up to?

I took a moment to compose myself and then went to the seminar room.

Two more classes and three more tutorial sessions. I just have to survive until Monday without completely losing my shit.

As I sat across from Cara later that afternoon, I contemplated my circumstances. If she thought Aubrey and I were together, then she must have figured Aubrey would have told me about their conversation. And yet there we sat, drinking coffee and exchanging fucking pleasantries. The situation was beyond screwed up. It was frigging surreal.

What I wanted more than anything was to fire questions at her.

What do you know? What was that warning to Aubrey all about? And what was with all the whispering in class today? Are you planning to ruin me? What the hell is going on?

But I wasn't about to reveal my hand — or my fear. No, I had to go about this carefully, maintaining the upper hand without showing any malice or giving her cause for defensiveness. I had to keep up the friendly but professional demeanor I'd used in all of our previous meetings.

"So, you and Mr. Ward are an item now?" I asked, trying to start things off casually before launching into full academic mode.

She blushed to the tips of her ears, taking me completely by surprise. I didn't know she had it in her.

"Um, yeah, I guess so," she said, playing with her coffee cup.

"That's great." I hid my amusement behind my mug and took a long swig. "He's a good guy."

"I know, right? He really is."

I crossed my hands in front of me. It was time to get down to brass tacks.

"And how did things go with your mom this weekend?"

She rolled her eyes. "Oh my God, it was super awkward, but she understood, I guess. I told her what you said—that thing about preparing the child for the path, not the path for the child. Remember?"

I nodded. What else do you tell a student whose mother insists on being *so* involved in helping her daughter revise an essay that she renders parts of the paper incomprehensible to the one who's supposed to have written it?

"I'm sure your mother meant well, but Professor Brown would have noticed the unique writing style of those two paragraphs. I don't know how understanding he would've been if he'd discovered your mother's involvement. This was a form of academic dishonesty, even if it wasn't your intention to deceive. He might have questioned your other course work or even pursued the issue with your other profs. I must admit, that thought even crossed my mind…"

I was embellishing, mainly for effect. I'd never had any intention of reporting her. I genuinely wanted to see her learn something from the process. I, of all people, understood the significance of second chances. But now there were new parameters to consider. I wanted her to feel the tenuousness of her situation and see me as her redeemer. The timing of her academic misstep couldn't have been better.

"My mom honestly hasn't done anything like this before," she said. "She helps me study for tests—like, talking about the books and stuff. But I think she could tell I was totally freaked about this essay. I let her get too into it. When I told her how stupid I'd looked when I couldn't even answer your questions about what those two paragraphs meant, she felt really bad. She told me to thank you for giving me this chance and not reporting this to Professor Brown."

"Tell your mother I have no desire to see someone lose their entire academic career over one mistake," I said. "Now, let's take a look at what you've come up with in your rewrite."

She sat back, ill at ease, while I read the new draft of her essay. It was an interesting paper, very different from her previous drafts.

"I like this angle," I said. "You've almost entirely reworked your thesis. It's got a sociological feel to it."

She shrugged self-consciously. "Remember you said I should write what I know? I'm not great with Shakespeare and the imagery and stuff, but I know sociology, so it kinda made sense to me to treat the characters and their problems like case studies, you know what I mean?"

"Absolutely. No, this is good." I turned to the third page of the essay. "I like what you've done with *Romeo and Juliet*—the way you've drawn analogies with contemporary issues. The conclusions you've drawn here are interesting too—your observations about the way love is often impeded by social norms." I looked over at her. "You believe what you've said here?"

"Yeah. I guess I'm a stupid romantic or something." She turned crimson again.

I smiled. "I don't think there's anything wrong with being a romantic, Miss Switzer."

"You don't?"

"Of course I don't. I happen to agree." I paused, choosing my words carefully. "Love is elusive at the best of times, don't you think? If you find someone with whom you might be happy, it's hard to accept the notion that, as you said in your paper, social codes—rules—might stand in the way of people pursuing that happiness."

"That's exactly what I meant," she said.

A beat passed as we looked at each other. A moment of silent understanding.

She knows. No doubt about it.

I cleared my throat and flipped through the last few pages.

"Well, I'd say you're in good shape to upload this to the plagiarism detection web site in plenty of time before Friday."

She sighed in relief. I reached over to my laptop bag and pulled the folder out, sliding the photocopied pages onto the table.

"It's very satisfying to look at this now and see how you've improved."

"What's that?" she asked, leaning over the table.

"Oh, it's just a copy of your last draft. I kept one for my files. One of the most rewarding things about being a TA is seeing the growth of students. Those light bulb moments—when students come to an understanding of something? Those are my favorite."

She looked at the essay, panic darting across her face. I continued to gaze at her impassively.

I really do love a good epiphany.

"Oh, don't worry," I said, striving to keep my tone warm and reassuring and not at all threatening. "I have no intention of sharing any of this with Professor Brown. I think you've dealt admirably with this dilemma. It's been a real learning experience for you. Had you followed through with the submission of this draft—" I tapped the papers in front of me "—we'd be having a different conversation, but you've worked hard to do the right thing. Please don't worry." I slipped the essay back into the folder.

Insurance.

"Well, um, okay," she stammered, watching as the damning evidence disappeared into the side pocket of my laptop bag.

"Really, there's nothing to worry about. I won't tell anyone about this. Not *anyone*," I said, emphasizing the last word and looking at her intently. "As far as I'm concerned, there's no harm done. This'll be our little secret. Deal?"

She looked across the table at me and stuck her hand out. She wanted to shake on it. I played along, more than happy to oblige. I grasped her hand firmly and held her gaze as we shook hands.

"So, this will all stay between us?" she asked.

I nodded. "Absolutely. All of it."

"Deal," she agreed.

The relief I felt after Cara left the Arbor Room was so palpable, I had to share it with Aubrey. An email wouldn't suffice. I went to the Hart House quad, eager for some fresh air. Without hesitating, I dialed her number. She answered on the third ring.

"Well, hello there, handsome. The rules have gone right out the window, I see?"

I let out a huge breath. Was it possible I'd been holding that lungful of air since two o'clock?

"You'll have to forgive me. I've had a stressful day. I—well, to be honest, I just needed to hear your voice. I'm sorry if I'm putting you in a difficult position."

"It's okay. How did your tutorial go?"

"It was fine. But I called to tell you that I met with Cara afterward. She just left, actually."

"Really? Shit, you didn't confront her, did you?"

"No, I didn't. We had a scheduled meeting to go over her paper one more time before Friday, but I think it's safe to say that we have an understanding. I'd be amazed if she said anything to anyone. Seriously. Put it out of your mind."

"I have no idea why you're so confident, but I have to admit, I think you're right. I can't imagine her throwing you under the bus. She may hate me, but she really likes you, and if she wanted to get at me for whatever reason, you'd end up as collateral damage if she reported us. I don't think she's prepared to sacrifice you to hurt me."

"Well, that's piqued my curiosity. What the hell are you basing that comment on?"

"I can't tell you."

"Oh, no you don't. No secrets."

She paused, and I listened to the dead air.

"Aubrey?"

"Yeah, I'm here. Look, there have to be exceptions. What if it's a secret that can't hurt you? There must be *some* things I'm allowed to keep from you. You seem to know something about Cara that you're not telling me."

"But that's different. It would be a conflict of interest. As a TA, I can't tell you what I know."

"Oh. Well, if you want to put it that way, then as a *student* I can't tell you what *I* know. But I promise this secret can't hurt you. In fact, I think you'll be pleasantly surprised. It's your turn to trust *me*, now. Do you?"

I rubbed my eyes in frustration, but I was also strangely intrigued. I had to believe she wouldn't withhold important information from me again, especially if it could affect my reputation or academic career.

"Yes, poppet, I trust you."

"Good. Then it's decided. You'll find out soon enough. Until then, you just need to have some patience."

"Patience? I'm really beginning to hate that word."

"Do your best, okay, sweet knees?" she asked.

"All right. Look, I should go. Will you email me later? Something to look forward to while I'm marking?"

"Of course. I'll drop you a line after dinner." I heard her take a deep breath. "I love you, Daniel."

I closed my eyes as her words washed over me.

"I love you too, sweetheart. I wish I could come over there right now and show you how much."

Tell me I can. Please tell me I can come get you and take you home with me—

Aubrey interrupted this errant thought, grounding me firmly in reality. "You can in fifteen days," she said. "I can be a slow learner, though. You might have to show me *several* times."

Oh, you can count on that.

CHAPTER 20

All's Well

Our wagon is prepared, and time revives us:
All's well that ends well; still the fine's the crown;
Whate'er the course, the end is the renown.
(*All's Well that Ends Well*, Act IV, Scene 4)

I had mixed feelings as I walked to Hart House for the final Friday tutorial. We'd been through a lot together as a group, especially with the loss of Mary at the beginning of the term. These Friday tutorials had been the highlight of my week for months now, and I'd be sad to see this group go. This feeling was compounded ten-fold as I sat at the table with everyone.

"Well, here we are. Our last tutorial, then one more class and you're finished. How do you feel?" I quickly took attendance before settling back in my chair.

"Weird," Trina said. "I can't believe I'm almost done with university."

"I remember that feeling," I said. "The thought of entering the real world was so terrifying that I decided to stay in school. I may never graduate."

This wasn't a joke. Sometimes the doctoral process seemed interminable.

"I don't think I could afford to get my master's, even if I wanted to," Vince said. "I'm so in debt."

A few people around the room nodded in agreement. Aubrey looked sideways at Julie. No knee tapping today. Perhaps they'd made a pact to be more discreet than usual. I noted the weariness in her eyes. She'd mentioned a potential all-nighter in an email the day before. The end of semester crunch was taking its toll.

"The sooner we get this tutorial over with, the closer you'll be to finishing." I flipped open the text and scanned my notes. "Let's start with genre. *All's Well that Ends Well.* Comedy or tragedy?" I opened the question up for debate. The answers were predictable.

"Neither." This from Shawn.

"Both." Neil's rebuttal.

"Neither and both," I mused. "That's an interesting dilemma."

Julie frowned. "I don't know — it's like Professor Brown was saying today, it's a problem play, right? I suppose that's part of the problem, trying to pigeon-hole it."

"I agree, Miss Harper. It is hard to categorize. It's neither a typical tragedy, nor a definitive comedy."

"I came across some interesting critiques in doing my paper," Aubrey said. "Shakespeare might have been experimenting — trying out a new form or structure when he wrote this. The themes and ideas he's exploring in *All's Well* predate some nineteenth-century drama — with female protagonists pushing the envelope and the conclusions of the plots being open-ended. Audiences back then didn't care for the headstrong female."

Even when she was wiped out, she was still able to rise to the occasion.

"You're absolutely right, Miss Price," I said. "Jacobean audiences found Helena too forward in her comments about sexuality and her frustration with the lack of control over her own fate."

Aubrey's tired eyes came alive with enthusiasm. "Helena does seem to set a precedent for Ibsen's heroines if you think about it. Even Strindberg's and Chekhov's female protagonists. Shakespeare was so ahead of his time in his thinking."

This was another thing I'd miss about tutorials — seeing Aubrey's mind ticking over during these discussions. This was the last time I'd get to watch her in action.

"So, Shakespeare's not a misogynist, Miss Price?" I asked.

She shook her head, eyes sparkling mischievously.

"I'm so glad he's off the hook. And you make some excellent points." I looked around the table. "That's one of the reasons you don't see many staged productions of this play. In the seventeenth, eighteenth, and nineteenth centuries, Helena was a very difficult character to sell. Many critics still don't buy the way the king and the countess characterize her as wholly virtuous given the things she says and the way she uses the bed-trick to fool Bertram into consummating their marriage. She's a perplexing character, especially on paper."

"Daniel, are you saying that this play isn't fully realized until it reaches the stage?" Aubrey looked at me with a cheeky grin. I'd never forget this line — the basis for our first clash of opinions.

"Yes, Miss Price. I suppose I *am* saying that, and this time I don't think I'll let you talk me out of it. It takes a very fine actress to reconcile the two distinct aspects of Helena's nature — her quiet virtue and her willfulness and sensuality — but, done properly, the play works much better on the stage than on the page."

Aubrey may have had a ready rebuttal, but she didn't have a chance to share it because Shawn elbowed Cara and said, "Hey, Cara, it's that thing you were talking about yesterday. What did you call it?"

Cara scowled at him. Apparently she didn't want to share. I wondered if she'd shown him her paper. She'd made some insightful sociological observations about the relationships in *All's Well*. Did I dare ask? Oh, what the hell. Last chance to have a little fun.

"Something interesting you could share, Miss Switzer?"

"Go on, Cara. Tell him," Shawn said. "It *is* interesting."

"Well." She looked reluctantly around the table. "From a sociological angle, you'd call it the Madonna-whore complex," she said.

"Hey, I've heard of that," Vince said. "A lady in the streets, but a freak in the sheets."

I shot him a look. He really seemed to enjoy courting castration. Trina sat up. She ignored Vince's comment and looked at Cara.

"Right! Feminists argue that it's wrong for women to reject their sexuality because it validates the societal view that a woman who is comfortable with her sexuality is a slut, right?"

"Yeah, basically," Cara said. "Sexuality is one of the layers that should be, like, integrated into her personality. If you say a woman can only be sexy in private but she should be all lady-like in public, that creates this thing, it's a sociology term, a *bifurcation* of her identity, so she can never really be herself."

Around the table, jaws dropped as, one by one, Cara's classmates struggled to come to grips with the fact that she'd just used a couple of four-syllable words and seemed to know what they meant.

I wasn't surprised. We'd had several discussions about sociology in the last couple of weeks, and I was becoming aware that the girl wasn't stupid — she just didn't intuitively understand Shakespeare and exacerbated the problem by disguising her literary ineptness as ditziness. But Julie and Aubrey were stunned, looking as if Cara had just told them that the world *was* flat after all.

I glanced at Shawn. He was giving Vince an I-told-you-so look. Perhaps he'd also discovered that Cara's brain wasn't *actually* pea-sized. Cara clamped her mouth shut, seeming to have surprised herself in addition to everyone around the table.

"That's a really astute comment, Miss Switzer," I said. "This sociological lens you've been using to examine Shakespeare's works is an effective analytical approach. And, yes, a feminist lens works really well here too, Miss Collins."

"I don't know about all that," Lindsay said. "All I know is the characters are weird. I don't get why Helena wants to be with that Bertram guy even after he's so nasty to her. She's sorta lame."

"It's no different than a girl having a major crush on a guy and seeing past all his faults because she's so infatuated," Julie said.

Lindsay shrugged. "Whatever. I still think it sucks that he's forced to marry her and it's not till the very end that he sees that she might be worth his time."

Cara turned to look at Lindsay. "Sometimes guys are so dense, they totally can't even see what's right in front of them."

Lindsay smiled and raised an eyebrow. Shawn rolled his eyes and swatted Cara's hand. How entertaining. Out came the dirty laundry, and thank the Lord, for once it wasn't mine.

"And they had sex for the first time without him even knowing it was her! He honestly thought he was with that Diana woman. That's the most unromantic thing ever," Cara said, this time responding, true to form, by seizing on the romance angle.

"Maybe that's why she's still into him at the end, though," Vince suggested. "She does say he was great in bed."

"God, shut up, Vince! You're such a knob," Trina complained.

"Well, she does," he protested indignantly.

Trina had apparently reached the end of her tether. Her face was almost as bright as her magenta hair. Maybe the pent-up stress of the week was getting to me, but I couldn't help bursting out laughing. Everyone turned to me, as surprised by my outburst as they'd been by Cara earlier.

"I'm sorry," I said. "Phew, stressful week. I needed that." I rubbed my eyes and looked at Vince. "Comic relief is definitely your forte. Oddly enough, you have a point. If anyone wants to verify Mr. Costa's claims, check Act Four, Scene Four. Helena definitely enjoyed consummating the marriage."

Vince smiled and shrugged. "Sorry, Trina. Guess I'm not talking outta my butt this time."

She rolled her eyes and crossed her arms. I looked at my watch and scanned the table. There was plenty of time left, but the tone of the discussion had gone downhill, and I wasn't sure I'd be able to get things back on track, even if I wanted to.

"I know you're all stressed with final papers and exams coming up. What I'd suggest at this point is getting your notes in order and making sure you set up an appointment with either Professor Brown or me if you need to work anything through before the exam. Would everyone be okay with wrapping up early?"

Of course there was a unanimous nodding of heads and murmured assent.

"In that case, let me just say it's been a really interesting semester. I know it's been difficult, with the loss of Mary, but I've enjoyed my time with you and learned a great deal through this process. I wish you all good luck in your final exams and whatever the future brings."

I expected them to all start packing up and pushing their chairs back, but no one moved. Aubrey and Julie looked at each other. A few people glanced over at Cara. She stood up self-consciously.

"Um, before we go, Daniel, there's something I wanted to say. It's kinda on behalf of all of us." She reached into her bag and pulled out a small wrapped gift with a card attached. "We got you something. Well, my mom got it, but we all chipped in, and everyone signed the card, and, well, yeah, it's just to say thanks. We had a good semester. And you helped us a lot. Well, I know you helped *me* a lot. So, yeah."

She walked around the table to hand me the present. I was utterly shocked.

"Thank you." I took the gift and sat there feeling awkward and strangely ill. "This is, well, unexpected. Should I open it now?"

Everyone nodded encouragement. I removed the card from the envelope. It was full of signatures along with some personal messages. I would read them later. I ripped open the wrapping of the gift and found a small box, "Sheaffer" inscribed on the top. Nestled inside the silk lining was a brushed silver pen, mechanical pencil, and letter opener set. My name was engraved on the side of the pen. The pencil and the handle of the letter opener were similarly engraved. A lump formed in my throat.

I shook my head and looked up and down the table. Aubrey smiled encouragingly, probably sensing how overwhelmed I was. Suddenly I realized that this is what she'd been keeping from me—the secret that, as a *student*, she hadn't wanted me to know. This is what Cara had been up to all week. Collecting donations.

"Everyone, this is…really…very nice. Thank you so much. And thank you for organizing this, Miss Switzer. I don't know what to say."

"Well, since you're speechless, can I make a request?" Julie asked.

"Yes, of course," I replied.

"Could you lose the whole last name bit before we go?"

I laughed. "Too much?" I looked around at the vociferous nodding. "My apologies. This was my first real experience as a teacher's assistant. The formality seemed like a good idea at the time. I suppose there was as much of a learning curve here for me as there was for all of you. So, yes, *Julie*, I think I can oblige."

"Ah, thank you, that's so much better!" Julie sighed and relaxed back in her chair, eliciting laughter from her peers. Aubrey clasped Julie's hand tightly and smiled.

"Oh, and speaking of my failings." I reached into my bag and pulled out a large manila envelope. "I almost forgot. The English department has asked you to fill out these questionnaires to give me some feedback on my performance as TA. It's not mandatory, and they're anonymous, but if you'd like to complete one and bring it to class on Monday, Professor Brown will collect them. Try to be nice. Think about all those good things Cara just said, okay?"

I handed the pile to Neil, who took one and passed on the remaining sheets. Everyone packed up as the pile of questionnaires traveled around the table. One by one, people wished me a good weekend, and Neil actually shook my hand before exiting. At the door, Aubrey subtly bobbed her head at the hallway — an invitation to leave together. I shook my head, just as inconspicuously, and she sighed in frustration.

She tossed her bag over her shoulder and reluctantly followed Julie toward the door. The only people left were Cara, Shawn, Lindsay, and Vince. I interrupted them as they headed out.

"Cara? May I have a word?"

"Sure. I'll catch up with you guys back at the Kap house."

"You want me to wait out here for you?" Shawn offered.

"No, that's okay. Go ahead."

She waved them off then turned to look at me.

"I wanted to reiterate my gratitude," I said. "For the gift. It was very thoughtful."

"It's okay. Everyone said it was a good idea. No one needed to be talked into it or anything like that."

"You've made a lot of progress this term. You should be proud of what you've accomplished."

"I meant what I said before. I know you went out of your way to help me. I'm sure I was starting to, like, get on your nerves or something. This stuff doesn't come easy for me like it does for people like Shawn, or Aubrey…"

Aubrey. Her name hung in the air between us.

"Yes, well, I suppose that makes your achievement all the more satisfying. You've, ah, you've worked hard for it." I was struggling to speak coherently.

She shrugged. "Thanks."

She watched me expectantly while I tried not to betray my mental gymnastics, sorting through the potential consequences of what I was about to do.

Oh, fuck it.

I opened the flap of my bag and took out the folder.

"Look, Miss Switzer — Cara. I've been thinking about your essay. I hope you realize I had no intention of showing it to anyone. In fact, there's no need for me to hang on to it. So, here." I pulled the essay from the folder and handed it to her. "You can have it back."

She held it in her hands, looking down at it for a moment as a voice in the back of my mind shrieked, "*Noooooooo, what have you done?*" But it was too late. It—whatever *it* was—my fate perhaps—was in her hands now. Literally.

She rolled it up and curled her hand around it. "Thanks. That does make me feel a bit better. Well, I guess I should go," she said, taking a few steps backward. "Have a good weekend."

"You too," I barely managed to choke out.

I spent the rest of the afternoon castigating myself for giving Cara her essay back, but as I sat at my desk that evening, gazing at the engraved pen set, I couldn't help thinking my worries were completely unfounded. Would she have gone to all the effort of collecting money and buying me a gift if she was harboring ill will against me?

When I opened my email account and found a message from Aubrey—the one I'd been waiting almost a week for—all thoughts of Cara evaporated immediately. I knew as soon as I read the subject line what was in store for me:

From: Miss_V
To: Jung Willman
Date: Fri, Apr 17, 8:47:56 PM
Subject: "Wilt thou hear some music, my sweet love?"

Okay, mister. You seemed a little melancholy today at the end of class, and I decided you must need a little pick me up. So, grab that CD, make yourself comfy, and open the attachment. I hope you enjoy listening to this as much as I enjoyed the one you made for me.

Love & hot, wet kisses,
Your Poppet

After being momentarily distracted by the thought of Aubrey's kisses, I found the disc and inserted it into the CD drive of my laptop.

I opened the attachment and flaked out on the couch, alternately closing my eyes to listen to the songs and reading the notes she'd included. Her words took me on a little journey through our relationship thus far, this time from her perspective.

Listening to that CD was easily the best seventy-five minutes of my week. The songs she'd picked were a perfect escape. In fact, the message she'd written to accompany the last song filled me with so much hope that I could barely contain my desire to steal her away somewhere.

I love Ingrid Michaelson, Daniel, but I may regret ending the CD with the song "Overboard." In fact, I already feel my stoic pride-or whatever the hell it is that makes me so stubborn and determined to do everything for myself-rearing its ugly head and trying to beat me back down. I'm choosing to ignore it. Like Ingrid says in the song, you can catch me, Daniel. I will let you. That's how much I love you. I hope you understand the significance of those words and how hard they are for me to say.

All my love, Aubrey.

The CD finished. The words ended. I wanted both to go on forever. Now I understood why Aubrey had said the CD I'd made for her had been the best gift she'd ever received.

You can catch me.

Did this mean that she would let me help her? Allow me to make her life easier? I snatched my phone off the coffee table, determined to get clarification, but as I passed my thumb across the display, I realized the inadvisability of doing that. This admission wouldn't have been easy. No. I wouldn't push the issue. I'd let things be.

That didn't mean I couldn't call her, though. If she was going to let me catch her, it wouldn't hurt to remind her that I was there, right beside her, behind her, wherever she needed me to be.

CHAPTER 21

Passions and Plots

O world, thy slippery turns!…so, fellest foes,
Whose passions and whose plots have broke their sleep…
(*Coriolanus*, Act IV, Scene 4)

J ulie put her hand on mine and squeezed it gently. "You okay?"
"I'm fine. I just wish Daniel would get here already."

I looked over her shoulder at the courtyard doors and checked
the time again.

"He'll be here soon. I doubt he'll drag this last tutorial out, especially knowing you're up here waiting."

"You're right."

I sat back in my chair and tried to enjoy the sun on my face.

"What exactly did you tell him in your email this morning?" she
asked.

"I just said I had some good news and some weird news. I didn't
want to freak him out by saying bad news…"

I lost my train of thought as Daniel emerged through the doors
and began walking across the courtyard. He was wearing his sunglasses and had a jacket slung over his shoulder, sexy as hell.

"God, I love those jeans," I whispered.

Julie smiled. "Can't say I blame you. He definitely puts the 'tight ass' in TA."

I snorted with laughter. "Don't I know it. He makes my ovaries ache."

"That sounds like PMS to me." She chuckled.

I swatted her leg, shifting my chair around so that Daniel could sit between us. He put a take-out cup of coffee on the table and stowed his bag under his seat.

"Do I dare ask what you two are giggling about?" he asked.

I shook my head. "Not a good idea."

"Yes, I get that distinct impression. Well, this was a great idea." He scanned the Hart House quad. "What a beautiful day."

"Yeah, Julie thought it might be quieter out here, too," I explained.

"Good point." He sipped his coffee and looked back and forth between us. "So? How do you feel? That's it. No more classes."

"I don't think it's sunk in yet," I said.

"It will. When you realize you don't know what the fuck you're doing with your life, it'll sink in fast."

Julie cocked her head.

"What?" he asked.

"You and the F-bombs. It's so not you."

"Julie," I said, patting her hand. "He's a foul-mouthed horn dog. Might as well accept that and move on."

"Thank you, sweetheart," he said, tilting his head and smiling graciously.

"You're welcome, dear." I beamed back at him sweetly, batting my eyelashes.

"You two are so adorable," Julie whispered. "I can't wait until you can be a real couple."

I shrugged. "Meh, whatevs."

He narrowed his eyes. "I'll make you eat those words."

My imagination quickly whipped up a variety of scenarios in which Daniel made me do all sorts of naughty things. "I look forward to it."

"Ahem, excuse me?" Julie knocked on the table. "I'm still here."

"You're right, Julie," Daniel said. "Aubrey gets carried away from time to time. I apologize on her behalf."

I rolled my eyes and settled back in my chair. The easygoing banter felt good. In fact, I was so relaxed, I'd almost forgotten the reason we were meeting. Daniel had not.

"As much as I'd love to sit here and shoot the shit for the rest of the afternoon, I've been on pins and needles all day thinking about your cryptic message. What the hell's going on?"

"You should tell him about your mom's email," Julie suggested.

"Okay, the good news," I said. "My mom wrote to tell me she and my dad are paying for my trip overseas — as a graduation present."

Daniel's face lit up. "That's amazing! You, of course, accepted this gift very graciously?" he asked, raising his eyebrow.

"I did my best," I said.

"Good. You must be relieved. I know you were worried about paying them back."

I tried to decide if he was getting in a subtle dig about my stubborn refusal to accept money from him, but he looked entirely sincere. I decided to take his comment at face value.

"It's a weight off my shoulders."

"No doubt. So, let's hear the weird news. You got a strange email, you said?"

Julie looked down at her hands in her lap, as if she felt like she was intruding on our conversation. I didn't feel that way at all. I was infinitely more comfortable with her there. I turned to Daniel and lowered my voice, which was completely unnecessary, but since Cara's warning I'd felt more paranoid than ever.

"I got an email from the English department telling me to go over there today to make an appointment. They want to interview me for some reason. My first instinct was that they're calling me in to question me about something to do with you — with us."

Daniel visibly blanched. The blood actually drained from his face. He took his sunglasses off and rubbed his eyes wearily.

"I wanted to wait until I knew more about why they want to see me," I said, "but I knew you'd be upset if I didn't tell you right away."

"No, of course, I'm glad you told me. You have no idea what it's about?"

"I made an appointment for the interview after class. Julie came with me. I asked the secretary what it was about. She said she makes appointments, but she's not privy to the reasons behind them."

"I thought maybe it had something to do with her GPA," Julie suggested. "You know, maybe they want to meet with students who are probably going to graduate with distinction —"

"But it's the *graduate* office, Julie, not the undergraduate office, so that doesn't make sense," I pointed out.

Daniel put his glasses back on and sighed. "When did you schedule it for?"

"Wednesday," I said. "After I finish work, I'm heading straight there."

"Well, don't waste time and energy worrying. I'm sure it's nothing to be concerned about."

"Are you just saying that to try to make me feel better?" I asked him.

He smiled wryly. "Yes and no," he said. "I have no clue why they want to see you, but don't leap to conclusions and start fabricating all sorts of crazy scenarios." He paused briefly. "That's *my* job." Even though he was smiling, I got the sense he was trying to placate me.

"But what if something really awful *does* come out of it?"

"Let's cross that bridge if we get to it," he said. "You need to focus on your exams. Your first one is Friday, right?"

"Yeah. I had to rearrange my work schedule for the next two weeks. I feel bad for Gisele — my exams totally mess up her routine, but I can't do much about it."

"And you're going to stick it out there until July even though you don't have to pay for your trip?"

"I have no plans to leave. I'd say things are pretty much back to normal with your dad. We're getting along great, so July will be a breeze," I explained.

"Mmm, we'll see," he said pensively. He sipped his coffee.

"Well, that was cryptic." I looked at Julie. She just shrugged.

"Sorry. I don't mean to be mysterious. I guess I've got a lot on my mind. Speaking of which, I can't stay long. Martin wants to sort out tutorial grades, participation, attendance, that sort of thing. He's expecting me any time."

Julie cleared her throat conspicuously. "I'm gonna scoot and give you two a few minutes alone. Is that okay, do you think?"

"I think it's fine," Daniel said. "I'll be leaving shortly, anyway. Thanks for being here today, Julie."

"No problem. Okay, if I don't see you before, maybe I'll see you at the exam?" she asked as she packed up her bag.

"I might drop by for a bit, I'm not sure. Once the exam is over, well, I imagine I'll see you then." He glanced at me, his mouth turning up in a small, secret smile. God, it was great to hear him say that.

I stood up to hug Julie.

"Let me know what happens, okay? And if you get any inside scoops on the exam, text me." She nodded her head at Daniel with a mischievous grin.

"She's the best," I said as Julie walked away. "Somehow having her here for a bit made me feel less like I'm letting your father down. That probably doesn't make any sense." I bit my lip. "So, are you worried about this interview thing?"

"I'm sure there's a logical explanation. Unfortunately, I don't know what it is."

"You don't think Cara said something?"

He laughed cynically and took his glasses off, rubbing his eyes once more.

"What?" I asked.

He shook his head. "Oh, God. Nothing. If this plot gets any thicker, you'll be able to stand a spoon up in it, that's all." He sighed. "Will you call me on Wednesday when you finish up with the interview? I know you've been avoiding calling, but I'd like to know what's going on as soon as possible."

He was right. With the exception of the panicky messages I'd left him when he'd disappeared for the weekend, I hadn't phoned him once since I'd promised his father I'd cease contact. It was ridiculous at this point not to agree to call him. It was difficult spending time with Dean Grant, knowing I was going back on my word, but it was harder still being cut off from Daniel. I'd simply have to live with the stirrings of my conscience. I couldn't have it both ways.

"Of course I will."

"Good. Thank you. I don't know how else I'll get through the next ten days," he whispered. "If I thought I couldn't talk to you…" He shook his head, reaching for his bag and rifling through it.

"Ten days," I said. "What are we going to do?"

"I've been trying not to think about it." He handed me a large envelope. "But maybe this will help."

"What's this now?" I sighed.

"God, woman, you are so infuriating!" he said in a tone of mock exasperation.

"Okay, don't get all Huffy McHufferson."

His brows shot up with amusement.

I laughed and shook the envelope. It was open at the top, so I peeked inside. It was filled with numerous smaller envelopes.

"There are ten in there," he said. "They're dated. You get to open one every day between now and next Thursday, starting tomorrow."

"Really?" My heart lifted a bit. "You're so thoughtful, you know that?"

"Not really," he said. "I'm actually a selfish bastard. This is to make sure you don't forget about me while we're apart."

I chuckled. "Don't even joke about that. That's not remotely possible." I glanced into the envelope again. "I'm so excited to have something to look forward to every day." I stowed it in my bag. "But I don't have anything for you. What will you have to look forward to?"

He licked his lips and made a great show of staring hungrily at my mouth before slowly lowering his eyes to my chest and then my legs.

"Don't worry, Aubrey. I think I have *plenty* to look forward to."

I was early. Too early. It was too late to walk around the block or something to burn off nervous energy, so I sat in the chair in the English department office waiting room. I clasped my hands together and tried to remain calm. It didn't work.

I thought back to my morning and the meeting I'd had with Dean Grant. He'd been awarded the provost position and was leaving Vic. He was thrilled; I was not. The student residence advisor, Elaine Armstrong, had been named his successor, and I was not a fan of her. Matt had experienced her wrath in his first year over alcohol infractions, and she'd been less than compassionate. In fact, she'd been a downright bitch. Working with her would not be pleasant — I was almost sure of it.

I groaned. Thinking about Elaine Armstrong was not inspiring calmness. I needed a distraction. I pulled my backpack onto my lap and fished around for the two envelopes from Daniel I'd already opened.

I took out Tuesday's card. A photograph Daniel had taken of Professor Brown's classroom was attached to the front. I peeked inside to re-read the Shakespearean quote he'd included with a comment underneath:

"Did my heart love till now?"
I'm with Romeo on this one. My unsuspecting heart didn't
know what hit it that day. Nine days, poppet. I love you.
~D

I ran my fingers across his words, marveling at the way he could communicate so much with the smallest gesture. He remembered everything; our earliest meetings and exchanges were just as etched in his mind as they were in mine. I popped the card back into my bag and took out the one I'd opened this morning before heading off to work. On this one, he'd attached a picture of the old seminar room to the front of the card.

I gazed at his accompanying words.

I was inexplicably drawn to you from the first moment I
saw you in Professor Brown's classroom, but everything
became clear when we sat together in that seminar room.
You were the beautiful, warm, outspoken, intelligent, sexy
woman I'd been looking for. I sat beside you, looked into
your eyes, and thought, "Well, there you are. Where've
you been all this time?" Eight days. So very close. ~D

I was snapped back to reality by the sound of the door opening along the corridor. A man's voice carried down the hall as he concluded a meeting with someone. The secretary summoned me, and I pushed the envelopes to the very bottom of the bag as I walked, almost crashing into Cara Switzer as she rounded the corner, exiting the office I was about to enter.

I froze.

I scanned her face, took in her raised eyebrows and small smile.

"Cara? What are you doing here?"

"Hi, Aubrey."

"Aubrey Price?" The man in the office doorway peered out.

"Yes, that's me, I'm just—"

"Good luck," Cara whispered. And then she was gone.

Good luck? What the hell for? I turned and made my way unsteadily to the office.

"Aubrey, I'm Aaron O'Connor, the teaching assistant coordinator for the English department. Please come in and have a seat."

This guy was the *TA* coordinator? Crap almighty. I sat down, my mouth suddenly dry and my pulse pounding in my ears. Was this how Daniel felt right before he had an anxiety attack? Was I about to have one? I wiped my sweaty palms on my jeans, waiting as the man before me, whose name I'd already forgotten, jotted notes on a piece of paper and flipped through some pages.

I tried to appear nonchalant as he lowered his pen and leaned across his desk. He had unnerving, beady eyes. I focused on the place where his shaggy eyebrows met at the bridge of his nose.

"I won't keep you long, Aubrey. I just have a few questions about Daniel Grant, the TA for the Topics in Shakespeare course you've taken this semester."

I tried to wet my lips, but my glands seemed to have forgotten how to create saliva.

"Sure. Okay," I said, trying to sound casual.

"I've read over a handful of the questionnaires submitted by the class, but I wanted to get a little more information—assemble a more detailed picture of how he did."

"Is Daniel in trouble?" As soon as the words were out of my mouth I wanted to stuff them back in.

"Why would you say that?" he asked.

"Oh, no reason. I've just never been interviewed about a TA before." That was better—a reasonable response. "And I like him. I mean, he did a good job."

God, woman, don't you know when enough is enough? Just shut your pie hole and let the man talk!

"I see. I certainly got the impression from most of the questionnaires that he was well-liked, with only a few exceptions. You got along well with him?"

"I guess so," I said vaguely, shrinking into myself. I couldn't decide what would be worse for Daniel, saying I liked him or saying he'd merely been tolerable.

"Did you find his evaluation of your work fair?"

Beady Eyes picked up his pen, ready to write down whatever I said. I'd have to be careful. I gathered my thoughts and did my best to tell a semblance of what I, as a student, saw as the truth. This was essential; if I started blatantly lying, I was sure to turn beet red and start stammering like an idiot.

"He took evaluations seriously," I said. "He was very concerned about impartiality. And if you ever had an issue with a mark or a question about something, he was more than happy to meet to discuss concerns."

I felt good about this answer. It was all true.

"And *did* you ever have cause to meet about an evaluation?"

Again I told the truth. "Yes. Once."

"And the basis for this meeting?"

"I was confused about the mark on a test that Daniel had evaluated." Once more, this was not a lie. So far so good.

He responded to my answer by raising a shaggy brow — or, rather, one side of his unibrow.

"So, you met with him so you could question him about his assessment?"

"Yes."

"And what was the issue, if you don't mind me asking?"

"There were two marks on my test, and I wasn't really sure what that meant. Professor Brown had changed the mark on the test."

"I'm not sure I'm following."

"Daniel had taken off a couple of points. Professor Brown didn't agree, and he ended up assigning me a perfect grade."

"Oh, I see. Would you have objected to this grade Daniel assigned if Professor Brown hadn't changed it?"

Wow. How was I supposed to respond to that? Visions of Nicola formed in my mind. Had people complained about Daniel giving them low marks? Had Cara? Is that why she was here? Was this the secret they shared? But how would that explain why he'd been so sure she wouldn't speak out against him or reveal our secret? I was beyond confused. I tried to focus on the question, formulating an answer that wouldn't set off alarm bells.

"It was only a couple of points. It wasn't a big deal," I claimed. "I think Daniel has higher expectations of a few of us in the class, based on what he thinks we're capable of."

I waited for his reaction, wary of saying more.

"Fair enough. Now tell me, where did you meet to discuss this evaluation?"

"In the Hart House library?" Why had I said it like a question?

I wanted to shift in my seat as he scrutinized me again, but I willed myself to remain perfectly still.

"And was the issue resolved satisfactorily?" he asked.

"Completely," I said. "Daniel was very receptive to my concerns. He explained that he was trying to hone his skills using rubrics and benchmarks and things like that."

Holy crap, that was a good one.

"And did you have cause to meet with Daniel on any other occasions?"

Oh, sweet Jesus. I couldn't fuck this up. *Truth, Aubrey. Find some truth to cling to.*

"Yes, we met to discuss my independent study early in the semester. And another student and I met with him on Monday—we had questions about the exam."

I was verging on half-truths now. Okay, maybe they were quarter-truths.

"And where did *these* meetings take place?"

I puckered my brow, trying to look as if I was struggling to remember—as if I couldn't recall every minute detail of each encounter Daniel and I had ever had.

"I believe I met with him at the Pratt Library at Vic. That was back in February." *Exactly fifty days ago.* "And then on Monday, my classmate and I met him in the Hart House quad."

"So, you never met with him in an office during office hours or anything like that?"

I shook my head. "Daniel insisted on meeting at the library or at Hart House."

"Okay. Well, is there anything else you might not have indicated on your questionnaire that you'd like to say about Daniel and his performance as TA? Anything about the way he treated students in tutorials? Any sense that he was playing favorites? For example, you work for his father at Victoria College. Did that pose problems?"

I wanted to laugh. Working for Dean Grant had posed all sorts of problems, but certainly not the type he was referring to. I frowned, trying to think of some constructive criticism—something that wouldn't raise red flags, something that might have come across in the questionnaires anyway which would still show Daniel in a positive light.

"I don't think my job at Vic had any impact on the way Daniel treated me. I honestly think he did a good job. He was always willing to help—he treated everyone with respect. If anything, maybe he was a little too formal. He was *very* professional. I mean he wouldn't even use people's first names. I think he could relax a bit. That's just my opinion. I have no idea how everyone else felt."

Mr. Unibrow nodded and wrote a few more lines as I sat, helplessly watching. After a couple of moments, he tossed his pen on the desk and stood up.

"Thank you for your time, Aubrey. You've been very helpful. As I mentioned earlier, I'm still working my way through the rest of the evaluations, but that's all I need from you at present."

I stood up and threw my bag over my shoulder, not entirely sure what had just happened—not certain what I would tell Daniel. I needed more information.

"Is this a new practice, sir? I've never heard of this sort of thing. I mean, I've done evaluations, but never been interviewed about a TA before."

He made his way to the door and opened it, ushering me through.

"I wouldn't call it standard practice, but Daniel has transferred from Oxford and this is his first time as TA here at U of T. We'd like to give him as much feedback as we can because his ultimate goal is to teach. I'm sure you understand," he said dismissively. Clearly I was taking up his valuable time.

"Right. That's a great idea," I said, as if he needed me to validate his policies and procedures.

"Thank you again for your time," he said.

I nodded, taking a quick look over his shoulder at the nameplate on his door.

Aaron O'Connor.

I hurried down the hall and pushed open the double doors, emerging into the afternoon sun. Feeling as if I was coming to the surface after being held at the bottom of a deep pool, I took a giant gulp of fresh air and propped against the wall to steady myself.

I had to call Daniel to tell him what had happened. Not that I even *understood* what had gone on in there. I dropped my backpack on the ground and fished for my phone in the side pocket with shaking hands. I was just about to dial his number when a voice behind me interrupted me.

"You okay?"

I whirled around, and there she was, sitting on the low parapet at the bottom of the stone steps. Cara. She'd been waiting for me.

CHAPTER 22

Confession

The fairest is confession.
Were not you here but even now disguised?
(*Love's Labour's Lost*, Act v, Scene 2)

I hastily put the phone in my pocket. Daniel would have to wait. I walked down the steps to join her.

"Cara, what are you doing here?"

"I had an interview, like you did."

Duh! Jesus.

"No, I mean, why are you *still* here?"

She rolled her eyes and crossed her arms under her boobs. God, they were huge.

"I was going to see if you were okay, but whatever. Forget it."

She stood and tossed me a contemptuous look before walking away. I narrowed my eyes as she retreated, remembering that Daniel had warned me not to talk to her. But if I let her go, I honestly felt like I'd never figure out what her deal was.

"Hey, Cara? Wait up." I caught up with her, and we quickly fell in step. I tried to soften my tone. "What's this all about? I can't imagine why you'd want to talk to me—why you care how I am."

She turned to look at me, chewing on the inside of her cheek like a chipmunk. Funny how I always seemed to associate her with rodents.

She gestured to a bench a little distance away, and we both sat. I waited for her to say something, but she had her eyes trained on the ground in front of us. The uncomfortable silence stretched on. Was she waiting for *me* to start talking? I was rooting around for something to say to break the ice when at last she spoke.

"Look, Aubrey, I know you don't like me, and I don't care. I mean, I don't really like you much either," she added.

For some reason, this admission struck me as funny. I laughed. She smiled wryly.

"Well, we don't have much in common," I said, aiming for a conciliatory tone.

She fiddled with the strap on her shoulder bag. "I guess not. Except maybe one thing."

Oh, this should be rich.

"And what's that?"

She looked straight at me. "We both really like a certain TA and don't want him to get in any trouble."

I tried to keep my face immobile. Was she trying to trap me — get me to confess something? Her warning and Daniel's cautioning words came back to me.

Don't let her bait you.

"He's been a good TA," I said guardedly. "I don't see why he would get in trouble."

"I figured you'd say that. I'm actually kinda *glad* you said that."

"I'm not sure what you mean."

"Well, I'm glad you're being more careful."

What the hell?

"Cara, you'll have to tell me what you're talking about. I'm a little confused."

She sighed. "I'm going to tell you something, and I don't expect you to, like, say anything or whatever. Actually, don't say anything. I don't want you to."

I sat back on the bench, crossing my arms. "Okay. Shoot."

"You probably don't know this, but I've liked Shawn for a really long time."

I had no idea what this had to do with anything, but I nodded.

"Back in February when I found out Shawn liked you, I was so mad. Well, first I was upset. Like, *totally* upset. It was bad enough that he liked someone else, but for it to be *you?* That sucked, you know what I mean?"

I nodded. What the hell could I say to that? She hated me and the guy she liked was interested in me. That would have been a total slap in the face.

"So anyway, a bunch of us got together for drinks before this event one night," she said. "Shawn was raving about how great you'd looked the day before, and how he thought you were really hot. Once we got to the actual event, I was so upset that I had to escape to the washroom. Pathetic, I know, but I've totally liked him since I met him at the first Kap party in frosh week, and he's never looked twice at me in four years. It didn't matter what I did; he never paid any attention. It wasn't fair that *you'd* get to have him when you didn't even seem interested."

"I'm sorry." I don't know why I was apologizing—I had no control over Shawn's feelings. I'd certainly never led him on.

"Yeah, well, it doesn't matter now. Anyway, that night, while I was in the washroom crying, I heard something that made me feel better." She looked at me pointedly. "It was at Brennan Hall. The night of that benefit thing for Mary?"

Holy shit! Suddenly, I realized *exactly* where she was going with all of this. What would Daniel say right now? Would he want me to shut her down? As much as I wanted to avoid pursuing this topic with her, I was burning with curiosity and dying to hear what she would say next.

"And what do you think you heard, Cara?"

"It's not what I think I heard. It's what I *know* I heard. You were talking to Julie Harper about this guy you were dating. A guy you probably shouldn't have been dating. And you definitely shouldn't have been talking about it, at least not out in the open like that. Anyone could've heard you. *I* heard you."

I weighed my options, trying to decide how to respond, but I didn't have a chance.

"You know who I'm talking about. And you don't have to deny it or whatever. I'm not fishing, and I'm not trying to get him in trouble. That's the last thing I want. He's been totally awesome to me."

I looked uncomfortably at my hands. "I really don't—"

"Just let me finish?" she interrupted me. "Seriously. Don't say any-thing."

"Um, okay."

"When I first found out you guys were together, I was stoked, 'cause that meant you were taken. But after a while, that sort of didn't matter anymore. I wanted him to be happy because he's a good per-son. He's really helped me. And I've watched you two all semester, ever since that night, and I swear there're times when it's so obvious you're into each other. That's why I warned you to be more careful. I should've said something earlier."

I looked at her impassively, trying not to look *too* interested in what she was saying.

"I felt kinda bad after I said that to you," she admitted. "You know, about being more careful who you talk about and where? But, really, I wanted you to be kinda scared. I figured it would make you realize people might be watching you. Julie was the one who said his name. You didn't say it once, but you still should've been more careful."

I squinted up at the sky for a second. I hadn't said anything in-criminating—hadn't confirmed my relationship with Daniel—but I wasn't denying it either. Wasn't my silence as good as an acknowl-edgment?

"I wanted to say something when I was talking to you about chipping in for the gift," she said, "but Shawn was there and it was awkward. Then later that afternoon, I had a meeting with, well, *him*, and I figured you must have told him what I'd said, and he thought I was gonna rat you guys out. I felt bad. I wanted you to be careful, but I never would do something that nasty to someone, especially not to him. And just 'cause we're not friends doesn't mean I wanted to screw *you* over either."

She looked at me expectantly. My mind was racing, trying to puzzle out what must have happened between her and Daniel. Had he confronted her?

"Cara, this is really awkward. I don't know what to say. I'm sort of confused. I don't get why you're telling me all this now."

She clasped her hands in front of her.

"I guess I'm kinda worried. That guy in there asked a lot of ques-tions about, you know, appropriate behavior and stuff. I'm scared they might know something. I don't want him to get in trouble. Do you think he's in trouble?"

"Look, we do agree on one thing—Daniel is a really decent person. It would be shitty if he got screwed over. But as far as I can tell, the university is just being thorough." I paused and then carefully emphasized my next words. "Unless someone said something to indicate *otherwise,* as far as they know, he's a first-time TA who has a few things to learn about evaluation and about building rapport with students."

She looked at me reproachfully. "All I did was tell that guy in there that Daniel was an amazing TA and that he went out of his way to help me."

I looked at her levelly. "And I said the same."

Her expression softened. "Do you think maybe everything's okay, then? Maybe it's just the university being hard core to help him and stuff, like you said?"

"I hope so. I don't know what else to say about it."

She nodded.

I mulled over her predicament, feeling a vague sympathy for her.

"You know what, Cara? I wish I'd known you liked Shawn all this time. Maybe I could've done something to try to help you."

"No offense, Aubrey, but I never would've told you something like that. You're not very good at hiding the way you feel about people. People you really like *and* people you don't."

"Fair enough, but I really have a hard time with the whole flirty, tits-first routine. I know it's not your fault for being well-endowed, but you're not a stupid person. I don't understand why you behave that way."

"That's how I survived in high school," she explained. "When you're a blonde with big boobs, everyone, like, assumes you're an airhead. It's easier to go along with that than to work to prove them wrong."

"See, in my opinion, that's all the more reason to prove them wrong."

She smiled. "That's what Shawn said. He said he feels like he's known me all these years and has never seen who I really am. He said he never thought twice about me because he figured guys were always falling all over me. Which is *so* not true."

"I'm happy for you. I'm glad you guys got together before it was too late. He's a great guy."

"I know, right?" She smiled in a self-satisfied way. "So, if we were in some cheesy movie, this is the part where we'd hug and decide to be best friends, right?"

"Probably."

She shook her head. "I hate cheesy movies."

I laughed. "Me too."

She stood. "When you talk to Daniel, can you let him know I said hi and that I hope everything works out, you know, with stuff?" she said.

"I will. Thanks."

"Okay. Well, see ya."

I held up my hand in a parting wave, and she took a few steps backward before turning swiftly and bouncing off down the street.

"Daniel, where are you? Your voice sounds funny," I said.

"I'm driving. I had to get out. I was going crazy earlier waiting for your call."

I closed my eyes. Of course. The whole time I'd been talking to Cara he'd probably been pacing, wondering what the hell was going on.

"Sorry I kept you waiting."

"I knew you'd call when you were ready. Are you okay?"

"I'm fine. Hey, if you're driving, you shouldn't be talking on the phone."

He sighed in mock exasperation. "Yes, dear."

"I'm not nagging. It's a law."

"Come on. You know me better than that. I'm using my Bluetooth. Where are you?"

"I'm sitting on a bench in front of Burwash Hall. I just had the most surreal morning of my life."

"Mine's been pretty interesting too, but you tell me about yours first. What happened at the interview?"

"I think it went okay. I met with a guy named Aaron O'Connor."

"Yes, he's the TA coordinator."

"Right. I got the sense he was trying to figure out if you'd done something inappropriate. I tried to defend you as best I could without going overboard. And you'll never believe who I saw while I was there — Cara Switzer! She got called in too. Apparently he asked her a lot of the same questions."

"Well, that all makes sense."

"It does?"

"Absolutely. Martin called me about fifteen minutes ago to tell me *he'd* been called by O'Connor first thing this morning. Turns out O'Connor is spearheading this campaign to make sure I haven't screwed up, given my so-called track record at Oxford. Martin thinks it's overkill, and he wasn't supposed to tell me, but he thought I had a right to know."

"Really? I can't believe they're being so anal! The accusation against you was retracted."

Funny how I seemed to have completely forgotten that Daniel had been breaking all the rules for weeks by dating me.

"Aubrey, anything that threatens a university's reputation is bad for business. They had to make sure I wasn't some loose cannon TA, running around trying to use what little power I might have to blackmail poor, unwitting undergrads."

"Don't even joke about that, Daniel. Seriously."

"I'm sorry. I don't mean to wind you up."

"I wish Professor Brown had known about this before. At least we would've known there was nothing massive to worry about. He could have put our minds at rest."

"There's no point bitching about it now. Anyway, it sounds like the interview was fairly straightforward. What made it surreal?"

"Well, the interview wasn't really all that strange. But talking with Cara afterward? *That* was surreal. She's not the person I thought she was."

"Did she give you a hard time?"

"Not at all. She was actually pretty cool. I've underestimated her."

"I told you she was an interesting girl."

"You were right on the money when you said she wouldn't want to report you. She's really concerned about you getting into trouble. She has known about us all semester, you know?"

"She told you that?"

"Yes. Point blank. She's known since the benefit for Mary. Just as I'd suspected."

"Sounds like a scary conversation."

"I freaked out a bit at first. For a minute, I had this image of her wearing a wire or something."

He laughed. "Jesus. Talk about paranoia."

"I know. I tried to stay calm. But, if anything, she was even more cautious than I was. Her discretion was impressive. The whole experience was very illuminating. Oh, and she asked me to say hi and to wish you well with everything."

"That's nice to hear. Thanks."

I took a deep breath and closed my eyes. "God, I feel so much better."

"Me too," he said. "You have no idea."

I could imagine how relieved he must have been. As my eyes drifted over to Northrop Frye Hall, I remembered the other big news of the day.

"Hey, by the way, your dad and I had quite the chat at work this morning."

"About?"

"His new job. He landed it, eh?"

"Yes, he told me on Monday. I wondered when he was going to tell you. How do you feel about it?"

"I'm happy for him, but that bitch Elaine Armstrong is taking over in a week and a half. I'm not looking forward to that."

"You'll be fine. You're a strong, intelligent woman."

"You have more faith in my abilities than I do."

"I'm the man who's in love with you. Of course I do."

I pulled my feet up onto the bench and hugged my knees. The emotional heft of his words made me smile.

"Hey, sailor? The card I opened today? The picture of the tutorial room and what you said about knowing who I was when you sat beside me? It's pretty awesome."

"You like it?"

"I love it."

"Good. I like making you happy."

"You know what would make me happier?"

"What's that?"

"If I could see you. Can you just drive by and wave or something?"

He laughed. "It might take me a while to get there. I'm on my way to Orillia."

"Orillia? Why the hell are you going up there?"

"Oh, you know. Gonna swing by Casino Rama. Feed my gambling habit."

"Come on," I pleaded. "What's really going on in Orillia?"

"Can't tell you—I'm afraid."

"You're such a hypocrite! How come you're allowed to keep secrets and I'm not?"

"What if it's a secret that can't hurt you?" he said.

I could hear the smile in his voice as he used my own argument against me. Damn.

"Does this have anything to do with next Friday?" I asked.

"Maybe."

"You're not going to tell me anything, are you?"

"Nope."

I huffed in exasperation.

"In fact, I have to go, love," he said. "I've got to stop and grab some gas."

"Not even a *tiny* hint?"

"You're going to love it. That's all you need to know. You *might* even love it more than you love me."

"Not possible."

"Good answer, poppet," he replied.

That evening, with my interview at the English office behind me, I finally allowed myself to believe that Daniel and I might actually make it to the end of the semester without being discovered. We'd made a pact to be extra cautious, resolving not to see each other until the exam was over, despite the misery the decision inflicted on both of us.

Without Professor Brown's classes to look forward to, which had afforded me the chance to gaze at Daniel from across the room, the next week would be a difficult one. I would simply have to dedicate myself to the task of studying with a vengeance. I got to work drawing up a detailed study schedule, using the comfort of a rigid routine to keep me anchored.

The sound of Joanna crashing through the door with an armful of bags interrupted my studying. I wandered into her room and leaned against the wall.

"There's my long-lost roommate. I was starting to forget what you looked like," I said, watching as she unzipped all of her bags on the bed.

"Hi," she said, smiling at me over her shoulder. "Still the same old me."

"Is everything okay with you and Stephen?"

"We're fine," she assured me. "We need some space during exams, that's all. I'm glad I kept my room here. This is one of those times when having a place to escape to is a real blessing."

"Well, that makes me feel special," I teased.

"Cripes, I didn't mean it that way," she said, putting her hands over her mouth in horror.

I waved off her concern, helping her put away a pile of T-shirts and jeans. "Don't worry about it, Jo. I'm glad you're happy. I don't mind playing second fiddle to true love."

"I think it is true love, Aub. We're making all these plans. It's pretty amazing."

She filled me in on their decision to go overseas for a year after graduation to teach ESL in Taiwan and come home to start their life together debt-free. While Stephen was heading back home after exams to stay with his family until convocation, Jo planned to stay in Toronto until they left so she could take an adult education course. They had all their ducks in a row. Exciting stuff.

Unfortunately, their plans only served to remind me how fuzzy my own future was. I resolutely pushed my concerns to the back of my mind. I didn't have time to worry about that now. I had to study for my Friday exam.

I returned to my room where I spent a good couple of hours sorting through my notes, highlighting exam outlines and trying to get a sense of how much work lay ahead of me. By eleven o'clock, I was wiped. I got ready for bed and then sat at my desk, intending to send Daniel a good-night email.

I waited for my laptop to power up and flipped through the pile of envelopes on my desk. How wonderful to have Daniel's lovely cards to look forward to every day.

"I'd say a penny for your thoughts, but I'd actually pay a shit ton more to know what's going through your mind right now."

Matt was standing in my open doorway, watching me moon over the envelopes in my hand.

"Hey, cowboy," I said, gesturing for him to come in.

He walked up behind me and rubbed my shoulders.

"How's studying?" he asked.

"My brain is mush. I've lost all ability to think." I rolled my shoulders. "That feels good. I had no idea how sore I was until you started doing that."

He laughed before patting my back.

"What's this all about?" he asked, gesturing to my hands.

I smiled secretively. "They're from Daniel."

"Well, I figured as much." He snorted. "Doesn't he believe in emails? Texting?"

"For your information, I won't get to see him until next week. There's a card here for me to open each day between now and next Thursday. Something to look forward to."

"Man, why do I feel like I should be taking notes?" he said.

I laughed.

"Have you told Jo about Daniel yet?"

"She hasn't exactly been around long enough for a heart to heart. I'll let you know when I've told her everything, okay?"

"Fair enough." He watched me for a moment as I looked down at the unopened cards. "You miss him, eh?"

I nodded. "Part of me wants to open them all right now." I wasn't joking. It was all I could do not to tear through them like a five-year-old on Christmas morning.

"You wouldn't do that, would you?"

"It's tempting." I picked absently at the seal of tomorrow's envelope.

"You let me know if you're having a weak moment, and I'll talk you off the ledge." He ruffled my hair and crossed the room, closing my door quietly behind him. How did I get so lucky? Great friends and an incredible boyfriend. I snapped my laptop closed and grabbed my phone instead, quickly typing out a good-night text to Daniel.

Hey, handsome! I wanted to say again how glad I am that everything seems to be okay. If I thought something we'd done (or worse, something I had done) would lead to heartache for you...I couldn't forgive myself. Sleep well. I love you so much. Almost forgot--how'd things go in Orillia? Details please! -Poppet

A few moments later, my phone buzzed.

I'm relieved too, believe me. Please know this--the only thing you could do to cause me heartache is to leave me. As for my trip to Orillia...you'll see soon enough. Goodnight, sweet Aubrey. I love you too. -D

Was he crazy? I couldn't even take the idea of me leaving him seriously. And I couldn't leave it alone.

Leave you? Ha! Rest assured I did not wait all this time to have some hot shmexy times with you, just to walk away before getting any action! ;) Goodnight. -A

I flopped back on the bed and had just managed to get comfortable when my phone rang. I smiled as I answered.

"Hello?"

"Miss Price, what am I going to do with you?"

"Who is this?" I asked coyly.

"Only the man who's counting the hours until he can be with you—so he can touch you, kiss you, taste you, love you—spend the night with you in his arms."

I squirmed under the covers. "Mmm, yes, I do have a vague memory of this man."

"Only a vague memory? What does he have to do to jog this memory of yours?"

I pulled the blanket up under my chin. "Gosh, I don't know. If I could kiss him, I'm sure it would all come back to me..."

I heard him breathe deeply. "He wants to kiss you, too. Desperately."

"Daniel, I miss you so much. I don't know if I can do this."

"We agreed this was the best decision. If we stay apart, there's no way we can screw anything up. We're so close now, love."

"I know. It's just hard." I rolled over onto my side. "Are you really counting the hours?"

"Maybe."

"How many?"

"I think it's something like two hundred."

"*Two hundred?*"

"One day we'll look back on this and laugh." He sighed.

He was right, but somehow knowing I'd be laughing next week didn't make me miss him any less.

CHAPTER 23

Dressing Old Words New

O, know, sweet love, I always write of you,
And you and love are still my argument;
So all my best is dressing old words new…
(*Sonnet 76*)

During my time apart from Daniel, the first thing I did every morning was clamber out of bed to grab the day's envelope, then eagerly crawl back into bed to open it and pour over the contents.

The cards got sweeter every day. The pictures on the front gradually moved away from Professor Brown's classroom to include Daniel's parents' house, our table at the Gardiner Museum, and the arch under the Vic Gatehouse. The words he included inside each card were just as thoughtful, liberally sprinkled with romantic poetry and personal messages of adoration.

We talked on the phone every day and sent each other plenty of emails and texts, but it was the cards that made each day special. I lined them up on my bookshelf, returning to them frequently to re-read his lovely words.

When I woke up on Sunday morning, it was already light in my room. I peeked over at my alarm clock, refusing to move the rest of my body unless it was past ten o'clock. Ten seventeen. Nice. I'd slept like the dead.

I yawned and stretched, frowning at the dull beating in my temples—most likely my monthly PMS headache. In the bathroom, I popped a couple of Tylenol and returned to my desk, excited to open Sunday's card. I was just about to tear the envelope open when a voice at my ear almost made me leap out of my skin.

"Aubrey, can I borrow a highlighter?"

"Jesus, Jo, you scared the shit out of me. Don't creep up on me like that."

"I wasn't creeping, I was walking." Jo gestured to the card in my hand, scanning the other cards lined up on my bookshelf. "What's this all about?"

"It's, um, nothing really. Well, that's not true." I shook my head. "It's a long story."

"Okay," she said. She looked at me for a few seconds, and after perhaps deciding I wasn't going to say more, she turned to walk out of the room.

"Hey, Jo, wait. I need to tell you something."

She examined my face. "Is everything all right? You seem out of sorts."

"I'm okay, really. Come here for a sec."

I pulled the bedspread over my pillow, and we both sat cross-legged on my bed. I grabbed the framed picture of Daniel at Oxford off my nightstand and handed it to her. She blushed furiously.

"I saw this yesterday when I was stealing a few sheets of computer paper. I wondered when you'd tell me about him. He's absolutely gorgeous. Who is he?"

I bit my lip and smiled. "Daniel," I said. "That's Daniel. My boyfriend."

Daniel. My boyfriend! The words sounded foreign coming out of my mouth. Had I actually not said them out loud until now?

"Holy moly! How do you have this incredibly good-looking boyfriend and I don't know about it? What the heck?"

"Like I said, it's a long story."

"In that case, let me get comfortable."

She flopped back on the bed with a contented sigh and looked up at me expectantly. I laughed and proceeded to tell her the story of the handsome TA, his adoring student, and the terribly ill-advised relationship they'd embarked upon in February. Her eyes widened at various points in the narrative, and I let her grab my hand at the particularly harrowing parts.

"And so now we're just…waiting," I said. "The exam is on Thursday, and on Friday we'll finally be able to be together. I was just about to open today's card."

Joanna stared at me in wonder for a moment. "Goodness, why didn't you tell me?"

"I don't know. You always do the right thing. I didn't want you to judge me—to think I'm a bad person. And to be fair, Jo, you haven't been around much."

"Aubrey, I've basically been living in sin with my boyfriend for three months. My parents are paying for my apartment here, and I'm hardly ever in it. I'm not a saint. Do I really come across as that judgmental?"

"I'm sorry. I didn't mean it like that. To be honest, I had to respect Daniel's feelings, too. The more people who knew, the more dangerous it would be for us—for him."

"I suppose so. Gosh, I've been so out of the loop. I wish I'd known. I would have been there for you. How awful not to have been able to talk to anyone."

"I did tell Matt. I had to. It was impossible to keep it from him, being around him all the time." I watched as she registered the fact that Matt had known while she hadn't. "You didn't know it at the time, Jo, but you *were* here for me. Remember the week I was upset about an argument with a friend? The friend was Daniel. We'd had a bad fight. You were here, and you did comfort me. You did my hair for the Kap party, remember?"

She smiled sadly. "Of course. I've never seen you so upset. It sounds like the last couple of months have been horrible."

"He's wonderful, and we've had some lovely moments, but they've been rare. When you really want to be with someone and you're made to feel like everything about your relationship is wrong? Well, it's been shitty. Hell, it still is! We're going to have to be discreet for a little longer. To let the dust settle, you know?"

"So, you really like him, huh?"

"You have no idea. I'm totally in love with him. He's fantastic—too good to be true sometimes." I put his picture back on my nightstand. "I'm glad you know. I'm happy you're back, too." I reached for her hand. "I've missed having you around. You make really good coffee."

Jo knew me well enough to interpret my bravado as an admission of how much she meant to me. She squeezed my hand, and out of nowhere, I started to cry.

She sat up and rubbed my back gently. "Oh my goodness, Aubrey. Look at you. I've upset you."

"No, it's not you, really. I think it's PMS." I reached for a tissue and blew my nose. "Well, I guess it's not just PMS. I miss him. It's hard being apart."

"When was the last time you saw him?"

"Last Monday."

"Holy crow! So, these cards he's given you to open—it's like having a little piece of him with you every day."

"Exactly."

"Well, look on the bright side. It's Sunday. You'll see him soon."

"I know." I nodded, flicking at the envelope's seal.

What I was actually thinking was, *Soon just isn't soon enough.*

"I'll leave you to open that." Jo pushed herself off the bed and snagged a pink highlighter from my desk. "And any time you want to talk, I'm here, okay?"

I nodded and waited for her to close the door behind her before tearing the envelope open. On the front there was a picture of the bookcases in the Hart House Library and inside another one of Daniel's lovely messages.

I know you remember our first exchange in the library as vividly as I do. I made it clear that day how much I wanted you, and now I'm counting the moments until we melt together as one. In a few short days, my body will be yours. My heart and soul already are. ~D

On Monday, my routine was turned upside down. My shift at the registrar's office was relegated to the afternoon because of my morning exam. This meant working two hours longer than I was used to, but I didn't care. I was positively giddy as I went through my day.

By the time I headed home from my exam at ten forty the next morning, I was *beyond* giddy. Just knowing that Daniel and I would have only two days to get through once I put the large red X on my calendar Tuesday night had me—well, I was at a loss for a suitable adjective.

I breathed deeply as I walked, rolling my shoulders and neck to work out the kinks that had settled into my muscles after sitting in the same position for two hours. I went through my bag and retrieved the card I'd opened that morning. A picture of the corner table we'd shared at the Four Seasons hotel was attached to the front. I smiled as I re-read Daniel's message.

Time can't go quickly enough. I look forward to seeing you, being with you, talking with you, touching you. All of this—and more—in two days.
Yours, in every way, ~D

I'd already tried unsuccessfully to call him as I'd left my exam room, but I took out my phone to try again. Once more he didn't answer. I'd emailed him before leaving for the exam to tell him I'd be calling around this time, but he hadn't answered my email either. I left another message. He was probably taking a long shower…

While I was trying to be rational, not being able to speak to him was making me antsy. Our evening conversation had been so brief on Monday—I'd been distracted by my impending French exam—and now I felt this incredible distance between us, a sense of detachment which was neither my fault nor his, but unpleasant all the same.

When I reached the Vic quad ten minutes later and again had no luck reaching Daniel, I began to get concerned. This wasn't like him. Rather than letting my imagination get carried away as I'd so often done in the past, I decided to give Penny a call to see if she knew where he was. It would be nice to talk to her and hear about her trip anyway. I dialed as I walked and took a seat on the empty bench in front of the Pratt Library.

"Hello?"

"Penny, hi, it's me, Aubrey."

"Oh my goodness, what a surprise! How are you, dolly?"

"I'm okay. How are *you?* How was your trip?"

"Oh, it was brilliant. I'm so glad I went. I missed Brad dreadfully, of course, but it was lovely to see my family and friends. And the wedding plans are ticking over perfectly. It was fantastic. I hear you're swamped with all of your finals?"

"Yes, it's a busy time. I'm staying afloat, though. Say, Penny, have you spoken to Daniel this morning? I can't get hold of him."

"I haven't spoken to him, no. We all had a bit of a booze-up last night and were up late."

"Ah, that makes sense, then. Did he seem okay last night? We spoke when I got home around five fifteen after my shift at the registrar's office, but then I didn't hear from him again except for a quick good-night text around ten."

"I think he's okay. He misses you. He sounded sort of down when I spoke to him after dinner last night, so I convinced him to come by to help Brad do some painting. They started drinking and got carried away. I had to take away the brushes. The two of them had turned into dueling Michelangelos. I hadn't really planned to paint the ceiling. Useless buggers. Anyway, how did your examination go this morning? You did have one, didn't you?"

"It was fine. I think I did well. I have another one tomorrow, but I need to chill out for a couple of hours."

There was a moment of silence on the other end of the line.

"Does this mean you're done for the day?" she asked.

"Um, sort of. I do have to study a bit more for tomorrow's exam, but I'm not super worried about it, so I'll take some time to unwind before getting back to it this evening. That's why I want to talk to Daniel. I miss him like crazy."

"I bet you do, love. Did you leave him a message?"

"Yes, a few minutes ago."

"I'm sure he'll be thrilled to have heard from you and he'll call you as soon as he can. So…what do you think of this? If you don't have any commitments this afternoon, would you like to come round here for a bit?"

"Come round? Visit you? At your place, you mean?"

"Yes, exactly. Only if you've got the time, of course. I can show you the house, we can have lunch, and there's something I wanted to talk to you about. I don't want to pressure you, but I'd love the company if you can wangle it."

I didn't even hesitate. "I would love to visit you."

"Well, that's marvelous! Can you come now?"

I laughed. Her eagerness was heart-warming. "I look a little rough. I've got the I-pulled-an-all-nighter look going on, but I'm just two minutes from the subway. I could head straight over, I guess."

"I'm so jet-lagged, I could fit several pairs of shoes in the bags under my eyes," she said. "Trust me, darling, come as you are. You'll fit right in."

Forty minutes later, I was stepping off the streetcar in front of Kew Gardens. Penny met me with a warm hug, telling me she'd missed me and thanking me for making the trip to see her. She didn't need to thank me. I was thrilled to see her, too.

"So, what do you think of the Beaches?" I asked.

"Lovely area. I can already see it's going to be fantastic in the summer."

"It is," I assured her. "Busy though. People from all over the city will come down here just to hang out. And there's a jazz festival in Kew Gardens every summer."

"Daniel told me about that, actually," she said, leading me around the corner and taking us south toward the boardwalk. "I think I'm really going to love living here."

She brought us to a stop in front of a lovely gabled house with a porch that skirted the width of the main floor. A stone path cut through a garden full of spring blooms.

"Well. This is it." She pushed open the little front gate and led me along the path. "Let's get inside. I'm famished."

I followed her into the house. I was pretty hungry myself.

"I'll give you a tour afterward," she said, closing the door with a quiet click and leading me along the hallway to the kitchen at the back of the house. "There's not much to it, but it's ours and it's far bigger than my mum and dad's place back in England, so I'm perfectly content."

The house had charm and character, but it wasn't at all what I was expecting. With Penny's "high-maintenance" look, I'd expected her to have an ultra-modern, polished taste, but I felt like I was in a French country cottage.

"Have a seat." She gestured to the kitchen table and then looked at me searchingly. "Would you like a cup of tea? Or would you prefer something cold?"

"Tea would be great, thanks."

"I've just boiled the kettle before I left, so this won't take long."

She pulled a salad and some sandwiches out of the fridge.

"It's nothing fancy. I had to make do with what Brad had stocked while I was away. I hope you like egg salad and salmon?"

"Both are great, really. I'm easy."

"That's not what I've heard, darling," she said with a saucy grin.

I scowled at her jokingly. "Very funny."

"I'm just teasing. I must say, though, listening to Daniel counting down the days is downright delightful. He's so bloody desperate."

I helped myself to a few sandwiches and grabbed some salad as she got up to pour the tea. "Believe me, I feel his pain. This is the strangest relationship I've ever had. I can't wait until we don't have to look over our shoulders all the time."

She handed me my tea and put the milk and the sugar bowl in front of me before joining me at the table.

"Aubrey, I wanted to ask you something," she said. "I don't want you to feel any pressure, but I have to ask."

She reached across the table, taking an envelope from a small box and resting it on the table in front of me.

"What is it?"

"Open it and see."

She nibbled at her sandwich, watching me as I tore it open and pulled out a lovely cream-colored card. A wedding invitation. Penny was inviting me to her wedding.

I covered my mouth with my hand, suddenly overcome with emotion. I hadn't had a chance to prepare myself for this gesture. But really, hadn't I been thinking about this for weeks, hoping against hope that I could go with Daniel to Penny and Brad's wedding?

"Oh, no, don't cry, love," Penny said, reaching across the table to pat my arm.

"I can't help it," I said, sniffing and trying to avoid ugly-cry territory. "I'm so happy you asked me."

"I'm so glad. I thought you'd be annoyed with me for hijacking your holidays. I know you're going over to visit family, but if you could get away for a couple of days, we'd love to have you." She squeezed my hand and smiled. "I wanted to ask you early enough so you can try to plan around it, if you're able to join us, that is. And I know Daniel would be over the moon to have you there with him."

"No, this is wonderful." I reached for a tissue and blew my nose. "I wouldn't miss it for the world." I dabbed at my eyes. "Good grief, I'm so sorry about this. Hormones. I've been an emotional wreck all week."

Penny opened her mouth to answer, but then my phone rang, making us both jump. I looked at the display. "It's him." She smiled knowingly and continued eating her sandwich.

"Daniel! I'm so happy to hear from you. I was worried," I said.

"Sorry, sweetheart. I just got your messages. I woke up this morning with the most outrageous hangover, courtesy of Brad and Penny. I took some Advil, drank a bucket of water, and went back to bed."

"You sound groggy. Are you feeling better?" I asked him.

Penny quickly finished her sandwich and got up to put her plate in the sink. She was watching me, a bemused expression on her face.

"Much better," he said, "but I need some caffeine in the worst way. I hope to God Penny has a pot of tea or coffee made."

And that's when I heard footsteps. In the house. Coming down the stairs. Penny's eyes darted to the ceiling.

"Daniel? Where are you?" I asked.

"Oh, I'm at Penny and Brad's," he said. "I hadn't intended to stay over, but I came by to help Brad paint, and by the end of the night I was in no shape to — "

He didn't finish his sentence because there he was in the kitchen doorway, staring at me as I gaped back at him, my phone pressed unnecessarily to my ear.

Golden Slumber

We may, each wreathed in the other's arms,
Our pastimes done, possess a golden slumber…
(*Titus Andronicus*, Act ii, Scene 3)

"**A**ubrey! What the hell are you doing here?" Daniel said into his phone.

"I think you can hang up now, love," Penny suggested.

He looked at her like he had no idea who she was or where she'd come from. He was speechless. Penny snapped into action.

"Well, I have a shite load of shopping to do, so I'll let you two get on with it, shall I?"

She dashed around the kitchen, grabbing her purse, keys, and jacket. "It was nice seeing you, Aubrey. Sorry to dash out like this, but something tells me you won't miss me *too* much." She hugged me and gave Daniel a quick kiss on the cheek. "Make yourselves at home. I've got my phone, and I'll be gone for *ages!*"

Daniel finally lowered his arm — phone still in hand — as Penny breezed down the hall and out the front door. He was almost moving in slow motion.

"What's going on?" he said.

He was wearing a pair of rather large PJ bottoms and a wrinkled white T-shirt. His hair stuck out in all directions, and he sported a healthy few days' worth of stubble. His eyes were red and bleary.

In short, he was a befuddled hot mess.

I tossed my phone on the table and crossed the kitchen in three strides, launching myself into his arms with such force that his back hit the fridge. I wrapped myself around him, and he buried his face in my hair.

"I thought I was dreaming," he murmured. "I can't believe you're here."

"Believe me, you're awake." I held onto him tightly. "Oh my God, I've missed you so much. This has been the longest week of my life," I whispered into his neck.

He breathed deeply, as if I was the oxygen he needed to fill his lungs. When I finally pulled back to look up at him, he took my face in his hands, his eyes burning. He rubbed the end of my nose with his, then kissed my forehead before gently tracing my lower lip with his thumb. I hummed, and he smiled broadly, realizing that we were alone in the safety of Penny and Brad's home.

"I'd dearly love to plant a wet one on you, but I really need to brush my teeth."

I laughed. "In that case, *please* tell me you have a toothbrush here."

"I'll fucking find one," he said, chuckling and guiding me out of the kitchen. He led me up the narrow staircase onto the landing and gestured to the room at the end of the hall. "Why don't you go in the spare room and wait for me? I'll be there in two minutes. Take this?"

I took his phone, smiling and hugging my arms around myself as he disappeared into the washroom. The guest bedroom was dimly lit and smelled vaguely of fresh paint.

The room was sparsely furnished. On one wall, there was a dresser with a portable CD player and a pile of CDs on top. Daniel's wallet and keys were on the small bedside table, and his clothes were neatly folded on the end of the bed, which he'd already made. Clearly, he was from another planet.

I reached under the blinds to push open the window, then put his phone on the side table and perused the CDs, squinting to make out the names of the bands. Metallica, AC/DC, Mötley Crüe, Guns

N' Roses—this had to be Brad's collection. There were a couple of homemade compilation CDs in the pile as well. I flipped one over. *"Jeremy is an Emo Fuck"* was handwritten on the back insert.

I scanned the list of artists. All mellow. Perfect. I popped it into the CD player and stood against the dresser as the first song started, a lovely acoustic guitar-backed vocal. Jeremy and I obviously had similar taste in music. Did that mean I was an emo fuck too?

I sat on the corner of the bed to wait for Daniel, jiggling my legs and smiling. How amazing of Penny to orchestrate this meeting between Daniel and me. There was no doubt in my mind that our lunch date was a way for her to get me here. She knew how much we were pining for each other, but she also probably knew that neither one of us would have proposed a meeting at this point.

I finally heard the bathroom door open, and then Daniel was standing in the doorway, leaning against the doorframe, arms crossed. He glanced over at the CD player. "Good choice," he said.

"It was either this or Ozzy."

He narrowed his eyes. "Ooh, tough call."

"I know. I had to do eeny meeny miney moe. So, all better?" I asked, gesturing to his mouth.

"Why don't you see for yourself?"

He summoned me with a playful wiggle of his index finger. As I took the few steps from the bed to the door, I raised an eyebrow and bit my lip. In return, I was rewarded with what had to be the best one-dimpled smile to date.

"Hey," I whispered, leaning into him and gazing up at his beautiful blue eyes with undisguised longing.

He glanced from my eyes to my mouth and then back again, caressing my cheek with the back of his fingers. "Hey."

I don't know what I expected. A small tender kiss perhaps, followed by another, and then his lips would gradually part and his tongue, tentative at first, would meet mine—this is what I'd become accustomed to, and the music was soft, gentle, soothing—but that was *not* what happened. As soon as our lips touched, he claimed my mouth—my whole body—kissing me with unrestrained passion.

One of his hands moved down my back, pulling me toward him and crushing my chest into his, while the other roamed shamelessly over my ass as he drew my hips forward. His moans and minty kisses made my head spin. Daniel pressed his lips to the sensitive hollow between my collarbones and then trailed back up to my throat along the line of my jaw to my earlobe, where he dropped a final soft kiss. "There's a bed right behind you. How do you feel about that?"

"I don't want to talk about *how* I feel. I just want to *feel*."

"Good answer," he breathed.

And then he lifted my leg, wrapping it around his hip and scooping me up so that I was forced to circle his waist to avoid falling. He pushed the door closed with his foot and lowered me onto the bed. I scrambled up toward the pillows, frantically tugging him with me.

Then we were kissing and rolling, all legs and arms, tongues and hips. I needed to touch him everywhere. I tugged at his T-shirt in frustration, and he quickly yanked it over his head and tossed it carelessly behind him before pressing his lips to mine again.

I ran my fingers and nails all over his back, making him shiver. His half purr, half growl was just what I wanted to hear. When his hand moved to unfasten my shirt, I froze, my chest rising and falling rapidly as he slowly released the top two buttons. His breathing was heavy, but his fingers moved gently, methodically, the frenzied clutching and grabbing suddenly replaced by a fervent but controlled passion.

"Should I stop?" he whispered.

"No, no, don't stop," I begged.

"Another good answer," he said.

As the last button slid free, he looked down at me with smoldering eyes and gently opened my shirt. I sent up a silent prayer of thanks that I hadn't worn a sports bra today. The one I was wearing wasn't exactly sexy, not black or lacy, but it was sweet—white with lemon yellow polka dots.

"I love polka dots," he said softly, smiling and resting his hand lightly on my ribcage before giving me another torturously slow kiss. I teased back, flicking his lip with the tip of my tongue, loving the way his breath tickled my skin and his hips pressed into me.

"Give me your tongue," he whispered against my parted lips.

He gently sucked it into his mouth with a soft moan. I may or may not have blacked out for a few seconds, because how the hell was I supposed to remain in my right mind when he was being so sexy? And now that Dallas Green was singing in the background, I was surely doomed.

His hand began to move upward, and I slid my fingers through his hair, guiding his mouth down to my neck where he alternated between sucking and nipping. At last, after following the seam of my bra with his finger for what seemed like a lifetime, he finally moved his hand up to trace the outline of my breast through the thin fabric. I shuddered with anticipation, and when he slipped his hand into the cup of my bra, running his fingertips lightly over my nipple, I gasped with relief.

For weeks I'd craved the feel of his hands on my skin, starved for his touch. And now here he was, peeling back the fabric of my bra and gazing down at me reverently. I struggled to meet his eyes, pushing back any feelings of self-consciousness that might ruin the moment.

To say I saw stars would be clichéd. But when he whispered my name and lowered his lips to softly suck on my nipples, my back arched off the bed so violently I thought I might actually levitate.

I wanted him now. I wanted everything, and he seemed intent on giving me what I needed, moaning and repeating my name as he kissed me. I clawed at his back, pulling his hips against me with a frantic need. Where was our good sense, our restraint? Gone. All gone. We both had checked our brains at the guest room door.

I rolled onto my side, and throwing caution to the wind completely, I moved my hand down between our bodies. I touched him slowly but firmly. Of the two of us, I don't know who gasped louder. All I could think about was how badly I'd wanted to do this for weeks and how desperately I wanted him this very minute. As for Daniel, he had his face buried in my hair, breathing hotly in my ear.

"Oh, fuck. Do that again," he urged me.

I repeated the movement, feeling powerful, needed, desired.

"Again?" I whispered.

"Fuck, yes."

He placed his hand on mine, encouraging me to use my whole hand as he moved rhythmically against me, pressing his chest to mine. Skin to skin. Divine.

We kissed each other like sloppy, crazy teenagers, our movements mindless and out of control, breathing raw and husky as we pushed and pulled, reached and grasped, sighed and moaned. I rubbed myself against his leg, aware of how ridiculously adolescent I must have seemed, but I couldn't help myself. Friction. I just needed friction. His fingertips slid purposefully down my ribcage toward the waistband of my yoga pants.

"Fuck, I love these," he whispered, slipping his fingers under the elastic with ease.

Apparently he'd wandered in the desert long enough and was heading straight for the Promised Land! My response was one part whimper, two parts moan, and a million parts *bring-it-on*. His hand moved lower, inching slowly across my tummy until he toyed gently with the little cotton bow at the top of my panties.

Bloody hell!

And that's when I remembered.

Bloody hell was right!

Oh no! Oh no, no, no! Fuck you, Mother Nature! Fuck you and your whole extended family!

"Daniel," I breathed, trying to guide his hand away.

"No, don't. Please—don't think." He kissed me and eased his hand from my grasp. "Forget logic, forget everything—I want to touch you. I *have* to."

His fingers resumed their journey, creeping under the seam at the top of my panties and his slow, sensual kisses almost made me forget myself. One, maybe two more inches…But no, I couldn't.

I backed away from his kiss. "Daniel, don't."

I grabbed his hand again, pulling it up to my stomach, and this time I threaded my fingers through his. He looked at me, his breathing labored, his expression betraying his bewilderment.

"Please stop. It's—it's just not a good time. I don't want you to do this…now. I mean, I *do*—I just can't. It's *bad timing*…"

I don't know why I couldn't just say what I meant. I was dying of mortification. He was poised above me, looking at me with furrowed brows, and then his eyes opened wide as understanding dawned on him.

"Oh, Christ, you have your period?"

"Yes." I closed my eyes, grateful that at least *he* could say the words that I'd been unable to spit out for whatever ridiculous reason.

He squeezed my hand and lowered his forehead to rest it against mine for a moment as he tried to calm his breathing. Then he rolled onto his side, facing me, and pulled my bra back into place before bringing the two sides of my shirt loosely together.

"Wow," he said, resting his hand on my stomach.

"Sorry. I'm *so* sorry. I completely forgot. I didn't mean to lead you on."

"It's okay. Stop apologizing." He kissed me gently.

I hooked my fingers into the waistband of his pants. "If you want, I could…"

He took my hand, threading his fingers through mine, mimicking the way I'd retrieved his hand a few moments before. Then he looked down at me, his face awash with emotion.

"This isn't about wanting to come, Aubrey. It's about wanting *you*."

I gaped up at him, speechless.

"Don't get me wrong, I'm fucking frustrated as hell," he said. "I feel like I'm about to explode, but I suppose it's for the best. This wasn't exactly how I envisioned things happening. I mean, not here, in Penny and Brad's spare room."

"I know. Me either."

He shook his head, casting his eyes up and down my body, taking in my mussed hair and partially clad state.

"You are so fucking hot. Now I *really* can't wait until the weekend." He cradled my cheek and gave me a sweet kiss. Then he narrowed his eyes. "About the timing—will you be, you know…"

"Will I be done by Friday?" I smiled. "The timing was shitty for today, but I started on Sunday. It'll be over by Friday."

"*Friday*. Right. About that…" He winced.

I pushed myself up onto my elbows. "No. Don't tell me…"

"I'm sorry, it's beyond my control."

"What is? What's going on?" I struggled to contain my aggravation.

He sighed and tucked my hair behind my ear.

"Martin has asked me to meet him at his office on Friday afternoon. He wants to compare notes and evaluate a few exams together. He said it would be a good exercise to do some comparative assessment."

"Okay, well, that's not a big deal. What about afterward?"

He shook his head. "It's my dad's last day as dean on Friday, and there's a reception for him at Vic from five fifteen until seven fifteen."

"There is?"

"University types, administration, that sort of thing. My family will be there too. After that, we're going out for a family dinner. I don't imagine we'd be finished much before ten thirty or eleven. I suggested you might be able to join us, but my mom's invited Verna and Bruce Atkins. They're Sabrina's parents."

"What? Why would they be there?"

"Bruce is my dad's best friend."

"Seriously?"

"They've been playing golf together for years. That's actually how I met Sabrina back in high school. Family get-togethers."

He grimaced, and I flopped back onto the pillow.

Don't over-react.

"My mom thought you might be uncomfortable if they were there, and I was inclined to agree. Was I right?"

I tried not to pout. But really, did I want my first public appearance to take place in a room with Sabrina's mother and father? Not really.

"Please don't be upset," Daniel said, pulling me back to lie on his chest. "I'll pick you up first thing Saturday morning. I know it's hard to take after all this waiting, but my hands are tied. You understand, right?"

I ran my fingers aimlessly through his chest hair, maneuvering myself so that I could take advantage of the opportunity to feel the warmth of his body against my bare skin.

"Yes, I understand," I said grudgingly.

What I understood was that the world was one big cock-blocking asstard, but I kept that opinion to myself.

"Can we sneak in a visit on Thursday afternoon? Technically that is after exams."

He shook his head. "There's somewhere I need to go on Thursday. It's important. There's no other time I can do it." In response to my inquisitive look, he swept my hair back off my face. "And no, I can't tell you. It's a surprise."

There was no point fighting with him. His week was mapped out.

"All right," I said. "You win. Saturday it is."

"I didn't win, sweetheart. This isn't about winning and losing. Just circumstances, that's all. Now can we try to enjoy our time together? I distinctly remember you once telling me you'd be happy to sit and watch paint dry with me. We could do that right now. There's some very fresh paint in here."

"I did say that, didn't I?"

"You did. So, what do you say? You up for it?"

I could either sulk like a petulant child, ruining whatever time we had left together, or I could enjoy the time we *did* have, even if we could only lie in each other's arms.

"Absolutely." I snuggled up to him as he ran his hand inside my shirt, rubbing my back gently. "Mmm, that feels nice." I sighed, pressing myself against him, the heat of his skin warming my bare tummy. I tried unsuccessfully to stifle a yawn and felt him chuckle.

"Am I boring you?" he asked.

"No, I'm just so comfortable, and that music is relaxing. What's this song called?" I asked, nestling my face into his neck.

"It's a remake of The Beatles' song 'Golden Slumbers.'"

"Mmm, slumbers," I mumbled.

"You tired?" he whispered.

"A little."

"You can take a nap if you want."

"No, it's okay."

"I don't mind. I'll even let you drool on me."

I smiled and tucked my right hand into his side, wrapping my other arm around him. "You must love me."

"I do. I love you more every day. Please don't feel bad if you fall asleep. You've been going non-stop."

"I *am* tired, but if I go to sleep I might miss something."

He brushed his lips against my forehead. "I promise not to do anything fascinating while you nap. You sleep, my lovely. I'll be right here when you wake up."

I wanted to object, but I couldn't. With Daniel rubbing my back like that, I was fighting a losing battle. I gave in to the feeling, relaxing with a contented sigh.

Daniel sang to me quietly as his fingers moved in gentle circles on my back. I was floating—hovering in that warm place between sleep and wakefulness. Then I crossed over, slipping into a lovely dream. Daniel and I were sitting under a tree in the Vic quad. He was kissing me, and we were both oblivious to the people walking past and staring.

We were in love, and neither one of us cared who knew the truth.

Love and Honesty

I know thou'rt full of love and honesty,
And weigh'st thy words before thou givest them breath,
Therefore these stops of thine fright me the more…
(*Othello*, Act III, Scene 3)

long the paths that crisscrossed Queen's Park, squirrels busied themselves among the gnarled roots of the trees while people jogged, walked, or stood talking in groups with friends. I passed all of this feeling entirely disconnected.

I was finished with university.

Now what? For the past four years, I'd had a purpose, a goal to achieve when I'd woken up every morning. What was my goal now? To bed Daniel on Saturday and then continue to do so as frequently as possible thereafter? A fabulous plan, but not exactly a *career* prospect. Talk about feeling aimless.

I reached Jackman and stood in the front hallway of the apartment for a moment, listening for signs of life. Nothing. I was alone. I sighed and made my way to my room, kicking off my shoes inside the door. A flash of color across the room caught my eye. There was a huge bunch of tulips and daffodils arranged in a cut-glass vase in the center of my desk. How beautiful! Two envelopes rested against the vase, along with a Post-it note in Matt's writing.

Jeremy dropped these off this afternoon. I'm at Sarah's. Talk to you later...or tomorrow. Oh, and congrats on being done. ~Matt

Jeremy had dropped off flowers for me?

I picked up the envelopes. "*Thursday*" was printed on one, and the other one read, "*Open on Friday, May 1ˢᵗ.*" I opened the smaller envelope to find a handwritten letter from Daniel.

Aubrey,

I know you've already opened a card from me today, but I had to mark this special day in some way. Remember Patty's story — how she'd received a bouquet of roses from my grandfather on the day she graduated? Waiting until June is not an option, so I chose to acknowledge today with flowers. And yet, thirty-one days ago, I made you a promise. I curse that promise every day, but I've taken such pains not to break it.

These flowers are from Penny's garden. I hope they lift your spirits and make you think of me. To plunder again...this time the words of Alfred Lord Tennyson: "If I had a flower for every time I thought of you, I could walk in my garden forever."

As you read these words, I would hazard a guess that I'm at Martin's office, having just returned from my day's "outing," and I'm now preparing to take home exams which I must mark my share of tonight. And you have just finished writing your exam — the final exam of your undergraduate career. Congratulations, my love. I'm sure you did well. I suppose I'll find out shortly, won't I?

I'm taking the evening to finish my course responsibilities, but I'll see you soon, sweetheart. Enjoy the flowers.

All my love, ~D
xo

"Thank you, Daniel," I whispered, immediately comforted by his reassuring words.

I picked up the other envelope. Another homemade card? A late addition in light of the fact that we wouldn't be able to be together tomorrow night as we'd originally planned? I would wait to open it—maybe save it for Friday evening when I was feeling sorry for myself, unable to join Daniel and his family at their celebrations.

I placed the envelope on my bookshelf, slightly bitter that I'd been left out of the entire evening's events. I paused again to look at the pictures on the front of the other cards.

As the week had progressed, the photos had continued to represent the places we'd been together, places that held significance, but today's card was my favorite—the fallen tree log in the woods in High Park where we'd first admitted that we loved each other. I needed to read it again.

When you open this, our time together will be mere hours away, so let me try to zero in on the thoughts that I know will occupy my every waking moment by quoting Gustave Flaubert: "I will cover you with love when next I see you, with caresses, with ecstasy. I want to gorge you with all the joys of the flesh, so that you faint and die. I want you to be amazed by me, and to confess to yourself that you had never even dreamed of such transports..."

Good Lord! How badly I wanted that! Amazed by Daniel? So far, all indications pointed to the fact that fainting was a *very* real possibility. From the very first time we'd brushed knees, to our first hug under the Gatehouse Arch, to our recent encounter at Penny's house, there was no doubt that we had incredible chemistry.

A good fainting spell would certainly be in order.

When I arrived at the office the next morning, the sight of Dean Grant's piled-up boxes almost brought a tear to my eye. I'd been trying to block his impending departure from my mind, but now there was no avoiding it. On Monday morning, I would have a new boss.

I gritted my teeth and crossed to my desk, ready to get to work. As I reached over to turn on the computer, I found an envelope addressed to me perched on the keyboard. I opened it quickly and pulled out an invitation to that evening's cocktail party to celebrate Dean Grant's years of service to the college.

I sat down, contemplating this turn of events. Why was I just receiving this invitation now? And did Daniel know about it? At that moment, Dean Grant came out of his office carrying a box which he deposited on the front counter. He turned to look at me, resting his hands on his hips. He was wearing Dockers and a golf shirt—his version of a slobby packing outfit.

"Good morning, Aubrey." He gestured to my hands. "I see you've found your invitation."

I held it up and nodded. "Yep."

Feeling like little more than an afterthought, I couldn't bring myself to smile. He must have sensed my disillusionment, because he sighed heavily.

"I can't blame you for feeling slighted. I haven't handled everything as gracefully as I should have over the last six weeks or so. I'm genuinely sorry. I should have given you the invitation to the reception on Monday when I first received it. I'm the one who requested you be put on the guest list in the first place, but every time I imagined you there with Daniel, surrounded by university administrators, knowing the way you two are when you're together…"

I suppose I could see his point, but did he really think I was so immature that I wouldn't be able to conduct myself appropriately? I frowned, perching my chin on my hand as he struggled to explain himself.

"I spoke with Daniel, and he indicated that not inviting you to tonight's gathering would be a terrible insult. He's right, of course." He paused for a moment. "I understand how difficult the last few months have been for you. I've tried to give you your space, tried not to lean on you too much."

He looked at me for confirmation. I nodded. This was true. He really had backed off.

"I won't put you on the spot today by asking how much contact you've had with Daniel over the last few weeks, but I have an inkling you've not been entirely incommunicado. All we can hope for now is that your conduct together hasn't raised any eyebrows."

I crossed my hands in front of me and tried to speak calmly. "I've done my best to live up to my promise to you, sir. I hope you know that. By the same token, Daniel and I have very strong feelings for one another, and it would have been impossible to brush those feelings under the rug completely—"

"Or to cut off communication entirely?" he asked.

I breathed deeply. "We *have* been in touch, but I assure you, we've been exceedingly discreet. Thankfully, the semester is over now."

He looked steadily at me, processing my words. "I assume that means full steam ahead?"

I smiled up at him. "Don't worry. We'll still be cautious on campus. At least until after graduation."

"Thank you." He returned my smile, gentleness settling into the creases around his eyes. He walked around the desk behind me to look out the window as he spoke. "May I ask a favor, Aubrey? Something for you to think about this evening at the reception?"

"Of course," I said, regretting the words as soon as I'd spoken them. What unrealistic promise would he wring from me now?

He turned slowly, regarding me wistfully.

"Gwen and I are thrilled that Daniel has found someone who cares about him as deeply as you do. I hope you know that. The disappointment I feel knowing you'll no longer be working for me is tempered by the fact that I'll see you a great deal, regardless."

"Thank you, sir," I said, touched by his words, but aware that he hadn't asked for his favor yet.

"Can you try to remember that there are some incredibly opportunistic people in this world? People who would go to great lengths to ensure their own gains, even if it means destroying someone else in the process?"

I sighed and rested my hands on the arms of my chair.

"This Nicola person at Oxford did a horrible thing," I said. "I can't begin to imagine the misery she inflicted on your family. But with all due respect, that was a year and a half ago. I think it's time for Daniel—for everyone—to look to the future and try to seek closure."

"I agree," he said. "I'd love nothing more than to forget the whole incident happened. Unfortunately, it's not quite that simple."

"You *do* know Daniel didn't do anything wrong to elicit those accusations, right?" I couldn't believe I was saying this to him, but I couldn't help myself.

He perched on the edge of my desk, folding his arms across his chest.

"Whatever did or didn't happen over there, he obviously put himself in a position where he could be taken advantage of by getting far too close to her. That's his nature. In time, he'll learn to maintain a distance. I don't think he's mastered that quite yet." He smiled at me knowingly. "But I wasn't referring to Nicola when I mentioned opportunistic people. There are a vast number of them in this world—a good deal of them right here at this university. I hate to be cynical, but my advice to you is to develop a healthy skepticism. It's lovely to try to see the good in all people, but not always realistic."

I laughed and leaned back in my chair. "I fear you're preaching to the choir, sir."

"I'm happy to hear that. Do me a favor and encourage Daniel to audition for that choir?" He glanced around at the boxes. "All right, I have to get these sorted out. I hope inviting you at the last minute like this doesn't mean you've made other plans. Will we see you at five thirty over at Old Vic?"

My plans for the evening had included a shaving and plucking session followed by a do-it-yourself manicure and pedicure. But that could all wait until after seven thirty.

"I'll be there with bells on," I said.

"Good. I'm glad. Penny will be happy as well. She speaks fondly of you. It will be nice for her to have someone to talk to."

He started to walk back to his office, but stopped at the door to turn back. "I'm glad you're going to be there tonight, Aubrey. It's been a real joy having you working here." He looked at me for another moment before closing the door quietly behind him.

I grabbed my purse and escaped to the washroom. I'd be seeing Daniel in eight and a half hours! Now there was no point in waiting to open my last card. I ripped open the envelope, gasping when I saw the photo on the front of the card. It was a picture of the two of us in Penny's spare room! I was lying on his chest, fast asleep, and his lips were pressed to the top of my head. He must have taken the picture with his phone. How adorable was he? I opened the card and stuck to the inside of the paper was a two-hundred-and-fifty-dollar gift certificate for La Vie en Rose—a lingerie store. On the bottom half of the card, Daniel had written:

Well, it's official. There simply can't be any more ways to tell you that I love you. And since I've run out of words, I'll borrow some from our beloved William: "true love...cannot speak; For truth hath better deeds than words to grace it."

Better deeds than words...I can think of some deeds that would be quite appropriate, can't you? In fact, to hell with words. I'd be fine with us not talking at all this weekend! Speaking of this weekend, see that gift card up there? I'm sure you're rolling your eyes, but I've kept my promise, poppet! So, now you need to brace yourself. All bets are off. La Vie en Rose is at the Eaton Centre. Spend it all this afternoon. Go crazy. Trust me—this is as much for me as it is for you. And just two words: polka dots. See you soon!
~D

I leaned back on the vanity. This was how things would be from now on. As Daniel's girlfriend, I'd have to graciously accept gifts, and lots of them. Was this something I could get used to? I peeled the gift card off and stowed it safely in my wallet. Then I grabbed my phone to send Daniel a text.

> **Good morning, sunshine! Looks like I have a busy day ahead of me...party, packing...polka dots. ;) -A**

A few moments later, my phone buzzed.

> **Good morning yourself, beautiful. Your text made me very happy. Party? I'm glad my dad got his shit together. Packing? Yes, I'll send a list shortly. And I'm thrilled to hear polka dots are on your to-do list. Can't wait to see you. Love you. -D**

I put my phone back in my bag, mighty chipper all of a sudden. A day that had seemed rather bleak when I'd gone to bed last night was looking up.

"Hey, Penny," I said, moving in for a quick hug.

"*There* you are." She sighed gratefully, kissing me on both cheeks and looking me up and down. "You look lovely."

"Thanks. I know I'm a little late. David was concerned about Daniel and me making a scene. Daniel suggested waiting for about twenty minutes for the crowd to fill in. How're things so far?"

"Well, I know nobody in the room except Brad and his family, the punch is plentiful but non-alcoholic, and the queue at the bar is ludicrous." Penny gestured to a line of rather desperate people across the room. "I'm bloody glad you're here."

I laughed and squeezed her arm.

A voice behind me interrupted our exchange. "Aubrey?" I turned and there was Gwen, glorious in a black cocktail dress, which was tastefully accented with a lovely necklace and pair of dangling earrings. Any uncertainty I might have had about how to greet her was quickly squashed as she pulled me into a warm hug. "It's so lovely to see you."

"Thanks, it's nice to see you too."

She was holding my wrist, gesturing to her husband who was chatting with three men near the punch table. He excused himself and made his way over to us. His face was flushed. He'd had quite a day between packing, fielding congratulatory calls from every cor-ner of the university, and now this — a celebration to recognize his work at Vic.

He bent forward and whispered, "I had no idea so many people would be here."

"Don't be absurd, dear," Gwen chided him, straightening his tie and patting his lapel.

"Dean Grant, you have to know you'll be missed," I assured him.

He pursed his lips and regarded me with an odd expression.

"Aubrey, I think you'll have to call me David from now on. Unless you'd prefer to call me Provost Grant."

"Good grief! That sounds pompous!" Gwen exclaimed. "I'd go with *David* if I were you," she said to me.

I laughed and nodded. "I think you're right."

"Well, there's the man of the hour!" a voice boomed behind us.

"Aaron!" David spun around to shake hands with the man who'd just greeted him. And what do you know, it was Aaron *Unibrow* O'Connor. Crap almighty! What was he doing here?

"So good of you to come," David said.

"Oh, I never pass up an opportunity to rub salt in my own wounds."

David chuckled and turned back to us. "Ladies, this is Aaron O'Connor. One of my rivals for the position of provost—"

"Yes, that's right," O'Connor interrupted, leaning forward conspiratorially. "I dug pretty deep trying to find some dirt on old David here, but, I'm sorry to say, his record is spotless. I didn't stand a chance."

While he was striving for a humorous tone, something about the way he spoke made me wonder how much of what he was saying was actually in jest. David laughed politely again and continued with his introductions.

"Aaron, this is my wife, Gwen, my soon to be daughter-in-law, Penny, and my employee—well, former employee now—Aubrey Price."

O'Connor shook our hands in turn, and when he looked at me, one side of his long eyebrow flicked upward.

"Aubrey Price? I believe we've met, have we not?"

"Yes, sir, I was in for an interview early last week."

"Of course, of course. Well, isn't *this* a coincidence," he said, glancing at David before smiling at me. The look on his face made me shudder. I suddenly needed to take a shower. I also felt a clutching in my chest. David was looking at me questioningly, no doubt wondering why I'd been interviewed by the man whose role at the university was to monitor the conduct of graduate Teaching Assistants.

We were distracted from O'Connor's cryptic comment and equally mysterious expression by Brad and Daniel, who were easing their way through a small group of chatting people to reach us.

"Boys, there you are," Gwen said as her two sons made their way over, each carrying three drinks in their hands.

"That line was brutal," Brad complained, handing Penny a glass of white wine and his dad a beer before taking a sip of his own beer.

Daniel quickly surveyed the group, his eyes darting across mine as he took quick note of the fact that his father was talking to Aaron O'Connor, the very man whose insistence on interviewing me had just about given us both heart failure the week before. For my part, I was trying to keep my eyeballs in their sockets. Suit-wearing Daniel was lethal.

"And here he is now!" O'Connor exclaimed, clapping Daniel on the back and pointing at the drinks in his hands. "One of those for me?" he asked.

Daniel stepped forward and graciously handed him a beer. "Mr. O'Connor, be my guest."

"Well, I was only kidding, but if you're offering." He laughed at his own attempt at a joke and took a long drink.

"Mother," Daniel said, handing her a glass of wine.

Daniel's eyes continued to flicker occasionally over to me, subtly taking in my outfit, my hair, the necklace that rested just above my cleavage. He looked absolutely gorgeous, but I contained both my expression and my desire to launch myself at him.

Go away, bushy brow, I thought, internally glaring at O'Connor. *You're cramping my style. Not to mention giving me the heebie-jeebies.*

As if he could hear my silent plea, O'Connor again congratulated David, said he was happy to have met everyone, and told Daniel he would be in touch soon to discuss TA positions for the coming year. Daniel nodded and said that sounded wonderful. And then, thankfully, Aaron O'Connor was gone.

David eyed me grimly. I couldn't help recalling his warning from earlier.

"Was it just me, or might you characterize that man as, I don't know, a little…opportunistic?" I asked him.

"You might indeed," he replied dryly.

"He took Jeremy's beer," Brad observed.

David laughed and placed his hand on his son's shoulder. "He certainly did."

"David, we should probably mingle," Gwen suggested.

"You're right," David said. "Have fun, everyone. Talk to you in a bit." He leaned over to murmur something in Daniel's ear which elicited an eye roll from his son, and then he and his wife moved on, quickly absorbed into another group of chatting people eager to offer their congratulations. Daniel watched his parents walk away and then regarded me with a concerned expression.

Brad, oblivious to the drama swirling around us, threw his arm around me and said, "So, how are you, Aubrey? All edjumacated?"

I laughed. "Just finished exams yesterday."

"No kidding! Well, cheers! Wait, you don't have a drink. Daniel, she doesn't have a drink."

"Let me remedy the situation, then. Would you like a beer or a glass of wine?" he asked.

I eyed the line and winced. "I'll have a glass of punch. Really."

"Are you sure?"

"I'm positive."

"We'll make up for it tomorrow, okay?" He winked at me slyly and headed over to the punch table.

"Tomorrow, eh?" Brad smiled at me lewdly. "Bow chicka wow wow."

I blushed and put my hands over my eyes.

"Aw, don't be embarrassed. You're gonna have a great weekend. You'll love—"

"Bradley, it's a surprise," Penny interrupted. "And this is not the right time to be discussing this."

Brad cringed. "Right, sorry. I forgot. You know what, beauty? Can you hold my beer for a sec? I gotta hit the washroom. I'll see if I can track Jeremy down, too."

Brad headed off through the crowd. "Jeremy went to call Julie," Penny explained.

"Oh, okay. I was wondering where he was. Julie's crazy busy with her showcase. You're coming with us to the show next weekend, right?"

"Absolutely. Can't wait to see Miss Bendy in action," she said, smiling. Her eyes flickered over my shoulder, and her smile withered.

"Oh, ruddy hell."

I turned to follow her gaze. A tall, very thin brunette was walking purposefully across the room toward the punch table—and Daniel. It was Sabrina. There was no mistaking it. That prom picture I'd seen at Patty's was indelibly seared in my mind. I'd need some serious brain bleach to rid my memory of it.

She reeked of money, her I-just-stepped-out-of-the-salon hair falling around her face in thick waves. The price of her shoes alone could have paid my rent for two months. I couldn't even contemplate her jewelry. The sight of her made me feel ill. What the hell was she doing here?

"That's *her*, isn't it, Penny?"

"Yes, that's Sabrina, darling. Those are her parents behind her."

I watched Daniel turn as Sabrina greeted him, invading his space and pressing her lips to his cheek. He shook hands with her father and kissed her mother on the cheek. Well, this was all kinds of heinous.

Daniel looked woefully in my direction. Part of me felt sorry for him. He couldn't exactly drag Sabrina over here to introduce her to me as his girlfriend tonight. The other part—the part that had once wanted to pierce Penny's eyeball with the heel of my shoe—wanted to punch him in the junk for failing to warn me she would be here tonight. Wasn't she supposed to be five hours away in Ottawa? Penny watched me, her face awash with sympathy.

"She's nothing more than a clothes horse, lovey. Don't give her a second thought."

I glanced back across the room to see her now hugging David and Gwen. My face burned. First Aaron O'Connor and now her!

"Breathe, darling," Penny whispered.

I followed her advice and took a deep breath.

"I think I need some air. Will you tell Daniel I'm going outside for a minute?"

"You *are* a little flushed. Go ahead. I'll talk to him."

I turned, and she grabbed my arm.

"Try not to let this ruin everything. He's got a lovely weekend planned for you. Don't let her cast a pall over your time together. He loves *you*."

"I know, Penny. I love him, too. I'm just not sure I can smile through this right now."

I made a beeline for the south exit and pushed my way through the double doors. I'd barely reached the bottom step when Daniel was beside me.

"Aubrey? Where are you going? You're not leaving, are you?"

"I don't know. Maybe it wasn't a good idea for me to come. I mean, what the hell is Sabrina doing here?"

He jammed one hand in his pants pocket and raked the other through his hair in frustration.

"Walk with me?" he said, bobbing his head toward the Pratt Library.

We walked the short distance and settled onto the bench we'd shared all those weeks ago when he'd first told me about Mary's death.

"I did *not* know Sabrina was going to be here, you know that, right?" he said.

"Are you sure? Is she going out with your family tonight? Is that the real reason I'm not invited to dinner?"

The muscle in his jaw jumped. "Of course she's not. Why would you say something like that?"

"Just connecting the dots, I guess. She lives in Ottawa. Why else would she be here unless there was a special occasion to come back for?"

"She's not going out for dinner with us. She was dropping off her parents, that's all. Her father's had a couple of weird seizures. He's not allowed to drive right now. Doctor's orders. Now that they're here, they'll get a lift with my parents to the restaurant."

"So, she came all the way from Ottawa to do weekend chauffeur duties?"

"Not exactly."

"Well, *what* exactly?"

"Fuck." He grimaced at the sky before looking back at me. "Sabrina is in town because she's moved back to Toronto. She didn't like living so far away while her father was unwell."

I slumped back on the bench. "Wow. That's *awesome*. How long have you known?"

"Since the weekend. I would have told you on Tuesday at Penny and Brad's, but I didn't want to ruin our time together. I wasn't sure how you'd feel about it. I wasn't sure how *I* felt about it." He looked at me apprehensively.

"Weren't sure how you felt about it—meaning what? Weren't sure if you were excited?"

"No! God, no. Just…it was easier knowing I wouldn't have to deal with her being around. My mom and dad are such good friends with her parents, and now that she's back, the likelihood of her randomly showing up places is a lot greater. But I did *not* know that she'd be here tonight. I assure you, I was completely taken by surprise when she walked in."

"Me too."

"I'm sorry. Look, she's gone now. She took two minutes to congratulate my father and left. End of story," he said.

But not before rubbing her perfume all over you and leaving a red lipstick mark on your cheek.

"This sucks," he said. "I was hoping we'd never have to talk about her again."

"She's a person, Daniel, not a dust bunny. You can't just sweep her out of the way. So, now that we *are* talking about her, is there anything else I should know?" I asked.

He closed his eyes for a second. "Let's just say I'll be buying new towels, sheets, and throw pillows before you come over again," he said. "Housewarming gift," he added.

"Wait—what? Are you saying I slept on sheets that Sabrina bought?"

"Technically, no. You slept *in a sleeping bag* on sheets that Sabrina bought."

I ground my teeth, letting this information sink in.

"What are you thinking?" he said.

"I'm thinking that's a very personal gift. Please tell me Sabrina never slept on those sheets."

"She didn't. Sabrina didn't even *touch* those sheets. She bought them online and had them delivered. You claim it's a personal gift, but I'd say it's one of the least personal gifts I've ever received."

"Okay, good. That's good. That makes me feel a bit better."

"Good." He expelled a deep breath. "Will you come back inside with me?"

"I don't think so. After bumping into Aaron O'Connor, and now this, I'm kind of rattled. I think I need to go home and get my head together. Plus, I have some packing to do."

"Are you sure?"

"I'm positive. You go and enjoy your evening. It's your father's night. I'll see you in the morning."

"Are we okay?"

"We're okay," I assured him.

"And you'll be at York Mills at ten o'clock sharp tomorrow?"

"I'll be there."

"I really do love you, Aubrey. Sorry I'm such an ass sometimes."

I shook my head. "I love you too, Daniel. *Despite* how much of an ass you are sometimes."

"I'm lucky you're so tolerant."

"You're right. You're also lucky you're so hot."

He smiled sadly. "Have a good night, okay?"

"I'll try. You too. Oh, and you've got some of her lipstick…" I pointed at the red mark on his cheek. As he frowned and rubbed furiously at his face, I turned and made my way back to Jackman.

CHAPTER 26

Fire

Who is so faint, that dare not be so bold
To touch the fire, the weather being cold?
(*Venus and Adonis*)

*S*top biting your damn nails, Aubrey!

I caught myself for the millionth time and jammed my hand in my pocket. Jo had given me a manicure and pedicure the night before, and I was ruining her hard work. But where the hell was Daniel? I continued pacing, looking at my phone every few minutes. He was the one who'd told me to be there at ten on the nose.

I thought grimly about the debacle of the evening before. Considering that we hadn't even really gotten our relationship off the ground yet, we'd certainly had our fair share of conflict. Being on speaking terms after all we'd been through was amazing enough, but the fact that we were still so desperate to be together was utterly remarkable.

My thoughts were interrupted by the sound of squealing tires as Daniel careened into the parking lot and pulled up to the curb. He hopped out and dashed around the car to join me.

"Jesus, I'm so sorry. The traffic on Yonge Street was a nightmare."

"That's okay. I was worried, that's all."

"Worst route ever." He looked down at my small suitcase. "This is it?"

"I could have fit a few pairs of panties in my purse, but I figured I'd better bring a bigger bag. You know, leave room for souvenirs."

"Good thinking." He winked at me and tossed my bag in the backseat, then opened the passenger side door for me. As he eased himself into his seat and saw me reaching for my seatbelt, he stopped my hand. "You know what? Just wait a second?"

He leaned over the center console, slid his hands into my hair and kissed me deeply. It was just what I needed. Sweet and sensual, it was a kiss that spoke of regrets, of longing, and ultimately of reconciliation and promises of things to come.

Dropping a soft kiss on my cheek, he continued to cradle my face in his hands. "Christ, I needed that. Especially after last night. That reception was a catastrophe."

"Only for us. I hope your father enjoyed himself."

"He did," he assured me, kissing me again softly. "So? What do you think? Ready?"

"I don't think I've ever been more ready for anything in my life. Let's get going to—wherever it is."

"I hope I haven't built this up too much. I'd hate for you to be disappointed."

"I won't be. I just want to be with you, Daniel. We could drive back to your condo, and I'd be perfectly happy. Of course, we'd have to go shopping for new sheets and towels first," I added, smiling at him cheekily.

He rolled his eyes. "We are *not* going back to the condo."

He snuck quick glances at me as he drove, and I found myself grinning despite the flock, herd, school, or whatever you'd call the group of butterflies dancing in my stomach. When he laced his fingers through mine, placing my hand on his thigh, I began to have wayward thoughts of caresses…his fingers exploring my skin. The girly bits started to dance along with the butterflies.

I sat back and tried to enjoy the drive, humming along with the music from his iPod and watching the scenery. We'd been on the highway for about forty-five minutes when he interrupted my daydreams.

"Are you hungry?"

"A little."

"Maybe we should stop and grab a snack?"

"Did you have something in mind?"

He beamed at me. "I think it's time we had our first date."

I returned his smile. "Oh, really?"

"Absolutely," he said, pulling off the highway. Two minutes later we stopped in the parking lot of the local Tim Hortons. "Do you remember that night after the Palais Royale? How I said I couldn't wait to do something as simple as hold your hand while drinking coffee and eating Timbits at Tim Hortons?"

"I do remember. Vividly."

"Well, no time like the present. Shall we?"

Daniel held the coffee shop door open for me, and we went up to the cashier, who looked at us expectantly.

"Can I help you?"

"Do you want a coffee, sweetheart?" Daniel asked me.

"Yes, please."

"Okay, we'll grab two medium coffees to stay. The first one we'll take with…two milks and one sugar?" He glanced over at me for confirmation, and I nodded.

"And the other?" the cashier asked as she punched the information into the register.

"Black," I said, smiling at Daniel.

It was ridiculous to be so ecstatic over ordering each other a coffee, but to me it meant we were a couple. This was so banal, so normal. So amazing. This was what we'd been waiting for. Among other things.

"Can we get some Timbits?" I asked him.

"Sure, we'll grab ten."

The cashier picked up a small box and a piece of waxed paper, waiting for directions.

"Make that five chocolate glazed." Daniel smiled at me again.

Five chocolate Timbits disappeared inside the box.

"And the other five?"

I narrowed my eyes. "Honey dipped?" I guessed, but Daniel shook his head. "Hmm. Sour cream glazed?"

He raised an eyebrow and nodded.

"Five sour cream glazed," I told the cashier, who was now looking back and forth between the two of us like we were aliens who had just emerged from the mother ship.

Humor me. We're on our first date here.

Daniel handed her a twenty dollar bill. "Why don't you grab a table, Aubrey?"

I nodded and started to make my way to the corner, but then I thought better of it and chose a table for two in the center of the seating area. I watched Daniel pocket his change, clasp our mugs by the handles, and grab the box of Timbits with his free hand. He scanned the room and sauntered over.

"Are you trying to make a statement, Miss Price?"

"You bet your sweet knees I am. And if you call me Miss Price again this weekend, I'll be forced to inflict pain on you."

"Is that a threat?" He sat and pushed my coffee across the table.

"I believe it's a promise, sailor."

"Will your nails be involved in the inflicting of this pain?"

"Possibly."

"Excellent. Duly noted."

He opened the box of Timbits, and we both picked up our mugs. I almost had the edge of the mug to my lips when he held up his hand. "Wait, wait, we need a toast, don't you think?"

"Okay. What should we drink to?"

"Hell, what *shouldn't* we drink to?" He chuckled.

"True."

He looked at me contemplatively. "I think we should drink to the man who brought us together."

"You want to drink to Professor Brown?"

He laughed loudly, his coffee swishing as his hand shook. "No, not Martin. I think we should drink to the man whose very words brought about our meeting on February second in a classroom at University College."

"Oh, I see. Excellent idea." I touched my coffee cup to his. "To Shakespeare."

"To Shakespeare."

We both took a drink and put our cups down, our eyes locked. His left hand was resting lightly on the table. My right one was as well. The tiniest details of our relationship flashed before my eyes. Clinking coffee cups in the Arbor Room in early February, lightly touching fingers at the Gardiner a couple of weeks later…

"Are you okay?" I asked.

"So far so good."

I looked down at our hands and stretched my fingers out to reach for his. He held my eyes and moved his fingers forward, stopping just short of touching me.

"Why do you look like you're afraid you might burn yourself?" I whispered.

He shook his head and then slid his hand forward quickly, entwining his fingers with mine. A fluttery feeling passed through my stomach.

We were holding hands.

In public.

Such a simple gesture, but for us? Epic.

"Are you sure you're all right?" I asked.

He looked at me steadily. "Better than all right. I love you, poppet."

"I love you too, sailor. This is the best first date ever."

He took a chocolate Timbit out of the box, bit it in half, and then reached over to pop the rest in my mouth.

"It sure is," he agreed, watching me lick the sugary coating off my lower lip.

"Are you going to tell me where we're going?"

"Nope."

We'd driven even farther north, and at first I'd suspected that Daniel was taking a second crack at a weekend at Taboo. But Taboo was in Gravenhurst. We'd already passed the exit for the resort and stopped at a supermarket about fifteen minutes north of the town.

"Daniel, please tell me where we're going," I pleaded as we loaded the groceries into the trunk.

"Nope."

He slammed the door and turned to take me into his arms, kissing me passionately right there in the Sobey's parking lot.

"I gather you're feeling pretty comfortable now?" I asked, a little breathless as he let me go.

"Actually, my heart feels like it's going to explode."

I examined his face, trying to decide if he was joking, but he merely ushered me into the car.

"I'm fine," he assured me. "I'll be even better when we get there."

I crossed my arms. "Wherever *there* is."

"Exactly." He laughed.

We continued north, and I saw the signs for the Muskoka Lakes, and then a sign for Lake Rosseau. That's when it hit me. Of course! How could I have been so obtuse? Daniel was whistling away, very pleased with himself. It seemed a shame to burst his bubble, so I kept my peace, continuing to look out the window with a clueless expression on my face. But when he pulled off the highway and the roads began to get narrower, I couldn't hide my excitement any longer.

"What?" he said.

"You're taking me to the cottage."

"Well, don't you have excellent powers of deduction?" He smiled. "How do you feel about going there?"

"Are you kidding? This is the best surprise *ever*."

"I'm glad you think so. I didn't want to do anything too flashy. I want you to be comfortable." He steered the car carefully along the road, which was now winding through a thickly forested area.

"Do your parents know?" I asked him.

"Absolutely. We have their blessing. I'm sure my dad is secretly relieved that we're so far away from the city."

A few moments later, we pulled into a deeply wooded driveway. Daniel drove slowly as small branches brushed the sides of the car. Then he swung over to the right and came to a stop. He pointed across the dashboard.

"The cottage is around this tree," he said. "The only drawback about coming up here in May is the potential for black flies. We're going to make a dash for it, and then you'll stay inside while I bring everything in, okay? We'll have to gauge the amount of time we can go out, depending on how bad they are."

"You mean we might have to stay in all weekend?" I asked.

"We might."

"Maybe we should just stay in *bed* all weekend," I suggested.

He leaned over to kiss me. "I love the way you think. Okay, grab your purse. You ready?"

"Yep."

We both climbed out and hurried along the gravel driveway toward a flagstone path. A few steps along the path, I stopped, stunned at the sight before me. Cottage? This was a *cottage?* This was so *not* a frigging cottage! It was a *mansion* that happened to be in cottage country. Daniel unlocked the door and turned to look for me.

"Poppet? You coming?"

"Yes, I…This isn't…It's so…"

He held out his hand. "I'm pretty sure black flies have teeth."

I willed my feet to move along the pathway and through the open door.

I slipped my shoes off and took his outstretched hand. "Here," he said, leading me into the kitchen. "Have a look around while I grab the rest of our things."

I was stunned. This was what he'd been referring to as the family *cottage?* I spun around in the middle of the kitchen. Hardwood floors, stainless steel appliances, wine fridge, stove with six gas burners, granite counter tops, large harvest table…

The door opened and closed several times as Daniel collected our stuff. Finally he brought in the groceries and deposited them on the large island counter.

"Well, this is it," he said, gesturing around him.

"It's…wow. Daniel, it's unbelievable."

He shrugged out of his jacket and placed it on the back of one of the kitchen chairs.

"Come on, I'll show you around."

He took me on a tour that had me gasping with surprise over and over again. I tried to keep track of everything as we moved from one area to another on the sprawling main floor of the cottage. There were five family bedrooms, two guestrooms, a nanny's quarters, four bathrooms — one with a claw foot tub, another with a Jacuzzi tub — and all hardwood floors throughout with sumptuous throw rugs everywhere.

The games room made the basement of the Grant home in Toronto look rinky-dink. It had to be at least fifteen hundred square feet and had every type of entertainment accessory conceivable. Most impressive were the cathedral ceilings and the floor-to-ceiling windows through which you could see the lake sparkling below.

"You must have had so much fun here growing up," I said as Daniel showed me the bar and then pointed out the hot tub outside the games room door.

"It *was* fun. I have some really good memories." He pulled me into his arms and leaned against the pool table. "And I look forward to making some new ones," he said, brushing my hair away from my face and kissing me.

When he took my hand to lead me back upstairs, I began to wonder how things would play out. As much as I wanted to run down the hall to his room and get started *making memories*, I also wanted this to be special. Daniel must have agreed because, after we'd unpacked and put everything away, he suggested an afternoon walk so he could show me the property.

"It's so beautiful out it seems silly to wear long sleeves," I said as I zipped up my hooded sweatshirt.

"You can always take it off if the bugs aren't a problem," Daniel suggested. "It's warm now, but I think I'll make a fire tonight," Daniel said. "The temperature will probably drop."

"That sounds nice."

"I hoped you'd think so. Those pillows around the fireplace are new," he said, smiling secretively.

"*Are* they now?"

Was this part of his master plan? A fire. Throw pillows. Fur rug.

"Penny helped me buy them on Thursday. She chose some new candles for the mantel, too."

"I see. So *this* is where you were on Thursday?" I asked, looking up at him as he guided me out to the pathway.

"That's right."

"You've had a busy week."

"You have no idea," he chuckled.

We walked hand in hand away from the cottage, with Daniel pointing out various noteworthy sites along the way — the big rock where he'd shared his first kiss with Nancy Dawson when he was nine years old; the hill he'd tobogganed down when he was ten, landing awkwardly at the bottom and breaking his arm; the trail the family enjoyed hiking on in the summer and cross-country skiing through in the winter.

"So, this is all your family's land?" I asked, gesturing around us.

"Yep. This isn't the original cottage though. The one Patty and my grandfather built was smaller. This cottage has been here for about twenty-three years. The nearest neighbor is about a quarter mile that way." He pointed back down the road.

"That's amazing. The privacy, I mean. Your family is very lucky. So, growing up, you came up here a lot?"

"We used to spend summers up here. We came up a few times for Christmas. One Christmas—I think I was seven—we got a huge train set and had it assembled in the games room. Man, I loved that thing. That was the year Santa brought me my first guitar as well."

I thought about Daniel strumming his guitar, looking hotter than Hades. I couldn't help sighing.

"I love Santa."

He smiled and threw his arm over my shoulder, leading me to the other side of the road to point through the trees. "Goldie Hawn and Kurt Russell's cottage is over there."

"That's cool that you share a lake with celebrities. I wonder if their daughter's ever been up here—Kate Hudson, right? Have you seen her around? *She's* quite the looker, eh?"

He shrugged. "Not really interested, to be honest. Besides, I happen to be a little distracted by this gorgeous green-eyed girl at the moment."

I smirked. "Really? Tell me about her."

He propped himself against a tree and hugged me close.

"Well, she's smart, stubborn as a fuck, and funny as hell. She's beautiful, and she has these crazy long legs that go on forever." He kissed me in a way that made me weak in the knees—all soft lips and gentle tongue. Then he pulled my hood back a little so he could whisper in my ear. "And her legs stop right here." He cupped one of my buttocks. "At this phenomenal ass."

"Wow. She sounds awesome," I said, holding onto his shoulders to steady myself.

"She is." His eyes were clouded with emotion.

We stood kissing under that tree for who knows how long. Finally, we headed back inside before the black flies started to eat us alive. Frankly, giant man-eating squirrels could have been feasting on my ankles, and I would have been oblivious.

"Happy tummy?"

Daniel was hugging me from behind and rubbing my stomach through my T-shirt as I dried my hands on a dish towel. I tossed the towel on the counter and spun around in his arms.

"That steak was incredible. My tummy is *very* happy."

"I'd like to make some other parts of you very happy," he said, nuzzling my ear. I shivered straight down to the tips of my toes. He brushed my hair away from my face and regarded me seriously. "It's about time I stopped making you *miserable*, that's for damn sure."

I pressed my fingers to his lips. "Daniel, don't. The past three months—everything was out of our control."

He lovingly kissed my fingertips. "I adore you." He shook his head. "Words. Not good enough."

"Maybe it's time for some of those deeds you were telling me about yesterday."

"You're right. There are a couple of deeds that might show you precisely how I feel. If you're interested—" his lips moved to my ear "—I'd love to try," he whispered.

I bit my lip shyly. "Is it okay with you if I change first? I was hoping to show you the dress and shoes I bought for our trip to Taboo."

"Even if you won't have them on for very long?"

I laughed. "Absolutely."

"In that case, can you do me a small favor? Can you put your hair up?"

"I'm sure that can be arranged."

"Did you want to have a soak in the tub or something? You can use the bathroom down the hall. I'll shower in my parents' bathroom, and then I'll get the fire going."

"Sounds perfect."

"So, you'll be all dressed up. What should I wear?"

I looked down at his jeans. "These," I said. "And whatever else you want. My only request is the ratty pants."

"Fair enough." He refilled my wine glass and handed it to me, his eyes shining. "I can't believe you're mine and this is finally happening."

He kissed me slowly, sucking on my tongue, tugging at my lip, moaning quietly into my mouth. Finally, he broke away.

"You'd better get going before I ravish you right here on the kitchen table."

"That doesn't sound unappealing." I playfully tugged at the top button of his jeans.

He slapped my ass, pointing down the hallway to the bathroom. "Go!"

I laughed, making my way to Daniel's room, grabbing my bag and taking it into the bathroom with me.

For the next half hour I soaked in the tub with my wine, moisturizing my skin liberally afterward and finishing off with a vigorous tooth brushing. I selected a black lace bra and accompanying panties, smiling as I anticipated Daniel's reaction to the hot pink polka dots. I slipped into my dress and shoes and arranged my hair in a loose bun, securing it with a clip. At last, I surveyed myself in the mirror and smoothed my dress.

"It's show time, Aubrey," I whispered to my reflection.

My shoes clicked on the hardwood floor, announcing my arrival. Daniel was sitting on the sofa in front of a roaring fire. A row of tea lights glowed across the mantelpiece. Smoky jazz music filled the room. He'd opened another bottle of wine, and two glasses sat on the side table. He'd thought of everything.

He turned as I crossed the room and then stood up, eyes wide. "Wow. You look stunning."

"Thanks," I said, trying to *own* stunning as I stepped into his embrace. He held me tightly and then moved back to take a closer look at my dress and shoes.

"Gorgeous. How do you feel?" he asked.

I smiled. I felt gorgeous. And sexy. And *ready.* "Nervous as hell," I said. "You?"

"Same."

"Any anxiety?"

"Only the performance kind."

I laughed lightly. "I don't think *that's* going to be an issue." I rested my hands on his chest. "But how are you feeling about losing your independence?"

He frowned and played with a loose tendril of my hair. "What do you mean?"

"Well, you've been *self-employed* for so long, I'm concerned you might have trouble getting used to having someone working *with* you," I teased.

He threw his head back and laughed. "Ah, I honestly don't see that as a problem."

"Are you sure?"

He nodded. "Oh, I'm sure."

He ran his hands down my back and rested them on my hips. Then he told me with his lips, his tongue, and his sighs exactly how much he wanted me. As our bodies pressed together, it became abundantly clear that, like me, Daniel was *ready*.

"This dress *is* beautiful, Aubrey, but unfortunately it's in the way of something I really, *really* need," he murmured.

"Zipper's in back." I slowly undid the buttons of his shirt, sliding it down his arms and tossing it on the couch. I snuck my fingers under his white T-shirt and rested my hands on his sides.

He looked into my eyes and found the top of the zipper, slowly easing it down.

"I can't wait to see you step out of this dress." He lowered his lips to my shoulder. "God, I want you," he whispered. He slid his hands down my back, cupping my buttocks.

"Daniel," I sighed, barely able to speak as he lavished my neck with kisses and brought one of his hands up, running his fingers lightly along my spine. "Daniel," I repeated, taking his face in my hands.

His eyes searched my face. "Are you okay?"

"I'm wonderful, but—would you do something for me?"

"Anything."

"Would you sit on the couch for a minute?"

He squeezed my hand and sat on the edge of the sofa, gazing at me with undisguised longing. Emboldened by his desire, I eased off my shoes, kicking them to the side. Daniel leaned forward eagerly. I slowly lowered the straps of my dress and then let it fall unceremoniously to the floor and stepped out of it.

His eyes traveled up my legs, lingering over my panties and then moving up my torso to check out my breasts. I didn't know what was making me warmer, the heat from the fire or the heat from his gaze.

"Do you have any idea how incredible you look right now?" he asked me.

I simply raised my hands to my head, unclasped the clip, and let my hair fall around my shoulders.

"Sweet Jesus," he breathed. "Aubrey Price." He looked me up and down again. "You are hired."

CHAPTER 27

Heavenly

Panting he lies and breatheth in her face;
She feedeth on the steam as on a prey,
And calls it heavenly moisture, air of grace;
Wishing her cheeks were gardens full of flowers,
So they were dew'd with such distilling showers.
(*Venus and Adonis*)

"**A**m I?" I asked, laughing at the naughty gleam in his eye.

"Most definitely." His eyes traveled down my body again, making my stomach flutter with excitement. "When can you start?"

I twirled a lock of hair around my finger. "How's right now?"

"Perfect."

I lowered myself to the rug, reclining against the pillows and holding my hand out to him. Something about the way he was worshipping me with his eyes made me feel completely comfortable despite my nerves. A strange expression crossed his face.

"Are you okay?" I asked.

"Yeah," he said quietly.

He stood above me and pulled off his T-shirt, blindly throwing it behind him. With his eyes locked on mine, he popped open the top button of his jeans. I drank in the sight of his bare chest, his tightly muscled abs, and the sprinkling of hair below his naval. As his fingers moved to the next button on his fly, I shook my head.

"No?" he asked, his hand hovering over the button.

"No." I held out my hand to him again. "Not yet."

He knelt down and stretched out beside me, resting his hand lightly on my stomach. Every nerve in my body strained toward him, eager for his touch, but at the same time I was paralyzed with anticipation, my hands fisted at my sides. Finally, after looking at me hungrily for the longest time, he placed his finger gently on my mouth, tracing the outline of my lips. I closed my eyes and breathed deeply, melting into the fur rug.

I kissed his finger softly, and when I opened my eyes he was smiling as he traced a soft line between my breasts and across my stomach, making me jump when he found the ticklish spot under my ribs. He toyed with the bow at the side of my panties.

"Do you know how many times today I wanted to tear your clothes off?" he whispered, running his fingers along the side of my thigh to my knee and back again.

"I'm surprised. You certainly didn't let on," I said, my voice wavering.

His beautiful eyes trapped mine intently. "I'm surprised too. Apparently I have supreme self-restraint."

"You must," I agreed, reaching up to run my fingers through his hair. "I hope you plan on losing it very soon."

"Yep. You'd better brace yourself," he breathed.

He licked his lips, and I found myself doing the same. And then he kissed me with a passion that swept me up like an undertow. I arched my back and clutched at his shoulders, gripping him tightly, unable to get my body close enough to his.

He slid his hand under my back, feeling for the clasp of my bra. I squeezed my shoulders together and he deftly flicked the clasp open, kissing his way down one arm and then the other as he slowly eased the straps off my arms. He held my bra, teasing the fabric with his fingers for a moment before tossing it over his shoulder.

"I love the polka dots, but I love these more," he whispered, lowering his lips while I threaded my fingers more tightly through his hair, holding him still as I pressed against the soft darting movements of his tongue.

As he licked and nuzzled, his hands began to roam. My entire body tensed, waiting for him to slide his hand inside my panties. Again, he toyed with the silky strings tied at my hip. "Are these just for decoration?" he asked, breathing hotly in my ear.

"No. Pull…"

He tugged harder, and the soft fabric slid open at the side.

"Fuck," he said, sinking his fingers into the bared flesh around my hip bone.

"Other side," I urged.

He opened the other bow, and I squirmed as he loosened the strings. His fingers grazed my inner thighs as he reached down to gather the fabric in his hand. I gasped and lifted my hips upward, but Daniel's hand was now hovering above my face, the black lace panties balled up in his fist.

"One pair saved from certain disintegration." He tossed the panties over his shoulder.

And just like that I was naked. And Daniel was not. He was lying there in his jeans, with the top button popped open, and somehow this was the sexiest scenario imaginable. I pulled at his shoulders so he'd roll on top of me, but he shook his head, determined to do things his way. His self-control was mind-boggling.

"Beautiful," he said, as his eyes feasted on me. "I imagined you lying here—like this—in front of the fire. My fantasies didn't even come close."

Was there any feeling in the world better than being worshipped by Daniel Grant?

"Your skin's so soft," he murmured, his hand torturously skimming my body.

"Please." I sighed, writhing helplessly, trying to make contact with his hand.

He responded to my whispered plea by tentatively running his fingers downward between my legs. His touch was agonizing in its softness and sent a piercing spasm of pleasure through my whole body. Was it possible to come from a single touch? His fingers had barely grazed me, and I felt as if I could fly apart at the seams.

"There's my sweet, wet velvet," he breathed in my ear.

I gasped while Daniel traced a tickling path across my skin. There was no rhyme or reason to his movements—just a delicious dance as his fingertips moved with no apparent rhythm. Then I realized there was a rhyme *and* a reason. He was trying to drive me mad!

"Daniel, please!"

"So polite, Aubrey."

"Not fair," I said, my voice barely more than a husky whisper. "You're teasing me."

"My apologies. How's this?" he asked, sliding his fingers across my sensitive skin.

"*Oh, God.*"

"Yeah? Just like that?" His voice was almost as hoarse as mine. He increased the pressure and speed of his fingers, moving them in deliberate circles.

Just like that.

I loved this man. I absolutely loved him. And his fingers? Oh, I loved them too. My love for his fingers quickly became adoration when two of them slipped inside me.

"Jesus!"

"Some time in the last couple of minutes you seem to have found God," he whispered.

Never mind *God*—Daniel appeared to have found me a direct route to heaven. The sensations he aroused were indescribable. I couldn't help lifting my hips to meet each lovely stroke.

"Oh, fuck, Daniel."

"So much for God," he breathed, claiming my mouth and kissing me hard as his fingers continued to drive me to distraction.

I was a quivering ball of need, making the most inhuman sounds against Daniel's lips, clutching him everywhere—his shoulders, his back, fumbling helplessly with the buttons on his jeans as I writhed and panted, curling my toes into the rug. He continued flicking my tongue with his in time with the movement of his fingers. Oh God, his tongue! I wanted his tongue on me!

I pushed at his shoulders.

"What is it? Tell me what you want," he said, still swirling his fingers, now wet and slippery between my legs.

"I can't...I can't."

"Of course you can," he murmured. "Tell me. I want to hear you say the words."

He stilled his hand, and his mouth twisted into a sly smile. Did he think that because his fingers were no longer moving that I could formulate thoughts? Didn't he realize how mortifying the idea of telling him what I wanted actually was? I could barely think it, never mind say it! I closed my eyes and swallowed thickly.

"I want…I need…" Nope. I couldn't do it.

"Yes?" he encouraged, licking his lips eagerly. "Tell me."

An epic blush crept up my neck and into my face. I needed an out. So, I plundered. I plagiarized. I cheated.

"'*Let lips do what hands do,*'" I said, pushing at his shoulders again.

He chuckled softly. "I can't believe you can quote Shakespeare at a time like this. Cleverness like that ought to be rewarded."

He kissed me gently, and I could feel his smile against my lips. And then he moved, his tongue darting across my skin as he made his way from my neck to my breasts, and then stopped to drop a circle of kisses around my belly button. His hands wrapped around my hips, holding me still, and his hair tickled my tummy as he moved lower and lower, slowly torturing me with anticipation, until finally there was no more teasing. There was only pleasure.

He anchored me with his mouth, and the whole universe was Daniel's lips, his tongue, his fingers.

I moaned, hardly recognizing my own voice as I laced my fingers through his hair, holding him in place. *Do that forever.*

Hearing Daniel's appreciative moans as his tongue darted against me with excruciating precision was too much. I arched upward and tugged his hair hard. He gripped my thighs, growling. *Fucking hell!*

I dropped my head to the side, vaguely aware of the jazz music in the background, feeling rather than seeing the flames leaping in the fire as Daniel's tongue coaxed me toward ecstasy.

I was there. I was *right there.*

All I had to do was let go.

I stroked Daniel's hair and heard myself saying his name repeatedly.

Close…so *close.*

With my heart knocking at my ribs, I opened my eyes, looking up at wooden beams crisscrossing above me, and I suddenly realized that this was all wrong because no, no, no…I didn't want to be staring at a ceiling right now! Not the first time. No, I wanted to look into

Daniel's eyes and feel him inside me—to feel not only physically satisfied but emotionally connected, too. I needed him to stop *now* before I was too far gone. I attempted to wriggle away from his touch.

"Daniel," I said, reaching for his shoulders, urging him to stop and move back up my body.

He hummed, his tongue still flicking deliciously.

"Stop. Please stop."

I lifted my head, and his eyes met mine. "Are you okay?"

"I'm—yes, I'm fine. But please, Daniel, I want you up here…"

He dropped a sweet, soft kiss on my inner thigh and then moved back up to lie beside me. "Are you sure you're okay?"

I nodded and kissed him fiercely, tasting myself on his lips and on his tongue. I reached between our bodies, pulling the rest of the buttons of his fly open, and he shifted his hips with the same sense of urgency I had. He helped me as I struggled to push his jeans and boxers down his legs. I didn't have the patience to tease him. I wanted to touch him. I needed him inside me.

I stroked him, closing my eyes as I felt him for the first time, bare in my hand, reveling in the silky smoothness of his skin while he pressed himself insistently into my palm, pleading for more pressure.

"Oh God, Aubrey," he whispered.

He propped himself up on one elbow, his other hand cupping my breast, pinching my nipple as I parted my legs and guided him between them. His eyes were clouded, his breathing faltered, and he was shaking his head in a way that usually meant *no,* but which, right then, could only be interpreted as *yes. Hell, yes.*

No more waiting. With a sudden sweeping gesture, he pushed aside the pillows scattered around us so that I was now lying flat against the rug. My heart beat madly, excited by his sudden urgency.

"Now?" he whispered.

Oh, God, finally!

"Yes!"

And with his eyes locked on mine, he eased himself inside me. All the needing and wanting, the months of waiting, crystallized in this moment.

"So perfect," he murmured as his lips sought mine.

His muscles worked beneath my hands as I arched my body to meet his every move. It *was* perfect. *He* was perfect. The tempo of the music dictated his unhurried pace, allowing for infinite sensation. Each movement was slow and exquisite.

I did my best to remember every detail—the fire, the music, the softness of the rug, the heat of his skin, the stubble along his jaw line, the straining tendons in his shoulders, his breathing, and, of course, the sweet union of our bodies.

His nose was barely touching mine, and our eyes were locked in their own heated embrace when he moved his hand to where we were joined and gently circled his fingers.

"Yes?" he said softly, brushing his lips against mine.

I nodded.

Yes. A thousand times, yes.

He smiled knowingly, intent on discovering what delighted me, what secret touches would make me come unhinged before him, and I knew without a doubt that his efforts would be rewarded. I stretched my arms above my head, straining upward, outward—seeking that perfect moment of bliss.

Daniel followed the lines and curves of my body, his mouth against mine, not kissing me but sharing my breath, reaching for one of my hands with an outstretched arm and threading his fingers tightly through mine. He stroked me with his other hand, devoted to a single-minded goal.

"I can't wait to watch you come."

His voice, low and husky, was my undoing. My whole body buzzed in anticipation. I tried to keep my eyes open, knowing he was watching me, wanting to share this experience with me as much as I wanted to share it with him. Every muscle and nerve in my body was directed inward as if by some magnetic force which then exploded outward in an exquisite rush of pure pleasure. Weeks of sexual tension were obliterated in a blinding flash of euphoria.

I quivered, breathing his name into his open mouth, and then I sighed, dropping my head back as I tried to regain my breathing.

He stared at me as I gradually floated back to earth.

"That was one of the most incredible things I've ever seen," he said at last, his voice thick with emotion. He brushed his thumb across my fingers.

"It felt pretty incredible, too." I rubbed the back of his leg with my toes. "Care to join me?"

He smiled lazily and then hooked his hand behind my knee and hitched my leg up. He brought his face close to mine again. "I thought you'd never ask." He moved slowly but rhythmically. Captivated, I watched the vein on his forehead straining, the muscle in his jaw jumping with his effort, his breathing becoming heavier, more rapid as he moved inside me. How many times had I imagined this moment, tried to picture Daniel's face contorting with ecstasy? My imagination was a poor substitute for reality.

I listened to his labored breathing and felt the tautness of his muscles straining against mine. I'd angled my face to kiss him when suddenly, with a sharp gasp, he rolled onto his back, pulling his hand free of my grasp and placing it over his chest, wincing.

"Daniel? What's wrong?"

"My heart," he said. "It feels like it's going to leap out of my chest. It's not right."

"That's normal. My heart is racing too."

He shook his head. "No, you don't understand. It's — fuck — it's too much like that feeling I get before I have an anxiety attack."

I moved in close to his side and placed my hand on top of his. "Breathe for a second. You're fine. I'm sure you're fine. An accelerated heart rate is a normal physiological response, right?"

He rubbed at his eyes in frustration. "I don't want to lose control. Maybe my subconscious…"

"This is right. It's perfect. Try to relax." My heart ached for him, but at the same time I was sure he was over-thinking things. I caressed his cheek.

He closed his eyes and swallowed, breathing deeply.

"Fuck, I'm ruining everything. I've tried so hard to stay in control all day."

I turned his face, forcing him to look at me. "Hey, you're not ruining anything."

"What if I lose —"

"Shh. You're not going to lose control. I don't think this is anxiety. You're second guessing yourself. But we aren't doing anything wrong. You know that."

He took my hand and threaded his fingers through mine. "I want this to be perfect for you."

"This *is* perfect for me. I want it to be perfect for you, too."

I kissed him again, teasing his mouth open with my tongue, trying to reassure him that our love was right—that we were meant to be together and there was nothing for him to feel anxious about.

"I don't deserve you," he said, shaking his head. "You're so incredible."

"Together *we're* incredible." I looked at him for a moment. "Why don't you let me take control for a few minutes?"

I sat up and moved over to straddle him, watching for any sign of objection. He swallowed thickly.

"Holy fuck, Aubrey."

I angled my body over his. "It's your turn," I whispered.

He moaned and gripped my thighs, guiding my movements. I tried to measure his expression for signs of anxiety as well as pleasure. God help me if I was wrong about this.

He cupped one of my breasts with one hand, holding my hip with the other. Suddenly he pushed me up to a seated position, moving with me and wrapping one arm around my waist. I ran my hands down his back, burying my face in his neck, feeling his pulse beating erratically under my lips.

"You feel incredible," he said.

"This is so right. You know it is," I whispered. "Just let go."

He moaned in response.

I dug my nails into his back.

"Oh, yeah," he urged me.

I dragged my nails up his back, all the way to his shoulders, feeling him arch upward with the movement of my fingers. Then, with a hoarse cry, he pushed into me hard, breathing my name. Those two syllables were the most beautiful sound in the world as he experienced physical release.

I held on to him for dear life, so relieved. His face was nestled in the crook of my neck as he rocked me. I ran my fingers through his hair, my heart flipping with pure happiness. We'd finally given ourselves to each other. Maybe it hadn't gone without a hitch, but I didn't care. It had been perfect.

"I love you so much," he said at last.

Tears welled in my eyes, and my throat ached with emotion. "I love you, too. More than ever." I remained cocooned in his warmth for a moment, and then I leaned back and placed my hand over his heart. "You scared me for a second."

He laughed softly.

"I scared myself. I don't know what came over me. But you know what? You were right. I am okay. I'm *more* than okay. I'm the luckiest man in the world. Thank you for keeping me grounded. But how are you?"

He ran his thumbs tenderly under my eyes, catching an errant tear. I shook my head as he reclined back onto the rug, and I lowered myself onto his chest.

"A little overwhelmed, I guess." I tangled my legs with his, rubbing against his glorious thighs and snuggling up into his side, already missing the intimacy of our joined bodies.

He stroked my hair gently. "I know what you mean. That was completely mind-blowing."

I grinned up at him. "It was pretty amazing. I think you've been holding out on me. You've got some mad skills, mister."

He laughed and tickled my back with his fingertips. "I thought I was fairly forthright about my manly prowess. But you're one to talk. You told me a little fib a few weeks ago."

I frowned at him defensively. "What's that?"

"Well," he said rolling me onto my back and trapping my legs with one of his. "You told me you've never been horseback riding."

"I haven't," I said. "I've never ridden a horse. I swear."

"Hmm." He regarded me suspiciously. Then, with a cheeky grin, he added, "After what I just witnessed, I find that *very* hard to believe, young lady."

Love Speaks

…when Love speaks, the voice of all the gods
Makes heaven drowsy with the harmony.
(*Love's Labour's Lost*, Act IV, Scene 3)

Did I look different? Was there anything about me that said, "*I just had awesome although slightly stressful first-time sex with Daniel Grant?*"

Not really, although my chin was pretty red. And this was no post-coital flush. This was razor-burn-red. I leaned into the mirror.

"You're just gonna have to toughen the hell up," I said to my rosy chin.

It glowered back at me. I quickly rubbed some moisturizer on my face and went back down the hallway to the living room where Daniel was waiting for me in front of the dying fire, now wearing a pair of cargo pants and a black T-shirt.

"There you are," he said, patting the cushion beside him and looking me up and down. "Hey, *that's* nice. Very sexy."

I snuggled into his side, pulling my feet up under me. The belted silk wrap hiked up, barely covering my ass. Daniel reached down to pull up the hem, sneaking a peek at the matching panties I'd put on. He whistled and squeezed my thigh.

"La Vie en Rose?"

"Uh-huh. You approve?"

"I do." He pressed his lips to mine, caressing my breast through the silky fabric. "So far I love what you picked out. I can't wait to see the rest." He rubbed his thumb gently across my chin. "Did I do that? I should shave."

"No, it's fine," I said. "You don't need to. I'll get used to it. Really."

He frowned like he wasn't convinced, but then he kissed me gently, trying not to rub his scruff against me. I cuddled up closer, sneaking my hand under his T-shirt and resting it on his heart.

"How are you feeling?" I asked.

"I'm fine. Sorry if I scared you."

"Daniel, it's okay. It was *real*. I'm not looking for something from a fairy tale or a movie. I've never wanted that. I just want you."

"How do you know just what I need to hear?"

"I've always thought that about you, too. I guess we're good for each other."

"I guess we are. Thank you for being so understanding. Aside from the fact that it was insanely hot watching you take control like that, I think you were right. I needed to stop analyzing everything. It was just such an unknown."

"What was?"

"Sex. With the anxiety issues. I didn't know what to expect."

I sat up. "Wait a minute, are you telling me you haven't had sex since you started having your anxiety attacks?"

He nodded and frowned. "Why do you sound so surprised?"

I blinked incredulously. "But that was last year."

"Right. I haven't been with anyone in almost a year and a half."

"But you're so…"

He looked at me, a bemused expression on his face. "So…?"

"So…fuck hot," I blurted.

He laughed. "Oh, poppet, you're so good for my ego."

"Well, it's true. That's just a waste."

He regarded me with mock seriousness. "So, by having sex with me, you're basically doing a public service? Making sure I'm put to good use?"

"Absolutely. Waste not, want not." *And I want. I really, really want.*

"Seriously, though," he said, looking at me earnestly. "You didn't take me for a...I don't even know the word."

"A man whore?" I suggested.

He smirked and nodded. "I guess that's as good a term as any."

"No," I assured him. "I mean, I'm surprised that you've been unattached all this time, but I guess I assumed..."

"Assumed?"

"I don't know. Sabrina...?"

He sighed and took my hand in his. "Don't even go there. We haven't been together that way in years. She was a supportive friend when I came back to Canada last spring, but I had no interest in any romantic liaisons, trust me. She's history, Aubrey. Ancient history."

And then he kissed me deeply, slowly, until I was sure I could feel his love filling every spare corner of my heart and squeezing out all of my self-doubt. I didn't have to worry about Sabrina, or anyone else for that matter. He loved *me*. He wanted *me*.

"You know what amazes me?" he asked. "I still can't believe we've made it. It's okay for me to love you, to make love to you. No one can do anything about it. I could make love to you again, right this minute. There's no reason to stop, no need to feel guilty. It's surreal, after all this time."

"It's pretty amazing, that's for sure." I batted my eyelashes at him hopefully. "So, do you want to?"

He chuckled and shifted his body so that his legs were stretched out and I was tucked between him and the back of the couch.

"Of course I do. But I also want to do a million other things—all the little things we haven't been able to do. I want to curl up with you and talk for hours, watch movies, drink wine, cook together, watch the sunrise, watch the sunset, sleep with you wrapped up in my arms." He tucked my hair over my ear. "I'm in love with you, Aubrey. I want to share everything with you, not just my body... *everything.*" He rolled his eyes. "God, that sounds cheesy. I'm sorry. Does this all make me less—what did you call me?"

"Fuck hot?" I laughed and shook my head. "Not at all. It actually makes me love you more, if that's possible."

He rested his hand on my hip and kissed my forehead. "Good."

I looked at him quietly, trying to digest all the wonderful things he'd just said.

He examined my expression, and his eyebrows furrowed. "You do believe me, right?"

"Of course," I said. "It's just…I have to admit it *did* cross my mind at one point that maybe the novelty would wear off. Like maybe part of my appeal was that I was forbidden — "

He frowned and interrupted me. "Do you want to know why I'm not tearing this incredibly sexy but ridiculously flimsy robe off of you right this minute?"

"I guess."

"Because we have all weekend together. And as much as I'd love to devour you, I think I'd rather savor you and enjoy every single moment." He punctuated his words with kisses.

He slid his hands inside my robe, finding the curve of my breast, teasing me until I was trembling and the familiar ache between my legs surged back with a vengeance. I moaned and slipped my hand up his thigh.

"I have a funny feeling you're trying to make it difficult for me to resist you," he murmured, running his nose along my cheekbone.

"I might be." I pressed myself against his hand, urging him to continue his caresses.

"It pains me to admit this, sweetheart, but I'm not seventeen. I do need a *little* recovery time."

He leaned over the arm of the couch and poured us each another glass of wine.

"Recovery time, eh?" I said, lifting my eyebrow.

"Uh-oh. Maybe I shouldn't have said that. Do you need to give this some thought now that you know I'm not Johnny Endurance?"

"Yeah," I said, feigning disappointment. "I don't know about Johnny Endurance, but you did sort of mislead me with the John Holmes thing. I guess I shouldn't have gotten my hopes up."

He snorted and squeezed my thigh playfully. "Okay, let me get this straight — you don't want something from a fairy tale, but you *do* want something from a skin flick?"

I shrugged, and he laughed.

"I may not be a porn star, but I guarantee I'll make you eat those words," he said. "Give me half an hour, and you'll be sorry."

"You promise?" I asked playfully.

"Cross my heart." He drew a little X on his chest.

"I look forward to it, Mr. Grant."

I made an exaggerated show of looking at the clock on the mantelpiece while I sipped my wine and stretched my legs out across his lap, occasionally rubbing my foot against his zipper. Though he resolutely refused to react, the shadow of a smile played on his lips.

He relaxed against the couch, running his fingertips lightly up and down my legs, making me tingle with every sweep. I marveled at how natural this all felt. It was as if we had done this every night for months. There was something to be said for getting to know someone before becoming intimate. We could talk seriously, we could joke around—everything was so easy. All of the turmoil we'd been through seemed to have brought us closer together, showing us the importance of being completely open and honest with one another.

He rolled his head to the side to look at me. "You've gone very quiet all of a sudden. What are you thinking?"

"About how happy I am. I'm comfortable here, and with you."

"I feel the same way. It's been ages since I've felt...*content*. I'm glad you like it here."

"It's perfect," I sighed as he massaged my calf. "Daniel, did you really think about us here? Me lying on the rug in front of the fire?"

"Honestly? I sat on this very couch when I was up here with my parents and imagined you doing exactly what you did earlier—holding out your hand to me, like I was the only person in the world that mattered. That's when I decided I wanted to bring you up here this weekend. Earlier I had to remind myself I wasn't dreaming."

"It's rare that things work out the way we hope they will. So, where else did you imagine us?"

"Everywhere! In my bed. In the shower." He chuckled and put his hand over his eyes. "Oh, God, if you only knew what went through my mind that weekend."

"Really? Well, we'd better get moving. Maybe we should head to the bedroom. Sounds like we have a few fantasies to fulfill. Once you've fully *recovered*, that is," I added with a wink.

He stood up and grabbed the bottle of wine.

"Okay, you insatiable wench. How do you feel about watching a movie in bed? I brought *Casablanca*. You told me you'd like to watch it together some time."

"I wouldn't mind watching the first *half hour* of *Casablanca*," I said mischievously. I glanced at the clock. "Nope, make that the first *twenty-five* minutes."

"Oh, come on, we have to at least watch Sam sing 'As Time Goes By,'" he insisted, wrapping his arm around me, the bottle pressing against my back. "That's my favorite part."

"I don't know. My favorite part of the movie has always been the opening credits. Once they're done…the rest? Meh," I said, smiling as I took his hand and led him to his bedroom.

Daniel rummaged around in his bag and tossed the movie on the dresser, then headed to the washroom. I took the opportunity to examine the books on his shelf and the photos perched here and there, mostly family shots of summers spent at the cottage—he and his brothers playing in the water, all tanned, with mops of sun-kissed hair; the family gathered around the barbeque; Daniel with his guitar beside a fire pit; Jeremy roasting marshmallows; their mom sitting in the screened-in porch, drinking wine; his dad snoozing in the hammock…

Irrational pangs of envy stabbed my stomach. I was coveting Daniel's upbringing. My own had been so different. Once my mom and dad separated, life became very much a case of plodding along, one day rolling into the next with little to distinguish one week from another.

Summers were long and boring. Part-time jobs were more and more crucial as my aspiration to attend university became firmly rooted in my mind, along with the realization that my parents' income wouldn't be enough to help me in any significant way.

I frowned as I thought back over my adolescence. The last truly carefree summer had been the one before I'd started ninth grade, but if I was being honest, once my father had left when I was eleven, I'd begun to dread summers. Being a latchkey kid and an only child made for a lot of very long, quiet days. Of course I had a handful of close neighborhood friends, but they would inevitably go away on vacation or head off to camp. It was no wonder I'd become such a bookworm.

"Hey, you okay?"

Daniel was behind me. I hadn't even heard him come back in. I was holding a picture of him sitting on the dock with his guitar, the setting sun in the background. I placed it on the shelf and turned, locking my hands around his neck.

"I'm fine."

"You sure? You seemed very deep in thought."

He looked over my shoulder at the picture I'd been holding and rubbed my back.

"I was thinking about my dad. When I was little, we used to go camping at Sandbanks. My dad would rent a boat, and we'd go out really early, just the two of us, to catch the sunrise. I loved watching the sun come up with the mist hovering on the water…" I shrugged. "It was *our time,* you know?"

"Those are special memories. I love being on the water too. Being out on the lake in a boat when everything is peaceful? Nothing compares, especially when the sun's coming up or setting."

He wrapped his arms around me, swaying gently. I was reminded of all the times we'd held each other, knowing an embrace was all we could share. I didn't want to let go, but finally I did, unlocking my hands and easing myself back.

"So, are we gonna watch this movie or what?" I asked.

He chuckled. "You really don't want to watch it, do you?"

"I'm a terrible actress, huh?"

"Not to worry. You have other *far* more interesting talents," he said, scooping me up into his arms and lowering me onto the bed. I scampered up toward the pillows. He stood beside the bed, rolling his shoulders and rubbing his neck. "Frig, my shoulders are killing me."

"Are you implying that I'm heavy, sunshine?"

"Not at all. I think it's from marking exams — being hunched over for hours in the same position. Occupational hazard, I suppose."

I resisted the urge to ask him how I'd done on my exam. The question had nibbled at the edges of my mind all day, but I was firm in my determination to avoid putting him on the spot or making any reference to the TA/student relationship which was, thank the freaking Lord, over and done with. Instead, I focused on his muscle pain.

"Do you want a back rub?"

"Are you serious?"

"Of course I'm serious."

"Fuck, yes, I would love one. I can't even remember the last time—"

I held up my hand. "Don't want you to remember the last time, sailor."

"Right. Sorry."

I shook my head. "It's okay." I patted the bed. "Lie down here, and I'll see what I can do." I cracked my fingers and shook out my hands, feigning an expertise I didn't actually have.

He grinned like a little boy on Christmas morning and peeled off his T-shirt, tossing it over his desk chair. He made a move to climb onto the bed, but I stopped him.

"You might as well lose the pants too. I mean, you *do* want to be comfortable, right?"

"Of course." He smiled knowingly, removing his pants.

I salivated at the sight of his long, toned thighs and the way his boxers sat just below his belly button, hiding what had quickly become my *new* favorite part of his body.

How much longer until he was suitably recovered? Surely he'd be good to go now? I had such a one-track mind. Was I really an insatiable wench? Pfft. Who wouldn't be, in my position? After weeks and weeks of delayed gratification, my patience had officially worn thin.

Daniel made a big production of getting comfortable, stretching out on his stomach and resting his head on the pillow with his arms underneath. I straddled him, first running my fingers up and down his back and then rubbing his shoulders, pressing my thumbs into his muscles. He moaned approvingly. I loved his back. So strong and lean. Unfortunately, right now he was also sporting some rather angry red marks.

"Wow, I did a number on you. I think I drew blood."

"I don't care. It felt amazing. I love it when you scratch me like that."

"Yes, you've made that abundantly clear."

He turned his head, trying to peer up at me. "Does that bother you?"

"Does what bother me?"

"Me being so vocal about what I want?"

"No, why would it? It's incredibly hot."

"I think so too." He was quiet for a moment. "Are you always so reticent? About asking for what *you* want, I mean."

I rested my hands on his shoulder blades. "I'm reticent?"

"A little. When you were pushing on my shoulders earlier, I got the idea, and hauling out a Shakespearean quotation was brilliant, but I'd much rather hear you *ask* for what you want."

I slid off and sat beside him.

"I don't know. I guess I was a little shy. It's been a long time for me, too — since I've been with someone. I didn't want you to think I was — I don't know." I covered my eyes with my hand, embarrassed again.

Daniel pushed himself up onto an elbow.

"You don't have to be shy with me, poppet. I love you. I want you to feel comfortable saying anything to me, sharing everything. I wouldn't think you were crude or crass or anything. You know that, right?"

I shrugged.

"Sex is an incredibly sensory experience. Different things appeal to different people. You felt *amazing*, and you looked incredibly sexy. I love the way you taste, the scent of your skin — but hearing you saying please over and over, and the way you reacted to my touch? You can't imagine the effect that had on me. I guarantee if you want to see me lose my shit, talk to me. Tell me what you want. Or tell me what you want to do to *me*. I'll be putty in your hands."

I nodded reluctantly.

All of a sudden, he started back-tracking. "But if it makes you feel awkward, of course, you don't have to. I'm sorry. I hope I haven't made you self-conscious."

"No, it's okay. I know what you mean about the effect words can have. When you touched me for the first time and said what you did — something about sweet velvet?" I smiled at the memory. "I just about fell apart."

"I did too." He kissed my knee, gazing up at me from under his beautiful lashes.

"I promise to try to be more communicative about what I want. I suppose I need a little more *practice.*"

He chuckled. "When was the last time you looked at the clock?"

"I hadn't even noticed that your half-hour recovery time will be up in four minutes."

"I'm starting to get the picture. You just want me for my body. It's okay, you can admit it. You obviously can't resist—"

"All right, on your stomach, Mr. Ego. Let's get on with this back rub."

He smiled wickedly and rolled over. I resituated myself and picked up where I'd left off, mumbling about insatiable wenches and recovery times. At first he snickered as he listened to me, but then he settled into the pillow with a sigh. I quietly rubbed his lovely shoulders, kneading his muscles and pressure points. He closed his eyes, moaning with satisfaction and occasionally flinching if I hit a tender spot.

As his breathing deepened, I congratulated myself. I was better at this than I'd thought. He was *really* relaxed. When I heard him make a funny little snuffling sound, I frowned. "Daniel?" I whispered, kissing him softly on the shoulder.

No answer. He was breathing deeply and steadily. Wait. He was snoring! The fucker had fallen asleep!

My knee-jerk reaction quickly gave way to guilt. Of course he was exhausted. He'd spent the week doing cartwheels to please everyone—frantically marking to meet Professor Brown's deadlines, attending all of his father's social events, driving up here on Thursday to get things ready for me, and then getting up early today to pick me up and driving another two hours. He must have been completely wiped. It was a miracle he'd lasted as long as he had without nodding off.

I carefully climbed over his body and tiptoed to the bathroom, where I got ready for bed and popped my birth control pill. I changed into a slinky nightie, figuring he'd at least get to see it in the morning.

Back in the bedroom, I turned off the bedside lamp and surveyed the bed. He was dead to the world and lying the wrong way around—his head where his feet ought to be. I grabbed a pillow and carefully settled in beside him. I hadn't really thought I was all that tired, but as I listened to his steady breathing, my own eyes drooped, and sleep quickly overtook me.

When a voice roused me from my sleep, I thought for a minute Daniel had woken up and started watching the movie after all, but the voice wasn't coming from the TV. Daniel was curled around me, his chest pressed against my back as he mumbled in his sleep. I peered at the digital clock on the nightstand. It was two in the morning. I snuggled back into his arms.

"You're mine," he murmured. Then he breathed deeply a few times. "You're mine."

We'd slept together twice now, and both times he'd talked in his sleep. This was obviously a nocturnal habit. What was he dreaming about? I wished I could be inside his mind, if only for a moment.

Once more he uttered the same two words and then sighed contentedly.

I smiled and turned my head. "You're right, Daniel. I *am* yours," I whispered.

CHAPTER 29

Not Imagined

The dream's here still: even when I wake, it is
Without me, as within me; not imagined, felt.
(*Cymbeline*, Act IV, Scene 2)

As soon as I woke up on Sunday morning, my first thought was of Daniel. This was nothing new. What *was* new was the fact that this morning I would open my eyes and find him right beside me. I smiled and rolled over, expecting to see pillow-tousled sex hair. I didn't. Instead, where his head should have been, there was a paper rose.

I reached out from under the blanket to grasp the paper. Origami? Seriously? I fought the urge to laugh, instead trying to focus on the effort he'd put into the gesture.

After a quick trip to the washroom, I headed down the hall to find him. He was in a sweatshirt and PJ bottoms, sitting on the sofa in the family room and quietly plucking away at his guitar, humming along. I'd wondered if I would get to hear him play this weekend when he'd brought his guitar case in from the car.

I couldn't bring myself to interrupt, so I wrapped my arms around myself and rested against the wall, listening to him strum. I didn't recognize the tune. After a few moments, I crossed the room and leaned over the back of the couch to lightly touch his sleeve.

"Good morning, handsome."

He glanced up at me, startled. "Hey, crazy legs. I didn't hear you."

"Sorry. I didn't mean to sneak up on you. That was a pretty song."

He waved his hand dismissively, propping the guitar on the coffee table and turning around to place his hand over mine on the back of the couch. "You must be freezing," he said, motioning to my nightie.

"A little. You don't have to stop playing, you know."

He made his way around the couch and hugged me, rubbing my back vigorously. "I can play any time."

"Oh, you're so warm." I sighed, gratefully burrowing into his neck. "I was sad when I woke up and you weren't there."

"Well, let's go back to bed and have a cuddle."

He took my hand and led me back to the bedroom. After putting the pillows back where they ought to be, he slid under the covers fully dressed. I crawled in to join him, snuggling into the warmth of his chest.

He flinched when I stuck my toes up the bottom of his pant leg. "Your feet are freezing."

"I know. Warm them up for me?"

"I'll try." He rubbed his toasty feet against the little blocks of ice at the end of my legs.

"Anything else need warming?" he asked.

"Mmm, my lips are a little chilly."

He smiled and kissed me slowly, his hands pressed into the small of my back, drawing my hips against his. I moaned and clung to his sleeve. And then, out of nowhere, my stomach made a loud gurgling noise.

"Someone's hungry," Daniel said.

"Stupid stomach."

He perched on his elbow. "Do you normally eat breakfast?"

"Yeah, I can pretty much eat any time," I admitted. "I tend to start with a coffee, though."

"Me too," he said. "I'll go grab us a cup. I made a pot a little while ago."

He started to get up, and I grabbed the sides of his sweatshirt. "In a minute, okay? Can we hang out here for a bit longer?"

"Of course." He settled back into the pillow and gently brushed my hair off my face. "Did you sleep okay?"

"Yes. Really well. You?"

"I slept all right. Woke up really early and couldn't get back to sleep, though."

"I hate that."

"Me too. It happens to me a fair bit. I've never been a great sleeper. Sometimes my brain just won't shut down. And I had this *very* sexy dream in the middle of the night. I couldn't stop thinking about it." He smirked.

"Really? I had a dream too."

"You did? What happened in your dream?"

"I dreamt that I was fast asleep, and you woke me up and ravished me," I said, snuggling even closer to him.

"Huh, that's very interesting because I dreamt that we were curled up fast asleep and then you woke *me* up and ravished me. Seems to me, you were pretty desperate. It was hot and *very* sensual."

I laughed and shook my head, abandoning the pretense of the dream. "I'm surprised to hear you say that, Mr. Chattypants. Because it was very *quiet*, if I remember correctly. I thought you were a big fan of dirty talk."

He nuzzled my neck and kissed my shoulder, right where he'd nibbled on me in the night. "You're right, it *was* quiet. I suppose as much as I love dirty talk, there's something to be said for communicating with your body. There was a perfect serenity about it. I needed that." He kissed the tip of my nose. "Thank you for giving me the space I needed to grapple with my demons last night."

"I *was* pretty understanding, wasn't I?" I smiled at him cheekily. "I love you, Daniel, but for the record, you can tell your demons to fuck the hell off, or I'll kick their asses."

"I'll be sure to pass that message along." He sighed contentedly, and we both lay for a while, lost in our thoughts. "You know, I don't think there's any better feeling in the world than waking up with the woman you adore cuddled up against you and knowing you can just make love to her there and then."

"I know. I'm *so* glad you woke me up."

"I didn't wake you up, you woke me up," he insisted. "I guess you figured I'd slacked off long enough."

"Maybe I wouldn't have been awake in the first place if you hadn't been talking in your sleep."

"Oh, shit, I was?"

"Yep."

"Uh-oh. Anything incriminating?" he asked, peering down at me.

"No. Unless you weren't talking about me, in which case it's devastating."

"Oh, really? What did I say?"

Now he wasn't just curious; he was downright fascinated. I threaded my fingers through his.

"You said, 'You're mine.'"

"Huh. That's interesting." He seemed to be rolling the words around in his mouth. "It's not surprising, though. You know how an idea gets kind of stuck in your head? I guess that's what happened. I may have been asleep, but my brain was still processing the idea."

"So, the idea of me being yours is something you've been thinking about a lot?"

"Let's just say there's a logical explanation for why those words were stuck in my head. But I can't tell you what it is. Not yet, anyway. It's a surprise. But I guarantee—I *was* talking about you."

"Does this surprise have anything to do with your trip to Orillia?"

"I was wondering if you'd ask about that. I thought you'd forgotten."

I shook my head.

"This surprise has nothing to do with it. But later on you'll find out about that, too."

"So, you're going to be full of surprises today? First origami, now this? You have so many hidden talents, Mr. Grant."

He laughed and patted my backside. "It would have been easier to buy you a dozen roses like my grandfather did when Patty finished her classes, but this seemed more original. And it was free." He dropped a gentle kiss on my cheek. "Okay, time for breakfast in bed. You stay here," he said, tugging the sheet up to my shoulders and tucking me in with a kiss and a wink that would have dissolved my undies, had I been wearing any.

While he whistled his way to the kitchen, I thought about Daniel's demons. Was he really at peace with everything? I was at a loss for what more I could do. I'd simply have to be patient and understanding. It went without saying that he was worth it. This sweet man had made me origami and was bringing me breakfast in bed! It was a no-brainer!

Again I was amazed that this was *my* life. I was here in this beautiful cottage, Daniel and I had made love in front of the fire, and I hadn't dreamed those incredible moments of intimacy in the night. I pinched my arm. Yep. I was awake.

This was my life.

He returned a few minutes later, carrying a tray with two steaming mugs of coffee, glasses of orange juice, and cinnamon buns with sliced honeydew melon on the side. Oh yeah.

"My lady," he said, placing the tray in the middle of the bed.

"Wow, thank you. What a treat."

I propped the pillow behind my head, and we spent the next half hour eating, drinking our coffee, chatting about nonsense, and dissecting and re-assembling the origami rose. Once breakfast was out of the way, I stretched lazily against Daniel's chest. I closed my eyes, basking in the feel of the sun warming my face as it streamed in the window and enjoying the heat of Daniel's body.

"Thank you for breakfast," I whispered.

"I know it wasn't fancy—"

"I don't need fancy," I assured him. "You should know that by now."

"I do know, and I'm learning to appreciate that."

"I love you, Daniel."

"I love you too," he said, giving me a kiss that quickly changed from playful to passionate. My heart raced as his hands slid down my back to pull me gently against his hips. "I love you a lot," he murmured against my lips. "You can't even imagine how much."

"I don't need to imagine. I think I can feel it for myself."

"I should hope so," he said.

As his tongue darted against mine, I imagined the soft wetness of it between my legs, remembering how he'd worshipped me with his mouth the night before. I wanted him again, and I wanted him *now*. It was time to cross another fantasy off his list.

"Daniel, are you feeling adventurous?"

"Adventurous?" His mouth turned up at the corner. "What are you thinking?"

I held up my hand. "In front of the fire," I said, counting on my thumb. "In bed," I added, counting off my index finger. I popped a third finger up, raising my eyebrow at the same time. "Shower?"

He wiggled out from under me, climbing off the bed and beckoning me to join him. I crawled to the edge of the mattress, and he picked me up and threw me over his shoulder. I giggled as he carried me all the way to the shower. We then proceeded to empty the hot water tank so that Daniel could prove once and for all that he'd kicked those demons' asses.

He also proved to have *very* strong legs.

A Compelling Occasion

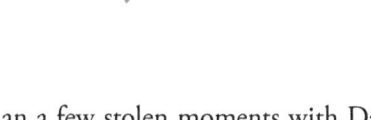

Under a compelling occasion, let women die...
(*Antony and Cleopatra*, Act 1, Scene 2)

Spending more than a few stolen moments with Daniel was a novelty, one which would take some getting used to. It seemed unreal that we had time to go for another leisurely stroll, to curl up on the couch and watch *Casablanca*, and to laze around in the great room, swapping sections of the newspaper. It was pure luxury to sit next to him, holding hands and knowing we still had hours and hours together to do more of the same.

We had a light lunch and planned the rest of the day, aiming to eat dinner at six thirty before we had to go back to Toronto. My mind wandered as we ate in comfortable silence, the music from the iPod dock wafting into the kitchen from the great room.

"You know what?" I mused. "Orgasms are weird."

Daniel spluttered, and I patted him on the back as he coughed and rubbed his eyes.

"Where the fuck did that come from?" He laughed.

"I was watching you pick the tomatoes out of your sandwich, and it made me think of Patty, which made me think of lycopene and oil changes, and then I thought about orgasms."

"That is…strangely logical," he said, chuckling and taking another bite of his sandwich.

"Patty wouldn't be pleased to see you doing that," I observed, pointing to the rejected tomatoes. "Aren't you concerned about your prostate's health?"

"Not any more I'm not," he said, chewing and smiling at me devilishly. "I've had my oil changed three times in the last sixteen hours. Frankly, I think Patty would be thrilled."

"You're probably right. You gonna call and tell her?"

He chuckled again. "I don't think so." He raised an eyebrow. "I think you should tell her. After all, you're the one who's so gainfully *employ*ed. You should call her tomorrow and give her all the details. I insist."

I kicked his foot under the table. "I promise not to tell her you're not eating your tomatoes if you promise not to make me tell her I'm changing your oil," I said, balling up the napkin on my plate.

"Deal."

Daniel cleared our plates and filled the sink with soapy water. Our morning cups and plates were still sitting unwashed on the counter. Obviously he couldn't bear to leave two meals' worth of dishes dirty. I joined him at the counter.

"How *is* Patty, anyway?"

"She's well. I spoke to her during the week and told her I was bringing you up here. She was happy to hear that."

I bumped him over with my hip, handing him the dish towel and taking over the washing. "Is she still hanging out with Gerald?"

Daniel leaned against the counter and smiled. "Yep. Still keeping him a secret, though."

"Why do you suppose she won't tell your parents?"

He shrugged as he dried our coffee mugs. "I'm not sure if it's because she thinks they won't approve, or if she's afraid of upsetting my mom, you know, as if she's somehow disrespecting my grandfather." He stowed the mugs in the cupboard. I watched as he spun every cup on the shelf so that the handles were all facing the same direction. Yep. Definite OCD tendencies.

I pulled the plug and rinsed out the sink, wiping the taps down with the cloth. Daniel handed me the dish towel, and I dried my hands.

"Your family just loves keeping secrets. I bet Patty would feel a lot better if she could unburden herself and tell your mom."

"You're probably right. Knowing Patty, she's probably waiting for the perfect time to spill the beans," he said, taking me in his arms and sliding his hands into the back pockets of my jeans. "But enough about my grandmother's love life. Can we back up for a second?"

"To what?" I asked, putting my hands around his neck.

"To your out of the blue comment a few minutes ago. Why do you think orgasms are *weird*? I think they're spectacular. And from my vantage point, it certainly doesn't seem like *yours* are weird. They look pretty damn amazing."

I laughed. "They are, trust me. I don't know. It's like, all that build up to this epic few seconds of such incredible physical pleasure."

"Maybe it's a good thing that an orgasm is only a few seconds long. What if the Elizabethans were right and orgasms really do shorten life?"

"*La petite mort?* You believe that?"

"I guess not. If it were true, most men wouldn't live past forty-five!"

We both laughed, and Daniel wrinkled his nose. "We talk about some of the oddest things."

I shrugged. "I don't know, I think it's kinda cool."

"It is. You're right."

He smiled, and I ran my fingers lightly under one of his eyes. "You look tired, sailor."

"I don't know why I'm so exhausted."

"You're burned out. It's been a long few months. Emotionally draining, too. Did you want to head back earlier? It's a long drive, and you were up early this morning."

"Nope. We can't leave until after dinner." He looked at me with a mysterious glint in his eyes. "Besides, there's a lasagna in the fridge that Penny made especially for us. It would be a shame not to enjoy it before we go."

"This is true."

I scrupulously avoided bringing up the topic which had been driving me crazy all day. He hadn't mentioned the surprises since this morning, and we only had the afternoon and a small part of the evening left. What was he planning?

I brushed the hair off his forehead. "Well, if you're determined to stay, how would you feel about taking a nap?"

"Seriously?"

"Why not? We can do whatever we want, right?"

"I didn't think you'd be into napping."

"Are you kidding? Sunday afternoon naps are the best."

"Especially naked ones," he said, smiling suggestively.

"You've got that right." I took a few steps backward, popping the button on my jeans as he followed me.

By the time we were halfway down the hall, we'd both discarded our jeans and T-shirts, and when Daniel carried me into his room and lowered me to his bed, we were both naked.

I pulled back the comforter and slid eagerly between the sheets.

He nudged my legs apart with his knee. "You know, I'm not sure if we should do this." His mouth traveled from my neck to my collarbone and between my breasts before flicking deliberately at my nipple. "Aren't you worried about having another orgasm? There's more precious moments I'll be taking off your life…"

"No, not worried." I parted my legs to welcome Daniel's lovely, long fingers.

"Well, in that case…"

He threw the covers back so his tongue could join his fingers as he worked his magic, bringing me to a quick, shuddering climax.

And then another. And another.

If this was shortening my life, then God help me, so be it. What a glorious way to go.

CHAPTER 31

Fantasy

Is not this something more than fantasy?
What think you on't?
(*Hamlet*, Act 1, Scene 1)

I woke and glanced at the clock radio—three thirty. I'd slept for almost an hour and a half. Sheer decadence! I slowly swung my feet to the floor and stretched. Daniel was still sleeping, lying on his stomach with his arms scooped under his pillow. I took in his strong shoulders and the dimples on his lower back, right where the sheet rested. He snored gently.

The man was incredible—adorable and hot as fuck all at once.

And he was mine. *Mine!*

And at this very moment, I was doing a very quiet—but *very* silly—happy dance in the middle of his room.

Buck naked.

I ceased my jig and looked for something to throw on without making too much noise. Daniel's black T-shirt was draped on the back of his desk chair. I pulled it over my head and checked out my reflection in the mirror. The hem came to rest just above my ass. I briefly considered panties but opted to stay commando. I was a little sore, and it felt good to let the girly bits breathe. And there were no neighbors for a quarter of a mile. No one would see me.

I crept to the door, but then felt bad about deserting him. After all, he'd given me three epic orgasms, turning every part of my body into rubber. After watching me stretch and yawn, completely spent, he'd been totally unselfish, encouraging me to curl up against his chest and sleep. He'd wake up and be looking for payback, and I wouldn't be there. That would be disappointing.

I decided to leave him a note. I quietly pulled open the top drawer of his desk and spied some paper beneath a couple of books. I slipped the paper out and wrote quickly.

> Hey, sleepy head. I had to get up. I couldn't lie there any more—I'm feeling a wee bit achy—haven't had a workout like that in a while.☺ I'm going to explore. Come find me when you're up. I think I owe you one...or three.
>
> P.S. You're snoring.
>
> P.P.S. I also think you're drooling. Very hot!

I folded the note into a paper hat, snorting quietly at my own ridiculousness, and then I left it on my pillow and quietly left the room. I picked up our abandoned clothes as I went, leaving them in a folded pile on the breakfast bar in the kitchen. Then I went downstairs to the games room.

I stood for a long while at the wall of windows with my palms against the glass, staring out at the lake. I could almost hear the echoes of laughter—Daniel, Brad, and Jeremy playing at the water's edge, jumping from the dock into the cold lake, canoeing, maybe even waterskiing. There was a large boathouse off to the side of the property. Surely there would be all sorts of toys inside, given the family's fondness for fun and games.

I turned to survey the room. Speaking of fun and games, if I was going to be spending more time with his family, I'd better get a firmer grasp on some of these pastimes. Brad would take great pleasure in mocking me for my inadequacies. I needed to practice. Where to start? I saw the pool table and smiled, remembering Daniel leaning over the table in his parents' basement. I'd drooled as I'd gotten my first glimpse of his bare forearms, admiring his broad shoulders and tight ass as he'd hitched his leg up to expertly execute the shot.

Two and a half months.

That's how much time had passed since that playful but very revealing exchange. It hardly seemed possible that it was so long ago. On the other hand, considering what had felt like a *lifetime* of waiting in the interim, it seemed like far more than nine weeks had passed. And now there we were—a couple—in every sense.

I crossed decisively to the rack on the wall and grabbed a pool cue. I chalked the tip and then took two of the scattered balls and lined them up at one of the corners of the table. This was a completely contrived shot, but I had to start somewhere. I leaned over and made a little bridge with my hand the way Daniel had taught me back in February. I brought the cue back and slid it forward, hoping to connect with the white ball and possibly sink the red striped ball waiting in front of the pocket.

Ha! Not only did I *not* sink the striped ball, I didn't even *hit* the white ball. Instead, I jabbed the end of the cue into the green fabric, leaving a blue, chalky smudge on the felt.

"Fucking piece of shit," I muttered.

"Aubrey, what are you doing?"

I whirled around, my hand on my heart. Daniel was standing against in the doorframe, watching me. His gray track pants hung low on his hips.

"Daniel! Crap, you scared me."

"Well, frankly, you're scaring me, too. What are you doing to the poor, defenseless table?"

"I was trying to get that stripy ball to go in the hole," I explained, pointing to the corner of the table.

"Ah, I see." He crossed the room and stopped in front of me. "This is very upsetting," he said, taking the cue out of my hand.

"I know. I'm sorry. The chalk will come out, right?"

I rubbed at the smudge, but he pulled me back.

"Don't worry about the table. That's not what I meant. I was actually talking about my teaching abilities. I thought I'd done a better job of instructing you, but that *was* a while ago. Perhaps you need a refresher."

Oh, *now* I saw where he was going with this. There was something in his eyes—that easy confidence. This was the Daniel that feared nothing and no one. God, how I'd missed him. I rested my hands on his bare chest.

"Don't blame yourself. As you say, that *was* a while ago. From what I remember, your instructions were outstanding. A refresher would be a good idea, though. You know, to *clarify* a few points."

He smiled at me—a slow, lazy smile, eyes hooded and playful. He placed the pool cue on the table and then reached around my waist, slowly slipping lower.

"Where are your panties, Miss Price?"

I made a big show of pulling up the hem of the T-shirt, feigning shock when I saw that I was naked underneath.

"I swear I was wearing panties a few minutes ago. It might have been that look you just gave me. I don't think they stood a chance." I snapped my fingers. "Poof!"

"I really *do* have quite an effect on you, don't I?"

"I suppose you do."

"Suppose? Can't you be more definitive than that?"

I took his hand and drew it between my legs.

"Definitive enough for you?"

"I'll say," he said, running his fingers along my wet skin. "You know the feeling's mutual, right?" he said, his lips close to mine as he moved his hand around to my lower back.

"Yes, I do think I feel something mutual, right about...*there*." I shifted my hips against his. He closed his eyes and moaned, his hand tightening at my waist.

"Last time I tried to teach you to play pool, we were rudely interrupted."

"I was very disappointed. The lesson was reaching a high point, if I recall."

"Would you be terribly disappointed if I put off this lesson in favor of—other pursuits? I gave you time off for good behavior earlier, but there's this very pressing *job* that needs to be attended to before we leave today."

His voice made me tingle down to the very tips of my toes. I quickly shed the T-shirt, throwing it on the corner of the table. As he looked me up and down, the saucy dimple came out to play. Sexy motherfucker.

"What if this job doesn't get done?" I ran my fingers under the waistband of his track pants and licked my lips.

"I'm afraid it would reflect badly on your performance appraisal, and that would be a shame. Things have been going so well."

He tilted his head and ran his fingers lightly up my sides, bringing them to rest at the swell of my breasts. It was all I could do to remain standing, never mind continue the suggestive banter, which was obviously one of Daniel's favorite forms of foreplay.

"You know, I have this overwhelming desire to please people, Mr. Grant. Would you be good enough to drop your pants so I can get to work?"

He smiled wickedly. "There's that initiative I so admire, Miss Price."

And then his pants were off and tossed aside. I patted the bank of the pool table and raised an eyebrow. Daniel scooted onto the edge. I pushed his shoulders, and he reclined, watching me as he moved. His words from the night before rang in my ears: "*I guarantee if you want to see me lose my shit, talk to me.*"

I gazed up at him from under my lashes.

Okay. Here goes nothing.

"I hope I haven't misunderstood. This is what you want, right?" I asked, running my hands up his thighs. "You want my lips right here?" I lowered my face slowly. "And my tongue here?" The tip of my tongue darted out, flicking him gently.

His hips jumped, and his hands moved to my hair. He moaned, dropping his head back and closing his eyes. I devoted myself entirely to pleasing him, and he said my name over and over as he encouraged my movements. I glanced up, watching his Adam's apple bob as he swallowed hard, the muscle in his jaw jumping.

His reactions spurred me on. I was enjoying the experience almost as much as he was. After several particularly deep thrusts into my mouth, his fingers tightened, scratching my scalp as he hissed.

"Oh, fuck, stop, stop," he panted, sitting up and drawing me close to kiss him. "You're so fucking hot."

In one quick movement, he was off the table and behind me, leaning me across the felt.

"Tell me you want me to make love to you," he said, urgently sliding his hand between my legs. "I want to hear you say it."

I shook my head.

"No?"

"No. That's not what I want." I moved frantically against his teasing fingers.

He hesitated. "You don't?"

I looked at him over my shoulder. "You've got me bent over a pool table. *Make love?* I don't think so."

"Jesus." He kissed my neck and then bit down on my shoulder. I moaned. "So, what you really want is for me to fuck you so hard the neighbors will hear you when you come?"

"Your neighbors are a quarter of a mile away…"

"Exactly."

He ran his other hand down my leg, circling my knee. His hot breath made the fine hairs on the back of my neck stand on end. "When I was giving you that billiards lesson in February, remember what I said about access?"

"Uh-huh."

He eased my leg up, resting my knee on the edge of the pool table, and then he was inside me in one swift, hard thrust.

We both cried out at the same time.

"That is called *perfect* access," he said through gritted teeth. Daniel's hands were firm on my hips as he sank into me, slowly and deeply, again and again. His chest pressed into my back.

Sweet Jesus…

"How about angle?" he breathed. "Do you remember what I said about that?"

I could do little more than sigh and moan. My fingers dug into the table, possibly making permanent divots in the fabric.

"You need to find the perfect—angle—to execute the shot."

Oh, he was working the angle. No doubt about that.

"Find that sweet spot every time, and the game…is…yours."

I nodded and moaned, pushing back and clawing the felt under my fingers.

My legs trembled. In fact, my whole body was quivering. I'd lost control of my limbs, and if it wasn't for the table, I'm sure I would've fallen over. Daniel reached between my legs, holding me against him, and the trembles became full-on spasms. My cries echoed around the room.

After a few minutes of potential unconsciousness, my cheek pressed against the table as I struggled to regain my breathing, I realized Daniel was draped over me, one arm circling my waist, the other stretched out along my forearm.

"You okay?" he asked, kissing my cheek softly.

"Are you kidding me? I'm great. That was...Wow."

"I didn't hurt you?"

"No, no, I'm fine."

"Good, because I'm not done with you yet."

"Really?" I'd been so wrapped up in my full-body orgasm that I don't think I would've known whether Daniel had come even if he'd used a bullhorn to announce it. I eased myself up and turned to face him.

"Hold on tight," he whispered. He lowered me on the table and pressed into me, haphazardly pushing billiard balls out of the way. Thumbs pressed into my hipbones, he moved slowly at first.

"Stretch your arms out," he said. "Like you did last night."

I looked into his eyes as I moved, feeling a billiard ball beside my right hand. Without breaking his gaze, I grasped it and rolled it around in my fingers. I brought one of my legs up to rest on his shoulder, trying to ease the overextended arch of my back.

He turned his head, brushing against my knee. "Oh God. I love your legs, Aubrey."

His tongue slid along the flesh above my knee. *Where was my camera when I needed it?*

"You look incredible, Daniel. Don't hold back."

And that was all I needed to say. All pretense of control vanished as he desperately chased release. He gripped my leg, his teeth sinking into my thigh and his other hand moving up to palm my breast as his hips drove against me. He swore and gasped, eventually collapsing onto me.

"You're amazing," he groaned, his chest heaving. A minute passed, maybe two. Finally, he lifted his head. Glancing up at my hand, he chuckled softly. "Do you know you're still holding the eight ball?"

I turned to peer up at the black ball in my right hand.

"Sink that ball at the end of the game, and you win. But you have to call it first," he explained. "Say which pocket you're aiming for."

"That one over there," I said, turning to face the corner of the table.

"Eight ball, corner pocket," he said, gently resting his lips against my cheek.

I angled my hand and rolled the ball toward the corner, where it dropped easily into the mesh bag below.

"For the win!" I grinned up at him.

I'd thrown Daniel's T-shirt back on and made a quick trip to the washroom to clean up, only to return to find him lying completely naked in the middle of the pool table, his hands clasped behind his head. I leaned over and ran my hand down his chest to the tight muscles of his abdomen.

"Comfortable?"

"Oddly enough, yes."

He patted the space beside him, and I climbed up to join him, burrowing into his side.

"Daniel, that was incredible."

"Another fantasy I can cross off the list." He put an arm around me.

"Did the real thing measure up to the fantasy?"

He brushed his lips against mine. "The real thing is *always* better, especially where you're concerned."

"I'd have to agree. Something about that position. It was amazing. I mean, *unnghh.*"

"*Unnghh?* I don't think I'm familiar with that word."

"*Unnghh.* The state and or condition of being so horny, you may or may not feel like you're going to explode."

"So, all this time I've been feeling *unnghh* and not knowing what to call it. You learn something new every day, I guess."

I smiled at him goofily, throwing my leg over his hips. "I guess we've both learned a lot this weekend."

He laughed. "When I woke up this afternoon and you weren't there, I thought I'd missed my chance for payback. I was happy to read your note and see that wasn't the case." He reached for his track pants from the corner of the table and pulled out the note I'd left him on my pillow. "What *is* this, anyway?"

"It's a *hat*. Duh!"

He laughed. "A hat?"

"Yes."

"What kind of hat?"

"Hell, I don't know."

"Can we pretend it's my TA hat for a sec?"

"Must we?"

"Yes." He scrunched it into a little ball and threw it onto the floor. "Ah, so cathartic."

"You're a wingnut."

He grinned and brushed my hair over my shoulder. "Speaking of my TA hat, can I ask you something? Seriously for a second. Something I've been wondering for a while."

"Of course."

"Have you ever considered doing post-grad work?"

I rolled onto my back, peering at the Tiffany light hanging above the table.

"Honestly? I would've loved to get my master's or something. I'm not sure in what." I sighed. "It wasn't financially viable, so I stopped considering it. I already have student loans to pay off. I don't want to spend the next ten years clearing debt."

Frowning, he leaned on his elbow as he peered down at me. "I hate that money has gotten in the way of you achieving what you want or pursuing your dreams. That's so wrong."

I shrugged. "It is what it is."

"So, now what?"

"All along I've been so focused on school, my GPA, the dean's list. I never really thought much about what comes after the finish line. I've known all along that I'll be staying at Jackman until I leave for England. I won't have to worry about life—you know, with a capital L—until I get back in August."

"I don't ever want you to worry about life, capital L or otherwise." He cradled my head in the crook of his neck. "We'll figure something out."

"Okay," I whispered, rubbing my nose against the line of his jaw as we cuddled quietly for a few moments.

When Daniel's phone rang, we both jumped.

"Shit." Daniel leapt off the table, fumbling for his phone in his track pants pocket. "Dad? Hi." He raised his eyebrows at me, communicating his surprise. "Yes, we're fine. Everything's great. Is everything okay there? Pardon? Hang on." He walked to the corner of the room. "How's that?" He took a few more steps, stopping at the bar. "Can you hear me now? Yes, that's better. Now I can hear you. Is everything okay?"

He looked over at me in a way that told me this call hadn't been precipitated by some sort of terrible emergency. Trapped beside the wet bar with his phone, he continued his conversation but gestured for me to bring him his pants. Being a complete shit disturber, I feigned confusion, looking at him with a puzzled expression.

"Yes, she's enjoying herself," he said to his dad. "We both are. It's very…relaxing."

He pointed to his pants again and looked at me beseechingly. I knelt on the table and held them up, mouthing, "These?" He nodded, so I pulled on the track pants myself, making a point of staring unabashedly at his dangly bits, licking my lips all the while. He narrowed his eyes at me and folded his arms across his chest, trying to look nonchalant as he stood there chatting, without a stitch of clothing on.

"No, the flies aren't as bad as I thought they would be. We went for a walk this morning. There were a few about, but not too bad. No, I made a fire last night. There's a bit of a chill in the air, but as long as you dress for the temperature, it's fine."

I couldn't help laughing as he glared at me playfully, poor thing. I climbed off the table and went to stand behind him. I put my arms around him, and he spun around, holding me while looking down at me with a glint in his eye.

Thanks a lot, his face said.

"Not yet," he said to his father. "Yes, I'm sure she will. At least, I hope so. Of course I'll be careful. I'll swing by in the morning and help you sort out the boxes, all right? Okay, Dad. Thanks for calling. Say hi to Mom. I will. Okay. Bye."

He hung up and looked down at me challengingly. "You're evil, you know that?"

"Oh, you love me," I said, kissing him sweetly. "It was nice of your dad to call. Everything's okay?"

"Yep. He was checking in to make sure we were doing all right. He says hi." Daniel patted my butt. "All right, young lady, drop your pants."

"My, my, Mr. Grant. So authoritative. What's come over you?"

"Goose bumps. All over my whole fucking body. Give me my damn pants."

I took a step back, hooking my thumbs into the waistband of his track pants, pretending that I was going to take them off, but then I took another step and turned.

"You'll have to catch me first!" I laughed, running across the room.

"Oh, you little —"

He chased me up the stairs as I squealed and tried to elude him. He caught me as I passed through the kitchen, about to dash down the hallway toward the bedroom. He trapped me against the wall, where he kissed me and laughed like a schoolboy who'd just won a game of kissing tag. Of course, in my limited kissing tag experience, I'd never had naked boy parts pressed against my tummy.

"You are so lucky you don't have neighbors," I said between giggles.

"No, *you* are so lucky we don't have neighbors." He undressed me and then put on his T-shirt, smiling wickedly as he drew the pants up his own legs. He picked me up and carried me to the bathroom, sitting me on the counter.

"Shit, that's cold," I squealed as my bare ass hit the marble.

"Serves you right." He stood between my legs.

"I'm sorry. Was that uncalled for? Doing that when you were talking to your dad? I guess I got carried away. It was pretty silly."

"Don't be absurd," he said, grabbing my silk wrap from the hook on the back of the door and helping me into it. "It was hilarious." He tied the sash of my wrap into a tidy bow. "It reminded me of the night in February — remember when I thought something had happened to you and I drove over to Jackman to make sure you were okay?" He cupped my face with both hands. "I was so jealous that night, listening to you and Matt. I wanted to be the one on the other side of the door, laughing and having fun with you. And now I am."

He kissed me tenderly, and I rested my hands on his forearms.

"So, yes, it was silly," he said. "But I need silly. I need someone to make me stop taking everything so seriously. Promise me you won't stop? You're so good for me."

"*Daniel…*" His name was all I could muster. I didn't know what else to say, so I hugged him fiercely.

"I mean it. I don't know how to explain how much you've changed my outlook on life," he whispered.

"You've done the same for me."

He shook his head. "I want to do more. Speaking of which, there are a couple of things I need to do right now. Why don't you freshen up and get dressed while I sort out some bits and pieces?"

"That sounds mysterious," I said, hopping down off the counter. "What could you possibly need to do?"

"Well, first I have to make the bed again, and then I need to alphabetize the soup cans," he said, smiling self-deprecatingly.

I knew he was joking. I'd be willing to bet a week's wages he'd already remade the bed. The can thing I wasn't so sure about, but there was no doubt in my mind that all the labels were facing the same direction.

CHAPTER 32

Yours

Lady, as you are mine, I am yours: I give away myself for
you and dote upon the exchange.
(*Much Ado About Nothing*, Act II, Scene I)

W e were cleaning up, this time for good. Dinner was done, and
we'd be leaving soon. I felt sad and dreaded our return to
Toronto. Our time at the cottage had been such a wonderful respite
from real life, and I didn't want it to end.

Daniel tied up a garbage bag, took it to the front door, and
returned to the kitchen to wash his hands. I stole a peek at the clock
on the microwave, and my heart sank. Five past seven. He'd told me
he wanted to get on the road by eight thirty at the latest.

"Aubrey, can you do me a favor while I think of it? Can you make
sure the windows of the great room are locked and then close the
curtains?"

"Yeah, no problem."

I crossed the room, stopping to rearrange and fluff the pillows on
the couch as I passed by. I tested the latches on all the windows and
found them all secure. As I reached up to pull the curtains closed, I
was distracted by the sky across the lake. The sun would be going down

soon, and by the looks of it, a gorgeous sunset was in store. Maybe we could sit on the dock and watch it together before we had to go.

That's when I saw it—a boat. A small cruiser that hadn't been there earlier was parked at the dock. When was the last time I'd looked out the window? When we'd been down in the games room? There hadn't been anything there at the time.

"Daniel, I think we have company," I called over my shoulder. When he didn't reply, I turned. He was standing against the breakfast bar in the kitchen wearing his gray hoodie, mine draped over his arm.

"What's going on? Are you expecting someone?"

He shook his head and held out his hand for me to join him. "We don't have company," he said, helping me slide my arms into my sweater.

"But there's a—"

"Come with me," he said, threading his fingers through mine.

He led me out of the cottage, around to the flagstone steps, and down to the dock.

"Well, what do you think?" he asked, bobbing his head at the boat.

"I don't understand," I said. "Where did this come from?"

"It's been in the boathouse all weekend, but originally, it came from Orillia." He looked at me expectantly. "You're looking at the owner."

"Wait a minute. Orillia? Does that mean…? Is this…?"

"Yes. It's mine. I bought it."

"You bought a *boat?*" I couldn't hide my shock.

"It wasn't as expensive as you think. It's only an entry-level cabin cruiser. It's not even brand new." His words poured out in a torrent. "But it's in great shape. I had the cabin overhauled, you know, with new fittings and fabrics. I want to take you out right now. I checked the Weather Network. The sun is going to set in about forty-five minutes." He stopped for a breath. "We can watch the sunset from the middle of the lake."

As he'd spoken, the expression on his face had changed from one of excitement as he described the boat to disappointment, thinking I completely disapproved of his purchase. And now he was gazing at me hopefully, pleading with his eyes for me to approve of his new toy and his plan to take me out for a private sunset cruise.

"Daniel, it's beautiful."

"Really? You don't think I'm crazy? I mean, I don't want to leave it here. I'm going to borrow Brad's pickup and bring it back to the city. I'd like to dock at Toronto Island. Then we can go out boating on the weekends. Our own little haven. I don't know…"

He shrugged uncomfortably. How could the man who'd been so commanding and sure of himself a few hours ago now be so incredibly vulnerable? And how could I be such an ass, letting him stand there and squirm? I smiled broadly and slowly put my arms around his neck.

"I think that sounds wonderful," I whispered, feeling the tension leave his body.

"Thank God." His eyes came alive with renewed excitement. "Okay, come on. Let me give you a tour."

He led me to the back of the boat and was about to help me climb aboard when he stopped and took a couple of steps farther down the dock, motioning me to join him.

"I almost forgot," he said, pointing to the rear of the boat. "See what I named her?"

Poppet. In red letters, outlined in silver. My heart lurched, the word *commitment* swimming before my eyes. He'd named his boat after me!

"Wow. I'm speechless. That's so…"

"Perfect," he said, smiling as he held out his hand to help me aboard.

I stood in the middle of the boat, listening as Daniel pointed out the raised helm seat, the frameless side windows, the benefits of the single-level cockpit floor, and the flat panel. We went down to the cabin where he drew my attention to the lifejacket cubbyhole and the lounge seating which converted into a small sleeper berth. There were compact bathroom facilities, a galley with flip-up extension, and the stainless steel integrated hardware, whatever that meant. My head was spinning. When he started rattling on about the fuel capacity, I zoned out entirely.

At some point, he noticed the glazed look in my eyes. "Sorry, I'm boring you."

"No, it's just a lot to take in. I didn't know you knew so much about boats."

"Are you kidding me? When someone gives me a nickname, I go out of my way to *own* it!"

I grinned at him and crossed my arms. "Very funny, sailor."

For the next half hour, Daniel toured me around the lake, showing me the neighboring cottages, some of which made the Grants' cottage look modest by comparison. He sat at the helm, and I stood beside him, my hand on his shoulder as he drove. He let me steer and explained the different dials on the flat panel. As we made our way back past their cottage and rounded the small peninsula, he reclaimed the wheel and expelled a quiet whistle.

"Look." He gestured across the lake.

The sun was beginning to set over the line of trees on the other side of the lake. It was breathtaking.

"Gosh, that is so beautiful."

Daniel slowed the boat and shifted in his seat, pulling me to stand sideways between his legs.

"I'm so glad you appreciate things like this," he said, tucking my hair behind my ear.

"How could I not? Look at that." I stretched my arm around his shoulders. We both turned to watch the clouds creeping across the sky.

"I love these kinds of sunsets," he said. "It's as if the clouds are paintbrushes. See the way they seem to dip into the setting sun to pull out the colors and then dab them across the sky?" He lifted his hand to trace a line across the horizon. "Orange, pink, purple. It's incredible."

"That was a really beautiful description," I said, leaning into him.

Daniel took my hand in his and looked at me earnestly. "I know you love mornings and sunrises, but those belong to you and your dad. Sunsets can be ours, okay?"

I swallowed hard, trying to chase away the lump that formed in my throat, overwhelmed by his thoughtfulness and concern for my feelings.

He scanned the horizon once more and turned off the engine. "I think this is the perfect spot," he said. He slipped out of his chair and led me to the cushioned bench at the side of the boat. "Sit here for a sec."

He disappeared inside the small cabin and came back out with his guitar. I clenched my hands together excitedly.

"You brought it! You're going to play something? Out here?"

His eyes twinkled as he smiled at me. "Yep."

He reached into his pocket and found a guitar pick which he placed between his teeth. He fished around in his other pocket, withdrawing a piece of folded paper and handing it to me. I opened it.

"What's this?" I looked down at the page. "Daniel, this is a Pablo Neruda poem. I *love* Pablo Neruda."

He chuckled. "I know. I've been picking Julie's brain. She told me he's one of your favorites. She said you two became friends in first year working on a group project in a poetry class."

"Julie told me once that if she could marry a poem, it would probably be one of Neruda's. I think she also found a poem she wanted to make babies with. As soon as she said that, I knew we'd be great friends."

"Oh, really? You can identify with wanting to procreate with pieces of literature?"

I laughed. "No, just with her sense of humor. Anyway, he's a very passionate writer. *This* poem is lovely. It's a paraphrase though — a translation. You know he didn't actually write this?"

"Really?" Daniel looked taken aback. "No, I didn't know that. What's it a translation of?"

"Have you ever heard of Rabindranath Tagore?"

"Tagore? That rings a vague bell."

"He was the first non-European to win the Nobel Prize for literature. He wrote a beautiful collection of poetry and prose called *The Gardener*. 'In My Sky at Twilight' paraphrases the thirtieth poem in the collection."

"Huh. Well, look at that. There's something else you've taught me today." He winked. "I'll have to look that up when we get home. Sounds like something I'd enjoy," he said. "Right now, though, *this* is what you need to look at."

He settled his guitar on his lap comfortably and tapped the loose paper with Neruda's poem. I looked up at him expectantly.

"I, well, I put it to music for you."

"Daniel, you didn't!"

He chuckled. "I did. Now, go easy on me. I'm a nervous wreck. I've been practicing, but I have a feeling it'll be different playing it with you sitting there."

I covered my mouth as he took a deep breath and began to finger-pick the strings. Right away, I recognized this as the song he'd been playing this morning when I'd come across him in the great room. When he started to sing, I wasn't sure what to watch—his lips or his fingers. Both were mesmerizing.

His voice soft and husky, and I shook my head in disbelief. What a romantic and thoughtful gesture. Plus, he'd gone to the trouble of choosing a poet *I* liked. His voice became stronger as he moved through the verses, his eyes closing when he reached the third verse in which the poet celebrated finally being able to call the object of his desire his own.

Then I understood.

You are mine.

That's why he'd said those words in the middle of the night.

By the time Daniel had finished playing, my heart was full and my eyes were teary. He gave me a half-smile and rested his guitar against the door of the cabin.

"I didn't think my singing was *that* bad," he said, inviting me into his arms and rocking me gently.

"Don't be ridiculous. You're awesome. That's the sweetest, most romantic thing anyone's ever done for me." I sniffed and rubbed my hands across my cheeks.

"It was a labor of love, believe me."

"I understand now why you were talking in your sleep."

"I worked on it neurotically all week, so it's not surprising the song's words were running through my head at all hours." He brushed my hair out of my eyes. "Is it okay with you if I say you're mine? I can't wait to tell the world."

"Of course. And I get to tell everyone you're mine, too, right?" I asked, tightening my hands around his neck.

"You know I'm yours. All yours."

"Daniel, does this mean we're going together?"

His laugh echoed around the lake.

"I haven't heard that expression in years. Going together, eh? Where do you want to go?"

"Anywhere. Everywhere. I don't care. Timmy's was great. The grocery store? Now *that* was amazing."

"I can't wait to walk with you everywhere at U of T, just holding your hand." He gazed over my shoulder at the sky. "I'm not sure how things are going to work once we get home. I guess we'll figure it out as we go along."

"I'm not worried," I assured him. "We did the right thing, Daniel. I'm glad we waited."

His eyes sparkled, and he looked so happy. I tried to memorize the expression on his face, wishing I could preserve it—something to bring to mind at low moments. I don't think I'd ever felt more at peace.

"And thank you for the song. It was beautiful."

"You're welcome. I'm glad you liked it."

I weaved my hands through his hair and kissed him the way he'd kissed me the night before—not as a prelude to sex, but as a wordless whisper aimed at your lover's heart. Kissing because you simply can't think of another way to show your love for the man you adore.

"See, if you'd done that to me back in February, I would have been completely snookered," he said, his smile softening as he pulled away.

I grinned, remembering how he'd jokingly referred to kissing as his Achilles' heel. He wrapped his arms around me, and we watched the sun slip behind the tree line, neither of us moving as the amber glow gradually faded. It was truly beautiful. But then, with the sun gone, the evening air cooled almost instantly. I shivered, dreading the return to reality. I wanted to stay here with Daniel forever. As if he could read my thoughts, he kissed my head and sighed.

"Well, poppet, I hate to do this, but we should probably head back. It's past eight o'clock."

"Are you talking to me or the boat? Man, this is so confusing." I rolled my eyes playfully.

"Very funny, but at this rate we won't be back in Toronto until eleven or so. You have to work in the morning, remember."

"Thanks for reminding me," I grumbled.

He looked at me pointedly. "So...quit."

"*Daniel.*"

"What? I don't see why you feel the need to torture yourself. But that's just my opinion. Ignore me."

"Don't be like that," I said, nuzzling his neck.

"I'm not being like anything," he said, his tone softening. "I wish you'd give your notice and let me take care of you, that's all. Maybe everyone else has left you to fend for yourself, but that doesn't mean I plan to. Tell Armstrong to shove the damn job and take some time for yourself. When you're ready, you can start thinking about a *real* job—a career—something that might actually mean something to you instead of subjecting yourself to that cow. You told me you'd let me catch you, but you're not letting me."

A flurry of retorts formed in my mind.

You can't catch someone unless they actually fall.

I can take care of myself.

Stop treating me like a damsel in distress.

"Maybe Armstrong won't be that bad." I struggled to maintain a casual tone, reluctant to end our weekend combatively.

He raised an eyebrow. "Don't get me wrong, I applaud your positive attitude. But spending five minutes in her company on Friday night was enough to last me a good long while. She's a condescending, patronizing, superior bitch."

I held my hand up to my ear, as if I were talking on the phone. "Yes, Department of Redundancy Department? I'd like to report an infraction."

He laughed shortly. "Yes, I guess those words *do* all mean the same thing. But that's my point. There aren't *enough* words to describe how haughty she is."

"Oh, so now she's a hottie?" I said, tapping my chin contemplatively.

He narrowed his eyes at me. "Haughty...H—A—U..."

"I know, I'm just—"

"You're just avoiding talking seriously about the topic."

He sighed, climbing back into the helm seat and restarting the engine. I moved back to join him, and he circled my waist with one arm while steering with the other, bringing the boat back around the peninsula toward the cottage.

"Okay," he said, patting my butt. "Hold on to me. I don't want you to get jolted or fall if the boat lists or bumps into something as I'm pulling in."

I wrapped an arm tightly around his back, widening my stance to better my balance as he confidently steered the boat. I wasn't jolted. I didn't fall. And even if the boat had listed or bumped into something, I'm sure Daniel would have been there, catching me before I'd even had a chance to stumble.

"Did you check to make sure you didn't leave anything behind?"

I nodded, pouting. The car was packed, the cottage was tidied, and all the windows were locked. I slipped my arms around his neck.

"I don't want to leave," I mumbled.

"I know. Neither do I." He rubbed my back. "You had a good weekend?"

I tipped my head back to look up at him. "Um, yeah, I'd say it was *very* good."

"Yes, it was." He paused for a moment. "You know, there's *one* more thing I want to do before we head out," he said.

"Daniel, I never thought I'd say this because God knows I can't get enough of you, but I honestly think the remaining surfaces we haven't christened are going to have to wait till next time. The girly bits are taking a nap."

He chuckled and clasped his hands around my waist. "I agree. Miss Velvet has every right to take a nap. She's had a busy couple of days."

"I'm thinking *crushed* velvet might be a more apt term at this point."

He winced. "Ouch, is it that bad?"

"A little tender," I confessed. "I think I'm the one who needs the recovery time now."

"Then *back in the saddle*, as it were?" he asked, raising an eyebrow suggestively.

"Absolutely."

"Well, that's good news. But I wasn't actually suggesting we take a turn on the kitchen table. I wanted to give you something."

He reached into his coat pocket and pulled out a small blue box.

"I'd almost convinced myself not to do this now — especially after our talk on the boat. I thought maybe we'd expended too many words on this subject already, but I've decided I don't care. I'm going to do it anyway. See, there is one very important word, something that's been sorely lacking in your life for the last year or so, and I'd like to discuss it a little more."

He passed me the box and then put his hands in his pockets. "Daniel, what is this?"

I looked at the box. Swarovski Crystal. What had he done? My mind raced with the possibilities. There was a *word* associated with this gift? One word? What word?

He shrugged and smiled. "I can only imagine what you're thinking. Don't freak out. It's just a little something. Go on. Open it."

I took a deep breath and cracked the box open. Whatever I'd expected, it wasn't what I found. Nestled in the blue satin lining was a key chain — the most beautiful key chain I'd ever seen. It was heart-shaped and studded with crystals and blue gems.

"Those are blue topaz," he said.

I nodded, watching the jewels sparkle as I moved the pendant in my hand. "This is, wow, really lovely. But I don't—"

"I figured you'd need somewhere to put these." He produced two keys and rested them on my palm, then closed my fingers around them. "One is the outer door to my condo building and the other is for my apartment. You're welcome to come over any time. You can let yourself in. You don't even have to call first, unless you want me to mess things up a bit before you arrive." He smiled gently.

My chin trembled. "Thank you, Daniel. I don't know what to say."

"Tell me you'll use the key ring. And promise me you'll *only* put these two keys on it."

"Of course I'll use it," I assured him. "It's beautiful." I threw my arms around his neck, and he hugged me close. "Why can't I put other keys on it?" I whispered.

He released me, gazing at me tenderly.

"Well, you can, but please don't put your residence keys on it."

"Why not?"

He opened my hand and turned the jewel-encrusted heart over. On the back, one word was engraved:

Home.

Acknowledgments

What a joy it has been to share the continuing story of Sailor and Poppet. Thank you to everyone who has cheered me on throughout the second part of this journey. My humble thanks go out to the readers who pass on recommendations to friends and take the time to write reviews on Goodreads or Amazon. I also owe a huge debt of gratitude to the bloggers who work tirelessly to spread the word about the books they love. Word of mouth is so important. Your impact is inestimable.

To Elizabeth and the Omnific team, I'm so grateful for your incredible efforts and hard work. To the editorial team, the art department, and everyone working behind the scenes—thank you.

Enn, amazing publicist and wonderful friend, thank you for everything you do. I love your "balls to the wall" attitude, but I know so much of your work is done quietly and without fanfare. Thank you—truly.

To my fellow authors, it's wonderful to be a part of a team where everyone is so supportive of each other's efforts. I feel blessed to have such lovely and generous people in my corner.

I must thank the loyal friends who stuck with me as I made the decision to publish. I've realized a lifelong dream, and having you there to encourage me and cheer me on along the way has made the experience all that much sweeter.

And to my husband—my partner in all things large and small—thank you for your unconditional love and support.

~GG

About the Author

Georgina Guthrie has been a self-professed book hugger for as long as she can remember. An avid reader and compulsive diarist, she is thrilled to be taking the leap into the world of publishing. GG resides in Toronto, Canada, but she still considers herself a Brit through and through and can often be found roaming the aisles of her favorite British import shop.

A graduate of the University of Toronto where she studied English literature, GG is happy to fill her hours reading and writing, but she's just as likely to be found enjoying a good film with her husband, dancing around the kitchen with her daughter, or hanging out with friends and family, almost certainly with a glass of red wine in one hand a bag of cheese and onion crisps in the other.

check out these titles from
OMNIFIC PUBLISHING

←⋯→Contemporary Romance←⋯→

Boycotts & Barflies and *Trust in Advertising* by Victoria Michaels
Passion Fish by Alison Oburia and Jessica McQuinn
The Small Town Girl series: *Small Town Girl, Corporate Affair* & *Keeping the Peace*
by Linda Cunningham
Stitches and Scars by Elizabeth A. Vincent
Take the Cake by Sandra Wright
Pieces of Us by Hannah Downing
The Way That You Play It by BJ Thornton
The Poughkeepsie Brotherhood series: *Poughkeepsie* & *Return to Poughkeepsie*
by Debra Anastasia
Cocktails & Dreams and *The Art of Appreciation* by Autumn Markus
Recaptured Dreams and *All-American Girl* and *Until Next Time* by Justine Dell
Once Upon a Second Chance by Marian Vere
The Englishman by Nina Lewis
16 Marsden Place by Rachel Brimble
Sleepers, Awake by Eden Barber
The Runaway Year by Shani Struthers
Hydraulic Level Five by Sarah Latchaw
Fix You by Beck Anderson
Just Once by Julianna Keyes
The WORDS series: *The Weight of Words* & *Better Deeds Than Words*
by Georgina Guthrie
Theatricks by Eleanor Gwyn-Jones
The Sacrificial Lamb by Elle Fiore
The Plan by Qwen Salsbury
The Kiss Me series: *Kiss Me Goodnight* by Michele Zurlo
Saint Kate of the Cupcake: The Dangers of Lust and Baking by LC Fenton

←⋯→New Adult Romance←⋯→

Three Daves by Nicki Elson
Streamline by Jennifer Lane
The Shades series: *Shades of Atlantis* & *Shades of Avalon* by Carol Oates
The Heart series: *Beside Your Heart, Disclosure of the Heart* & *Forever Your Heart*
by Mary Whitney
Romancing the Bookworm by Kate Evangelista
Fighting Fate by Linda Kage
Flirting with Chaos by Kenya Wright
The Vice, Virtue & Video series: *Revealed* & *Captured* by Bianca Giovanni

←⋯→Young Adult Romance←⋯→

The Ember series: *Ember & Iridescent* by Carol Oates
Breaking Point by Jess Bowen
Life, Liberty, and Pursuit by Susan Kaye Quinn
The Embrace series: *Embrace & Hold Tight* by Cherie Colyer
Destiny's Fire by Trisha Wolfe
The Reaper series: *Reaping Me Softly & UnReap My Heart* by Kate Evangelista
The Legendary Saga: *Legendary* by LH Nicole
Fatal by T.A. Brock

←⋯→Paranormal Romance←⋯→

The Light series: *Seers of Light, Whisper of Light & Circle of Light* by Jennifer DeLucy
The Hanaford Park series: *Eve of Samhain & Pleasures Untold* by Lisa Sanchez
Immortal Awakening by KC Randall
The Seraphim series: *Crushed Seraphim & Bittersweet Seraphim* by Debra Anastasia
The Guardian's Wild Child by Feather Stone
Grave Refrain by Sarah M. Glover
Divinity by Patricia Leever
Blood Vine series: *Blood Vine, Blood Entangled & Blood Reunited*
by Amber Belldene
Divine Temptation by Nicki Elson
Love in the Time of the Dead by Tera Shanley

←⋯→Historical Romance←⋯→

Cat O' Nine Tails by Patricia Leever
Burning Embers by Hannah Fielding
Good Ground by Tracy Winegar

←⋯→Romantic Suspense←⋯→

Whirlwind by Robin DeJarnett
The CONduct series: *With Good Behavior, Bad Behavior & On Best Behavior*
by Jennifer Lane
Indivisible by Jessica McQuinn
Between the Lies by Alison Oburia
Blind Man's Bargain by Tracy Winegar

←⋯→Erotic Romance←⋯→

The Keyhole series: *Becoming sage* (book 1) by Kasi Alexander
The Keyhole series: *Saving sunni* (book 2) by Kasi & Reggie Alexander
The Winemaker's Dinner: *Appetizers & Entrée* by Dr. Ivan Rusilko & Everly Drummond
The Winemaker's Dinner: *Dessert* by Dr. Ivan Rusilko
Client N° 5 by Joy Fulcher

Anthologies

A Valentine Anthology including short stories by
Alice Clayton ("With a Double Oven"),
Jennifer DeLucy ("Magnus of Pfelt, Conquering Viking Lord"),
Nicki Elson ("I Don't Do Valentine's Day"),
Jessica McQuinn ("Better Than One Dead Rose and a Monkey Card"),
Victoria Michaels ("Home to Jackson"), and
Alison Oburia ("The Bridge")

Singles and Novellas

It's Only Kinky the First Time (A Keyhole series single) by Kasi Alexander
Learning the Ropes (A Keyhole series single) by Kasi & Reggie Alexander
The Winemaker's Dinner: RSVP by Dr. Ivan Rusilko
The Winemaker's Dinner: No Reservations by Everly Drummond
Big Guns by Jessica McQuinn
Concessions by Robin DeJarnett
Starstruck by Lisa Sanchez
New Flame by BJ Thornton
Shackled by Debra Anastasia
Swim Recruit by Jennifer Lane
Sway by Nicki Elson
Full Speed Ahead by Susan Kaye Quinn
The Second Sunrise by Hannah Downing
The Summer Prince by Carol Oates
Whatever it Takes by Sarah M. Glover
Clarity (A *Divinity* prequel single) by Patricia Leever
A Christmas Wish (A *Cocktails & Dreams* single) by Autumn Markus
Late Night with Andres by Debra Anastasia
Poughkeepsie (enhanced iPad app collector's edition) by Debra Anastasia

·